THE LUPO STICK

Valerie Blumenthal

ISBN: 0995785309

ISBN 9780995785304
eISBN 978-0-9957853-1-1

ABOUT THE AUTHOR

 Valerie Blumenthal is the author of eleven criti-
cally acclaimed novels, several of which have been
widely translated. Her novel, *Saturday's Child,* sold
in the region of a million copies worldwide. She
has written features for the Times, Telegraph
and Mail on Sunday, published several short stories, and for four years taught creative writing in
a high security men's prison.

A third of the way through writing *The Lupo Stick,* Valerie was di-
agnosed with PCA (Posterior Cortical Atrophy), a rare form of
Alzheimer's, which strikes at a younger age. Writing *The Lupo Stick*
has been a labour of love, but also one that has been fraught with
frustration, as her condition altered over the six years it took to
write.

This book is dedicated to my wonderful husband, Christopher Yeates.

With thanks and much love also to my darling daughter,
Ingrid Stone, for all her support.

Thank you also to my new friend Celine Castelino
for all her technical input.

I would like to thank the following for their encourage-
ment: my lovely brother Adrian Blumenthal, Tina Betts,
Vanessa Lafaye and Silvia Miller.

Reviews for *'The Lupo Stick'*
"Valerie writes beautifully about the mother/daughter relationship, hidden secrets and Alzheimer's in her latest novel set in Italy." Tina Betts, Literary Agent.

"Having enjoyed Valerie's previous works and been drawn into the fascinating worlds she has created, I can't wait for this one to arrive and for me to leap inside." Dr Jonathan Romain, Rabbi, Author and Broadcaster.

"I've been a fan of Valerie's writing for a long time, so I'm thrilled to see a new book from her. I'm sure it will have the same mixture of heart-wrenching emotion and beautiful prose." Vanessa Lafaye, author of *Summertime.*

Reviews for her last novel, *'Saturday's Child':*
"Valerie Blumenthal explores her protagonist's dilemma with sympathy and tact, producing a very readable novel which makes some thoughtful points about the nature of maternal love." The Times.

"A sensitive portrayal of a woman struck down by love." Good Housekeeping.

"…Brings humanity to an imaginary case of child abduction…Valerie Blumenthal's morality play on mother love, abuse and abandonment is as touching as it's topical." She magazine.

"Unputdownable." Essentials magazine.

And for *'Kempton's Journey':*
"The honesty and humour Blumenthal brings to her subject and her hero's essentially likeable character make this more than just another chronicle of midlife angst. This is a book about ordinary people in everyday situations, described with a sympathetic insight, which makes even the most mundane events seem compelling." The Times.

"… A wise novel… shrewdly observed and lit by comic compassion." She magazine.

"*...A finely wrought work... Valerie Blumenthal's careful handling of characters and plot give events in the novel a wonderful emotional resonance.*" Edinburgh Evening News.

I wake, unable to breathe. Rubble everywhere.

'Mama! Mama!'

'It's alright cara. You're safe. You're dreaming. Mama's here. Always here.'

CHAPTER 1

NOW

ROSA

My stepfather's funeral. The four of us make up a sombre little band, bunched together in the front pew. Jack, my husband, takes my hand in his, and uncurls my tense fingers, one by one. Discreetly, he massages them, in silent consolation.

I can see the notes in Mama's hand quivering. She hasn't referred to them yet, and her voice, with its pronounced Italian inflection, is strong. She presents a tiny, stoical and isolated figure, standing at the pulpit.

'A charismatic man of gentle humour and integrity,' she is saying. 'Nobody could fail to be drawn to my husband's charm, or to that, mellifluous voice of his - I can hear it now. Rarely was it raised in anger; that is not to say, however, that he wasn't excellent at getting his own way.'

A titter of laughter around the packed church. My throat feels ragged. Gino, my brother, rubs each eye in turn. Billy gazes at the ground. He and his grandfather had been two of a kind.

She speaks for a further minute or so, when all at once she looks confused. 'I remember...' She breaks off, shaking her head, and her hat slips over her face. She adjusts it. Tries again: 'I remember...' She consults her notes for the first time, shuffling clumsily through them, before realising they are upside down. She rights them, but cannot seem to fathom them. I can feel her anguish.

'I've finished,' she says to the vicar, in an audible whisper.

Assisted by him, she descends from the dais and walks, slightly lopsidedly, back down the aisle. The only dry eye in the place is hers. Gino stands up to hug her, but she doesn't respond. Blindly, she feels for her seat next to him. Sitting very upright in it, she stares in front of her, toying with her embroidered handkerchief as though she were kneading pasta.

After the service, we traipse outside into the April drizzle. Mama follows the coffin on my son's arm. Seeing them like that, I want to cry; they look so sweet together: he bending from his great height to hold the umbrella over her; she dwarfed by him. In a few hours Billy will be on a flight back to New York, where he works. I know Mama is glad he could be here today.

As we approach the freshly dug hole, Mama's composure deserts her. Her mask crumples, and her legs seem to give way.

A little, choking sound escapes her. 'I can't bear it,' she says, on a gasp, staring into the pit with wild eyes.

Billy supports her before she can fall. He murmurs something to her. Whatever it is, it works, and she recovers her equilibrium, superficially at least.

'Ashes to ashes; dust to dust...' intones the priest's singsong voice.

Crouching, Mama tenderly lowers a single red rose into the grave.

When this part of the ordeal is over, more than three hundred people cram into the Oxfordshire hall for the next part. My cheeks become taut from sustained smiling, and I catch a whiff of my own perspiration while circulating with canapés. The jolly atmosphere of the wake feels wrong. There shouldn't be laughter.

And I glance across towards Mama, to see how she's coping. She is sitting in the corner of the long room, surrounded by a coterie of elderly widows and a lone widower, and I wonder what is going through her mind.

After an hour or so people begin to drift off. Mama gets to her feet; she puts on her jacket and picks up her bag purposefully, as though she is leaving. I follow her out of the room, worried she might be having one of her mental blips. Then she sees me, and her expression is that of a naughty child who's been caught out.

'Now don't be angry, *cara*,' she says in a wheedling tone which fails to reassure me.

'What are you up to? Where are you disappearing to?' I ask in Italian.

And calmly my mother informs me that she is off to her animal sanctuary to attend to a donkey in labour.

I stare at her, disbelieving. 'You *can't*. Not today. Please tell me you're not serious. What will people think?'

'Nearly everybody has left, Rosa. Anyway, I don't care what people think. Let them think what they wish. I've told the girls I'd come.'

'They rang you? They had no right.'

'Yes they did. I said they could in an emergency.'

'It's the day of your husband's funeral, for God's sake.'

'Don't you think I am fully aware of that Rosa? And let me tell you, *he* would understand. And approve.'

Which is probably true.

We glare at each other with mutual exasperation.

I try again. 'Why can't the girls see to the donkey? It doesn't have to be you.'

'Yes it does. She only came in two days ago. She won't let anyone near her. I'm the only one she trusts. She and I have a special rapport.'

'How can you have a rapport in two ...'

'Easily. This is my responsibility. Please don't tell me what to do, *cara mia.*'

It is pointless arguing with her. But I can at least have the last word.

'Why not? You tell me.' She smiles thinly.'

On her behalf, I lie to the dozen or so remaining guests: 'My mother apologises, but she's had to go home to rest,' I explain, crossing my fingers. And they commiserate with me, and make appropriate sympathetic noises.

'True or false?' My brother corners me.'

'What do you think?'

Gino, who is actually my half-brother, and considerably younger, gives a bark of laughter. 'I knew it. Good for her.'

'Well thanks a lot, Gino.'

He tilts my beret over my nose.

Jack, who over the years has learnt to detach himself from family quibbles, keeps his distance.

A couple of days later, having taken Lupo for his walk on Port Meadow, I settle to a morning's writing. Lupo circles a few times, only to flop down where he always does, on the rug by my feet. The book, a biography of a well-known international industrialist, is virtually finished, thank heaven - I'd been warned he would be vain, and demanding to work with - but there are some alterations my editor wanted me to make. Half way through the morning the phone rings. I ignore it, but a moment later my mobile rings. I take the call.

'Sorry to bother you Rosa,' says Liz, the manager of the sanctuary.

'No, it's fine. Has something happened?' I can feel the alarm gripping me already.

'We-ell, sort of. I'm a bit concerned about your mother.'

'Why, what's happened?'

'She didn't know where she was. She thought she was in Sicily.'

'Oh blast.'

If my mother only knew how I worry about her. She refuses to believe there is anything wrong with her. Her stubbornness drives me mad.

'I did try to put her straight,' Liz says, 'but she wouldn't have it. Then I changed the subject and a minute later she was back to normal. I mean, it could be all the stress, but...'

'No, it's something more than that. My stepfather thought so too. He kept badgering her to see a specialist. She's so good at bluffing, that's the thing... Has it affected her work?'

'Well, there have been a few incidents, but nothing ghastly. She'll cover it up and make a joke about a "senior moment." And one of us is always present when she's performing an operation - though her operating skills are as superb as ever.'

'Where is she now?'

'I insisted on driving her home. She wanted to drive herself, but I wouldn't let her. I know it's only a short distance, but in that state it would have been plain dangerous. She became quite bolshie. She threatened to walk back.'

'Oh God.'

'Anyway, I won in the end. But I wasn't her favourite person. You know what she's like.'

And don't I just?

'You're a star,' I tell her.

'It's nothing. We all love your mother. We so admire her. All her work. Setting up this place. It's amazing. This must be awful for her.'

I nod into the phone.

From our north Oxford home, to the village where Mama lives, is just a twenty-minute drive, depending on traffic. I park by the green, buy a box of Cadburys Milk Tray, which Mama loves, from the store, and let myself into the house. Tosca skids to the door, barking, then, realising it's me, she leaps up.

'Good girl. What a good girl,' I fuss her.

My mother rescued her from a scrap metal yard. She was skin and bone, and was kept on a chain by day, and by night roamed loose, behind the high barbed-wire fence. Mama told me how she had tempted her with food, used wire cutters for the fence, clipped a lead on her, and stole off with her into the night.

This was only about eight years ago, so she had already turned sixty.

She did not tell my stepfather what she was intending to do: 'He would have tried to stop me,' she said, with that mischievous smile of hers.

And that is the sort of fearless woman she was, and has been.

It was not long after taking the dog, that Mama realised it was pregnant. Tosca gave birth to a litter of German shepherd puppies. Only Lupo survived.

'Who is that? Is it you, Rosa?' she calls from her room.

'Yes Mama.'

I walk through the long, narrow house. Sunlight streams through the picture window. She is lying, clothed - except for shoes - on my stepfather's side of the bed, an open photo album on her lap. In her hand is the yellow rabbit her mother knitted for her when she was a child. I feel the tears gathering.

She lets go of it as she sits up, and holds out her arms to me.

'This is a nice surprise.'

She hugs me, with a strength you wouldn't expect for someone so small. Even in her late sixties she is still exquisite. Facial lines lend her dignity, and age has not altered her fine bone structure. But she looks exhausted.

'Oh *cara*.'

She says it on a protracted sigh. My heart breaks for her.

I sit down on the edge of the bed. 'I know.'

'I know you know. And his things are everywhere to remind me. I'll have to go through them. Sort them out. There's so much stuff.'

'I'll help you. We'll do it together. There's no rush.'

'I adored him. He was very precious to me... *Was*. I don't like the past tense.' She shudders. 'And the word "never". *Never* to see him again. It's unthinkable.'

We have lapsed into Italian, as we always do when it's just the two of us.

'Have you cried yet?'

'I can't, Rosa. I wish I could, but I can't... Where's Lupo?'

'I didn't bring him. You know how crazy the dogs get when they're together. I wasn't sure if you would be up to it.'

'Of course I am. Why wouldn't I be? Oh poor Tosca. She's really upset.'

I look at her, now in a mournful coil on the bedroom carpet.

'I'll bring her next time.'

Mama gets up from the bed and goes over to her dressing table. In the mirror I watch her brushing her still lustrous hair, which has only a few streaks of grey in it.

'Why do you think it is that you can't cry?' I ask her.

My mother puts down the brush and clips her hair into place.

'I suppose it's just the way I'm made,' she says at length.

'Uh-ha.'

I have two pressing matters I need to discuss with her, both which are bound to end in an argument.

The first: 'Mama, it's really time you saw a neurologist. You must be aware ...'

'I've seen one.'

'You - but ... Oh for heaven's sake, why didn't you tell me?'

'There was enough going on without making it worse.'

Without making it worse.

'Is it …?'

'Yes, Alzheimer's. It's probably been coming on for several years.'

'Oh bugger.' I say it in English, and her lips elongate into a grim smile.

'When did you find out?'

'Three months ago.'

'Three *months!*'

Aghast, I digest this. My mind is spilling over with questions I want to put to her: the implications. The prognosis. Her fears. The future. But now isn't the time.

'You shouldn't have had to shoulder this on your own, Mama. I'm so, so, sorry.'

She gives one of her shrugs. 'These things happen, *cara*. You can't predict them or account for them. You just have to get on with them.'

Out of respect I wait a few seconds before broaching the second matter.

'Mama, I would really like to write your biography.'

'What are you talking about? Why would you want to do that?'

'I don't mean for publication. This would only be for the family. Your life has been so interesting…' I can see her face darkening, but plough on. 'We'd use a Dictaphone and you could just talk freely and forget it was there. Think of it as a kind of legacy.'

'No way!' her fist bangs down on the dressing table with such emphasis that the hairbrush bounces onto the carpet. I retrieve it, and try to placate her.

'There's so much I don't know, Mama.'

But her stubbornness has not been improved by her illness.

'Good. That is how it should be. And how it will remain. Anyway you know most of the important facts.'

'No I don't. My real father, for instance.'

'Really Rosa, why bring it up now? Leave the past where it belongs.'

'You're being selfish.'

She turns on me angrily then. 'My life is my business, nobody else's. I refuse to be used as some kind of laboratory experiment to assuage your curiosity. And then you have the gall to accuse me of selfishness.'

I am nearly in tears. My mother has always had that power over me. She was so young when she had me, and we are almost too close. We laugh and squabble together in equal measures. And I simply cannot imagine life without her.

'It's because I love you. If we don't do it soon, one day it will be too late.'

Why did I say that? It was stupid.

'*Madre*, you are getting on my nerves, Rosa. I'm not dying, nor am I completely gaga yet. Though after another conversation like this I might well be. I don't *want* to do it, do you understand? I don't *want* to.'

She is becoming het up, which cannot be good for her. I wish I hadn't pushed her so hard. It was insensitive. I kneel by the dressing table and lean my cheek against hers, so that our faces are side by side, framed in the mirror, like a cameo.

'I'm sorry. I shouldn't have gone on at you like that. It was just an idea. I promise I shan't mention it again,' I say to her reflection.

She strokes my fingers. Hers are swollen and misshapen. 'My little Rosa.'

'Not little any more. Middle-aged and overweight.'

'You will always be *my* little Rosa, *cara*.'

We go into the small conservatory.

'Papa loves the fig tree. He'll be home soon,' she muses.

I do not contradict her.

I leave her dozing in the wicker chair.

The phone is ringing just as I'm opening my front door, and I grab it before the voicemail can cut in.

'I've spoken to Papa,' my mother says. 'And he thinks the book is a good idea. We have his blessing. When shall we start?'

And I wonder which Papa she means; which ghost she has evoked: her father, my stepfather, or the unknown man whose DNA I share.

It makes no difference.

I have been given *her* blessing.

CHAPTER 2

THEN (1958)
THE CHICKEN VENDOR

One night Beppe Lupo, the chicken vendor, had a premonition. Although it was the middle of the night he was definitely awake because the couple in the neighbouring *casetta* were making love and he could hear them through the open window. The wife was yelling her head off. It was not a dream, therefore, but a moment of awful clarity lancing into the heart of a man who had been dealt the card of death.

In the morning he paid a visit to his wife's sister, Annunciata Carluccio, a woman with a face as sour as ewe's milk left out in the heat.

'If anything should happen to Rosa and me would you promise to look after Graziella,' he asked her.

She prevaricated: 'Why would anything happen to you, Giuseppe?' She was a snob and never used the shortening of his name. Neither she nor her husband, the mayor, wanted a semi-literate chicken vendor as a brother-in-law.

'But *if,*' he insisted. 'For Rosa's sake.'

Grudgingly she agreed.

'As God is your witness?'

'This is ridiculous Giuseppe… Oh alright. As God is my witness.'

A week later, on a day so hot it flayed the hide off you, the chicken cart wended its way slowly up the steep, rutted coast road sliced into the mountain's flank, throwing up red dust behind it as it continued to climbed. Far below the fishing boats were out; dots of colour shimmering beneath the sun, seeming barely to move. The only sounds in the mind-numbing stillness were the intermittent screeches of circling gulls and chirping of crickets.

The chicken vendor squinted into the bleached sky. 'That's Stefano in his boat down there,' he remarked to his wife, squeezed up beside him.

He permitted the mule to rest for a few moments, as she was labouring and had dropped back with her load of dead birds. Despite the tassels fastened to the brow-band of her bridle the flies were plaguing her and she kept shaking her head. The chicken vendor leaned forward to sprinkle water from a bottle over her for temporary relief.

'It must be horrible for her,' Rosa said.

'I know, but what can I do?'

He took up the reins again and urged on the mule with a shake of them. Roused from her lethargy, she swished her tail and started forward, her ears flattening in protest.

'She's getting too old. It's not fair on her,' Rosa said. 'Maybe I should stop coming with you. It would lighten the cart for her.'

'But you weigh no more than one of those.' Beppe motioned behind him to the mound of feathers and beaks. 'And I like having you with me. You're right though. It isn't fair on her. I shall have to get another mule.'

'Mules cost money, Beppe.'

'We'll think of something.'

He had forgotten about his premonition and the conversation with his sister-in-law, and was looking forward to the future. At thirty-six he was still a young man.

They passed the old building that had once been a penitentiary, then the old monastery. This was the only road on the island and led to another, smaller, village. Now it looped back on itself. The lighthouse reared up like a stick of chalk against the volcanic rock of the headland, where only sheep and goats dared venture - and they were not always lucky; you would sometimes see a bloated corpse on the beach.

Round another couple of snaking bends. Here, scarcely visible through the screen of African Cypress trees, were the grand villas whose owners employed cooks, and menservants who wore white gloves, housekeepers and gardeners. A private chapel marked the entrance to this exclusive enclave, and a hundred metres below glittered a comma-shaped cove. Two years earlier, the mayor had installed a hydro-powered lift as an alternative to the five hundred and fifty steps leading to it. But this had cost a fortune, and many of the islanders resented their taxes being squandered on a facility that would be appreciated only by the elite few.

The chicken vendor's wife picked up the megaphone resting on her lap. For the past fourteen years, since she had married this man, she had called through it, and her voice could be heard rebounding from the mountainside to the harbour: *Freshly killed chickens, freshly killed chickens, freshly killed chickens!* They did other work too; the chicken business did not earn them enough to support themselves and their daughter, Graziella. Rosa took in sewing, while Beppe acquired bits and pieces here and there as a handyman. He also carved decorative walking sticks, a talent he'd discovered a couple of years previously. At his work bench, in the shade of the fig tree which grew outside his *casetta*, he would position the vice and whittle the wood into the forms of animals: horses, cockerels, rams with curling horns, dogs, hares, owls, eagles, two-tailed lizards, which brought good luck. Every gouge was made with tenderness, and beneath his calloused hands the creatures took on their personality. Considering the time each stick took to complete, Beppe barely made a profit from his carving, but this was incidental to him. He carved for the joy of it. And occasionally he would break off from his work to tug a plump fig from the branch, and while he ate it he would drink in the uninterrupted view of the towering mountains and the flat sea with all its riches, and be replete with a sense of goodness. The warmth might slip from the day and the sun shrink from the sky, but still he sat there. How could you put a price on such pleasure?

His own stick had the head of a wolf, to represent his surname, and was unique to him, and at the base of every stick he produced he carved his initials: B L, followed by a tiny wolf, as a trademark. He had debated whether it should be a G for Giuseppe, rather than a B, for Beppe; but as Rosa pointed out, the only people to address him by his full name were her sister and the mayor, who on principle would not buy a stick - and that had decided him.

Rosa had bumped into her sister only a day ago, on the steps to the cobbled *piazza*. Annunciata had, as usual, been unable to resist a jibe about Beppe. This time she was accusing him of having lost his mind: something to do with premonitions, but Rosa had been too incensed to listen.

'My husband's worth ten of that pompous one of yours, mayor or not,' she had defended him. 'Guido looks like a pig. I don't know how you can bear to wake up in the same bed as him. My Beppe is the handsomest man on the island, besides being a caring, considerate husband. That's more than can be said for some. And one day we will be rich. Everyone will want to buy his sticks...'

Over time, word of the chicken vendor's fine workmanship had begun to spread. Several of the villa owners could be seen strutting round the town with a stick made by the chicken vendor.

Tourists, too, bought them, though they were few and far between. Who, at that time, had heard of the remote *Isola delle Pecore*, a four and a half hour ferry ride from the coast of Sicily, with a population of twelve hundred and ninety-two? It belonged to no specific group and squatted in self-sufficient pride - a minute fleck in the Tyrrhenian Sea, seldom noted on the atlases.

Beppe was not without ambition, however. He might struggle to read and write, but his talent enabled him to hold his head high. It had elevated his status from lowly chicken vendor to artisan, and next month he planned to travel with Rosa and Graziella to Cefalù, where they would hawk his sticks to the numerous tourists. He would be able to charge them a higher price.

The final bend. From here one was afforded a spectacular view of the bay, its flat, turquoise sweep, and the domed outline of an islet visible through the heat-haze.

The mule was weary. The flies were driving her to distraction. A boulder lay in her path and she did not see it. The tip of her hoof caught on it, and she stumbled, causing the cart to jack-knife. For a moment it hovered; then slowly it pitched forward, over the edge of the mountain and somersaulted, hurling its occupants, the chickens, the braying mule, and a wolf-head walking stick, into the air and down the precipices to the sea below.

CHAPTER 3
THE LUPO STICK

The bodies of the chicken vendor and his wife were not re-covered, but the postmistress, Maria Alberta, had been on her round at the time and witnessed what had taken place. There had been a thunderclap of sound, which had made her almost fall off her bike, and she had turned round to see Beppe and Rosa Lupo flying through the air. The mule, still trussed up, was making an unholy noise, braying its head off as the cart bumped and bounced and rolled its rickety way down the precipice. The silence which ensued was terrible. Even the crickets shut up.

At first she had been unable to move, then she had cycled as fast as she could to the *Posto di Carabiniere*, where she recounted what had happened.

She was still off work, suffering from shock.

For days after the accident planks of wood from the cart float-ed to the sea's surface and were washed up onto the beach, and this evidence, combined with Maria Alberta's graphic account, sat-isfied Lorenzo Torre, the sole *carabiniere* on the island, that there were no suspicious circumstances surrounding the disappearance of Beppe and Rosa Lupo.

Graziella, thirteen and a half, with black eyes the shape of eucalyptus leaves, went to live with her aunt and uncle and their twin son and daughter.

Set back from the bustle of the harbour, the six-bedroomed house sat square and solid, like the mayor himself, behind a bougainvillea-draped courtyard. Its very foundations emanated respectability, an impression enhanced by the pair of brass carriage-lamps which illuminated it at night. To the rear sloped large gardens whose high hedges and giant cacti lent it privacy, and a further acre of land was given over to fruit trees. The interior was crowded with dark, heavy furniture, and a portrait of the mayor dominated the drawing room. He gazed down from his gilded frame, puffed out with smugness in his ceremonial regalia. Beneath it stood a glass-fronted cabinet containing his wife's *Capo di Monte* figurines, each on its own doily. Nobody other than herself was allowed to touch them, and every Monday morning she took the shepherds and shepherdesses from the cabinet to dust them with a soft brush; and the hatchet features of this woman, who was completely devoid of compassion, took on a rapturous expression as she was transported into the realms of their romance. Graziella liked to fantasise about cutting the wire from which the picture hung. Down the mayor would crash, onto the cabinet, defacing the portrait and smashing the figurines in a single satisfying sweep.

This highly polished prison became her home, and sometimes it seemed to her that the walls were stealthily closing in on her, preventing her from breathing.

Her bedroom was a sweltering box room filled with mysterious shapes beneath dustsheets, and on her third day at the house curiosity got the better of her and she peeled them back. Amongst the assorted oddments were journals, discarded household equipment, a commode, a chair leg, boxes full of photos, an old camera, and a canteen of tarnished silver cutlery. There were also two suitcases. She opened the larger first. Inside was a clothes bag, and she partially unzipped it. Out sprang a froth of white net, and she realised that it was Annunciata's wedding dress. Why had she kept it for all these years? Did it mean that her aunt possessed a sentimental streak after all? On second thoughts, maybe she was saving it for her daughter. Yes, that was more likely. She pitied whoever married Nina. Her cousin was as horrible as her aunt.

Using a knife from the canteen, Graziella pierced several holes in the fabric, then fed the dress back into its bag and zipped it up. The smaller case contained nothing but a stuffed squirrel. It had soft russet fur and she presumed her uncle had shot it. Perhaps he had intended to have it mounted in a woodland scene, within a glass dome. How could he have derived pleasure from killing such a pretty creature? What a senseless waste of its little life.

With all this paraphernalia occupying space there was little room for Graziella's few possessions; but at least she could grieve for her parents in privacy. Nobody could intrude upon her thoughts; not that anyone took an interest in her. And she missed laughter and freedom, and being able to express herself. And touch. Most of all she missed touch: an impulsive hug, a soothing hand, a tender caress. Who now could provide these? Certainly not Annunciata. She was unwanted. An *orphan*. The word itself seemed shocking to her; it belonged in storybooks. Never could she have conceived it would apply to herself. This total absence of love was the hardest thing to bear. She pined for her old life, her stolen joy. From being a lively girl she became withdrawn and silent. And each night she went to bed with her yellow rabbit tucked beneath her arm, and an ache in her lungs; and each morning she woke up with the ache still present.

'She makes me feel uncomfortable in my own house. I can feel her watching me the whole time and I don't know what she is thinking,' her aunt complained to her husband. 'She prowls around like a ghost, and demonstrates no gratitude that we've taken her in and pay for her keep.'

'We could send her to an orphanage,' the mayor suggested.

For a moment Annunciata's long face brightened, then she shook her head: 'No, for my sister's sake I can't. I gave my word. God was my witness.' She glanced fearfully behind her, as though He might appear at any moment.

One Saturday afternoon, several weeks after the tragedy, when the household was just stirring from siesta time and the shutters were still closed, Graziella heard a tentative knocking on the back door. Nobody else seemed to have heard it, so she opened it herself. There stood Stefano, the fisherman.

'*Ciao*, Stefano,' she greeted him, in surprised pleasure.

'Ciao, Graziella... That's lucky. It's you I came to see.'

He seemed ill at ease, standing on the step, his right arm tucked behind his back, and she smelt fish on him, and diesel from his boat.

'Me? Why? Oh - aren't you going to come inside?'

He moved from the step onto the door's threshold, but no further. 'I don't think I should. But here - look what I've found.' With a flourish he brandished a walking stick with a wolf's head from behind his arm.

Graziella clapped her hands to her mouth. 'Papa's stick!'

He passed it to her. She took it as though it were a gold sceptre, and ran her fingers over the carved head. The nose had nostrils; and her father had conveyed the effect of fur by cutting striations into the wood. She liked the eyes best; he had not gouged out holes, as he might have done for ease, but fashioned proper eyeballs and sockets. She used to marvel at his patience.

She bent her head and gave in to tears.

'Ah, *poverina!* I didn't mean to upset you,' Stefano said.

She pulled herself together. 'You haven't. I'm just happy you found it.'

'Ah, that's good then. I spotted it when I was out on the boat yesterday. It was bobbing along on the sea. I've cleaned the seaweed and barnacles from it and revarnished it so it's as good as new,' he said gruffly.

'Thank you.' She kissed his cheek.

'It's a pleasure Graziella. Your papa was my oldest friend.'

He started to reverse away from the door, eager to be gone. A few months ago he had drunk too much in Mama Lucia's café-bar, and had got into an altercation with the mayor about the cut in fishing subsidies. He had spent the night in the cell.

He departed in the nick of time, leaving behind a lingering odour of fish.

As the mayor descended the staircase he caught a glimpse of his back.

'Was that Stefano Vento skulking off?'

'Yes, but he wasn't skulking.'

'What did he want?'

'He found my Papa's stick.' She could not contain the excitement; was bubbling over with it. 'He's cleaned it and varnished it.'

'Let me see.'

She had been about to show him, but something in his tone alerted her. She remembered her father referring to him once as "*un tipo viscido*" - a slippery eel.

Graziella clutched the stick tighter.

'I said, let me see.'

And before she could prevent him, he had torn it from her. He was a stout, fleshy man and she had a ballerina's slightness. Agitatedly she jigged on the spot.

'Give it back to me! Give it back to me!'

'You don't need a walking stick. What do you need a walking stick for? You're a child,' he taunted, revealing three gold teeth in a grin.

'It's mine! It belonged to Papa. It's a *lupo*, like my name. It's *mine*.'

She attempted to snatch it, but he lifted it high, out of her reach, and twirled it.

She pummelled his barrel chest. 'Give it to me! Give it to me!'

'What on earth is going on', Annunciata demanded, coming into the kitchen, with both Graziella's cousins in tow.

She swung round to her aunt. 'He won't let me have my walking stick.'

'What are you talking about? What walking stick?' Then she saw the walking stick in her husband's hand. 'How did that thing get here?' she asked him.

'Stefano Vento found it evidently and brought it here. I teased Graziella that she had no use for it at her age, and she lost her temper,' the mayor explained in a rational manner.

'Quite so. Walking sticks are not for children, unless they are disabled. Which you are not, Graziella.'

'I'm not a child. You've got to make him give it back to me. He stole it, and it belongs to me. It was Papa's,' she shouted, becoming pink with rage. Again she tried to wrest the stick from the mayor.

'You see?' he said, grabbing her wrists.

'I told you she was a savage,' Nina remarked to her mother.

'P-perhaps you ought to give her b-back the stick,' Giorgio stammered.

Annunciata disregarded both of them and Giorgio left the room.

'I'll not tolerate this behaviour, Graziella. We have taken you into our home, you live here under our roof, share our meals, and this is how you repay us? Really, it is too much. You will apologise immediately, then if you ask politely you may have the stick.'

'I won't apologise. It's his fault.'

'Then you cannot have the stick.'

'*Che brutta!* Evil woman! I hate you. It's you who should be dead, not my mama and papa.'

Her aunt's hand flew to Graziella's cheek. It left behind a fuchsia coloured impression.

As punishment she was dragged, sobbing and kicking, to the cellar.

'You have your mother's temper. She was always free with her tongue,' Annunciata said, before bolting the door.

CHAPTER 4

THE ENGLISH FAMILY

To begin with, Graziella only saw blackness. It was all encompassing. She heard the scampering feet of mice near her, then something landed on her head, becoming entangled in her long hair, scratching her skull. She cried out, frantically brushing it away with her fingers, and the cockroach fell to the floor with a clack. She sobbed into the darkness. It was cold in here, in stark contrast to the paralysing heat outside. Her imagination took wings: what if no one let her out of here? Who would find her? Who would miss her? She would starve and die in this horrible, damp place.

Gradually her eyes adjusted to her surroundings. It was not as dark as she had thought. Slivers of daylight filtered through from beneath and above the doorframe and from the floor-grate; rotten bits of the architrave allowed further light to seep through. She could make out a dead rat near the step where she was crouched; another, which was very much alive, watching her. It did not seem in the least afraid, and once she became used to its apple-pip eyes fixed on her she ceased to be perturbed by it. It was quite pretty really, except for the bald pink tail, and she liked its twitching whiskers. Then, without warning, it placed its front paws on her and sprang onto her chest. She stifled her cry, holding her arms wide, but it did not bite her and simply perched there, as though in a trance and she released her held breath. Her slight movement must have frightened it, as then it darted along the length of her arm like a squirrel on a branch, jumped down and disappeared. Its feet tickled her as it ran, and she felt sorry for it all at once. It was not the creature's fault it was a rat, yet people were always trying to shoot them, or poison them, or lay traps, or set cats or terriers or ferrets or pine martens on them. Teenage boys thought it fun to bash them till their heads split; then string them up, sometimes still alive.

She wondered if the dead rat was the mate of the live one. That would be sad. She thought of her parents then. Perhaps it was best for them that they had died together. It was impossible to think of one of them without the other. Perhaps that had been God's intention.

A conversation with her mother came back to her: *You were born with passion in you, cara,* her mother told her. *Remember, your heart doesn't lie, but it may lead you astray. You have a powerful heart.*

Is that good or bad? Graziella had asked.

Both. And the job of your head is to decide when it is a good thing and when it is a bad thing...

The chain of Graziella's thoughts lead her a circuitous route, to the English family who had settled on the island for a few months. They had arrived in the early part of Spring, a year and a half ago, when the almond trees were in blossom. The husband was a softly spoken artist of enormous height and girth, while his wife, who was seldom seen without her guitar slung over her shoulder, was thin as a wraith and possessed a whimsical beauty. They had a son. His hair was gold and he had eyes that laughed. He wore a calliper. Their living accommodation was two tents, which they pitched close to Graziella's home, in a wild, elevated spot above the *Convento del Santo Bambino.* From here hibiscus-lined steps wound down to the village clustered below in colourful tiers, the houses stacked one upon the other, like irregular rows of teeth.

Hidden by a boulder, Graziella had lain down on her stomach in the long, coarse, grass and watched them set up camp. Their conversation drifted across to her, none of which she could comprehend, and she continued to spy on them as they unpacked their rucksacks.

'Boo!' a voice behind her exclaimed.

She turned, to see the boy grinning at her, shading his eyes from the sunlight with his hand. She sprang up and smiled back, then she thought she might get into trouble, and fled down the hill.

Word spread quickly of their arrival. Initially the locals had regarded the family with hostility, but then, a week into their stay, an incident occurred. It was early one Sunday morning. The village - or town, as some preferred to refer to it - was still cloaked in a silver sheen. The boy had got up to relieve himself, and in so doing disturbed a viper coiled on the rock which anchored down the tent. Surprised from its sleep, it sank its long-hinged fangs into the boy's arm.

The father had run through the silent village, in and out of a labyrinth of dark alleyways, cradling his son, calling, *Dottore! Dottore! Vipera! Vipera!*

Dogs barked in a syncopated chorus, shutters and doors were flung wide, and half clothed villagers gathered in the cobbled *piazza* to see what the commotion was about. Amongst them was the doctor, who even in his drooping underpants possessed dignity, and he hushed everyone up, told them to return indoors. It had been touch and go whether the child would survive. He owed his life to the power of prayer and to the antivenin, which Dottore Rugolo kept locked in his surgery.

After this incident everyone had rallied round and a constant stream of well-wishers had taken gifts to the family: homemade wine, homemade grappa, bunches of basil, salamis, olives and olive oil, the soft, pungent *formaggio di pecora*, ciabatta spiked with rosemary.

Graziella's father had made a stick with a wolf's head for the boy; by coincidence *Lupo* was also the family's surname, except it was in English. Wolf. Graziella had been curious to meet the boy again after that first encounter and had insisted on accompanying him. With her schoolteacher acting as interpreter, he had explained to the boy that he'd not yet cut the stick to its correct length because he needed to take measurements.

'But I would like you to leave it long please, for when I grow,' the boy said, via the teacher.

He and Graziella became friends. They saw each other every day, and wherever he went, he took the stick with the *Lupo* head.

'If you grasp it in the centre like a pole, rather than by its handle it won't trip you up,' she suggested when he kept stumbling; and she demonstrated what she meant. His name was Robert, but she called him Roberto, and he was exactly a year older than her - they were both born on January the first. They taught each other words from their respective languages, combining mime and gestures for clarity, though they understood each other instinctively. When he started at the local school her hand had shot up straight away, before anyone else had a chance to beat her to it: 'I must sit next to Roberto,' she informed her teacher. 'It's logical that I should as we are already friends.'

Her teacher had agreed that this made sense, despite the female protests, and Graziella exchanged places with the girl three desks away. The girl pinched her arm. Graziella poked her tongue out in return. Except for her friend, Raffaella Falcone, the girls were jealous of her and whispered about her behind cupped hands. She disregarded them. They were immature, giggly creatures.

Roberto proved to be a fast learner, and it was not long before he could converse in basic Italian, albeit with many errors.

Graziella was a hard taskmaster: 'It's not *"questa pomeriggio"*, it's *"questo"*. *It's masculine...*' Or, 'It's *"L'una e mezza"* not *" Luna mezza,"'* she would say.

When she deemed it appropriate she asked him what was wrong with his leg.

'I had polio,' he told her.

'Does it hurt?' she enquired.

'Not constantly, but sometimes it does. And if I do too much exercise, I get dreadful cramps. I used to feel as though I had insects crawling up and down me, but I haven't had that for a while. I nearly died, though.'

'That's twice you've nearly died,' Graziella commented. 'I'm glad you didn't.'

A couple of months passed. The air was sultry; the oranges on the trees ripened, and the grapes on the vines were becoming fat.

'We could take the mule cart and I could show you the vine-yards and orange groves,' Graziella suggested to Roberto.

'Are you allowed to go on your own?' he asked, impressed.

'Yes, as long as I don't go on the coast road, as it's so steep,' she said.

'Then I should like to come with you very much. Thank you,' he added, in that earnest manner which he had; and she smiled at his politeness, and also the mistakes in his Italian.

The following morning was a Saturday, and with both sets of parents observing, she harnessed the mule then hitched her to the cart. She demonstrated to Roberto the technique for climbing on.

'You have to lever yourself up onto the running board, then you just swing round onto the seat,' she said.

She saw his hesitation, and demonstrated again.

'You see? It's easy Roberto,' she assured him.

But it was not easy for him. The calliper was always in the way; and his mother looked on anxiously as, time and again, he attempted to replicate what Graziella had shown him. Twice he almost fell backwards.

'That's enough,' his mother insisted, holding her hands out in a plea.

'We could lift you on,' his father offered.

Roberto shook his head forcefully. 'No, I want to do it myself, stop fussing.'

The mule stood docilely as he made several further attempts. His forehead shone with perspiration. Graziella wished that she had not suggested the trip in the first place. This was her fault. It had seemed such a good idea though, and until now she hadn't realise the full extent of his disability; he had made such light of it that mostly she forgot about it. He was just Roberto. And she wanted to cry for him, and had to turn away, unable to bear his tortured expression, or watch his repeated, brave efforts. But Roberto had a stubborn streak and was not prepared to give up. Finally, using every last scrap of willpower that he possessed, he succeeded in hauling himself onto the running board; from there he half rolled, half scrambled onto the seat of the cart. He looked utterly spent, but he was laughing, and his eyes were alight with victory.

'*Bravo!*' they cheered him. '*Bravo Roberto!*'

'It will be easier next time,' he said.

Then Graziella had hopped nimbly onto the driving seat, and the pair of them posed while Roberto's father took photographs of them together.

They set off at a lazy pace, leaving the coast behind and passing the site for the football stadium, which was in the early stages of construction. It had been the mayor's brainchild; a trump card he had played shortly before the elections.

Within minutes they were in untamed countryside punctuated by a scattering of smallholdings. A ramshackle stone chapel, reached only by an overgrown footpath, sat at a midway point between them. Outside her shack Adelina Ferrara, dressed from head to toe in black, was hoeing her vegetable patch. Her face was as brown and cracked as the soil. A pregnant sow snuffled about amongst the geese, and a piebald goat lay on the dusty ground, its only sign of life being the twitching of its tail.

'*Buongiorno Signora*,' Graziella called. But the old woman did not glance up, and drove the hoe viciously into the ground.

'She looks angry like a crow,' Roberto observed.

'People call her that. "The crow",' Graziella said. 'I'm sorry for her. She must be lonely.'

'If she was nice she wouldn't be lonely.'

'Not necessarily. Maybe she's like it because people poke fun of her. My papa says she had a husband once. He was a drunkard and only married her for her patch of land.'

Roberto became thoughtful, and made a moue of his lips. 'Back home in England other children sometimes make fun of me because I'm lame,' he admitted.

He looked directly in front of him as he spoke, and she could sense his shame, and the pain in him.

'They copy how I walk. I try not to mind, but…' The rest of his sentence dangled poignantly in the air.

'If I were with you when that happened I would kick that person's shins,' Graziella said stoutly, and urged the mule forward with a growl in her throat as she had seen her father do.

He laughed. 'You are funny, Graziella.'

'Why?'

'You can sound so fierce sometimes, and you look so pretty and delicate.'

Flustered, she didn't know how to respond. She thought about correcting his Italian, but that seemed mean under the circumstances, so she merely shrugged. However, she was left with a peculiar feeling in her tummy.

They turned off the island road, onto a dirt track. Lentil fields stretched across the horizon in seemingly endless green waves.

Roberto took a bag of aniseed balls from his shorts' pocket and gave her one, before taking another for himself. She was struck again by his good manners, and wondered if all English people were like it. She felt inexplicably happy with him beside her.

They continued along here for a kilometre or so, sucking the sweets in companionable silence, interrupted only when a silver wild cat shot out from a thicket and ran across their path, a dead hare swinging from its jaws.

'*Che bello!*' Graziella crooned, at the same time steadying the alarmed mule. 'You hardly ever see them. They're very shy,' she told Roberto.

'I wish I had borrowed my father's camera,' he lamented.

'But the cat would have been gone before you could take a picture.'

'That's true. You're always logical. You always think of things before I do, Graziella, and I'm a year older.'

'Yes, but I'm a girl,' she said.

They made another turn, following an even narrower track that was shaded by tall, overhanging eucalyptus trees. The mule plodded on; she knew this route well and stopped of her own accord when the track petered out.

'This is it, we can't go any further,' said Graziella.

Through an archway of trees a breathtaking vista met the eye, of vineyards and orange groves against a backdrop of sweeping mountains and round-nosed hills. The vines on the lower slopes seemed to stretch forever; row upon uniform row of them, glistening from a recent, localised shower. A rainbow illuminated the orange groves, which sat on a raised plateau, their fragrance carried on the air in pungent bursts. Behind them soared *La Montagna della Madonna,* and in the shimmering light it seemed that her eyes were cast down in prayer. Halfway up the flank of the mountain, a small flock of sheep with lambs grazed peacefully.

Graziella dropped the reins and swivelled round to Roberto. He was gazing around him, awestruck.

'It's amazing,' he said quietly, in English.

The word was new to her, but from both his tone and his expression she could guess its meaning.

She looked about her and saw the familiar surroundings, which she had taken for granted all her life, through the freshness of his vision. She inhaled the intoxicating scents.

'*Si*,' she said slowly. 'Is a-maz-ing.'

She knew she would remember today for ever, even when she was as old as Adelina Ferrara.

And Roberto liked to play card tricks, but she could not understand how he was always able to guess the card she held in her hand and had picked at random.

'You have to concentrate very hard so the waves from your brain will go into mine,' he said, tapping her forehead.

'Show me the trick,' she begged.

'I've told you - it's not a trick. It's telepathy,' he insisted, his eyes laughing...

And he was a good swimmer, far better than her. His upper body was beautiful; it was golden and strong, and he swam with an elegant style. In the sea he was not lame. He would discard the calliper at the water's edge, throw himself in with a whoop, then she would watch him swim far out until he was a dot, and she became worried for his safety.

Then, on the second of November, seven months after the family had arrived, he came to see her and told her they were leaving the island; taking the ferry the next day. Returning to England.

Tears stood out in his eyes, and he kept spinning the wolf-head stick first in one direction then the other in his awkwardness.

Her mouth fell open. 'For good, you mean?' she asked, in a wavering voice.

He thrust his hands in his pocket. He could only nod.

Just twenty-four hours previously they had been celebrating All Saints' Day; the smell of incense lingered in her nostrils, together with marzipan fruit made by the nuns and coloured with vegetable dye, still hung from the bare branches of the trees. Absently she pulled off a marzipan lemon, which fell to the ground. Neither of them picked it up and it lay there between them, uneaten.

'But why?'

'My father wants me to have further medical treatment on my leg. And also my mother says she misses England.'

'But *I'll* miss *you*,' she blurted out.

'Me too.'

They stared at each other miserably. The laughter had left his eyes and she noticed green in them, and gold flecks. She had always thought they were grey. The lashes were as long as hers.

'I'll write to you,' he said. 'And you can correct my Italian. And when I'm a grown up I'll come back.'

When I'm a grown up. It seemed an impossibly long way away. An eternity away. She wanted to tell him that losing him was akin to losing a part of herself. She wanted to say so much, but the feelings within her were tangled up like the worms her father used for fishing bait and she was unable to articulate them.

Shyly he kissed her goodbye, lightly on the lips, and she smelt aniseed balls on his breath and sea salt in his hair.

She did not go to the harbour the next day to wave him off, though usually she found it a thrill to watch the ferry arrive and depart every Saturday morning. First the lorries with freight would drive off, then the odd car, and finally it was the turn of the passengers on foot. She liked to see them pouring off with their assorted luggage - smart suitcases, tatty bags, bulging parcels done up with string, gifts, pieces of furniture. There would be families, and men in formal business attire, lovers running into each other's arms, holidaymakers in rumpled shorts, men guiltily visiting their old widowed mothers. Off they streamed, all with their own stories, which Graziella wove in her head. There was hugging and weeping, and joy and sadness, and the volume of noise was immense: men unloading or loading cargo, shouted orders, excited chatter, the cranking of winches, a cacophony of bleating and clucking, braying or mooing; and sometimes livestock would break loose, and everyone would be running around trying to recapture the terrified escapees. Then the new passengers embarked, and a ramshackle queue would form, and there would be much pushing and barging, and heightened tempers.

However, this Saturday Graziella kept well away. To have stood on the dock watching her Roberto being consumed by the throng would have been too distressing. Instead she grabbed the mule from its corral, vaulted onto its back and rode to the vineyards. From here she would be out of earshot when the ferry's funnel bade a retreating farewell.

She had received more than a dozen letters from him over a period of nearly three months. They were on thinnest blue airmail paper, and always at least three pages long. In artistic, pointy writing, and grammar that became increasingly lax, he would relate his news to her: things he had done, places he had visited, funny incidents. She would try to picture him, to imagine his life in England but could not. He made no mention of his medical treatment, nor did she ask. On their joint birthday she had received a card from him with a picture of a horse on it.

I couldn't find a card with a mule, so this is the best substitute, he wrote. *Happy birthday and have a nice time. I miss you.*
Love, R xx
I miss you too, she had written in return.

They had corresponded until a couple of months ago; then, for no reason she could think of, his letters had stopped. She continued to write for a few weeks, and every morning she would demand of Maria Alberta, the postmistress, whether there was a letter for her, but there never was. So she gave up writing. What purpose was a one-way correspondence? It was demeaning. He had forgotten she existed and she must rid him from her mind. Nevertheless, she was hurt and sad.

Boys are funny creatures, her mother had attempted to console her, only days before the accident.

Yes, but he isn't. He wasn't like that, Graziella had said.

And now she remembered his polite manners, the card tricks, the soft pressure of his lips when he kissed her goodbye. She had kept all his letters and the card in an aniseed-ball tin, along with the snapshot of them together on the cart. They looked so happy, grinning into the camera lens. Even the old mule looked happy and alert.

Poor mule. Poor, loyal mule.

CHAPTER 5

RAT

Her attention returned to her current situation. She had noticed a large earthenware crock near the grate and realised now that it must contain her *zia's* famed cherry-liquor compote of which she was immensely proud. Graziella knew that in a few days she would be serving it up at a dinner party to which a number of illustrious guests were invited; a gleeful smile spread across her face, as an idea took shape in her mind. She stood up and lifted lid. In the dim light, the compote glistened like a dark pool of blood. She walked back to where the dead rat lay. For an instant, she fancied that it moved. Maybe it was alive after all, and was just in a deep sleep. She touched it with her fingertip. The stretched-out body was as stiff as a stale loaf of bread, and she could make out its teeth, bared as though in pain. Without question it was dead, poor thing; but at least its death would not have been in vain. Graziella picked up the corpse by its bald tail, carried it over to the compote and, giggling aloud, dropped it in. She had thought it might sink, but it floated in a circle on the surface, as though it had returned to life.

She pictured her aunt serving up the rat to the party guests: the whole evening would be in tatters.

Oh. The shock, the embarrassment.
The *shame.*

⊨⊨

She was released from the cellar after two hours. Annunciata had been making pasta and the tip of her long nose was daubed with flour, like a clown.

'I hope that has taught you a lesson,' she said, standing over Graziella in the kitchen and wagging a floury finger at her like a metronome.

Graziella stared through her and thought of the rat.

'You may go to your room now,' Annunciata said, lowering her eyes to escape her niece's unsettling gaze.

'Where is my stick?'

'I am not prepared to discuss the matter now. Go to your room please.'

For a few seconds Graziella stood her ground. She considered refusing to budge until she received an answer; but her aunt would only call the mayor. She could smell the smoke from his cigar through the open door to his study. He had the wireless on with the news, and above the newsreader's voice she heard the creaking of the wood floor and his heavy feet as he paced up and down; a habit of his when he was angry.

Reluctantly, she obeyed.

On the landing she encountered Nina, who was on her way downstairs.

'So you've been released,' she jeered.

Graziella was not in the mood for confrontation.

'Nina, please would you move so I can go to my room?' she requested in a reasonable tone, as Nina barred her passage.

'Technically speaking it is not your room. It belongs to my parents,' Nina said.

'Then technically speaking the same applies to yourself,' Graziella retorted.

Her cousin's eyes narrowed. 'You think you're so wonderful, don't you?'

'I don't anything of the sort.'

'Yes you do. Well I'm more than three years older than you, and you must do as I say. 'Nobody wants you here. My parents only took you in because of a premonition your father had, that he and your mother would die. He made my mother promise before God. Otherwise you'd have gone to an orphanage.'

'I don't believe a word you're saying. Now please let me pass.'

Nina continued to lean against the banister and smiled unpleasantly. 'Would you like to know what my papa did with your precious walking stick?'

'What did he do?' Alarm tugged at her tummy.

'He set fire to it. There is nothing left of it except ash.'

Graziella's mouth became dry. 'You're lying.'

'It's true. He burned it with the other rubbish. I saw him do it. Check the incinerator for yourself if you want.'

Graziella stared at her a moment longer. Her cousin's smile didn't waver.

With a cry, Graziella elbowed her aside and hurtled down the stairs. Her breath came in snatches as she ran, through the house - sweeping a vase of flowers from the window ledge in her flight; past the mayor's study, through the hall, through the arched doors to the courtyard, then down the garden to the end, where the incinerator was kept.

It was still smouldering, and smelt of charcoal. Puffs of grey smoke rose from it. At first all she could make out was a mound of ash; then she peered more closely, and she saw, poking out, the blackened remains of the wolf's pricked-up ears.

Her brain felt like a fat, overripe melon that would burst.

'*Bastardo,*' she screamed at the top of her voice. '*Bastardo.*'

She had never before used such a word. It carried across from the mayor's respectable house to the neighbouring houses, and brought her aunt running from indoors.

Her punishment this time was to go without supper. Not that she cared; she wasn't hungry. Her belly was brimful with hatred and grief.

In her room she lay on her bed, crying into the pillow. Then she stopped, and sat up. An invisible presence seemed to be caressing her, and she knew it was her mother.

You have to play a clever game, Graziella. You must plan your strategy. Stop thinking with your heart, the inner voice advised her.

A sense of calm washed over her. The feeling reminded her of when, as a young child, she had been stung by a medusa jellyfish; she had let the tide lap over her toe to soothe it. It felt like that now. Lifted from her despair, she made a resolution to herself: never again would she give the people whom she hated most in the world, the satisfaction of seeing her shed a tear. She would speak when spoken to, comply with what was asked of her and would even smile - but only with her lips. They would think they had won, but she would know otherwise. Then one day, however distant, she would have her revenge.

A griping pain stabbed her belly, and she felt a wetness in her knickers. She got up from the bed. She was bleeding between her legs. Dismally, she surveyed the red stain, willing it to disappear. It had gone right through the mattress, as though it had been stamped. Its shape was like a wolf's head, she thought.

She could not walk about bleeding. There was nothing for it: she would have to tell her aunt.

With her hand pressed between her legs, she crept downstairs.

CHAPTER 6

THE DINNER PARTY

'I am daring to hope that a Certain Person's behaviour has changed for the better,' Annunciata remarked to her husband, as, they waited for the guests to arrive.

'That's good,' he replied absently. He was reading an article about Silvio Milazzo, the regional president, in the *Giornale di Sicilia*, which was balanced on the mound of his stomach like a tray. He had met Milazzo recently at a function in Syracuse and found him to be very agreeable, but the article was scathing. He loathed journalists. You couldn't trust them not to twist everything you said or did. They should try running a government department; having to keep everybody happy. He had thought carefully before including the editor of the *Gazzetta* on the guest list for to-night's dinner party. There were pros and cons on both sides, but he had decided that on balance it was a good strategic move. He would ply the editor with good food and fine wine, slap him heartily on the back, generally flatter him, and just hope the little weasel did not bring up the unfortunate fiasco of the football stadium.

It was now ten months since its completion, and it stood disgraced and redundant, a graffiti-daubed folly which mocked the islanders every time they had to pass it. The owner of the construction company came from Taormina and had seemed to know what he was talking about; a nice backhander for the mayor had clinched the deal. However, as it turned out, he might as well have hired a bunch of baboons. The building had taken well over a year to complete; then, a matter of weeks after the inaugural match, with all its razzmatazz, there had been the tiniest of ground tremors, no bigger than a mouse's fart; half way through the day he got a call from his deputy, to say that cracks had appeared in the structure's brickwork. An independent inspection confirmed that the foundations had not been dug sufficiently deep. The indignant islanders had demanded answers, his opponents had bleated that he should resign; his colleagues from the *Consigliore Regionale* insisted he sue the construction company. But this was out of the question for the mayor, because of his "arrangement". The whole blessed thing was a mess.

For a while he strung everyone along. Then, conveniently, the owner of the construction company was discovered murdered in bed with his whore, and shortly after this the company was declared bankrupt.

Those who had their suspicions did not voice them.

But the mayor's popularity withered, and louts even vandalised his almond orchards, which was his main business. The stadium and what to do with it remained a noose round his neck. To knock it down would cause an outcry, but in order for the building to be made safe the foundations would require underpinning, which would cost a fortune. It was all a far cry from that joyful inauguration when he had presented the trophy to the winning team, and afterwards had been borne aloft on their shoulders, round the pitch.

'Of course it's too soon to tell, but I think the showdown the other day may have taught the young miss a salutary lesson,' Annunciata said. 'She told me she would like to pass round the platters of *antipasti* to our guests tonight, and I agreed to it.'

'That's good,' the mayor said again, having lost the thread of the conversation.

'It started me thinking - well she could be a useful extra pair of hands around the place. It would be a way of earning her keep.'

The mayor put down the newspaper with a resigned sigh. He wished his wife wouldn't witter constantly. She was wearing the sapphire choker he had presented to her on her last birthday. It drew attention to her scraggy neck - but it looked impressive, which was what counted. In fact it had not cost him a *centesimo*. He had acquired it from a jeweller in Palermo, who happened also to own a brothel. The mayor had put considerable business his way over the years.

'Did you listen to me?' Annunciata demanded.

He made himself appear interested. 'Yes. Earning her keep, you said.'

She nodded. 'So, I thought she could help the maid. You know some light housework after school. A bit of ironing. It would be good discipline for her. She's been allowed to run wild, that's her trouble. And then, when she is fifteen and finished her schooling, we could dispense with the maid. It would save money.'

'Why not?' the mayor answered. He was all for saving his money.

≈+ +≈

Graziella changed into the black skirt her aunt had insisted she wear, and tied the white, frilled apron at the back.

'Why do I have to dress like a waitress? I'm only helping,' she had protested.

'You will do as I say, without argument.'

Annunciata had put her fingers to her temples as though she had a headache and Graziella was its cause. The wattle beneath her chin quivered in irritation.

You look like a guinea fowl, Graziella thought.

She made a contrite face. 'I'm sorry, *Zia,*' she said. And she caught a whiff of her mother's lavender water, as though she had just glided past.

Annunciata considered her with knotted lips. 'Very well. But your hair should be in a bun. I shall do it. I don't trust you to make a proper job of it.'

Graziella's eyes had streamed as she prodded and spiked her scalp with pins, to anchor the hair in place. She was sure her aunt was relishing inflicting the torture. The pain was made bearable by thinking of the surprise that lay in store for her aunt. At this moment the compote stood at the back of the kitchen, surrounded by blocks of ice to keep it cool.

She went downstairs. Nina was in the hall, adjusting her dress in front of the mirror, tugging it down over her knees. Graziella recalled her mother remarking that the mayor looked like a pig. In that case his daughter resembled a piglet, in the too-tight pink dress which strained against her chest.

She saw Graziella in the mirror, and turned round.

'What are you staring at?'

'Nothing. I wasn't staring.'

'Yes you were. Anyway, I don't know why you're looking so pleased with yourself. You aren't even going to the dinner.'

'That's alright. I didn't expect to be asked.'

Nina glowered, peeved. 'Don't you mind?'

'Not in the least, why should I?'

In a further effort to rile her, Nina chanted: 'Little miss nobody, little miss nobody. That's what you are. A nobody. A maid.'

And though her fingers itched to pull her cousin's hair by the roots, Graziella kept her temper.

'Have a nice evening, Nina,' she said equably.

She opened the door to the kitchen. Lucia Penta, who had been hired to cook for the party, was there, stirring the glaze for the boar. It had been shot by the mayor, and hung from a hook in the cellar, its mouth snarling in protest. She looked up as Graziella entered, and moved from the window. Instantly, the evening sunlight, which had been obscured by her enormous bulk, infiltrated the room. She kissed Graziella on either cheek. 'Eh, that's good, Graziella. You're in time to help me,' she said.

Known to everybody as Mama Lucia, because for many years she had been a midwife, she owned the most popular café-bar on the island. Graziella's father would meet Stefano there most evenings for a glass or two of Grappa and a game of backgammon.

'I'd like you to continue stirring the glaze, please Graziella, whilst I make the truffle sauce,' Lucia said. 'Let it thicken and reduce but it mustn't bubble or the honey will burn.'

Graziella took the wooden spoon from her. As she slowly stirred, steam curled and escaped through the open window, carrying her memories along with it. Instead of her aunt's modern kitchen, she saw the one in the *casetta*, her mother stirring *brodo* on the wood-burning stove, throwing in lumps of meat, root vegetables and bones for flavour. It would simmer for hours in the cauldron, and they would have it for their evening meal, dipping in chunks of bread and raw garlic. They had no electricity, and when dusk descended, they lit the oil lamps, which gave off an orange glow and made shadows on the whitewashed walls. Then, one weekend her father announced he was going to make a cooler. He dug a deep square hole near the well, swinging the pickaxe rhythmically into the concrete-hard earth, before exchanging it for a spade. The sun had burned down, but the only time he broke off was when Graziella brought out a bottle of *limonata* for him. He had gulped it down in a second, and resumed work. When the hole was dug he then had to line it. He had donned gauntlets to protect his hands from the flame of the gas torch, and as he cut through the metal sheeting it sparked and hissed, and red-hot, molten globules fell, spitting, to the ground. Graziella stood a safe distance away with buckets of water from the well in case of a mishap. The heat was immense and her father had removed his leather apron and stripped to the waist. Sweat poured from him and his muscles gleamed. She thought he looked like Odysseus; she had seen an illustration of him in a book she had borrowed from the library van, which came on the ferry each month.

It's as efficient as anything you'll see in a swanky shop, and what's more, when there's a power cut my cooler will still function, he boasted, when the cooler was completed at the end of the day.

Her mother had kissed him full on the lips, and there was a look in her eye which Graziella was beginning to understand...

'Have you fallen asleep there, Graziella?'

Mama Lucia's voice, rough-edged from smoking, cut into her memories. She blinked to re-orientate herself.

'No, Mama Lucia. Nor have I burnt the glaze.'

Lucia chuckled and tweaked her chin. 'Eh, I was joking.'

She lowered her head to the saucepan to sniff the contents. The slab of her backside was not unlike the boar, rotating on the spit, Graziella thought.

'Eh! *perfetto.* You have done well, little one,' Lucia approved, and taking hold of the handles, she poured the glaze over the boar. It sizzled and spat onto the tray beneath it as though it had come to life. She wiped a trickle of perspiration from her face, and glanced at the clock. '*Porca miseria* - they'll be here any minute. I must push on...Take out a platter of *antipasti* would you? Lord knows where the maid has got to.'

The guests had been invited for seven thirty, and at seven thirty-three they began to arrive. First Doctor Rugolo and his wife, followed almost immediately by the attorney Pedro Mendolia and his wife. Padre Alberto came next, and then the widowed Contessa Leonora D'Alesandro, who lived with her gigantic mastiff dog in one of the grand villas on the coast. Nina had been given the task of welcoming guests and taking the ladies' shawls. 'Good evening, it's a pleasure to see you,' she recited to each; and bobbed in a curt-sey when the *Contessa* dropped her shawl into her arms.

La stupida, Graziella thought, from her assigned spot, by the statue of Pan. *Look at her simpering and kowtowing.*

The *Contessa* shook hands with the host and hostess, and pro-ceeded down the garden. In readiness, Graziella held out the plat-ter of *antipasti* for her; but then it slid from her grip.

The *Contessa* steadied her by the arm. 'That was close,' she com-mented dryly.

'I'm so sorry,' Graziella apologised. She imagined what her aunt would say, if she heard of this.

The *Contessa* peered down at her. She was taller than most men, and must once have been very beautiful. 'What is it? You look stricken,' she asked.

'Your stick - my papa made it.'

'Your father was the chicken vendor?'

'Yes *Contessa.*'

She helped herself to a *melanzane* and *ricotta* parcel. 'The stick was my late husband's. I commissioned your father to make it for him.'

'I know.'

She could recall her father returning home that day, full of himself.

You'll never guess, he said. *The Contessa has commissioned a ram's head stick from me for her husband, Il Conte! Her mother had clapped her hands: Oh you are clever. I must go and tell my snob of a sister,* she exclaimed.

'Your father was a true craftsman.'

'Yes he was. I loved watching him work.'

'I heard about the accident. You poor child, what a shock for you.'

'Yes, it was. *Orribile.*'

The kindness of this haughty woman was unexpected, and she felt herself on the brink of tears. But just then she caught her cousin's astonished expression, and the moment passed. Oh how jealous Nina must be.

The *Contessa* helped herself to another *antipasto.*

'What is your name?' she asked, in her direct manner.

'Graziella.'

'And your age?'

'Thirteen and a half.'

'So young? Why are you working here as a waitress?'

'I'm the niece of Signora Carluccio. They took me in.'

'Did they now? Well, Graziella, you are an extremely pretty girl. I would like to offer you a word of caution. There are certain unscrupulous people who, given the chance, will take advantage of one. Don't let that happen to you.'

She lit a cheroot, took a languid drag of it, plucked another antipasto from the platter, and limped off to talk to Signor Tebaldi, the *direttore di banca.*

Five minutes or so elapsed, during which Carlotta, the maid, turned up, sporting a black eye, which the patch across it was unable to hide. The other guests trickled in at intervals, one of the last being the editor of the *Gazzetta.* It made Graziella smile to herself to see the fuss the mayor was making of him, thumping him on the back as though they had been best friends. By eight o'clock all of the twenty guests were assembled on the terrace.

'You may circulate with another platter of *antipasti,*' her aunt said. 'But before you go, what were you speaking to the *Contessa* about? I hope you weren't being a nuisance.'

'No *Zia.* She asked my name and I told her. I said how kind you had been to me, taking me in, as you've done. She said I was very fortunate and should be grateful, and I told her that I was.'

Annunciata looked sharply at her, her lips puckering into a sphincter. But Graziella maintained her fervent expression.

'Well she is right of course,' her aunt said. 'I'm pleased you are beginning to appreciate it.'

Graziella went from group to group with the platter. She could feel the men's eyes following her, and shrank into herself. Lately she had become aware of this happening, and it unnerved her; it felt intrusive, and somehow sinister. Even Padre Alberto, who had an eye which wandered disconcertingly, got a look in his good eye that was less than holy when it alighted on her.

As you grow up you will find yourself looked at by men, her mother had told her on her thirteenth birthday. *Ignore them as though they were just annoying ants.*

Graziella re-adjusted her posture, making herself as tall as she could. Snippets of conversation flitted in and out of her conscience: *Fancy permitting a servant to turn up with a black eye... He won't get in for another term.... I'm thinking of running for office myself... So pretentious... The football stadium... You won't find a white wine in Sicily better than my Grille ... What á little beauty that young maid is. I tell you, I wouldn't mind...*

She shut her ears. With the exception of the *Contessa* there was nobody here tonight with a genuine soul. They were here for what they could gain: the men with their prosperous stomachs, their boasting and posturing; the women with their chignons and heavy bracelets and artificial laughter. Graziella could almost feel sorry for her aunt. Not one person here cared about the other, though they pretended to. And she might be young, but she could see it for what it was.

She extricated herself - and almost fell into the arms of her cousin Giorgio. He was offering round glasses of Bellini and had been tailing the vineyard owner, Dino Lombardo, reluctant to interrupt him in the middle of recounting an anecdote; when, finally, he had been noticed, he'd backed away in relief.

'Oh s-sorry Graziella. I didn't see you there,' he apologised, blushing.

'It's fine, Giorgio, honestly.'

Poor Giorgio, he looked so pained, with his skinny shoulders curved inwards, as though it might make him less visible. She knew he would have been dreading this evening. She felt sorry for him. He could not be blamed for his parents and sister. His father continually belittled him, addressing him as "Moron" - which he definitely was not.

'You mustn't worry Giorgio. In a few hours it will be over.'

'I wish it was over now. I won't know what to s-say to anybody. I shall s-stammer and make a fool of myself.'

'Why don't you pretend everyone is a different animal?' she suggested.

He laughed. 'Is that what you do?'

She raised a cryptic eyebrow by way of reply.

'I'm s-sorry my parents and sister are so vile to you.'

She was taken aback. 'It's hardly your fault, Giorgio.'

'No, but I just wanted to tell you that.'

'Thank you.'

'I think they feel threatened by you.'

'Threatened? By me? But why?'

'They b-believe that your father's background reflects badly on them… And you are v-very, well, pretty, and my sister is jealous, and my mother is worried no-one will look at her with you here.'

'You worked that out?'

'Yes. It's obvious.'

And thinking about it now, it *was* obvious.

'I think you're very clever, Giorgio.'

'Thank you. That means a lot to me.'

'You'll be off to university in another year or so.'

'If I pass my exams.'

'You will.'

'I c-can't wait to go - leave the island, get away from my parents. They m-make me absolutely sick,' he said, with a vehemence which quite surprised her.

At eight-fifteen on the dot, the white-gloved butler, in reality Antonio the gardener, rang a hand-bell and announced that dinner would be served. Supervised by Annunciata, guests were ushered indoors. The dining room looked splendid, she thought: two long tables, covered with white damask cloths, formed an 'L'; the silver gleamed, the cut glass sparkled, the red and gold dinner service was reflected in the Venetian glass candelabras. A display of orchids at the far end of the room provided the final touch. Who could fail to be impressed?

Padre Alberto said grace and they sat down, the host and hostess at the opposite ends of the table. Carlotta and Antonio carried in the first course. It was unfortunate about the maid's eye; you couldn't ignore it, but, that apart, the evening was running to plan; the swordfish, in a caper and lemon sauce, was delicious, the guests appeared to be enjoying themselves, and conversation flowed. Buoyed up by two glasses of *Grille*, she began to relax. Her husband had no idea how stressful it was organising an event of this kind. He seemed to think it happened by magic. Table plans were always tricky, and this one had been a nightmare. At the last minute two of the guests had had a spectacular falling-out, which meant that their wives weren't on speaking terms either. It had been most inconvenient, as she had put them next to each other, so it entailed a complete reshuffle.

The empty fishplates were removed and the boar was wheeled in. Mama Lucia made an appearance, and the mayor demonstrated his magnanimity by pouring her a glass of Grappa. Conversation grew louder and lewder, as more bottles of wine - a plummy *Nero d'Avola* to accompany the meat - were opened. The mayor found an appropriate moment to air his views on Silvio Milazzo, and so far nobody had brought up the subject of the stadium, at least, not within earshot. The evening wore on…

From the landing, concealed by a yucca plant, Graziella watched the theatre. Time was passing with aching slowness. She thought she would go mad with her impatience. Her body felt as though it was inhabited by a thousand vibrating cicadas. This prompted her to think of Roberto. He had loved their song; marvelled at how it struck up in unison, as though synchronised by clockwork.

It's the male which makes that sound, she told him. *They've got a kind of plate beneath their abdomen which makes it.*

I thought it was the legs rubbing together, he said.

No, that's a cricket.

How do you know all these things, Graziella?

I just do.

The table was being cleared of the main course, and the compote was brought in on a trolley, along with two almond cakes.

Beside herself with anticipation, Graziella watched her aunt rise from the table and walk over to the sideboard, with a queenly expression.

Any minute… Any minute…

Slowly, as in a ritual, Antonio lifted the lid from the compote and set it down for Annunciata. She peeped into its depths. An opaque skin had formed across the top, but she was unconcerned. Sometimes this could occur. She picked up the heavy silver ladle, waited a few seconds to prolong the drama; then, in front of all these dignitaries, she plunged it in, and ladled out the soggy rat.

Her shriek was that of a pig being slaughtered, and she flung it in the air, in a dripping arc. It landed in the lap of the diplomat's wife, who shook it off her with a screech. And soon the sound of women's screaming filled the room, as though a massacre were being carried out, and for a few seconds the scene resembled a game of pass-the-parcel, as the rat went from person to person. Then the inebriated men joined in the rumpus, kicking the corpse about like a football; glasses and crockery were smashed and the room was in uproar.

Amidst the uproar the editor of the *Gazzetta* slunk away, unnoticed, to write a satirical piece which had surely been sent to him by the gods; the *Contessa* wiped away tears of mirth and lit another cheroot; and, on the landing, hidden behind the yucca plant, Graziella rocked with laughter.

CHAPTER 7

NOW

ROSA

'Oh, that's fantastic. So funny.'

'Yes, it really was.'

And my mother's eyes are wet with laughter. Her laughter is beautiful: a youthful, joyful trill, full of mischief, now captured forever on this little machine. One day in the future I shall sit, listening to the recording of that laughter, over and over again. I shall be able to remember the real woman, before she became a shadow.

The laughter fades.

She looks out of the window, at Lupo and Tosca chasing round the garden, playing hide and seek.

'There was this dog,' she says in a distant tone.

'What dog?'

'He was one of the many strays on the island. I could tell he was blind in an eye, as it was opaque, and he was a tiny, pathetic, scrap of a thing, covered in sores. I could tell he was old, and his coat was like wire wool. I was so sorry for him... I took food from the house to feed him and cleaned his wounds. I called him Beppe

… No I didn't; that was my papa's name, wasn't it? You remember Papa, don't you?'

'No Mama, I wasn't born at that …'

'And I loved Bernardo, yes, that was his name. The wonderful thing was it was reciprocated. His little tail wagged as soon as he saw me. And I had a purpose in life again. He gave that to me. It made me smile just to think of him. Love is everything Rosa, whether that of a mongrel dog or a human. Poor Adelina Ferrara was not loved by a living soul. Not even her sow, who had eaten half her face by the time her body was discovered…'

I have noticed that increasingly my mother's conversation veers off track; and she will bring up names from the past which I have never heard of before and pertain to her own childhood.

'You were telling me about Bernardo, Mama.'

'Yes… He became *my* dog. And he was very clever. He'd wait for me in the morning, always a short distance away, as though he understood that it would be risky, and he would follow me to school. He learned what time I finished, and there he would be, by the gate, waiting for me. But then after a few weeks my aunt caught me taking salami from the larder, and I had to explain. I pleaded with her but she fetched my uncle. He forced me to bring Bernardo to the house, then he fetched his gun and he shot my dog in front of me. The only consolation was that his death was instant.'

'The bastard.'

'Yes. *Veramente.* Anyhow, I apologised for my crime and pretended to be repentant. I would not let them see that I was broken hearted, though my whole being was screaming. Day in, day out, for another year, I hid my feelings and played my part, waiting for my moment of revenge, which I knew would come… And a while ago you asked me why I cannot cry: I think that is the reason.'

She cannot, but I can.

On the pretext of needing the loo I head for her bathroom, where I sob quietly. Then I flush the cistern to avoid my mother's suspicion, and run the tap to rinse my hands. The *"His"* and *"Hers"* towels on the rail make me smile in recollection. They were an anniversary gift from myself. Her towel is pristine, whereas my stepfather's is damp and grubby; she must be using his. And his face flannel too, by the look of it. I leave the towels just as they are and dry my hands on my jeans. My stepfather's navy velour dressing gown hangs from a hook on the door. It is stained with Mama's red lipstick. Oh my poor Mama. I hurt for her.

The upper shelf of the rattan chest is taken up with his personal bits and pieces. Mama has the shelf below. And amongst the creams, lotions and oils I notice a pill dispenser. Closer inspection reveals the pills to be *Donepezil.* After hours spent on the computer, to find out what I could on the subject of Alzheimer's, the name is familiar to me. There is no cure, but pills work as inhibiters apparently, and can slow down the deterioration. But the dispenser is all very well, until the day she forgets to look at it. I shall have to come in daily. Or organise a carer. And I can envisage the resistance, and the battles ahead. My head is bursting with imponderables.

'Where were you?' Mama asks me, when I return to the living room. 'I was worried you'd gone.' Her voice is fuzzy with sleep.

'I only went to the bathroom,' I tell her, sitting down.

'Oh yes. I must have been dozing. I'm not sleeping well. I have dreams…'

She looks out of the window again. The dogs are lying side by side on the lawn, panting.

'Liz has promised she will keep the sanctuary going when I am no longer capable,' she says, staring ahead.

I clasp her arm.

'Oh Mama.'

There is nothing I can say.

CHAPTER 8

THEN

NEW DECADE

1960 was ushered in with a carnival and street party. The *piazza* was adorned with bells and balloons and bunting, and the village illuminated by lanterns and fairy lights strung from one end to the other. Tables heaving with food stretched as far as one could see. Young men on Lambrettas and Vespas eyed up women, lovers canoodled, laughing groups of girls linked arms, families were out in full force: wailing babies in prams; children tearing about in masks; toddlers riding piggy-back on their fathers' shoulders. Graziella could remember peeping down at the world from aloft her father's shoulders; his hand would be locked around her ankles, her arms gripping round his neck. How secure she had felt, high up there. Nothing could ever harm her.

She wandered about, losing herself amidst the throng. She had set off from the house with Giorgio and his friend, Paulo, but the latter had kept pestering her, and she had detached herself from them. He was vain beyond belief and couldn't pass a mirror without stopping to admire himself in it.

At seven o'clock, heralded by a fanfare of trumpets, the carnival began. The brass youth band lead the procession, wending its way through the alleys and up the steps, lustily playing their instruments, though not always together or in tune. Hot on their heels were members of the armed forces, in an impressive march. A succession of flower-bedecked floats followed: small children, dressed as characters from history, garlanded girls in white dresses, women in national costume tossing confetti into the crowds, nuns from the convent, masked harlequins. There were puppeteers and jugglers, a suitably fat Roman emperor and his empress, gladiators with rippling biceps, and Old Father Time with a beard down to his toes. Even the mules and donkeys conveying the floats had been spruced up, and looked as fine as Arabian horses with their gleaming coats and feather plumes - marred only slightly by the shitting and braying. Then came the carnival queen, borne along on a glittering throne, waving as she passed. Graziella's teacher had offered her the role, but Annunciata had forbidden her. As it happened she hadn't wanted to do it anyway, though that was not the point. Her friend Raffaella Falcone had been chosen instead, and Graziella was glad for her. She was a timid, and trusting girl, with a speech impediment and slow manner, and was picked upon by her classmates. Graziella would intervene on her behalf.

It's alright Graziella. I don't need protecting, Raffaella told her.

But they shouldn't get away with it.

It doesn't matter. I don't mind.

Recently, she'd announced that she was leaving school to become a novice with the *Ordine del Santo Bambino.*

'But you can't.' Graziella had protested, stunned and dismayed.

'I have to. It's a calling.' Raffaella explained.

'I'll never see you.'

'Yes you will. The convent isn't a prison. You would be able to visit.'

'You're my best friend, and we'll lose touch. It's inevitable.'

'No it isn't. It's up to you,' Raffaella replied.

In that moment Graziella had realised that she needed her friend more than her friend needed her.

On foot, headed by the mayor and Padre Alberto, came the dignitaries of the island. An egg whizzed through the air, splattering the edge of the mayor's robe. For a second he faltered, then he continued, reddening in anger as cheers went up.

When the last float had disappeared from sight, people helped themselves to the food, tearing into it like hyenas at the kill, pushing and shoving to get to it, loading their paper plates until they resembled castles. The men got drunker and drunker and the usual scuffles broke out, though nothing too serious, and Lorenzo Torre, the *carabiniere*, made no arrests. Then the band struck up and the dancing began. The celebrating reverberated from the square to the harbour, and the hills beyond.

In her shack Adelina Ferrara, "The Crow", dimly heard them. Her embittered heart had given up and she lay on the earthen floor dying of old age and prolonged disappointment. She drew her last, rattly breath to the tune of *"Volare"*, leaving behind a sow, a goat and three geese to mourn her passing.

Sitting alone on an upturned crate, her plate of uneaten food on the sandy ground beside her, Graziella saw Stefano approaching. He was with a woman, and in his hand was a bottle of Peroni. He stopped by her feet, slopping beer on his shoes and hers.

'Graziella, Graziella, where have you been? I haven't seen you for ages,' he said, slurring his words.

She stood up, laughingly ducking from his alcoholic embrace. 'Nowhere,' she said. 'I've not been anywhere. And you could have visited me.'

'I don't think I would have been very popular, Graziella.'

'No. On second thoughts, maybe not,' she agreed.

'But look at you!' Stefano gave an appreciative whistle. 'The *piccolina* is all grown up and beautiful in that lovely dress.'

It was Nina's pink dress, which she'd salvaged from the bin, and dyed red.

'Thank you,' she said lightly. She felt awkward; not because the compliment was inappropriate - he'd known her since she was born - but because of the woman's eyes boring into her.

'Oh this is Donatella,' Stefano introduced her at last. 'Did you know I have got engaged? Finally the fisherman has been hooked.' He laughed at his own joke.

Graziella congratulated both of them. Donatella continued to stare at her.

'Yes, isn't she wonderful, aren't I the luckiest man?' He pulled his fiancée against him. Her smile was wooden.

'Why don't you join us Graziella? We must have a dance? Yes, really you must. Wouldn't that be nice?' Swaying on his heels, he turned to the silent Donatella.

'I'm tired, Stefano. I'm going back to the house.' Graziella said.

'But you can't. It's not midnight. And there are the fireworks to come.'

'Let her go if she wants to,' Donatella said; the first time she had spoken.

He looked surprised. 'Well of course... Ah, but it is so good to see you, though, *piccolina*. Such a young woman, now. I miss your father, you know. I think of him often. He was my best friend.'

'Let the girl go, Stefano. She has told you she wants to,' Donatella said.

'Of course, of course. But it's such a shame.'

Clumsily he embraced her again and they parted.

In bed, she clutched her yellow rabbit and listened to the revelry. A huge cheer went up as the church clock struck the hour, then the sky was illuminated with fireworks. She wanted to cry, but couldn't. What would the new decade hold for her? And in the morning it would be her birthday. In fact it already *was* morning, therefore it was also her birthday. She was now fifteen.

CHAPTER 9

THE MAID

She slept for an hour or two. Dreamed of her father. He sat at his workbench, carving. It did not seem strange to her that he was dressed in naval uniform.

She ran to him: *But you're alive! I had a terrible nightmare that you were dead. Where is Mama?*

Your Mama was killed by an octopus but I am bringing her back to life. See?

And he showed her his work. It was the form of a woman, but instead of wood he was using sheets of airmail paper with words on it that she could not decipher.

She was woken by the howling of the wind, coupled with rain battering down. The storm sprang up from nowhere, when the revelry had reached its peak, putting paid to the music and dancing, driving everyone indoors. In another display of pyrotechnics, lightning shot through the night, and thunderclaps shook the heavens. The wind roared and screeched round corners, bending the naked trees as though they were made of rubber, toppling power cables, ripping up canopies, tearing off roof tiles. Shutters banged open and closed, window panes shattered, metal signs swung to and fro, and a thousand paper plates and a thousand paper cups were scattered across the island. In the belfry, exposed by an avalanche of tiles, the bells rang on their own, like a ghostly call to mass. The sea reared up, crashing onto the shore, spewing creamy foam as high as the harbour wall, setting free the rattling, fishing boats which had been hauled onto the beach.

Then, at around six in the morning, the ferocity of the storm abated, and an hour later it had all but died.

Graziella had been up for several hours, unable to return to sleep. The electricity to the whole island had been cut off and she had got dressed in darkness, using her torch to see. Now dawn was breaking. She was curled up on the window-seat in the parlour, straining to read a large book. *Animals of the World,* it was entitled. Her teacher had lent it to her. It was the most beautiful book she had ever seen - better than anything the library van could offer, on its fortnightly Wednesday visit - and must have cost a great deal of money. The glossy pages were packed with photographs, illustrations, diagrams and fascinating facts, and an entire section was devoted to animal behaviour.

'I know you will look after it,' the teacher had said.

'With my life,' Graziella, replied, hugging the book to her.

As it grew lighter the villagers stumbled outside, most of them hungover or still drunk, to assess the damage to their properties. Through the window Graziella watched the shadowy figures wandering back and forth despondently, gesticulating and pointing, and she could hear the subdued murmur of their voices. They did not stay outside for long and, disheartened, they returned indoors, probably to bed.

The mayor's house remained impervious to the weather's vagaries, and except for a few broken terracotta pots, incurred no damage.

The mayor descended the stairs now, with a heavy tread. He showed no sign of having seen her, and marched through the hall and out: A man with a purpose. From the way he slammed the front door she guessed he was going to the football stadium, to learn its fate. He drove off in his Alfa Romeo, though it was only a ten-minute walk there.

Her aunt came downstairs next, in her quilted housecoat.

'Good morning Graziella. What a storm… And goodness knows when the electricity will be repaired.' Her friendly tone changed and became imperious: 'Stop reading please. I have something I wish to talk to you about.'

Forewarned that whatever it was, she would not like it, Graziella laid the book down on the chest. She raised an eyebrow in query. 'Yes *Zia*?'

'Don't do that,' Annunciata said.

'Don't do what *Zia*?'

'Raise one eyebrow like that. It's insolent and off-putting.'

'I'm sorry *Zia*. I didn't know I did it.'

'Hmm.' She sat down, tucking her slippered feet beneath her. Her bunion protruded through the fabric. 'Anyway, I was about to tell you that you will not be returning to school.'

'What do you mean?'

'Precisely what I said.'

'You mean I am leaving school, for ever?'

'That is what I mean, yes.'

'But why? I want to stay at school. I want to go on studying and become a vet. I don't want to leave. Why should I leave?' Her words tumbled out in a heated stream.

'I want, I want, I don't want, I don't want,' Annunciata mimicked her. 'You are not in a position to make demands, Graziella. We all want things we cannot have.'

Graziella let her eyes wander round the room; it exuded middle-class affluence, with its highly polished furniture, fussy ornaments and photograph of the mayor shaking hands with the Italian prime minister.

'What did *you* want that you could not have, *Zia*?' she asked, unable to conceal her bitterness.

Instead of the reprimand that Graziella had anticipated, her aunt became reflective. A wistful expression blurred the sharpness of her features. In a moment of insight Graziella knew that more than anything in the world Annunciata had wanted to be beautiful. As a child she would have prayed nightly to be transformed into a swan. Then, as she grew up, she would have prayed for love. Both had been denied her. They had been the privilege of her younger sister.

Graziella took advantage of the moment.

'Please let me stay on at school, *Zia*. I would like to go to university one day. My teacher says I stand a good chance of a scholarship if I continue as I am.'

The glimpse of her aunt's vulnerability was short-lived. Her face resumed its habitual sourness.

'There will be no further discussion on this matter. I have already informed your teacher you won't be returning. And I have dismissed the maid.'

Graziella pressed her knuckles into her cheeks. 'But *why*? And what has Carlotta got to do with ...'

'I have a present for you.' Annunciata cut her short.

'For me?'

'Yes. For your birthday.'

She had noticed a large, gift-wrapped box beside the ironing board, but it had not occurred to her it might be for herself. Never before had she received a gift from her aunt, and she watched suspiciously as Annunciata heaved it up from the floor onto the table. It was clearly heavy, and she set it down with a relieved sigh, and her knees creaked.

Graziella made no move.

'Well open it,' Annunciata said.

Curious, despite herself, she untied the red ribbon then tore off the festive paper and lifted the lid. Dumbfounded, she stared into the box. It was packed with cleaning materials of every description, and each item had been artfully arranged between layers of red tissue.

With a sickening realisation, she comprehended why Carlotta had been dismissed.

She was to be the new maid.

How long had her aunt been planning this?

Despair rose in her. For more than a year and a half she had played her role, consoling herself it was a means to an end. A game. If she could bide her time, if she could restrain her temper, then eventually, she would be rewarded. Meanwhile, at least she had school and her studies; and she'd clung on to her dream of university, as though it were a lantern which never dimmed. What now, of those severed dreams? If this was a game, then it was a one-way game and she had been outwitted.

There was not a person to whom she could turn.

And where was her mother's voice? Why was she silent?

She continued to stare into the box. She wanted to throw it with all her strength at her aunt; the tin of floor polish would strike her head, which would crack open like a nut. She would fall to the ground, and blood would worm down the side of her face…

Annunciata mistook her lack of response for overwhelmed delight.

'You will be taking over from Carlotta, and as such it seemed appropriate to present you with your own cleaning materials on your birthday. You will be earning your keep, which is high time, and I am putting my faith in you. After an unfortunate start - and the less said about that, the better - you have shown yourself to be quite capable of undertaking the household duties and …' She broke off, frowning. Twin lines, which looked like a bird's claws, formed across the bridge of her nose.

'Well, what do you say?'

Strega brutta! Ugly witch! I wish I could poison you.

She collected herself.

'Thank you *Zia*. You've been very generous,' she said, and pressed her hands together for added effect.

Her aunt gave one of her grunts. 'You may have two afternoons off a week, and pocket money for basic requirements. I think you will agree that is generous. I would not wish it to be said that you were being exploited.'

'Nobody could think that, *Zia*.'

Brava cara! You did well. Believe in yourself. Your chance will come.

Her mother was there after all. And it occurred to Graziella that this had been a test, and she had passed it.

That afternoon the mayor's twin sister, Camilla, brought *Nonna* Anna for tea. The old lady sat, mute, in her wheelchair, staring vacantly ahead, her purple-blotched hands trembling on the swell of her lap. Her ancient Chihuahua lay across her white-stockinged feet, guarding her like a caryatid. She had suffered a stroke when, after her husband's death, her son had turfed her from the house and taken it for himself. It was much too big for an old woman on her own, the mayor had justified himself to critics. She would be better off living with her daughter, who could look after her.

Wearing her new apron, Graziella poured bergamot-scented tea into cups; she dropped a sliver of lemon into each, with a pair of silver tongs. Signorina Camilla slid a straw between her mother's lips and held the cup steady. Graziella could see the agonisingly slow passage of the liquid through the clear straw. She would not want to live like that, she thought. This wasn't life. She would beg someone to put a pillow over her face. Oh, but that wouldn't work, since in order to make the request she would have to be able to speak. *Madre*, what a ghastly fate.

Signorina Camilla had acquired the martyred look of a woman who'd had duty thrust upon her. Baking was her only pleasure, and today she had brought a lemon-thyme cake which was golden and moist with the fruit. Graziella cut it into portions and offered the first slice to the mayor.

He bit into it, dropping crumbs from his overloaded mouth as he masticated. 'Mm, *delizioso*,' he commented, smacking his lips. 'As sinful as the kiss of a virgin.' As he spoke he looked hard at Graziella.

There followed a stunned hiatus. Annunciata glared at her husband; Signorina Camilla's head jerked backward; *Nonna* Anna may or may not have blinked; and Giorgio writhed in his chair.

Graziella imagined her uncle's gold teeth and slimy-slug lips pressed to hers, and shuddered.

The mayor laughed, like a whinnying horse. 'Look at the lot of you. Where's your sense of humour?'

Nobody dared say anything. He was not in a reasonable mood after his visit to the football stadium. Its walls had been forced further apart, but the wretched edifice was still standing.

In a show of solidarity with her father, Nina laughed. They had always been close. Recently she had become engaged, and was even more obnoxious than before. An unflattering photograph of her had been in both the *Gazzetta* and the *Giornale di Sicilia*, and the wedding plans included a parade through the streets.

She took a slice of cake from Graziella.

'*Grazie*,' she said, exaggerating the first syllable. And beneath her breath she muttered: 'Maid.'

'*Prego*,' Graziella replied, sanguine in the knowledge that she had surreptitiously spat on Nina's slice of cake.

She glanced across at *Nonna* Anna. A glint had appeared in the old woman's eyes that had previously been absent. Her mouth seemed to have lifted fractionally. She was smiling! Was it possible she was smiling? Graziella was sure she was, and she smiled back at her.

Conspirators, they shared their tiny moment in silent communication and mutual approval. Graziella realised that although she was trapped within her carapace, capable only of observing and listening, she understood more than anyone else in this gloomy room. Her loyal little dog knew it.

CHAPTER 10

NOW

ROSA

My mother's voice dies away. She looks drained, her cheeks divested of colour. Though she won't admit it, the effort of concentration must tire her. I have learned, over the weeks that we have been doing this, not to rush her but to go at her pace, with all its circuitous diversions.

'You must have felt so alone, Mama. You were a child, for goodness sake.'

Her arched eyebrows rise further in surprise, as though she has never considered it before. 'Alone? Yes, I suppose I did. I was sad when Giorgio went away to university. He had been my ally. He became a lawyer.'

'I don't know how you bore it.'

'What choice was there? I just had to go along with it, *cara*.' She shrugs.

'I can recall your aunt, but only dimly the mayor. He looked rather like a pig, didn't he?'

My mother doesn't answer. An unfathomable expression flickers in her eyes, and all of a sudden an incident from way back surfaces to my memory. The *Isola* was small - you couldn't avoid running into people, like it or not - and one afternoon we had just left the café and there was her uncle outside, talking to someone. I remember how she took my hand and almost dragged me past without a word; I could sense her tension, and wondered about it.

There is so much I want to know, and fear I never will. And I realise, that some of her reminiscences will be inaccurate or skimped, while others will be embellished.

We go to her local pub for lunch. It is a Monday, and quiet. Only half the tables have been set up. Mama goes to sit where there is no place laid.

'Not there Mama,' I correct her.

'Why not?' she demands loudly. 'Surely I can sit where I want.'

'There isn't a place laid there,' I explain, conscious of sideways glances.

'Yes there is.' And she reaches across the next table, and lifting up a fork, waves it in the air.

A girl comes over to us, armed with cutlery and a mat. Clearly she had overheard our exchange.

'It's fine,' she says. 'I'll lay another place. It's not a problem.'

Mama turns to me: 'You see?' she says archly.

I bite my tongue.

We both choose the soup of the day, from the board. It arrives with a roll each, and I push the butter towards her - and watch, shocked, as she proceeds to spread it all over the plate. I say nothing, not wishing to humiliate her, and she bites into the dry roll.

'I buttered it, I know I did,' she mutters, half to herself. Then, obviously mortified, she sees what she has done. I go on talking and pretend not to have noticed anything amiss and after a few seconds she dips her spoon into the soup and takes a mouthful. But her hand trembles as it travels from the bowl to her mouth, and several drops spill onto the table mat. Without looking at me she says: 'You should have told me. Next time tell me please.'

However, it is hard to know when to prompt her, and when not.

Above all, Mama detests pity. She can't bear to be seen as weak, but sometimes it all gets too much for her. The other day I assured her that we all love her, and would always look after her, whatever happened. She regarded me with an expression that was difficult to read, but there was no anger in it. 'I do not want to be looked after, *cara*. Please understand that,' she said. 'I want to look after myself, thank you.'

'Well yes, of course. But when...'

She cuts across me: 'When I am shitting in my bed and no longer recognise you it won't make a scrap of difference who looks after me. It may to *you*, but not to me.'

'That could be ages off.'

'I prefer not to talk about it, *cara*.'

So we don't. Which helps *her* but not me. The list of subjects we *can* discuss is shrinking along with her brain, and I find myself struggling for things to say which aren't taboo. And when we do commence down a seemingly innocuous avenue, somehow invariably it meanders back down the forbidden territory. Frankly I'm scared. This affects all of us, all our futures. So next week Gino and I are meeting up to discuss matters. Mama would be furious if she knew.

She insists on paying for lunch, and we prepare to go. Every time I leave her I am filled with sadness for her lonely widowhood, and her lonely illness.

'Would you mind dropping me off at the sanctuary, on your way home?' she asks.

'Of course not.'

And that is another thing. She recently learned that she mustn't drive. If she did and she were to have an accident, her insurance would be invalid. She is reliant now on other people, which, understandably, she can't stand.

'It's ridiculous, I should be allowed to drive a couple of miles to the shops, or to the sanctuary,' she fumed the other day.

'The specialist did say you could have a driving assessment,' I pointed out.

'I'd never pass it.'

'There's your answer.' And I took away the car keys because I didn't trust her.

When she discovered what I had done she was livid.

'I'm not a child whose life you can just take over.'

'I know that. It's just in case you forget you shouldn't be driving.'

'Of course I won't forget. I wish you'd stop interfering.'

'I'm not. I'm *trying* to be practical.'

'Well you're not. You're being disrespectful to your mother. Sometimes I don't like you.'

Which cut through me.

'The feeling's mutual,' I threw back at her.

We did not speak for three days. Then we had dialled each other simultaneously. I had repeatedly got the engaged signal, as had she. When we realised, we dissolved into laughter.

Back home I make myself a coffee, sit at my computer, and press the 'play' button of the recorder. Mama's light tones are like stars dropping into the quiet of my study, bringing to life the island where I spent my childhood.

CHAPTER 11

THEN
TWO ENCOUNTERS

It was Saturday afternoon; the day after her birthday, and she set off for her old home, to check if there had been damage to it. She had been back only once, and that had been the day after the accident, to collect her possessions. Her aunt had gone with her and Graziella, in a state of shock, had gathered items randomly. Since then she had passed the *casetta* countless times but always scurried by. To linger would have been too painful.

The village was bustling with activity and the islanders were out in full force. Armed with brooms, buckets, hammers and screwdrivers, they were in good spirits, and a party mood prevailed. The mayor had organised a communal clean up and was in his element, presiding over groups, issuing instructions, waving his hands like the conductor of an orchestra. For the benefit of a press photographer he snatched up a broom and pretended to sweep - throwing it down when he departed.

The harbour area was less hectic, though no less industrious than the *piazza*, and Graziella spotted her schoolteacher amongst the helpers near the quay. Intent on avoiding her, she tucked her hair into the hood of her windcheater, bent her head forward, and tried to hurry past, but the teacher had seen her.

'Graziella!' Propping the broom against a door, she walked towards her.

Graziella moulded her features into a smile and went to meet her. Broken glass crunched beneath her feet.

For a bit they discussed the weather; when that was exhausted, the teacher said: 'I'm so pleased we've run into each other. I'd been intending to visit you before term starts. Graziella, what's all this about not returning to school? You can't leave. You're the best student I've ever taught.'

She was lost for an answer; unable to meet her teacher's concerned eyes. She said hesitantly: 'It's just … well, how things are now.'

'Your aunt assured me the decision was yours. Is that correct?'

Stunned, Graziella's mouth fell open. She was on the point of blurting out that it was a lie; that she had pleaded with her aunt to let her remain at school - then clamped her lips together. If her teacher were to become involved it could rebound on herself. Annunciata might throw her out of the house, then where would she go? And whilst she longed to leave, it would be on her terms only.

'Yes, it was my decision,' she said. And felt as though a porcupine spine had lodged in her throat. Now the teacher would think badly of her.

'But why? I don't understand.'

'Well… Lots of reasons.'

'Such as?' The teacher would not give up.

Graziella rotated her shoulders and did not answer.

'*Ayah!*' came a cry from nearby, and she transferred her attention to the clean-up operation. A young man had cut his arm on glass and was bleeding. Graziella could tell the injury was minor, but he was behaving as if he'd been mortally wounded, with his *Ayahs* and his groaning. It was obviously a ploy to exempt him from further work, but his wife was taken in. '*Povero, povero,*' she crooned, assisting him into one of the cottages.

Silly woman. How could she not see that her husband was a good-for-nothing shirker? She, Graziella, would never allow herself to be submissive to a man.

She turned back to the teacher.

'I'm bored with studying.'

'But you've always enjoyed it.'

'Not any more.'

'You're only just fifteen. You're too young to make such a decision.'

'Most girls leave school at fifteen, even thirteen or fourteen.'

'Yes, but not girls like you. You are outstanding. You're two years ahead for your age. Think - in only another year and a half you could be going to university. I know you could get the grades. You could train as a vet. That's what you always wanted.'

'Well I don't want it now. And I don't want to go to university.'

The teacher persisted: 'But you *do*. We were only speaking at the end of last term, about the likelihood of your getting a scholarship. Something or somebody has made you change your mind. What has changed since then?'

Everything.

The pain which blocked her throat could no longer be contained, and in the absence of the real target of her anger, she turned it on her teacher.

'Why must you go on and on? You asked me the reason and I've told you. School is boring. BORING. Studying is boring. That's all there is to it. What more can I say?'

Her teacher's body seemed to contract into itself.

'Nothing. You've made your decision quite clear, Graziella.'

Graziella's shoulders drooped in shame. 'I'm sorry.'

The teacher's eyes held her a moment longer. 'So am I Graziella. I don't recognise this girl, and it saddens me greatly. I wish you happiness with your life. I'm sure we shall see each other from time to time.'

'I've got that beautiful nature book you lent me. I shall return it to you.'

'Keep it.'

'But I couldn't.'

'Think of it as a souvenir.'

Graziella extended a conciliatory arm, but the teacher ignored the gesture. Stiff-backed, she re-joined the group of workers.

For a while Graziella hovered nearby, hoping the teacher would come back. They would start afresh. In her head, she played out how it might be.

I haven't changed. It was my aunt's idea, not mine.

Then you must continue your studies. If your aunt throws you out you can live with me.

The teacher did not come over to her. She did not look up from sweeping the debris.

Graziella roughly brushed away tears, and set off again.

She came to the *Chiesa della Madonna,* and, on an impulse, walked along the mosaic path leading to the church's pillared portico. The doors to the vestibule were open, and she went in. The usual notices were pinned to the board, and she glanced cursorily at these then took a candle from the wooden box next to the stack of dog-eared bibles. She had no money on her for a donation, but that wasn't her fault, was it? Jesus would understand. Crossing herself, she pushed open the heavy double doors.

The combined spicy aromas of incense, musty wood, and communion wine clung to the air, permeating the thick white walls and wrapping round her: familiar, though not always loved.

Nobody was about, and she let the silence seep into her, before walking down the nave to Our Lady's Chapel, avoiding pieces of gesso, which had broken off from the frieze. Her feet squeaked on the tiles, and it seemed to her that a thousand eyes were spying on her from above.

Several candles were already burning in the chapel, and she lit hers from one of them; the tiny flame danced into life, its magnified shadow leaping against the walls. She crossed herself again before the life-sized statue of Mary, and recited the *Ave*, her fingers kneading the rosary beads that she was never without. It occurred to her that for centuries, people had lit candles in this very spot. They had knelt in genuflection on the hard ground, as she did now, their lips moving imperceptibly in prayer, like a ventriloquist's. But how could praying to a man made statue invoke the real Mary, she wondered, not for the first time. And that aside, how could Mary interpret everyone's thoughts? All at once she felt absurd, as though she were praying to a doll, and she tiptoed back down the nave, accompanied by a new sense of loss.

Her parents used to sit towards the back of the church, on an end pew, and she sat there now. The only sound was that of the doves chortling in the dovecote and she attempted to draw calm into herself. Christ's lugubrious features bore down on her in all their stoic agony from the Stations of the Cross wall paintings. Did He know she had not been to confession for more than three weeks? Did he know that she doubted his immortality?

She thought about ringing the brass bell to alert Padre Alberto that she wished to confess, and then enacted a possible scene in her head.

Bless me Father, for I have sinned, she would commence, from behind the anonymity of the confessional curtain.

Have you come to confess your sins, my child? He would ask in his nasal voice.

Yes Padre. I have not confessed for more than three weeks. And I have offended my teacher and hurt her feelings, though she was trying to help me and has only ever been kind to me.

He would ask her the reason and she would explain what had led to it; then she would go right back to when the mayor had burned her father's Lupo stick, and out her grievances would tumble, in a torrent.

But the padre might not consider her aunt and uncle's treatment of her to be unreasonable. Leaving aside the mayor's financial contribution to the church, which was bound to influence the padre's opinion, it was probable he would share their view that women had their place and it was in the home. They did not go to university or become vets.

Are they cruel to you? he would ask. *Do they beat you?*

She would have to concede that apart from the once, when her aunt had slapped her, they did not beat her. But cruel? What constituted cruelty?

I hate them, she would say.

That is a wicked statement. Hatred is both unhealthy and dangerous. You must purge yourself of such a cancer.

He would prescribe the appropriate number of *Aves*, as both her penance and her cure, she would picture him behind the curtain, his roving eye circling its own orbit; and she would be bursting with irreverent giggles.

Graziella stood up from the pew, intending to leave, when the she heard the shuffling of feet, and the vestry doors creaking open. Flustered, she saw that it was her aunt's ex-maid.

Carlotta appeared equally taken aback.

They addressed each other simultaneously:

'*Buongiorno*, Graziella.'

'*Buongiorno*, Carlotta.'

There followed a strained pause.

'How are you?' Graziella asked, to fill it - then wished she hadn't. Carlotta looked as haggard as an old woman. Her leg was bandaged and she was resting it, standing like a stalk.

'I'm fine, thank you Graziella,' she answered, her quavering voice belying her words.

'I'm sorry about you losing your job,' Graziella said awkwardly. 'It had nothing to do with me. I wanted to stay at school.'

'I guessed as much. The *Signora* is a bad woman. And now my husband is very angry with me for not having work.'

'But you can't help it. It wasn't your fault.'

'He says it was. He says I'm lazy. He poured hot oil over my leg.'

'*No!*' Graziella's hand shot to her mouth. 'That's dreadful.'

'I try my hardest to keep him happy, but it is never enough.'

'You should leave him. Why don't you just leave him?'

Carlotta gave a bitter little laugh. 'And go where? I have two children and no money. What can I do? Anyway he'd come after me. No Graziella, I'm trapped. You and I are both trapped in our different situations.'

'I won't let them get the better of me. I won't let them rule me,' Graziella said.

'But they already do.'

Vehemently Graziella shook her head. 'No. It might seem like it, but they don't. It's part of my plan.'

'What plan?'

'It will present itself to me when the time is right,' she said.

The ex-maid regarded her with a look that might have been pity, then rang the bell for the priest.

CHAPTER 12

THEN
THE CASETTA

Unsettled by both her unfortunate encounters, Graziella hurried from the church into the chilly air. She passed the convent - then thought sadly of her friend Raffaella within the confines of its walls - and climbed up the last few steps until they petered out. She continued along the track. Normally it was hard with compacted soil, but it was now churned up and slippery from rain. The terrain became more rugged, and she scrambled over stones and boulders, wind whipping her hair. It was always windier up here, and it whistled round the bare trees, and the bleached grass lashed her legs.

Rounding the bend to the *casetta*, her excitement and trepidation intensified in equal measures; but as she approached the rear of the stone building, the landscape that met her was very different from the one she had last seen a year and a half ago. A wilderness had sprung up around it, virtually eclipsing it from view. The hectare of land was overrun with weeds, some taller than herself. The *casetta* seemed to have merged with the landscape, and the paved path had disappeared. The neighbouring *casetta* had fared even worse; all that remained of it were a few broken bits of timber. Graziella had heard that the husband was in prison and the wife had taken up with another man.

She had not expected this. In her mind's eye she had envisioned her home as she had last seen it: a magical place untouched by time and circumstance. She was tempted to turn tail and bolt. But if she did she might never return. The *casetta* would be swallowed up. Grass would grow over its tiled roof. All you would see would be a mound, like an ancient burial site, which hikers would trample over. It would be as though it had never existed; as though a family had not lived there contentedly, and a man with life before him had not carved walking sticks beneath the shade of the fig tree.

She owed it to her parents - and herself - to prevent that from happening. The *casetta* was her property now. Nobody could steal it from her.

Her property.

It was an extraordinary thought. It changed everything.

She pulled her hood low to protect her face, and fought her way through the nettles, sliding in mud, ducking under branches and brambles, trying to disregard the pain from a hundred lacerations. Progress was further hindered by vine-like creepers which entwined round her legs and seemed intent on tripping her up. A large frog sprung out in front of her. Dripping from its head to its webbed toes with mud, it looked as if it had been coated with dark chocolate. It hopped alongside her keeping her company for a while, before disappearing into the slough again.

When she reached the yard she let her arms dangle for a minute, then, slowly, stood upright again. Her ripped flesh burned, her ankles were blood-speckled, her feet squelched within her sodden shoes, but she had made it.

La mia piccolina, hai corraggio, her father used to say, compressing her cheeks between big hands.

The air seemed fresher up here, cleansed by the storm, and carried the scent of wild thyme and rain-drenched grass.

'I did it!' she shouted to the racing sky. Her voice boomeranged back to her from the mountains: *Did it, did it, did.*

Her mood sobered. She wandered about, taking stock, avoiding shards of glass and pieces of corrugated metal, which stuck up like shark fins between the nettles. She righted her father's old wheelbarrow, which lay capsized on the ground, then picked up his spade and leant it against the wall. An oil drum, which had been used as a water container, rattled and rolled with each gust of wind; a metallic, lonely sound. Further along, the vegetable plot had been eclipsed by weeds, as had the mule's corral; and the olive tree had been split in two by lightning. The chicken coops had blown over, but the panels appeared to be intact and only needed reassembling. The gate was buckled and hung, from a single hinge; a bar had broken off and lay in the mud. It would do for beating down the weeds on the way back, she thought. The mule's shelter was still standing. Brambles precluded entry, but some lower slats were missing, and if she pressed her face to the gap she could peer through. A head-collar, and pair of blinkers, green with mould, hung from a nail. The blinkers had seldom been worn: the mule, a "Molly", had only worn them during her oestrus cycle, when she became skittish. She had been an affectionate creature, Graziella recalled. She would doze in a dark corner, flicking away the pestering flies, resting a hind leg, but if you called her she would emerge with a whicker, which vibrated down her nostrils, and would poke out her ungainly head for her ears to be scratched.

Amongst the saturated straw was a fossilised clump of shit, and for some reason this remainder of the mule's bodily functions seemed ineffably poignant.

From the yard, she walked round to the front of the *casetta.* Here was the view her father had loved: the mountains behind you, and the sea before you. Here was the veranda where he had carved his sticks. And she half expected him to appear. Perhaps none of the bad things had happened. Perhaps she was existing in a dream and she would wake from it… *Chickens, chickens,* her mother would cry, and, they would hear her voice and, silly trusting birds, run to her, without an inkling as to their fate.

She closed her eyes and counted to ten. Opened them.

The blustery sky greeted her.

At the door to the kitchen she wavered. They had never used to lock it; crime was rare on the island, besides, they possessed little of worth. Now, she braced herself for what she might find. The handle was stiff from lack of use, and the door had warped; in order to open it she had to push her weight against it. She entered her old home like a thief.

At a superficial glance, the kitchen appeared to be as her mother would have left it; but the illusion was swiftly dispelled, as her eyes swept round the room, and took in the layers of dust and soot which coated every surface. Skeins of grey cobwebs stretched the length of the room, enshrouding the four chairs, the table and attached meat grinder. Spiders ran amok, peeping from corners, weaving exotic patterns. The cast iron pot, containing the congealed remains of *brodo*, had sprouted a fungal beard. The walls were slimy and speckled with mould. Rat and mice droppings carpeted the floor, like black olive pips. And while Graziella stood there, in the middle of the room, a pair of rats shot past her, and sprang onto her mother's treadle sewing machine.

A sickly, rotten odour pervaded the room and she went over to the window. The decomposing body of a jackdaw lay on the fly-scattered ledge. In its panic it must have knocked over the oil lamp, which lay, smashed, on the stone floor. She imagined how the poor thing would have suffered, beating its wings against the glass.

The smell was awful. She opened the window wide, and threw the bird out.

Her glance lit on familiar objects: the metal bath, like a cap-sized boat, suspended from the ceiling hooks; the washboard and wringer; the bellows, which used to remind her of a wheezing pigeon. There was a large space on the wall, by the wooden crucifix: the megaphone had hung there. Now it resided at the bottom of the seabed. What did the fish make of it? All that would remain of her parents would be bones. Their corpses would quickly have been stripped by sharks and barracudas. It made her feel ill to think of them like it.

Her father's fishing rod leant against a wall, and beside it, his rubber boots. He had used to take her on expeditions to *Laghi dei Gemelli*, where he taught her to fish for pike and carp. He had made her a scaled down rod of her own from split cane. The two lakes met, to form a figure of eight, and it was an isolated spot, barren and stark, except for the odd, misshapen tree clinging to the cliffs where eagles made their nests. One of Graziella's earliest memories was of her fascination at seeing her reflection in the water.

Look Papa, I've got upside down legs, she had exclaimed.

And look, I've got upside down legs too! He had responded, laughing.

'Oh.' Her sigh fanned out, full of longing, and she sank into a cobwebby chair and wept for everything that was lost.

She caught sight of her distorted image in the smeary bath. A filthy, wild creature stared back.

She walked through to her bedroom. Like the kitchen, it was draped in cobwebs and peppered with mouse droppings; other-wise, except for an absence of possessions, which she had taken to the mayor's house, it was as she remembered. Even after all this time she could detect the faint sweet-sickly whiff of chickens. Until she turned seven she had slept in her parent's room that had origi-nally been a hay loft; then one day her mother had gently told her that this could no longer continue and she would have her own room.

Why? she had asked.

Her mother had explained it was because she was growing up.

Her father had converted for her the small adjoining barn where the chickens had been kept, and made new coops for the birds. Graziella had helped him paint her new room.

You're my best assistant, he told her.

I'm your only assistant, she pointed out.

True enough. But if that weren't the case you would still be the best.

He made her a small table and chair, and a cupboard with shelves; her mother sewed yellow curtains and cushions, and made a sheepskin rug for the uneven floor. When the moving-in day came she presented Graziella with a yellow rabbit she had knitted.

It's to keep you company, so you don't get lonely, cara.

And to begin with it had felt strange, sleeping on her own. She missed the reassurance of knowing she could reach out to touch her parents, or climb into their bed if she had a bad dream. She missed her father's snoring, and the mysterious sighs and grunts in the night, which sometimes woke her, and she hugged the yellow rabbit to her. But she would watch the patterns the moon drew on the thin yellow curtains and the way the stars seemed sometimes to fall out of the sky, and in time she grew to love her room. She now understood the significance of her mother's sighs and her father's, harsh animal grunt that had woken her most nights. She was a young woman - the same age her mother had been when she had fallen in love with her father. Could that happen to her? Who would her suitor be? How would she know it was love?

She climbed the ladder to her parents' room. The single, small window meant it was deprived of natural light, and it took her a moment to adjust her vision. Rodents had gnawed through sections of the mattress, exposing the straw, and wisps had drifted round the room, settling on furniture and on the quilt. It prompted her to think of the money hidden there. Kneeling, she rummaged beneath the mattress. Her fingers came into contact with a metal tin, and she pulled it out. The wad of her parents' savings was intact, the lira notes fastened by an elastic band, and a separate pouch contained *monete*. In total it amounted to more than she had expected. She hid the tin beneath the infested mattress again.

It was draughty in the room, and she saw that the pane was missing from the window. This must have been how the jackdaw had entered. Another intruder had also found its way in. In the penumbral light she could make out the furry hump of a Lesser Noctule bat, attached upside down to a rafter. She smiled. Bats did not worry her; they'd always roosted in the *casetta*. Her father had made a box for them.

They have as much right to exist as we do, he said. Graziella had never met anyone as humane as her papa. He might have earned his living from the chickens, but during their lifespan they were as pampered as a beauty queen. And though he always carried a shotgun and had taught her how to use it, he killed in order to provide, not for amusement. *I see no sport in death; no pleasure in watching the eyes of an animal glaze over,* she could remember him saying.

There was a sense of tranquillity in here. Perhaps it was due to poor natural light, but it seemed to her the room breathed. She'd often thought that the *casetta* had its own personality, and had the impression now it was waiting for its occupants to return and fill it with laughter. She moved softly round the room so as not to break the spell, touching familiar objects. Memories jostled for ascendance, carrying her back; images flitted past like dancing motes, overlapping before she could catch them.

Beneath the window stood a table, shored up by wooden blocks and covered by a cloth to disguise the fact it was an orange crate, and seeing the personal items on it, she became tearful again. She slipped her father's penknife into her pocket, then picked up his jar of hair cream. He had used it daily to smarm down his curls, which he hated. Her mother would tease him, mussing his hair when he had just flattened it, and he pretended to be annoyed: *Leave it alone,* he protested. *It's my hair.*

But women know best what suits men. I think your curls are sweet.

I don't want to be sweet, he growled.

Graziella unscrewed the lid and held the jar to her nostrils. The ferny aroma she had always associated with him made her reel. A curious thing happened next: the light in the room altered, assuming a lime-green hue. It lasted about a minute, and she stared into its vortex until, bit by bit, it disappeared. What had it been? Could it have been a manifestation of her father's soul? Or was it merely a trick of light? There was no way of telling, but she felt comforted, and she screwed the lid on the jar again - tightly so that the smell of him would be preserved.

Her mother's brush lay on the table. Long strands of her hair were caught in its bristle, and tenderly she disentangled them, winding them round her finger, like a ring, before stuffing them in her pocket, with the brush.

She went over to the wardrobe. It was a fine piece, at odds with the other furniture, and had been bequeathed by her grandmother to her mother, indicating she had finally forgiven her daughter for her lowly marriage.

She opened the pair of doors as though her parents might jump out. Her father's clothes were on the left, her mother's the right, and were separated by a calico curtain: her father's work overalls looked spookily like a headless person. Her mother's section was ablaze with colour. Graziella ran her hands down a floral dress; it had a full skirt and wide belt, and her mother had looked like a girl in it. She had made every item of clothing the family possessed, and long after Graziella had gone to bed and recited her prayers *(Please God, look after Mama and Papa and don't let them ever be harmed)*, her mother would remain in the kitchen at the sewing machine. Graziella would drift off to sleep to its whirr. Eventually the oil lamp's amber line of light beneath the door would extinguish, and the *casetta* slept…

Her shoes stood in a row beneath the dresses: a smart black pair with heels, a pair of sandals, and a stout, outdoor pair. She tried these on; she had long outgrown her own, and they chafed, despite having cut the backs off. She massaged animal fat into her feet to soothe them and, when possible, went barefoot. Her mother's shoes fitted. It was like walking on a cushion, and she laughed with pleasure.

She noticed something sparkling on the floor, and bent to look more closely. It was her mother's gold chain and cross. Aside from her wedding ring and watch, it had been her sole piece of jewellery and she never took it off. Why had she not been wearing it the day of the accident? But when she picked it up, she realised the chain was broken, and she pressed the two pieces to her chest, imagining it resting against her mother's warm breast. There was a jeweller in one of the alleys, a tiny, squeaky-voiced man. He would repair it for her. She would wear it herself; feel her mother's heart beating next to her own.

"REPAIRED".

The word sang out, and she knew what she must do. Why had she not thought of it before? She would make the *casetta* habitable again. She would put her aunt's gift of cleaning materials to good use and scrub, dust, and polish every surface, every object and piece of furniture. She would cut down the weeds with her father's scythe, plant flowers and grow vegetables. A cat would take care of the rodents. Then she would move back into *her casetta*. First, though, she would take her revenge.

Dusk was fast falling; the bat stirred into life, flew past her and out through the window, fanning her with its wings.

She gave a final look round the darkened room and descended the ladder.

CHAPTER 13

NOW

ROSA

Gino is late. No surprise there.

I feel conspicuous, I'm sitting on my own in the foreignness of the hotel bar, trying not to look as though I'm on the game. A few feet from me, an elderly pianist is playing Chopin. Apart from myself, nobody in the room seems to be paying him a scrap of attention, talking and laughing over him. I feel for him, for his misplaced talent. He may as well be playing for himself. Then it dawns on me - that's exactly what he is doing: playing for himself, as if he were alone in the room. The piece comes to an end, and I clap softly. He looks up surprised, and gives a terse nod, as though I had intruded on his privacy, and lowers his head to the piano again.

My cheeks are still burning when, thank heaven, Gino arrives, in a whorl of apologies.

'Sorry I'm late. I went to the gym and lost track of the time,' he says, embracing me. His hair is wet and he smells of shower gel.

'Why aren't I surprised?' I comment. But he possesses his father's boyish charm, and I can never be cross with him.

He wanders off to the bar, and returns with a drink and a large packet of salted peanuts. With a big grin, he waves it in front of me.

'That's cruel. I won't have any.' I tell him.

My brother pulls down his mouth comically. He opens the pack, and we delve into it as though it's a race.

'How have you been - I mean, *really* been?' I ask him. 'I know we've spoken, but it's not the same.'

'To be honest, I miss Papa like hell,' Gino says, his voice thickening.

'Of course you do.'

'He looked so shrunken at the end, didn't he?'

'Yes, but I don't think he was in too much pain.'

'I hope not…. Mama always says he was one of life's special people. I just hope he wasn't disappointed in me.'

'What are you talking about? He thought the world of you.'

'I know that, but I'm not sure he regarded teaching PE as a proper job.'

'How can you say that? He was so proud of you - what you do for all the kids; way beyond your remit.'

'Thank you. That makes me feel better.'

'Don't thank me. It's true.'

'Well the same goes for you.'

I think of my dear, kind stepfather, who legally adopted me shortly after Gino was born. 'Sure, but it can't have been quite the same for him. I mean me not being his own child.'

'I assure you Rosa, that as far as Papa was concerned it *was* the same. Believe me, he regarded you as his daughter. He loved us equally.'

I resist tears: 'He and Mama never stopped being besotted with each other. You could see it in their eyes. They had a special look which they reserved for one another.'

'There is nothing each wouldn't have done for the other. It's a tough act to follow,' Gino observes.

We both reach for the peanuts.

'Anyway, how's the book going with Mama?'

'Interesting, shocking, sad, funny. No self-pity as you'd expect ... but I'm no closer to discovering who my real father is - or was...'

He stares at me, taken aback.

'I never realised it was important to you. You've not mentioned anything.'

I detect a faint note of hurt in his tone, and take his hand.

'It wasn't before. At least not to the same extent. It was more of a mild curiosity, which tweaked in me from time to time. But now, with Papa gone, and Mama... Well, it seems to be consuming me.'

'I can understand that. But for Mama it's early days yet. I'm sure she'll tell you in her own time.'

'*I'm* not sure.'

'Well if she doesn't it's probably because she is trying to protect you.'

'From what?'

'Perhaps she's afraid you'll be disappointed.'

I have considered as much myself. I've played out various possibilities in my head, then asked myself how I would feel if, say, my father turned out to be a criminal, or he simply wanted nothing to do with us and fled.

'It's my right to know, Gino.'

'Yes, but – and I don't mean to sound callous - by the same token, presumably she think it's *her* right to keep schtum.'

And I cannot argue with that.

'She wants us to help go through Papa's clothes,' I tell him. 'There may be the odd tie or jacket ...'

'Can't it wait?' he says. 'More than anything, I dread going through his clothes and personal stuff.'

'Me too. But we can't shirk it, if that's what she wants.'

'No - of course not. You're right.'

'Do you think she has deteriorated recently,' I ask him.

'Yes... And you?'

'Yes.'

We look hard at each other.

'She must stay in her own home for as long as she can, with extra support if necessary,' I say.

I hate having this conversation behind Mama's back. It makes me feel terrible; deceitful; as though I am betraying her.

'This is horrible,' I tell Gino. 'I know it was my suggestion, but I can't bear it.'

'I know,' he says gently; and his eyes are pink, and he looks drained. 'It's utter shit, and I wish we could bury our heads in the sand - to resort to the dreaded cliché. However, I don't think we should.'

So we talk about carers, and agencies and power of attorney, until I really cannot talk about it anymore, and nor can he.

I stand up:

'This is *Mama* we are talking about, making plans for. It feels so wrong.'

He shuffles to his feet: 'I understand. Well, we won't need to discuss the matter again for a while anyway. Let's just see what happens.'

'Yes.'

We hug goodbye. Drive off in different directions, back to our own lives.

CHAPTER 14

NOW

GRAZIELLA

Today has been a bad day.

I wake at about six, after a listless night, and reach out for my beloved husband, before remembering. The pain of missing him is excruciating and unending. When eventually I force myself to get up, I cannot find the light switch. I know the general area it's in, but for the life of me, I can't locate the blasted thing. I feel for it with my fingers, like someone blind, and finally discover it, inset into the wall, nearly a foot away from where I'd been fumbling.

The same thing happens when I go to run a bath: I simply cannot find the tap. It's as though someone or something is playing tricks on me.

Later, I cross the village lane to go to the shop - and narrowly miss being run over.

'Stupid bitch,' yells the driver, as he screeches to a halt. 'Why don't you watch where you're going?'

I sit on the bench, next to the shop, breathing deeply to recover; then go inside. They have changed the layout again. I wish they would stop doing that. Just when you get used to where the items are, they move them. I have only come in for a bag of sugar, but can't find it. I go over to the young assistant at the till, whom I've not seen before. Other than myself, there are no customers, and she is poring over *Hello*, and may as well be wearing a Do-Not-Disturb sign round her neck.

'Would you happen to know where I will find the ...' I begin. But the word has gone from me, and I stand there stupidly. 'It sweetens things,' I explain.

'The sugar and sweeteners are up the flight of steps, on the right,' she informs me, without interest.

Sugar. Sugar. Sugar.

I find it, and also buy a sweet, to save face, then make for the short run of steps. All at once they take on Everest proportions. I stare at them. How am I going to get down?

Gripping the railing with one hand, and the sugar, the other, I make my descent.

I pay with a ten pound note, even though in the purse section of my wallet I have the correct change. I know I would dither.

Back home, I realise I am shaking, and lie down on the bed. Tosca joins me. Like me, she is getting old.

'Ah, Tosca, he's gone. He's gone.'

I feel as though I am a phantom. Maybe I am. Maybe we are all phantoms.

But he was not. He was real.

Oh, he was so, so real.

CHAPTER 15

THEN
BLACKMAIL

Tension was running high in the Carluccio household and the mayor was irritable, his temper unpredictable. It was nearing election time again, and unless he could sort out the infernal football stadium problem between now and the end of the month he stood no chance of retaining his seat. His chief opponent was his deputy, who had defected to form his own party. Every evening Graziella could hear the mayor pacing up and down his study, and the house was enveloped with his cigar smoke.

He campaigned relentlessly to woo voters. Leaflets were put through doors, he visited individual homes, promised to review the fishing subsidies, spoke of building a fish canning factory, which would create employment. Pictures of him looking avuncular were pinned to walls and hoardings and if they were pulled down or defaced were hastily replaced. He refused to be outdone. When a photo appeared in the *Gazzetta* of his opponent pushing his disabled wife in her chair, the following week the mayor matched it with a picture of himself wheeling his speechless mother in hers. There was another of him awkwardly cuddling twin babies, one in each arm. Whom they belonged to, nobody knew, and the story went round that the parents had been paid. The ploy backfired as the article likened the mayor's sickly smile to King Herod's before he went on his killing spree.

'*Good people of Isola delle Pecore! Vote for me, Guido Carluccio, and you shall have your football stadium, that is a promise!*', rang out his amplified voice, competing with the honking horn of the official Fiat, as demonstrators tried to block its passage. The car had been bedecked with patriotic red, white and green ribbons, and its aged driver hunched tensely over the steering wheel, negotiating the tortuous lanes and alleys unsuited to vehicles.

Later that day he held a rally in the *Municipio*.

'I have a five part plan to develop tourism. It will bring prosperity to our island and put money in your pockets,' the mayor proclaimed, from his plinth.

'Your promises are like the stadium: they are made of cardboard,' yelled a heckler, joined by others in sympathy. And from another corner somebody called: 'You don't care about us, you just want to save your own skin,' which elicited further cries of agreement.

'I shall not let you down,' he assured them, hugging the microphone as though embracing a woman.

Others were prepared to give him a chance: 'How do we know that we can trust you?' one man demanded.

The mayor assumed a sincere expression. 'Because I have learned from you, the people, what *you* want. You have been good teachers and I have listened and am humbled by you. With regard to the football stadium, I can reveal that I have been in negotiation with a reputable contractor and will be signing the minute I am re-elected. But make no mistake - it *will* happen. The football stadium will rise again.'

A flurry of excitement followed.

'Will you be shoving up our taxes to pay for it?' challenged Stefano, elbowing forward.

The mayor retained his equanimity. 'No, because tourism will fund it. I expect it to double in the next twelve months. Thereafter? Well, there are no limits. I have big plans, practical, workable plans, and I want to share them with all of you.'

He paused for impact, his smile making him look like an alligator.

'Do you really want a turncoat as your mayor?' he proceeded, his voice climbing high. 'Do you really want to place your future in the hands of someone whose politics change on a whim, whose allegiances seesaw first to the right, then the left and no doubt back again. As for the football stadium: without a qualm, he has admitted that he would demolish it. He does not care what *you*, the people want. Wouldn't you prefer to have at the helm a mayor who is loyal to you and has *your* interests at heart? I repeat: you will have your stadium, financed by the tourists who will flock here, bringing with them prosperity for each of you. That, my friends, is the way forward.'

Aside from the same hecklers as before, general applause followed the mayor's oration, albeit muted, and, for the next twenty minutes, questions were slung at him from all directions. For each he had a credible response.

When, shakily, he dismounted from the plinth he looked wrung-out, and nobody could have failed to notice the sweat dripping from his forehead. He suppressed a belch, and tossed a peppermint into his mouth.

The crowd dispersed. Graziella slipped away, back to the house. Her aunt and Nina stayed behind, posing for the cameras. They wouldn't know she had been gone.

The following morning the family prepared to drive to the north of the island to campaign there; they would not be returning until the evening. Nina and the mayor were already in the car, he beside the driver, and Graziella saw him lower his head to his watch then glance impatiently towards the house.

In the hall Graziella buttoned the back of her aunt's dress, deliberately leaving one undone. 'Have you fastened the hook at the top?' asked her aunt.

'Yes *Zia*.'

Annunciata turned round to her. She was wearing too much powder; it had clogged in orange blobs round her pores.

'You are sure you will be alright on your own for that length of time?'

'I shall be fine, *Zia*.'

'And no skiving just because I won't be here.'

'Of course not.'

'It will be an opportunity to give your uncle's room a thorough clean, but please ensure you put everything back exactly how it was.'

'You can trust me, *Zia*,' said Graziella. And made her long, eucalyptus shaped, eyes as round as possible.

She watched them depart, a whole day to herself! She had seldom been left alone for more than an hour or two; somebody or other was always about. Today would be her chance for a good prowl.

She waited a while, in case for any reason the car should return unexpectedly, and switched on the Bakelite wireless. "*Volare*" was playing, and in a breathy voice she sang along to it.

> *Volare... oh, oh! cantare... oh, oh, oh, oh!*
> *Nel blu, dipinto di blu, felice di stare lassù....*

When she could be confident that the family was well and truly on its way, she switched off the wireless and opened the door to the hallowed domain of the mayor's oak-panelled study.

It stank of cigars and farts, and grimacing, she flung open the windows. His flatulence was terrible. He suffered from bowel problems and chronic indigestion, and you could hear his explosive belches throughout the house. Recently, convinced he had cancer, he had consulted a physician in Palermo, only to be told that stress was the cause, and he should change his lifestyle. He had returned home in a worse mood.

Anyone would think he wanted to have cancer, Annunciata grumbled to Graziella, to whom she sometimes unloaded her grievances when there was no one better to hand.

The first task the mayor performed each morning was to wind the old clock with a brass key; his second, to change the date on the perpetual calendar; and she altered the latter, back to the previous day. She imagined his bewilderment when he glanced at it: he would recall having changed the date as usual, yet clearly he was mistaken. And then he would worry that his mind was going.

The small, cluttered room portrayed a man always in a hurry: newspapers, journals, medicines, scrunched-up paper balls which had missed the bin, vied with discarded clothes. He had a passion for crocodile shoes, and his latest pair jutted from their box. Taking her father's penknife from her pocket, Graziella made a cut in them. Framed maps and photographs occupied a wall: a group one of the family - how ugly and smug they all looked, Graziella thought; a photo of the mayor's late father with his Spinone hunting dog; himself shaking hands with Sophia Loren; and in pride of place, himself as a young *Regia Aeronautica* pilot, wearing a flying helmet and goggles and standing beside the *Savio Marchetti* aircraft he had flown. He looked pleased with himself, even then.

A model of the plane was suspended by a wire above his desk; he liked to spin it when he was bored. Graziella lowered herself into his leather chair, giggling as air was expelled and it made a sounded like the mayor farting. She placed her elbows alongside the chair's arms.

'I am the mayor,' she said in a deepened voice, and pretended to draw on a cigar. 'I can do as I please.'

She prodded the model plane into motion, watching it, as it rose up and down. What must it have been like to have lived through the war? Her father, a boy at the time, had seldom spoken of it; but her uncle was older and, as a pilot he would have flown for nearly two years on the side of the Germans. He made no secret of the fact he had wanted them to win.

The surface of his Rococo desk was hidden by papers and a jumble of stationery that spilled out from a pewter mug. Bills and receipts were anchored down by a marble paperweight next to his leather diary, and she thought that she may as well start her search with these. She had no idea what she might discover but knew, beyond doubt, that in this room would be something incriminating. She flicked through chits, but the trips to Palermo, silk shirts, shoes, restaurant meals and hotel suites did not strike her as out of the ordinary. She could be pretty sure he hadn't spent the nights in hotels on his own, but this was insufficient ammunition to use against him. He would hardly be the first unfaithful husband on the island.

A scruffy buff folder lay beneath the desk. It was labelled "Correspondence", and she lifted it onto her lap with a flaring up of optimism. It made tedious reading, however, covering matters from mayoral duties to arguments about land boundaries. It would have been too easy, she reasoned to herself, putting it down. But suppose there was nothing after all? And according to the clock, she'd wasted nearly hour.

Patience cara, her mother reminded her. And something brushed her face, like a wisp of hay.

She walked over to the filing cabinet, but found it locked. Of course, it was bound to be. And she stared at it, as though it might magically open. Well that was it, wasn't it, she thought, despondent. There was nothing more she could do.

She was halfway out of the room, when she remembered something from the last time she had dusted it: she had discovered two keys on a ring tucked behind the photograph of the mayor's father and his Spinone, and had wondered what they were for. Now it occurred to her that one of them might be the key to the filing cabinet; the other was likely to be for the gun cabinet.

She felt behind the picture. They were still there. And, crossing her fingers for luck, she inserted the smaller of them. It turned easily. Scarcely able to suppress her excitement, she read the labels of various files and binders: Fishing. Tourism. Tax. Staff. Almond business. Mayoral business. Household. Insurance... Football Stadium. With a quickening of optimism, she pulled out the heavy file and, sprawled on the oriental rug, waded through page after page. But again she met with disappointment. And she had wasted a further half hour of precious time. Her earlier optimism was fast fading. Despondently, she returned the file to its place. She had been so certain.

'*Dove sei? Dove sei?*' she muttered.

She went through several more files, replacing each when she had finished with it, and was growing ever more frustrated, when her gaze fell upon a black, box file, ambiguously labelled "Miscellaneous". It was secured by a metal clip, which she pressed to release. The file fell open on her lap, and out slid a thick, un-labelled envelope, sealed with red wax, like a globule of blood. A frisson ran through her. Instinctively she knew that this was what she had been looking for.

She took her father's penknife from her pocket, and broke the seal.

The envelope contained the correspondence, originals and carbon copies, between the mayor and the *Direttore di Banca*, each in order of date.

"*Dear Signor Tebaldi,*" she read from the copy of the mayor's first of the letter, on headed paper.

"Re: Football stadium

I was glad of the opportunity to talk to you at our meeting last Thursday, on the above matter, however, bearing in mind the timescale, I am surprised that I have not yet received a response from you. Indeed, I have telephoned you on several occasions without success. Two days ago I came to the bank in person, to be told you were "unavailable". You will appreciate that this is a matter of urgency, as campaigning will start in earnest in a fortnight. As such I would request a response by return.

Yours respectfully,

Guido D Carluccio
Mayor, Isola delle Pecore"

The next letter bore the bank's insignia at the top.

"16/2/60
Dear Signor Carluccio,
Re: Football stadium
    Thank you for your letter of 13/2/1960.
    I have now had a chance to look into the matter of your loan application. Regrettably, having taken into consideration your adverse credit history, the bank is unable to comply with your request on this occasion.

Yours sincerely,

A.M. Tebaldi
Banca di Sicilia"

Graziella could well imagine how incensed the mayor would have been with such a casual brush-off, and this was apparent in his reply, which was again hand-delivered.

"Dear Signor Tebaldi.
<u>*Re: Football stadium*</u>
Further to your letter, dated 16/2/1960, I wish to express my displeasure at your decision. Having outlined my business plan to you, and in view of our long-standing business relationship, I fail to comprehend the reasoning behind your refusal of a loan, which would be to everyone's advantage. I would urge you to re-consider your decision. I hope I make myself clear.

I am, Signor, yours respectfully,

Guido D Carluccio
Mayor, Isola delle Pecore"

⊷⊶

"19/2/60
Dear Signor Carluccio,
<u>*Re: Football stadium*</u>
Our records over a period of several years show a pattern of financial instability and reckless unsupported spending of public money, of which you were warned, yet disregarded, on several oc-casions. With municipal funds significantly overdrawn, I regret that the bank is unable to offer further financial assistance for the substantial sum requested. I am not confident you would be able to honour your repayments, and as such the risk to the bank would be far too great to contemplate.
This decision is final and not open to negotiation.

Yours sincerely,

A.M. Tebaldi
Banca di Sicilia"

⊷∔∔⊷

The copy of the mayor's response to this was dated the same as the letter received. Graziella guessed he would have dashed it off in a rage. Hereafter, all correspondence between the pair was hand-delivered.

"Dear Signor Tebaldi,
<u>*Re: Football stadium*</u>
    Thank you for your letter.
    I am deeply disappointed by your lack of cooperation, regarding a loan for the above. Perhaps you will reconsider your decision and be more open to "negotiation" if I remind you of a particular incident which took place in Palermo, in October of last year. I had been dining at the Meridiana, on the edge of the Parks, after attending a conference, and was returning to my hotel via a short cut which took me through a back street of the red-light district. Such is life's quirkiness, that, I ran into you as you were propositioning a "ragazzo di vita". The boy was, at the very most, thirteen or fourteen and your arm was around him at the time. Your embarrassment at seeing me was apparent, and to save you from further discomfort I inferred that your private life was of no concern to me, and assured you of my discretion.
    It is strange, is it not, how one's attitude can change? I am now of the belief that such depravity must not go ignored and should be exposed. The public deserves to be informed of this unfortunate incident. Let people judge for themselves whether their Direttore di Banca is the appropriate man in whom to entrust their finances.

Yours respectfully,

Guido D Carluccio
Mayor, Isola delle Pecore"

><++>

"20/2/60
Dear Signor Carluccio,
Re: Football stadium
    I would be agreeable to a meeting with you tomorrow, 21/2/60,
at ten o'clock, to discuss matters.

Sincerely yours,

A.M. Tebaldi
Banca di Sicilia"

><++>

"Dear Signor Tebaldi,
    I am glad of your change of heart. I look forward to our meet-
ing, tomorrow. 21/2/60, at ten o'clock.

Yours

Guido D Carluccio
Mayor, Isola delle Pecore"

><++>

She picked up the final letter.

"22/2/60

Dear Signor Tebaldi,

I was glad of our very fruitful meeting yesterday and it is good to know that we have reached such a satisfactory understanding and are on the same wavelength. I am sure you would agree the outcome was mutually beneficial.

I am delighted, too, that you have agreed to favourable terms for an extension to my own property, and for the building of a swimming pool at the rear. As I mentioned, I may wish to prevail upon your good self from time to time with regard to further small requests.

You see, Signor, the validity of "negotiation" after all.

Yours respectfully,
Guido D Carluccio
Mayor, Isola delle Pecore"

⊷╋╉⊷

Graziella locked the cabinet and hid the keys again behind the picture.

She remembered to close the study windows, fed the letters into their envelope; then, with the package tucked beneath her arm, she left the house.

CHAPTER 16

THEN
THE JOURNALIST

The office for the *Gazzetta* was sequestered away in a stinking, dead-end alley past the harbour. The drains there always seemed to be clogged up with effluent, which bubbled up from the slaughterhouse, no matter what anyone did to try to alleviate the problem. The day was sultry and overcast, and the thick, stench-filled air combined with her nervousness, made her feel queasy. A middle-aged man whistled at her as she passed, and she shot him a furious look. '*Pederasta*,' she slung at him over her shoulder. Stefano lived in this area, in one of the terraced cottages. He fancied himself as a bit of an artist and had painted the exterior with fanciful murals, and one minute you would be pitched into the jaws of a shark, the next you found yourself in a meadow of grazing sheep. She wondered how he could stand the odour. She certainly couldn't imagine Donatella living here. Maybe, eventually, you became impervious to it, though she didn't believe she ever could.

The newspaper office was a narrow building up several uneven steps, whose rusty rail wobbled when she leaned against it. A pile of back-copies, bound with coarse string and sodden from the overflowing gutter, awaited burning, and from within filtered the sound of a typewriter in action. Graziella jumped over a fetid puddle to get to the door, and pressed the bell at the side.

'It's not locked,' called a bad-tempered voice.

She went in.

The journalist's head was bent over a typewriter. He made no effort to peer up from it and continued tapping, using two fingers with impressive speed, like frantic worms. Her nervousness grew and also her annoyance at his arrogance. The only clues she could gather, as to his appearance were his dark auburn cap of hair, and a well-muscled back beneath his short-sleeved shirt; there was also a fine covering of hair along his exposed arms. She thought that he must be tall, as his legs stuck out either side of the chair. Smoke rings from his cigarette spiralled diagonally towards the naked light bulb which swung gently beneath the rotating ceiling fan. She looked past him, down a flight of steps, into the basement print room, and made out the press: silent now.

At last he deigned to look up, and when he did her stomach gave a lurch; but this had nothing to do with the drains. In fact you could scarcely smell them in here, and the fan kept the room pleasantly cool.

He was in his early twenties, and she had seen him about. He was the oldest of three brothers, one of whom had been in her class at school. He seemed as taken aback as herself and got up from his chair with a suddenness that almost bowled it over. He rubbed the side of his temple. 'I wasn't expecting anyone,' he said, with a skewed smile.

'I'm sorry to interrupt you when you're so busy.' Her voice sounded foreign to her own ears; husky, artificial, as though she were propositioning him rather than excusing herself.

'I'm always busy, there's never a good time. There's only me here this afternoon.' Then he remembered his manners and bounded forward. 'Gino Terrasini.' He extended his hand to her.

'Graziella Lupo.' She extended hers in turn, and his fingers curled round hers with a confident grip.

'I know who you are.' His sleepy, heavy-lidded eyes drove into her.

'Oh.' She experienced the same quickening of the heart as a moment earlier, and her face became hot.

Their hands were still attached and she didn't know what to do. Was he waiting for her to slide hers from under his, or would that be rude? Should she wait for him to withdraw his hand first? How were you supposed to know such things? But then it became clear he simply hadn't realised, as a second later he abruptly released hers with a flustered apology.

He resumed charge: *'Dunque...* How can I help you?'

And she smiled to herself, because he was so obviously trying to sound businesslike. Whilst her opinion that he was arrogant had not altered, she could see past the swagger to an impression-able boy who could easily be crushed.

'I found some letters you might be interested in.'

'What are...' he began.

She made an impatient gesture. 'You have to read them. Right now, however busy you are. They are self-explanatory.' She took the bundle from under her arm and passed it to him.

He looked amused, but she did not care; there was no time to waste. 'Please. It's urgent.'

'I'm intrigued,' he said. He settled himself behind his desk again, motioning for her to take the spare chair, which, like his, was plastic and smeared with stains and finger marks.

Leaning tensely forward, she watched as he opened the enve-lope, and was gratified to notice his eyebrows shoot up when he registered whom the correspondence was between. He held the first of the letters close to his nose, as though he might be short sighted, uttered an 'Mm-hmm,' and put it to one side. He read the subsequent letters much more slowly, and she observed the chain of his reactions with each new revelation: tutting; rubbing his long-ish jaw; banging down his fist on the desk; sucking in his breath; whistling through his teeth ...

When he reached the end of the correspondence he sat for a second or two, not moving, then he sprung up from the chair, his eyes alight, and he burst out laughing.

'This is superb. Oh really, it's too superb!'

And hauling her to her feet, he waltzed round the little room with her, whirling her at a dizzying speed.

'Enough!' she protested.

He let go of her. 'Sorry, sorry. But really this is fantastic. You clever, clever girl! How old are you Graziella?'

She hesitated.

No Graziella, don't lie, warned her mother.

She looked at him defiantly. 'Fifteen.'

'And I am twenty-three,' he lamented. 'People would disapprove if I went out with you.'

'I don't care what people think of me.'

'I do. When is your birthday?'

'January the first.'

'Ten and a half months away. We shall go out on your birthday. Celebrate the New Year and your coming of age. If a film is showing we will go and see it together.'

'I might say no.'

'Well that would be your prerogative... But I hope you don't.'

Graziella tilted her head.

'Is that a yes?' he asked.

'It's a maybe.'

'How maybe?'

She laughed again, and relented. 'Alright.... very maybe.'

And she was already willing away the weeks and months.

His expression became serious. 'Will the mayor guess it was you who passed on the letters, do you think?'

'I don't think so. Not immediately, at any rate.'

'You know this will destroy him. And Tebaldi of course. But it's your uncle that bothers me. If he realises it was you he'll go crazy.'

'Let him. I shan't be living there anyway. I'm going to move back into my parents' *casetta*. I have been making it nice again.'

'But you can't live there on your own in that isolated spot.'

'I can.'

His eyes fastened on her. 'You're quite something, aren't you? Very brave.'

She shrugged. She was simply getting by as best she could. But sometimes she was weary of the continual battling.

The shadows in the room fell across her, playing on her features.

'Brave and beautiful,' Gino said. He sensed a change in her, and stroked her cheek. 'If there is anything I can do...'

The tenderness in his small gesture made her gasp. She resisted touching the spot where his finger had lain.

'There is something,' she said. 'You could...' She faltered.

'Go on, tell me.'

'You could pay me... For the letters, I mean,' she added with a wan smile, in case he misinterpreted her.

'But naturally. That's only fair. It won't be much though, I'm afraid. The boss is pretty strict on that front. And we don't keep money here.'

She looked crestfallen, and he thought for a moment: 'I tell you what. I could pay from my own pocket, then get it back, from him.'

'Are you sure? I don't want...'

'I insist.' He drew several notes from his trouser pocket and counted them out in front of her. She was too embarrassed to look and, flushing, took them from him. She felt cheap. What must he think?

'I have to go.'

'And I've got work to do. An article to write, thanks to you.' He indicated the letters, safely on his desk.

She gave a querulous smile.

'Ten and a half months then,' he said. 'Is that a date?'

Her spirits lifted. 'Yes.'

'Good. I'll hold you to it.' He kissed her hand then sought her eyes.

'Please take care of yourself, Graziella.'

She walked back down the alley, hardly noticing the stink. She felt jubilant. Was this Love? Was this how it had been for her parents?

The money rustled in her pocket. She would use it to buy a hen and cockerel at the market.

CHAPTER 17

NOW

ROSA

'What's your daughter's name?' my mother asks, at the end of another session.

'I don't have a daughter, Mama.'

'Don't be silly, of course you do.'

'Mama, it's me, Rosa.'

'You're not Rosa. Rosa was my mother. Stop muddling me.'

This has never happened before. It's as though someone has flicked on a switch in her and I don't know what to do. Feel like shaking her back to normality. How can I leave her like this? I uncurl her hand and slip mine into hers. She tilts her head, in question. Her eyes are puffy.

'You look tired,' I tell her.

'That's because Papa took up most of the bed last night and I hardy slept. I kept prodding him and tried to push him over to his side, but he wouldn't budge.'

Don't contradict her. You must resist contradicting her.

'That would have been Tosca, Mama.'

'*Porca miseria*, I know the difference between my husband and my dog, Rosa.'

But at least she realises it is me; and a second later she is herself again.

'I have to go, Mama. I have some work to do.'

'Oh that is a shame. I was hoping we could go to the sanctuary and I could show you some dangers... the chambers... *Madre*, Graziella, what is wrong with you today? I mean *changes*. I wanted to show you some of the *changes* we've made.'

How can I refuse her?

'That would be lovely then,' I tell her.

WELCOME TO PAWS FOR THOUGHT, ANIMAL HOSPITAL AND SANCTUARY, the sign above the wrought iron entrance gates says. And I drive over the cattle grid and park.

She hangs on to my arm as we tour round the grounds of the visitors' area, pointing out new "residents", and recent improvements: a bird of prey centre; a terrapin aquarium; additional hedgehog huts; a stall selling organic produce. Outside the donkey and pony paddock anarchy has broken out between half a dozen or so preschool children over whose turn it is for a ride.

It's my turn... No it's not, it's mine...I was there first...I hate you, you've stopped being my best friend...

Soon they are all in tears or having a tantrum, and their fraught parents drag them off in disgrace.

Mama has forgotten her stick and walks slowly, as though unsure where to place her feet or how far the ground is beneath her. Our circuit takes twice as long as it should, and I ought to go. But I can't rush her. If it's frustrating for me, what must it be like for her?

She stops in a wooded part of the nature trail to watch a pair of fox cubs frolicking, one with a missing eye, the other a missing leg.

'They were hit by a car,' she says. 'We're running a children's competition in conjunction with the *Oxford Times*, to name them.'

'Was that your idea?'

'Yes. It's... Well it's free... pub... free... ...'

She flounders for the word, and I willing it to come to her. Her face has become distorted with effort and I can feel her frustration.

'Publicity?' I suggest.

'Yes. Publicity. Thank you Rosa.' She says it grudgingly.

'It's a terrific idea.'

'It all helps.'

It must be six months since I was last here. We came as a family: Billy, Gino, myself, Mama, Papa. His health was deteriorating and he leant on his stick - the one Mama now uses, when she remembers it. Each of us knew it would be our last excursion all together.

She has lost weight, I notice.

'Are you eating properly, Mama?'

'Of course I am. Why?'

'You look thinner.'

'Well you look fatter.'

That stings me. She knows I've never felt good about my body. I can feel tears smarting behind my eyes. Momentarily, I dislike her, and detach my arm from hers. *It's her illness*, I remind myself. But she can be so cutting.

Considering that it is mid-week, the centre is buzzing. Encouraged by the May weather, visitors have gravitated to the outside café, and almost every table is taken. In the gift shop a queue has formed.

Starting with the concept, everything here was created by my mother. The success of this place is due entirely to her vision and her determination and hard work. When my stepfather brought her to England she studied for years to gain her qualifications, before founding the animal sanctuary. Never did she waver from her objective. And those character traits of hers which anger you, exasperate you, and sometimes wound you, are the very ones for which you love, admire and respect her.

I recall her as a young woman - little more than a girl - when we were living in the *casetta* on *Isola delle Pecore*: everyone was against her but her self-belief never flagged. I remember how she held her head high as people gossiped about her. I remember how she battled against adversity, this tiny, exquisite, indomitable woman. Above all I remember her fierce love. She would have done - and did do - everything within her power to protect me, to keep me safe.

Mama! Mama!

It's alright, it's alright. You're safe now cara. Your Mama's here. You're safe.

I take her arm again and hug her.

'What you have achieved with this place is magnificent, Mama,' I tell her. And I realise that whilst I may have thought this many times, I have never before voiced it. She is not a woman who expects or seeks praise - though she has lavished both on me.

'Thank you, *cara mia*. And you are magnificent. You know how proud I am of you,' my mother says, clearly having forgotten her remark.

While Mama is deep in conversation with a visitor, Liz gets me on my own.

'I'm not sure if your mother told you, but she has stopped performing all surgical procedures. It must have been a hell of a decision.'

'Oh God, it must have been. I ...'

Too choked to continue, I squeeze my eyes tight. All those years of study and work; everything she had ever wanted and striven for - pulled from beneath her. I can only imagine how she must be feeling. And I want to rage at whoever may or may not be up there: *It's not fair!* But, as Mama taught me, fairness rarely enters the equation.

'I'll keep this place going, whatever it entails,' Liz assures me, pressing my hand in understanding, because I don't reply.

'I'm so grateful to you,' I manage to say, when I feel more composed.

I glance in the direction of my mother. She is still talking to a visitor.

I slip away without saying goodbye to her.

CHAPTER 18

THEN

HOW THE MIGHTY HAVE FALLEN

T wo days later, on that Friday in May, the story broke.
Graziella brought the mayor his breakfast on the terrace as usual. He always took this meal alone in order to think and mentally prepare himself for the day ahead. The last thing he wanted was to have to listen to female chitchat at that hour of the morning. He ignored Graziella as she laid out the things from the tray and put the *Gazzetta*, folded inwards, on the table beside him.

'*Buon appetito,*' she murmured, and left him.

The mayor poured himself a cup of coffee, buttered a chunk of *muffoletta*, lavishly coated it with honey, and sank his teeth into it. He masticated it ruminatively, then unfolded the *Gazzetta* and shook it out.

Come Sono Caduti I Grandiosi!!

In disbelief and horror he read the headlines, beneath which was an enlarged picture of himself, and beside it, another of Signor

Tebaldi. The bread he had been enjoying, oozed from his mouth and the honey dripped onto his silk trousers.

'Ma no!' Stupefied, he read on, in such a state that the words leaped like fleas on the page, and he had to keep re-reading passages for verification.

> *"This is a tale of greed and corruption, politics and ambition, rent boys and blackmail, to rival the best fiction. However this story, uncovered by the Gazzetta, is not a work of fiction. Its two protagonists are none other than our illustrious Mayor of Isola delle Pecore, Guido Carluccio, and the equally illustrious Direttore di Banca, Signor Alfonso Tebaldi.*
>
> *The tale unfolds in a series of letters between the pair, and it all began with an ill-fated football stadium…"*

The mayor released a trumpeting bellow, like a felled elephant. Then he called for his wife.

She had been rearranging her Capo di Monte collection, having acquired another figurine, and did not immediately hear him.

'ANNUNCIATA!'

This time his roar penetrated her daydreaming. Hurriedly she shut the cabinet and ran to her husband.

He looked awful; his complexion had turned a jaundiced yellow, interspersed with liverish blotches. Fearing a heart attack, she knelt down beside him; her knees cracked painfully.

'What is it? What's wrong?'

In response he motioned to the newspaper, now lying in disarray on the ground, and she picked it up to see what it was that had so upset him.

Eventually she staggered up from her uncomfortable position. Her legs felt as frail as a newly born foal's. They were ruined, of course. It was a scandal from which they would never recover.

There would be no more parties. Their friends would desert them. Nina's wedding would be called off. This would wreck her chances of making a good marriage. Her big bosoms would be her only hope.

The mayor was loudly sobbing, his head buried in his hands, and Annunciata surveyed him objectively. Her sister Rosa had been right, Guido did resemble a pig.

But love struck at strange moments and was indiscriminating.

She brought one of the rattan chairs close to him. Leaning forward, she pulled his head towards her and opened her arms for him to go into.

He wept against the empty sacks of her breasts.

'I did it for the people of *Isola delle Pecore*,' he blubbed. 'Everything I did, I did for them, for the good of the island. It was never for myself.'

She stroked his sparse hair and dabbed at his tears with her handkerchief she always kept tucked into her clothing. 'Of course it was not. You are the victim in this,' she consoled him.

'Nobody will believe me, despite all the years of slog that I have put in.'

Never had she loved her husband more than now, his hour of disgrace. At last he needed her. And to be honest, she had grown tired of parties and entertaining. She had never fully recovered from the rat incident.

'I believe you.'

He disentangled himself from her. What had come over him? *I am lumbered with this hag forever,* he thought.

Annunciata stood up.

'I know who is responsible for this,' she said, in a decisive tone. And went in search of Graziella.

But Graziella was nowhere to be found.

CHAPTER 19

THEN
SACRIFICIAL LAMBS

'*Buongiorno*, Graziella' a voice near her said.

She wheeled round, dropping the aubergine she had just pulled from the soil, and squinted into the afternoon sunlight. '*Madre*, you gave me a fright,' she reproached Gino.

'Sorry, I didn't mean to scare you.'

He was holding a bouquet of flowers, which she pretended not to notice, and he was trying, but failing, not to stare at her in her shorts. The aubergine lay between them like a phallus.

'How long have you been standing there?'

'No more than a minute. You were utterly engrossed.' He retrieved the aubergine and she took it from him and dropped it into her basket along with the other vegetables.

'*Grazie.*' She murmured. She wished her old shorts were not so skimpy. And she felt dirty; sticky with perspiration. Her fingernails were thick with soil.

'*Prego,*' he said, with a mock bow. 'Oh … these are for you.'

He presented her with the flowers. From the clumsy manner with which he thrust them at her, she realised he had not bought a girl flowers before, and her heart became full.

'They're beautiful.' She buried her face in them. The carnations bore no scent, but the narcissi smelt of honey. She peered up from them. 'I've never been given flowers before.'

'I've never given them before.'

'Then they are extra special. Thank you.'

' I'm glad you like them.'

She searched for something to say that was clever or amusing; a remark to impress him with. But her brain wouldn't comply. Gino, seemingly equally at a loss, kicked a stone with the toe of his shoe, and looked about him, as though for inspiration.

'I must admit, this is very impressive Graziella.' He gestured to encompass the vegetable area with its netted rows.

'I like doing it. I used to help my papa and mama.'

Gino gave a respectful nod at the mention of her parents. 'Do you miss them a lot?'

'Every minute of every day.'

'That's awful. If I lost my parents - well, I can't imagine it. I mean you think your parents will always be there, don't you?'

'Well they're not, and that's just how it is.'

'I guess so. I'm never going to die, though. I've decided I'm going to be immortal.'

'Don't be silly. Everyone dies.'

'Not me.' He looked pensive for a second or two then plucked a cigarette from behind his ear. It took him a few goes to light it with his Zippo, as it was nearly out of fuel.

'Want a puff?' He offered it to her.

'*No, grazie,* I don't smoke. Smoking makes me cough.'

'That's a shame. I could imagine you in a beautiful dress, and you'd have … one of those long cigarette holders… Oh - you don't mind if I smoke, do you?'

'No, no, that's fine.' And she thought it nice that he had bothered to ask. It showed he was considerate.

'Well, Graziella, by the looks of it you really are coping on your own.'

'I told you I would, Gino. Anyway …' she threw him a sideways glance 'why are you here? By my reckoning it's been a week, not ten months.'

'Is that all? You see how you've bewitched me. I couldn't stay away. *And* you've got a black cat. That's proof.' He pointed to it, sitting on the wall, watching the hen and cockerel scratching about the yard.

She laughed, beginning to relax. His being here ceased to feel strange.

'His name's Caspar.'

'That's a good name. And you're smiling at last. You looked quite fierce before.'

Who else had told her that? Then she remembered. It had been Roberto: *You can sound so fierce sometimes, and you look so pretty and delicate,* he had said, the day they had driven the mule to the vineyards. The recollection made her smile - followed by a pang of yearning; such innocent happiness. She felt old by comparison to that girl.

'I don't mean to,' she said to Gino.

'It wasn't a criticism. You're lovely as you are. Don't change for anyone. Always be yourself.'

She was still holding the flowers, and he watched her as she carefully laid them across the water butt.

'I'm not sure who "myself" is any more. I seem to have lots of selves,' she confided.

'And they are all different aspects of you, rolled into one delightful, exciting package,' Gino said. 'Oh Graziella, if only… '

'What?'

'It doesn't matter.'

121

But she knew. He had been going to say, *If only you were older.*

'Have you seen or heard anything of the mayor?'

'No, nothing. I left the morning the article came out in the *Gazzetta.* That was so funny, what you wrote, Gino. Really clever.'

'Thank you. I'm glad you approved. That means a lot to me. I must admit, without boasting, it *was* rather good.'

She gave him a push. 'That *is* boasting.'

He looked contrite. 'I'm learning I can rely on you to put me in my place, young lady. And I think I like it,' he said.

He inhaled on his cigarette. His voice took on a serious note: 'I'm relieved the mayor hasn't been harassing you. I was afraid he might do. He's a bad man Graziella. There's nothing I would put past him.'

He contemplated her with a grave expression.

'What's happened,' she asked sharply.

'Actually, there is another reason for coming to see you,' he admitted. 'I wanted you to hear it from myself…Signor Tebaldi, the *Direttore di Banca,* is dead. He hung himself.'

'*Madre.*' She made the sign of the cross and perched herself on the edge of the rusty barrow. He joined her.

'I never thought… I didn't intend… It's my fault.' She put her head in her hands.

'Graziella, don't.' He tilted her chin upwards so that she had to look at him. 'You mustn't blame yourself. None of it is your fault. These are nasty people. They live in a murky world. Tebaldi was as odious as the mayor. '

'A man died and I played a part in his death.'

'That's rubbish Graziella, and you know it is.'

'So why did you bother to tell me?'

'Because I knew how you would react when you heard. And I was correct.'

'Has anyone told you that you're arrogant, Gino Terrasini?'

'That's unfair.'

'So have they?'

'Perhaps.'

She laughed then, and he drew her to him, gently pushing her head down, onto his shoulder.

'I want to look after you forever,' he said.

She knew he was about to kiss her, and felt dizzy in her expectation. She licked her lips. He moved closer to her, but as he did the wheelbarrow tipped forward, breaking the spell.

He stood up. 'No Graziella. I wish it - but no. Because we both know it would not stop there.'

She got up also, averting her eyes so that he wouldn't see the tearful disappointment in them, and rubbed flakes of rust from her legs.

Tenderly, he took hold of both her hands. 'Look at me, please, Graziella. It's not that I don't want to. You know that. It's because I respect you.'

She nodded, clenching her jaw.

He is a man of strong principles. I approve, her mother said.

He did not stay long after that.

'I shall see you from time to time. I shall hide in the bushes, but you won't see me. I'll be your invisible guardian.'

She couldn't muster a smile. 'You'll meet another girl. You'll forget about me.'

'Nobody could forget about you, Graziella.'

Fleetingly, she thought of Roberto again. He had forgotten.

'I swear I will wait for you. You are well worth waiting for. One in a million,' Gino said.

He trailed a finger down the long line of her throat with a moth-like touch which took her breath away, then kissed her on either cheek, chastely.

'*Ciao, bella.*'

And he was gone, waving behind him. At the brow of the hill he turned. She could just make out his figure. He made a funnel of his hands: *'Penso che ti amo,'* he called out at the top of his voice.

Happiness flowed through her. *'Anch'io,'* she shouted back.

But the hill masked him from sight and she could not be sure he had heard.

She arranged the flowers in a jug, keeping back a narcissus to press, in the book her teacher had given her.

I think I love you!

Had he really called out that? And now her happiness of five minutes ago was marred by longing. Ten *months.* Time would tick by to its own rhythm, without regard to impatience or love.

A rustling came from outside, followed by a clang, as though a bucket had been kicked over, and Graziella ran outside, with a smile because she thought that Gino had changed his mind and returned.

You couldn't even last ten minutes, she would tease.

And he would take her in his arms, like in a romantic film …

'Gino?'

The air was empty. Maybe Caspar, the cat, had been up to mischief. But now her keen ears detected a faint sound from the mule shelter, and she crossed the yard to investigate.

At first she did not see him, crouching in the shadows where the mule used to take refuge from the flies. When she did it was too late.

A stocking was pulled over his head, in a ludicrous attempt at disguise, and in his hand was the kitchen knife her mother had used for chopping meat.

She registered these details in the same second that he lunged at her. There was no chance of escape, no time even to vent her scream, as he captured her ankles. She fell to the ground, landing heavily on her elbow, and he jerked her to her feet by the hair, tugged her head back so far that she thought her neck would snap.

Her eyes felt as though they might pop out of their sockets, but all she could do was flail her hands like useless wings, and the only sounds of protest she could produce were tiny, terrified, squeaks.

'Puttana! Donnaccia!'

He spat twice in her eyes, and the stinging globs slithered down cheeks.

'Puttana!' he reiterated in a snarl, his chin pressed up to her, and he shook her like a dog would shake a hare. The violent movement caused the stocking to slip off, but if the mayor noticed he did not care. He toyed with the knife, watching her with a cruel expression, swivelling it close to her nose, playing with her. Frozen with fear, she shut her eyes. She felt the flat of the cold blade circling the hollow of her throat precisely where, not long ago, Gino had traced it with his finger, and she held her breath. Then his grip of her head slackened and she opened her eyes. His hand slammed into the side of her face.

Pain shot through her, and she gave a sharp cry, reeling from the impact.

'Make another sound and you're dead,' he rasped, and hit her a second time, across the mouth.

Stifling her cry, she tottered forward. The mule shelter seemed to tip towards her, and the sea roared in her ears as her head struck the wall. She could taste blood, and sank onto the floor, where she cowered in the corner. Normal, everyday life filtered through her conscience as if from another planet: the church bells ringing for three o'clock mass; the odd, distant car, or scooter, or mule and cart; faint voices; the bleating of sheep; bird song…

Her chattering teeth.

His breathing.

As though this were happening to someone else, she was aware of him yanking off her shorts, then her knickers. Her head felt too big for her body. She began to shake; couldn't stop shaking.

'Not a sound,' he reminded her.

Through her tears and snot, she watched him undoing the buttons of his trousers. He forced her slender legs wide apart and straddled her. His erection was huge, and he ripped into her, puncturing her protective skin, biting her nipples till they bled, crushing her with his weight. Faster and faster, harder and harder, he bounced on her, as though she were a trampoline, until with a yowl, he climaxed, and his semen spurted into her.

Graziella curled up like a mollusc. Through the slits of her swollen eyes she could see the mayor struggling with his trousers. They were wound round his ankles and he kept trying to pull them up, but one of the legs was inside out. While he fought with them the knife had temporarily been forgotten. It glinted on the ground, between them.

Surreptitiously, she slid out her hand and grasped it.

'*Ey! Che cosa fai?*' he exclaimed, alert all at once.

He made to grab it from her. But, she sprang up and, hindered by the tangled trousers, and by the confined space, he tripped.

Quick as a viper, she jabbed the knife into his thigh.

He gave a high-pitched squeal, and stared at the blood spurting.

'*Cagna!*' he swore at her, hopping from foot to foot.

Strength came to her from nowhere.

'Get out of my *casetta*, get out, get out, get OUT.' She waved the knife wildly at him. 'Don't come near me. I swear I'll kill you.'

And, though she could barely stand, and the knife shook in her clasp, she must have convinced him. He managed to pull on his trousers, and, calling her a variety of coarse names, dripping blood, he left.

Graziella walked slowly to the *Gazzetta* office. A month had elapsed. This was her first excursion in that time, and her heart raced. Every so often she would glance behind her to ensure she was not being followed. Only a tiny, diamond-shaped scar, unnoticeable unless you knew it was there, remained as physical evidence of her ordeal. Her mental scars were a different matter.

She rang the bell, trying not to retch from the stench of the drains. A silver-haired man came to the door, looking harassed. She recognised him as the editor of the paper.

'Yes, Can I help you?' he enquired.

'Could I see Gino please,' she said.

The man studied her in a strange way.

'You haven't heard?'

'Heard what?'

'Oh dear, you must be the girl he couldn't stop talking about. You must be Graziella.'

She nodded, and licked suddenly dry lips.

'He had an accident on his Lambretta.

He died. Nearly three weeks ago.'

CHAPTER 20

NOW

GRAZIELLA

My daughter switches off the Dictaphone. It is tiny. Hardly bigger than my thumb. All these gadgets nowadays are quite baffling. When I think how primitively my parents lived it seems quite extraordinary.

'So, Gino is my father?' My daughter asks.

'Yes,' I affirm. Let her believe it. The truth can be too brutal. You have to shave it sometimes. Please God, she will never find out.

'Did you love him?'

And did I? It was so long ago. Were those youthful yearnings and mesmeric gazes love? It was not the same, deep love that I bore for my darling husband. That was a love where you knew each other so well that your thoughts were interlocked. And perhaps your heart did not race, but you felt complete. Without him now I have been left stranded. There again, there are different kinds of love and one's perceptions of it change and fluctuate.

'Yes, I loved him.'

'But why didn't you tell me about this before?'

She is frowning. I know that frown of my daughter's. It is the precursor to a barrage of questions.

'I'm telling you now.'

'There must have been a reason.'

'It was a different era... And I didn't want to hurt your stepfather.'

'I don't understand. Why would it have hurt him? You're entitled to have had a relationship before you met him. As far as I know he never resented you for it. Or me, for that matter. And he obviously didn't mind you naming our Gino after him. There's something you're holding back from me Mama. You promised you would tell me everything. And what happened to the mayor? I can't believe he just went quietly to ground after you shopped him to the press.'

'He didn't go quietly to ground. He took his revenge on Gino, and therefore, indirectly on me. His death was no accident. I am convinced of it.'

Surely that must have assuaged her curiosity? But she is still frowning. I can sense further questions. My head hurts: needles scratching the inside of my skull.

'I don't wish to talk anymore. Have you any idea how tiring it is, regurgitating the past like this?'

'Of course I do. It's me who always suggests that we should stop.'

I wish she wouldn't wear that aggrieved expression. It gets on my nerves. 'Anyway, I've got to pack. I still haven't packed for tomorrow,' I tell her.

'Why, where are you going?'

'Now you're being silly. You know perfectly well we're going to the *Isola*.'

'You mean *Isola delle Pecore*?'

What on earth is wrong with my daughter today?

'Naturally.'

'But Mama we're not. We haven't been back there since ....'

'Why do you always have to argue? It is so draining Rosa.'

'But I'll show you your diary if you like.'

'Oh do be quiet. You're becoming very tiresome.'

Upstairs I fetch my suitcase from the spare room, and start by putting my underwear into it. My head is throbbing.

Papa is smiling at me:

Graziella, piccolina, he is calling to me.

Papa...

Everything is fuzzy. Images collide, toppling in a waterfall of names and faces and ghosts. *Don't go. Papa don't go.*

An abyss of loneliness engulfing me. And cold. It is so very cold....

'Mama it's alright. Mama, please Mama.'

Rosa's lovely, frightened face bending over me. Her pansy-soft eyes.

'Where... I don't...' My lips are having trouble forming words. What has happened? Why is the suitcase in the middle of my room with my underwear inside, as though I have been packing?

I stroke away my daughter's tears.

'I'm here, my little Rosa. Don't be sad. I'm here.'

Another "blip", as we refer to them. Such an innocuous little word for something so gargantuan.

One day it will swallow me whole.

CHAPTER 21

NOW

ROSA

I feel awful, leaving her on her own today. I should stay. I *could* stay; for a while, longer anyhow. I offer to take her to the cinema, to an early film, but she declines. Offer to take her to the sanctuary, but she declines that also.

They can cope without me, are her exact words. Never did I think I would hear her utter them. She must feel so purposeless, so redundant.

'I've got a lot of things I must do. Paperwork to sort out,' she says.

'I could help you.'

'No *cara*. There are matters only I can deal with myself.'

'Well, if you're sure…'

But the truth is I cannot wait to leave, and that fills me with guilt.

I drive home in torrential rain. Spray from the lorries makes it difficult to see, and despite the fan going at full blast, the windscreen keeps misting up with condensation and I have to rub at it with the dog towel. The traffic crawls along, stopping and starting, and the hypnotic rhythm of my wheezing wipers could send a person insane; but at least the appalling weather forces me to concentrate, diverting me from the weight of my thoughts.

Back at the house I all but collapse onto the sofa. Lupo jumps up beside me and rests his long head on my lap. He smells of wet dog.

'You're not allowed up here, you know that,' I tell him, cuddling him to me.

Mixed messages - I can imagine Mama chiding me.

I call my husband, but he is at a meeting. What can he do or say, anyway? This is something we must learn to live with.

The question circles relentlessly in my mind: *is* the man my brother was named after, indeed my father, as Mama claims? Or is that what she wished? Was the mayor linked to the accident which killed him? And scrolling back to my childhood, I remember again her expression that day we left the café and encountered her uncle. I realise now, what it represented. It was fear. My mother, who was afraid of nothing and no one, was afraid of him.

And now I ask myself: is there any point continuing with this project - turning down paid work in order to do so - if, when all is said and done, it becomes little more than fiction?

The house feels oppressive. I have to get out.

The phone. Mama. She sounds her normal self.

'It's stopped raining and I'm going to do a spot of gardening,' she says.

'Good.'

We chat for a while, mainly about the garden, which she and my stepfather transformed over the years from a virtual wilderness.

'I'm sorry *cara*,' she says.

'What for?'

'Letting you down. Having this wretched disease. Being awkward at times.'

For a few seconds I don't trust myself to speak; then, adopting a bright voice, I retort: 'You haven't let me down - that's ridiculous. You can't help having this horrible disease. And you've always been awkward.'

She chuckles, and I can picture her.

'Ah, my little Rosa, you have no idea how much I love you - though sometimes it mightn't seem like it.'

'But I *do* Mama. Of course I do.'

'Good. That's all that matters,' she says.

'And Mama - you know it's reciprocated, don't you?' I ask her.

'Yes, *cara*. Indeed I do,' she says.

A short lull in the conversation follows, then Mama says: 'I do realise how difficult my illness is for you. But I don't want you to worry.'

'I can't help it. It's natural that I would.'

'Well, there's really no need. I've seen to everything. It is important to be pragmatic.'

'What do you mean?'

She evades the question.

'One day at a time, *cara*.'

It's what my stepfather used to say.

And of course I must continue with my mother's story. What does it matter that fiction may be woven among the facts? It will be fiction through *her* eyes: as narrated by her. It is no less valid for that.

It is her entitlement.

CHAPTER 22

THEN
THE HERMIT

I t was the end of June; more than three months had passed since
that day which had changed Graziella forever.

The new mayor had been sworn into office, wearing a pair
of scuffed shoes beneath his robes, and in the packed *Municipio*,
where the other mayor had delivered his impassioned swan song,
he confirmed his plans. His first task would be to overhaul the tax
system - there were cheers here; his second to restore fishing subsidies - more cheers; his third, to demolish the football stadium,
with the assurances that should there be a financial recovery he
would consider a new site. No cheers greeted this announcement,
but neither were there groans. It had been anticipated. Meanwhile
- the dour little man continued - the old site would become a nature reserve, encouraging tourism. With this in mind, he would
impose a ban on the killing of certain species of wildlife.

His pragmatism and rumpled appearance came as a relief to
the majority of islanders. The day had been declared a national
holiday, and they poured out of the *Municipio* to get drunk.

Graziella had left halfway through his address. Crowds intimidated her. She rarely went out in public nowadays, and each day merged into the next. Sometimes she had the feeling that she was a ripple being carried along on the current of monotony.

She slept in her childhood room, with her yellow rabbit and her father's shotgun next to her. The cat, Caspar, slept on the bed also. Halfway through the night he would slink away to hunt, reappearing with a sequence of yowls, signifying his success.

For Graziella sleep had become a thing to dread. She was besieged with nightmares from which she would surface with a scream on the edge of her tongue: disembodied hands pressing down on her shoulders; her teacher drowning her in the tin bath; her uncle incarcerating her in a white, windowless building, and she realised it was a gas chamber; Gino sweetly kissing her, but when he turned she saw that half his face was missing.

When she awoke there was no sense of relief that it had been a dream. Her reality was no better. She felt dirty; indelibly sullied. No amount of washing could cleanse her. Her own body had become repugnant to her. She read and re-read the account of Gino's death in the back edition of the *Gazzetta* which the editor had given her. *A tragic accident,* the feature reported. *A promising journalist with ambition killed in his prime.*

Had his ambition lead to his death? Had she led him there? The mayor had been questioned, but released without charge. The gnarled remains of the young man's motorbike provided no clues, and though the coroner admitted the circumstances were "mysterious" - lack of evidence meant he had no option but to reach a conclusion of accidental death. A photograph of Gino, head thrown back in laughter, was printed at the top of the page. She had cut it out. The print had smudged where she kissed his picture each night.

From day to day she hardly saw a soul. She felt disconnected from the world, and lived like a hermit; like Adelina Ferrara, whose body had been discovered half eaten by her sow.

She clung to her routine. Discipline camouflaged her pain and temporarily blotted out her thoughts. She tended to the chickens, and the vegetable plot, cleaned the *casetta*, made *brodo* and *polenta*, and fished, and foraged. Sometimes she swam in the lake. Its coldness reminded her she was alive.

...I'm never going to die.... I've decided I'm going to be immortal, Gino had said, shortly before he was killed. And before he left her that day: *I shall hide in the bushes, but you won't see me. I'll be your invisible guardian.*

But the whispering bushes frightened her; and if Gino was in heaven - whose existence she doubted - then why did he not send her a sign? Her mother, too, had vanished; her voice silent. This had happened before, but never for so long. And Stefano had broken his word that he would visit; but she knew that would be down to the shrewish Donatella.

One person Graziella did see occasionally was her old school friend, Raffaella, and whenever she passed the convent, she was prompted to think of her behind its cloisters. The first time she had seen her had been on her way to the market; Raffaella was with two other novices, and their light laughter sounded so happy and pure, that it made her wistful. They had spoken briefly, but Graziella had felt inhibited by the presence of the others - as though she was intruding - and had excused herself. Another time had been through the collapsed stone wall of the convent; Graziella had glimpsed her in the yard, pegging out laundry from an enormous basket, singing as she worked. She had paused to stretch, then, noticing Graziella, went up to the wall.

'It's good to see you Graziella,' Raffaella said. 'But I can't chat. It's Mass soon and ...' She motioned to the basket of laundry.

'I understand. But that was lovely - hearing you sing. You sounded so happy.'

'I am. And I'm training to be a midwife.'

'You'll be good at that.'

'Well I'm not clever, like you, Graziella. You could do anything.'

Could she? Even now? The remark had sparked her with hope. They spoke for no more than a minute.

'I have to go, Graziella. But I often think of you. Please visit. The hours are on the board outside the gates.'

She went back to her laundry and her singing.

Inspired by Raffaella, the next library day Graziella had borrowed three books: *The Evolution and the Anatomy of Vertebrates*, another entitled *Learn to Speak English* and a novel, *Il Gattopardo*, by Giuseppe Tomasi di Lampedusa. For the next fortnight she read and studied voraciously, and as she immersed herself in books again she was able, for an hour or so at a time, to leave grief behind.

She had seen Raffaella on two further occasions, but both times she had been in the company of others. Then, early one morning, before the blistering heat set in, Graziella had been on her way back from collecting firewood when someone called out to her. Looking round, she saw Raffaella puffing up the hill, also lugging a sack of wood, and she waited for her to catch up.

'I thought it was you in the forest, but you disappeared,' Raffaella said.

'I didn't see you,' said Graziella.

They studied one another. In her white habit Raffaella presented an ethereal figure; a serenity shone from her, making her plainness almost beautiful.

'I've missed you,' Graziella said.

'I was hoping you would visit,' Raffaella reproached her.

'I can't.'

'Why not?'

'I have lost my faith. It would feel wrong.'

'Ah, Graziella.' Raffaella shook her head. Her lashless eyes filled.

'You see? I knew you would disapprove. It's why I didn't want to tell you.'

'I don't disapprove. You should know me better than that.'

'I'm sorry. I didn't mean to sound angry.'

'It's fine. But you're my friend. I would never judge you. I'm sad for you, that's all. At least you still wear your cross.'

'It was Mama's.'

'Oh, of course.'

She was looking at Graziella in a strange manner, with an intensity which made her smile.

'What?'

'Can I ask you something? Promise you won't be offended?'

'I promise,' Graziella agreed, laughing.

'Are you pregnant? I promise I shan't tell anyone, but *are* you?'

The laughter was erased from her face.

'No! Non è possibile!'

Raffaella observed her with a sorrowful expression. She touched Graziella's arm. 'I'll pray for you Graziella, even if you don't want me to,' she said.

Now, Graziella lay on her bed, in a stupor. It should have occurred to her. How could it not? The olives should have alerted her. She had never liked their sharp, acidic taste. Then, inexplicably, she had developed a passion for them. She would walk to the olive groves, where overhanging branches dripped with ripe fruit, and when she shook them olives rained down into the cup of her hand.

But the olives apart, there were no specific symptoms. Her periods had always been irregular, she'd experienced no sickness, and her tiredness she attributed to her depression. The likelihood of pregnancy had, quite simply, not occurred to her. How naïve she had been. Not that it made a difference to the outcome: *his* baby was growing in her womb, feeding off her.

Without warning, bile rose to her mouth and she vomited on the spot, heaving, spitting and raging.

'God, if you're there, how could you have done this to me?' she shouted.

God had deserted her.

CHAPTER 23

THEN
OMENS

The weeks and months went by. She dragged herself about in a fog. Then one morning in early October, she awoke refreshed. It was the same the next morning, and the following one, and the one after that. Then she realised: the nightmares had ceased.

Simultaneously, she felt a fluttering between her ribs and, at first, did not comprehend its significance.

Hello cara.

Her mother's lavender scent pervaded the room; her voice was as though she were standing beside her; as though she had not been absent for months.

A surge of happiness rushing through her.

'Where have you been? I needed you.'

I was here, but you were too sad to sense me.

There it was again: a fluttering. Like a butterfly. Unmistakable! Life affirming.

It's a girl, cara.

'Are you sure?'

Yes.

She was filled with relief. Had it been a boy she would not have kept him. She would have deposited him at the foot of the steps of the convent. He would have grown up to be like his father. Like all men: weak, drunk, unfaithful, violent. Her father and Gino had been exceptions. She had planned that should she give birth to a son she would carry him to the convent at night and leave him there.

A girl was a different matter. How could she give away a little girl? She would lavish her with love. It would be just the two of them. Her daughter would be more precious than anything in the world, and she would protect her from harm. And out of the bad, would come good. She was done with moping. It was time to emerge from her self-imposed exile.

In her parents' room she riffled through her mother's dresses for something suitable to wear.

The one with the roses on it, her mother said.

'It will be too tight. It will show my tummy.'

They will all know soon anyway. Be proud. You've done nothing wrong, cara.

She squeezed herself into the dress, and was about to close the wardrobe, when her mother stopped her.

Wait. You must look amongst your papa's things.

'Why?'

Look behind his shoes.

'What am I looking for?'

But her mother had gone.

She opened the wardrobe door to her father's section and hauled out his shoes. What enormous feet he'd had, she thought; and remembered how, as a young child, she would slip her feet into his shoes and try to walk with them, shuffling around like a penguin.

The poor light in the room was almost obscured by the open wardrobe door, but right at the back, she noticed the silhouette of something bulky; it had been partly hidden by his overalls. Her excitement quickened, and she dragged out a large, hessian bag, made heavy by its contents. Through the coarse fabric she could feel several oblong shapes.

'Please, please, please,' she murmured.

The bag had been tied at intervals with cord, and she picked at the knots with her ragged nails, suspense making her fingers clumsy. In the end she cut through the remaining knots with her father's penknife.

Four walking sticks rolled onto the floor, all different. One had the head of a horse; another an owl; the third, a curly-horned ram; and lastly was a two-tailed lizard, which had been painted in iridescent shades of green. Carved into the base of each were her father's initials, BL, and beside these, a small wolf's head. His trademark.

Each of the sticks told a story, and revived a memory, and Graziella sobbed with joy. For a long while she remained sitting there, surrounded by the sticks; touching them, revolving them between her hands, not trusting that this wasn't one of her dreams, and any moment the sticks would metamorphose into snakes which would sink their fangs into her. But nothing of the sort transpired. They were real and solid and smelt of the forest.

She stood up. Nobody would steal these from her or set fire to them. It was a pity there wasn't a Lupo stick among them, but the two-tailed lizard would bring her luck.

And it was surely no coincidence that, as she picked her way down the hillside towards the village, a two-tailed lizard should saunter across her path. It paused to blink at her through its scaly lids, as though relaying a secret message, before resuming its leisurely passage. And if this was not a good omen, she thought, then what was?

As she descended the steps to the *piazza* her confidence wavered. Everything was frighteningly familiar; nothing had changed. Why would it? Only she was different. Lambrettas, Vespas, mule carts and small Fiats were parked in the alleys; the last of the tourists wandered aimlessly, weighed down by photographic equipment; the usual gossips were gathered in their spot, by the telephone box - and as she passed their jaws dropped. The same three wizened men sat in their braces outside a small bar, drinking grappa and playing dominoes. She could see the butcher in his open-fronted shop chopping meat and wiping the blood from his hands down his apron. An emaciated donkey was tied to a ring next to the newspaper kiosk; cats and dogs sniffed about.

A little further on she came to a fenced-off, grassy area, sheltered by cypress trees. Several youths were kicking about a football, churning up clouds of dust which rose into the dry air. They were egged on by a group of raucous girls, whose faces were pressed against the wire fence. Graziella stopped to watch. All had been in her class at school; they were her age - fifteen - but they seemed much younger than herself. They were children, unencumbered by responsibility. They had never had to fend for themselves, rely on their wits, or battle daily in order to survive. She envied the ease of their normal lives.

One of the boys was Gino's brother, Tonino, and as she watched, the ball arched in the air and he threw himself towards it, his lithe body extending to reach it. A bolt of shock ran through her. He looked so like a younger version of Gino.

She ached to rush over and speak to him. Talking to him would make her feel close to Gino. She wanted to hear his name iterated aloud by somebody dear to him. Tonino would provide a link. He would comprehend her pain.

Did he die instantly? She would ask.

She would enquire about the accident and perhaps learn more about the circumstances. But the reality was that even had Tonino been alone she would not have gone up to him. It was unlikely Gino had mentioned her to his brother, and he would wonder at her interest. He would tell his parents, who would then believe their dead son to be the father of her baby.

Oh how she wished that were the case. How she wished she could lie to them; to all those who would point their fingers at her. Most of all she wished she could lie to herself.

'Go for it, Tonino,' the leader of the girls shouted.

With a stab of jealousy, Graziella realised he was her boyfriend, and for a moment it felt as if Gino had been stolen from her anew.

She was about to slink away, when the girl saw her. They were old adversaries, and a look, first of shock, then delight, spread across her features. Nudging her friends, she said something to them, whereupon they span round in unison.

'Prostitute! Not so grand now, are you?' jeered the girl, amidst laughter. The boys did not join in; they looked embarrassed.

'Stupida!' Graziella flung at her.

It sounded lame by comparison, and the girl's insult vibrated deep in her. She knew it was how she would be looked upon by the entire community.

It was market day, and she threaded between the stalls, pretending to be interested in the produce, conscious of heads swivelling and incredulous stares. Her fixed smile hurt her gums, and she realised that she was trembling. She was no longer sure that coming here, openly flaunting herself, had been the right decision, and wanted nothing more than to run back to the *casetta*, like a rabbit to its warren.

She concentrated on the colourful displays of fruit and vegetables, and the noise around her: the cries of the traders, honking of geese and clucking of chickens. A chained ram kept up an incessant bleating and charged anybody who came near it. Casually, Graziella picked up a watermelon.

'You like them big?' the middle-aged stallholder said, leering at her across his stand.

'*Vaffanculo*,' she hissed - softly, so nobody else would hear the vulgar expletive. Men! They were all alike, she thought, for the second time that morning. She was still smarting, when she came face to face with her schoolteacher. The latter's friendly smile died as she took in Graziella's fecund belly. Her hand leaped to her throat and her lips formed a silent "Oh". She seemed about to speak, then changed her mind and dodged by.

Graziella's eyes prickled. Of all the people she knew, the only one whose opinion really mattered to her was her teacher. The October air felt chilled with hostility and her bravado ebbed. She wished now that she hadn't worn that dress. She may as well have strutted naked up and down the *piazza*; or pasted a notice on the billboard outside the *Municipio,* where every month a film was screened.

GRAZIELLA LUPO IS PREGNANT, the title would proclaim.

She was on the point of turning for home, when she again felt that tweaking within her. It seemed to her that her unborn daughter was seeking to comfort her.

Let them all talk about her and think whatever they wished. They couldn't hurt her. She would name her daughter Rosa. They would look after each other and have no need of anyone else.

Her head lifted and she continued her circuit of the square.

CHAPTER 24

THEN
NO SHAME

The news had circulated around the village: the chicken vendor's daughter had got herself pregnant.

'There she goes!' the gossips exclaimed to each other, as Graziella sauntered by them.

And they beat their rugs harder, scrubbed their doorsteps violently and jabbed their crochet hooks in and out of their balls of yarn with ferocious speed. She was shameless with her lofty head-carriage, swaying hips and long eyes that never lowered in modesty.

'She had no morals. Look at her, brazenly exhibiting herself as though it were something to be proud of,' commented the florist.

'Her parents were decent folk,' the postmistress said. 'They must be turning in their graves.' She crossed herself and shuddered, remembering the awful image of Beppe and Rosa Lupo being hurled into the air, and the unearthly braying of the mule as it bumped with its cart down the rocks.

From her darkened bedroom, which she scarcely ever left, Annunciata observed her niece as she passed, and rued the day that she had taken her into her home.

There was much speculation as to who got her pregnant. Was it the son of Dino Lombardo, the vineyard owner, or even Dino Lombardo himself? Or maybe Giacamo Dattalo, the handsome butcher who chased anybody in a skirt under the age of fifty? Or perhaps it was the fisherman, Stefano; everyone knew he had a soft spot for her. Or it might have been a passing yachtsman who'd dropped anchor overnight. Or one of the youths who hung about, revving their Vespas. In fact, it could be anyone. There wasn't a man on the island who didn't look at young Graziella Lupo with longing.

Sanctimonious old prunes, Graziella thought, hardening herself against the venomous glares. She had just passed the *Posto di Carabiniere,* when a petulant voice arrested her.

'You silly man. Didn't you listen? I told you I wanted a square diamond engagement ring, not a round one. You'll have to go back to the shop.'

'I'm so sorry, my angel. I'll take the ferry to Palermo on Saturday and exchange it,' came the conciliatory response.

'I'm not waiting that long. You'll have to hire a private boat...'

Seconds later her cousin, wrapped in mink, came into view. An elderly, papery-complexioned man with lachrymose eyes hurried to keep pace with her furious feet. Graziella had seen him at the mayor's house on a few occasions: he was the attorney, Pedro Mendolia, whose wife had died the previous year. He must be Nina's new fiancé.

'Hello Nina,' she said equably.

Her cousin blanched, and made a choking sound.

'You!' she exclaimed.

She swung her handbag as if to hit Graziella with it, but lost her balance, and slid on the cobbles. The heel of one of her stiletto shoes became lodged in a drain.

She leant against the wall for support.

'Well don't just stand there gormlessly. Do something,' she shrieked at Mendolia.

Obediently, he bent down tugged at the shoe. His veined hands trembled. How could he let himself be humiliated like this? Graziella wondered. How could a man of his intellect and status have fallen for Nina? Did a pair of voluptuous young breasts completely override his brain's function? She would demolish him for breakfast, then take him for every *centesimo* he had. It would serve him right: he was no better than any other man, the old lecher.

He straightened up. 'I'm afraid it's wedged firm,' he said.

'Oh dear, you could be stuck here forever, Nina,' Graziella remarked.

'Whore,' her cousin screamed, disregarding the onlookers who'd stopped to see what was going on. 'Horrible little pregnant slut.'

Graziella tucked her thumbs in her pockets and surveyed her: 'It's you who is the whore,' she said, speaking in a tone of quiet contempt. 'You, in your ridiculous shoes, your fancy fur, and silk dress - bought, no doubt, by your *boyfriend*.'

Someone clapped; she didn't see who. Her cheeks felt like red flames. She was trembling with anger.

Brava, cara, her mother soothed her. *You handled that perfectly.*

Stefano's *ape* was parked in the alley opposite Mama Lucia's. The narrow, open-backed vehicle was stacked with chunks of barracuda, and beside it stood Stefano.

'Pesci! Barracuda! Venite, Signore!' he cried out, whilst wrapping fish in newspaper for a customer. *'Pesce! Barracu...'* Then he saw Graziella, and his voice faded. He took a long swig of *Peroni*, and wandered across the road to her. He wore a slightly sheepish expression.

'I've been meaning to come and see you,' he said.

She smiled; he was so obviously trying to avoid looking at her stomach.

'You say that whenever we bump into each other, Stefano.'

'Do I? I'm sorry... It's ... well ... difficult.'

'I was teasing.'

'Were you? That's alright then.'

'That's a lot of fish you've got there.'

'I caught it yesterday evening.' Stefano looked proud. 'It was quite a battle. I was almost pulled off the boat.'

'You must be careful. You've got Donna to consider now.'

'Often I think she'd be glad to be rid of me.'

'I'm sure that isn't true. You're a good man. A kind man. Papa often said it.'

The mention of her father set him at his ease. 'And you're a good girl, little Graziella. I *know* you. What happened to you?'

'What do you think happened, Stefano?'

He looked sorrowful.

'Things will work out for you. Don't let them upset you. And I *shall come and see* you. This time I really shall. If Donatella doesn't like it, well it's too bad. Quite honestly I am fed up of being bossed about. If there is anything you need, anything I can do to help you, well you let me know. I have let you down and I'm sorry.'

He glanced over to the *ape*, in time to see a skinny dog scampering off with a large cut of barracuda.

'*Porca miseria! Cattivo...*' he yelled, and charged across the road in pursuit.

Graziella was still laughing as she pushed through the fly curtain, which hung in gaudy plastic strips in front of Mama Lucia's open doorway. It flapped in the breeze, and her hair became entangled in it.

None of the tables outside were occupied - it was too blustery - and to her relief, inside was almost empty. Two local businessmen sat at a long table, playing rummy, slapping down cards at a rapid speed. A carafe of wine, three-quarters drunk, stood between them, and next to it, an untidy pile of coins. Immersed in their game, they did not glance up as she entered. Apart from them there was a young German couple, feeding each other *cassata* ice creams while gazing hungrily at one another. Through the steamed-up glass door, which divided the kitchen from the bar, she was able to see the top of Mama Lucia's head bobbing about. She could hear the hissing of the espresso machine and clinking of cutlery; and the cheesy-garlicky aroma of stone-baked pizzas drifted her way, making her ravenous.

She waited by the jukebox for Mama Lucia to come out. It was playing *Love Me Tender*. Graziella could sing all the words in English. She still remembered the vocabulary Roberto had taught her, and any words she did not know, she looked up in her dictionary. What was Elvis Presley really like, she wondered? He was handsome of course, but with every girl in the world swooning at his feet he was bound to be conceited, wasn't he? But she thought that he looked kind. And he sang of love.

> *…Love me tender,*
> *Love me dear,*
> *Tell me you are mine.*
> *I'll be yours through all the years,*
> *Till the end of time…*

The words were beautiful. They made her want to cry. She and Gino would have been like that. They would have got married. They would have been as happy as her parents had been.

The music came to an end as the kitchen door burst open. Cigarette between her lips, Mama Lucia carried out the pizza to the men. 'The plates are very hot,' she cautioned, brushing a tail of ash to the floor. Then she saw Graziella. Her eyes widened in surprised.

'Graziella!' She walked over to her and enveloped her in a sweaty embrace then held her at arm's length. 'I was hoping you would come to see me.' She sat down as she spoke lighting another cigarette.

Graziella sat down also. 'I wasn't sure I would be welcome. I didn't know if ...' She glanced towards the German boy and girl, and the card players, in case they were listening.

'Don't worry about them,' Lucia jerked her chin in their direction 'they aren't interested in us. As for being welcome - you're always welcome. Whatever the circumstances.'

'*Grazie mille, Mama Lucia.*'

Lucia waved a dismissive hand, and appraised her. 'Are you about seven and a half months gone, Graziella?'

'Six and a half.'

'That's all?' Lucia drew on her cigarette. 'Anyhow, you look well enough.'

'I am. I eat lots of fruit and vegetables, which I grow myself.'

'You're a brave girl.'

Gino had said that, the day she went to his office with the letters. Her thoughts always reverted to him. When would that stop? Would it ever?

'Everyone's talking about me. They think I don't care, but I do.'

Lucia shrugged her big shoulders. 'So what? Have people got nothing better to do than gossip? This will blow over. They'll soon get bored and find another subject to talk about...*piccolina*, I have to ask you - and it makes no difference to my opinion of you... the act which made you pregnant - did you consent to it or was it against your will?'

Graziella sucked in her breath. Her mouth trembled. She remembered the crunching noise her jaw made when the mayor hit her; the searing pain as he ruptured her hymen; his crushing weight sprawled across her. Mama Lucia watched her struggling with her emotions. She knew that haunted look; had seen it more than once, as a midwife.

'Ah ... it was like that.' She reached for Graziella's hand. 'Will you have it adopted?'

151

'No. It's a girl. If it had been a boy I would have given him to the nuns. But it's a girl.'

Lucia nodded. She did not question how Graziella could be so certain. But she knew that the labour would not be straightforward.

'You must come and find me the second the pains begin. Will you promise me you will do that?'

'Yes, I shall. Thank you.'

'You are not alone anymore, Graziella.'

⇥⇤

On New Year's Day, her sixteenth birthday, Graziella went into labour. She set off to summon help, but had not gone far before she doubled over. It chanced that the Contessa Leonora D'Alesandro, out walking her mastiff came across her, and alerted Mama Lucia.

Graziella gave birth to a daughter, who squawked in deafening protest at being disturbed. Ten minutes later she gave birth to a son. He made no sound.

Mama Lucia wrapped the girl in a shawl, and put her to her mother's breast. Raffaella Falcone, whose help had been enlisted, wrapped the tiny, lifeless boy in another shawl, and crossed herself, before taking him away.

CHAPTER 25

NOW
ROSA

A Sunday lunch. All of us round the table: myself, Gino, Billy - home for a few days, Jack, Mama. She is quiet, gazing round the room as though she has never seen it before, smiling with the polite detachedness of a stranger. Her old leather bag is on the floor beside her, and she keeps picking it up and rummaging through the contents, to reassure herself nothing is missing. Gino fetched and brought her to our house. She arrived with her shoes on the wrong feet, and her dress on back to front.

For more than two months she was laid low with bronchitis. Typically, she ignored it. It was just a "little cough" she claimed. And off she would go to the sanctuary, using the services of a local taxi company with whom she'd come to an arrangement, when Liz and I both refused to take her.

Then, one morning, she couldn't breathe. Thank God I was there. She was rushed into the John Radcliffe by ambulance, everything flashing and blaring.

I thought she would die.

After a fortnight in hospital, she was sufficiently recovered to leave. I drove home a frail, confused woman who had aged a decade. And so she has remained.

Since then, I've been driving back and forth to see her every day - sometimes twice a day, taking her meals, running errands, checking she has taken her pills, ferrying her about. I don't know which of us is the more fraught, her or me. And when I let myself into the house each morning, I'm terrified of what might greet me; that she'll be lying on the floor dead or unconscious. And I find myself resenting her, wishing unspeakable things, then hating myself for my thoughts.

During this period we have not worked at all on the book; but now that a soggy spring has given way to balmy summer, and some of her strength has begun to return, she has dropped the odd remark, indicating she would like to resume. Jack pours more wine into my glass. 'You look as though you could do with it,' he remarks, bending to my ear.

Billy attempts to engage Mama in conversation. Chatting in Italian to her, tells her about New York.

She frowns: 'Why do you have to work in New York? Your family is here. What's wrong with Britain?' she demands, sounding normal, and echoing my feelings.

'It's a fantastic opportunity, *Nonna*. I'm working under one of America's leading heart surgeons,' he explains.

'My papa was a heart surgeon.'

I shake my head at him, before he can contradict her.

'And do you have a girlfriend now, *caro*?' she enquires judiciously.

'Yes, *Nonna*,' he replies.

'Do you have sex?' she asks. 'Good sex is very important.'

Gino gives a smothered laugh.

To divert her, I offer Mama more pasta.

Shortly after lunch she starts rustling around her bag again, with a worried expression.

'What are you looking for?' I ask her.

'My car keys. I have to go now and I can't find them. They're not in my bag.'

'I drove you here, Mama,' Gino reminds her.

Her brow furrows. 'No you didn't, I drove myself.'

Everyone makes a pretence of searching for the keys.

'They're bound to turn up,' I try to soothe her. 'You could stay a bit longer.'

'No I can't. I've got a lot to do.'

'Let me take you back Mama,' Gino says. 'We'll sort it out later. I promise.'

'Very well,' she concedes.

We walk outside. The August sun is still warm.

'It was a delicious lunch *cara*. Thank you.' She says, with that abrupt switch of personality I have grown used to. She kisses Billy and Jack. I can see that she is impatient to be gone.

'What's the urgency, Mama?' I ask, as I walk with her to the door.

'But I told you,' Mama replies. 'I'm writing a book.'

CHAPTER 26
THEN
MISTERO

'What shall I tell Rosa when she asks about God, Mama?'
'Tell her the word "God" means something different to everyone.
When she is older she may decide for herself what it means to her. But she
should say her prayers nightly in case he is listening.'

'Should I have her baptised?... Mama? Please don't disappear... Tell
me what to do...'

⊱——⊰

'*Uno, due, tre, quattro, cinque, sei, sette, otto, nove, dieci,*' counted the child, as they descended the steps.

'*Brava, cara mia.* And if you had another ten steps how many would you have altogether?'

The child tucked in her lower lip and counted on her fingers. 'Twenty. And twenty is double of ten.'

'That's right. How clever you are.' Graziella hugged her then adjusted her straw sun-hat. She loved the feel of her daughter's fingers woven between hers. Their padded pinkness reminded her of a starfish.

Several heads turned as they walked by. After four and a half years, interest in her had waned, but the gossips' tongues still wagged.

'It's her lack of humility which most infuriates me,' the florist remarked, watching them cross the *piazza*.

'You never see her in church,' the baker's wife observed.

'And the child hasn't been baptised,' said the postmistress. 'What chance does she stand in life?'

'She will grow up a slut like her mother,' sneered Donatella, Stefano's ex-fiancée, who blamed Graziella for the demise of their engagement.

'You only have to look into the poor little mite's enormous, soulful eyes, to know she is sad,' commented the hairdresser.

'What rubbish you do talk.' Carlotta, ex-maid to the Carluccio household, had just joined them. 'She was born with those eyes. Anyone can see she's well looked after. Also I happen to know she *was* baptised. Her mother is no slut.'

Graziella was later than usual. Tuesday was her sausage-making morning, in readiness for the next day's market. She made them to her mother's recipe, and they were rich with pork meat and pungent with herbs. She used the old, unwieldy, grinder that was attached to the table, cranking endlessly, until her arms ached. But she herself did not do the selling. Her friend, Raffaella, sold them on her behalf, and people were happy to buy them, believing the nuns to have made them.

The August sun burned down; no hint of a breeze to relieve its harshness. The air vibrated with the buzzing and humming of insects. The bars were doing a roaring trade, as were the gift shops. In the last four years, since the old mayor had been deposed and his replacement had taken office, tourism had doubled. It had not harmed the island's reputation when a famous Italian pop star had built a villa high above the coast road, to use as a summer retreat. Mostly he kept to himself, though there were rumours of wild parties and orgies. Occasionally you would catch a glimpse of him in the town, dressed from head to toe in white, face hidden by dark glasses, a gold medallion dangling from his neck. He had a speedboat called *Ti Amo,* and sometimes you would see it streaking across the bay in a spray of white foam, like an irate shark. It would be a full five minutes before the ruffled sea calmed again.

But although buildings were springing up the length and breadth of the island, this did not detract from its beauty. You could still find solitude on the beaches, or in the hills or the forest; and if you stood at the foot of *La Montagna della Madonna* you might well find yourself alone in your daydreaming. The foreigners who holidayed here were respectful towards the inhabitants. By and large they were British, Dutch, and German, with the odd American among them. Mostly, they were students or young professionals with an adventurous spirit; and though, initially, the girls shocked the locals with their skirts that hardly covered their buttocks, the consensus of opinion now was that the town had been enhanced by the influx of tourists. It had been injected with a new lease of life, without sacrificing its core, and every new building project was subject to stringent regulations. The previous mayor wrote a letter to the *Gazzetta*, stating that the current prosperity was thanks to his vision five years previously; it was he, not his successor, who deserved the accolades. The other man had stolen his ideas. But who, now, took a scrap of notice of him? And in the following week's edition a cartoon depicted him treading grapes and spitting them out. *Sour grapes,* ran the caption.

During the summer months the ferry service was extended to run on a Wednesday, besides the usual Saturday, and another bus was acquired. Sometimes, on the switchback bend of the coast road where Graziella's parents had met their end, the two buses would pass each other, barely a centimetre between them, and the drivers would give a friendly honk of their horns to each other, laughing at the terror on their passengers' faces.

Owners of the smallest cottage with a room to spare would rent it out for bed and breakfast at an inflated price; if they had no spare room they would vacate their own and sleep on a mattress in a loft. When the ferry trundled into the port they would wait for the ramps to be dropped down, then swoop like vultures on the weary tourists, vying with each other for the business.

Vieni - I have perfetto room for you, very chip price. They offered mule trips round the island, fishing expeditions, walks to the vineyards - with picnic included and drives to the north of the island in old Mercedes cars with worn upholstery and which rattled and reeked of diesel and cigarettes. Stefano had acquired another boat from his uncle, who had recently died, and had had the idea of making the underside of the hull a glass panel, through which a whole secret world could be marvelled at. It seemed that everyone had become an entrepreneur. Local boys fell in love with English girls; money jangled in pockets. And with the growing prosperity, another *carabiniere* had to be employed, in case of increased crime.

They left behind the square and the shops and came to her old school. It was the holiday season and it was shut up for the summer, though the football pitch was available for anyone who had the energy to kick a ball in the sweltering sun. It stood quiet today, and the ghostly clamour of young voices played in her ears. Next year Graziella's daughter would be attending this same school. Her old teacher would one day be Rosa's teacher. It was an extraordinary prospect.

They walked along the esplanade. The harbour area was lively, and the cries of children playing in the sea extended to the thin strip of sand where sunbathers lay prone beneath bright umbrellas.

Graziella noticed the longing in her daughter's face.

'We can go in the sea later, *cara mia,*' she said.

'When you have finished working?'

'Yes.'

Despite the competition from the other café-bars, Mama Lucia's remained the most popular. It might not have gilded lettering above the awning, or serve fancy cocktails which cost as much as a fisherman earned in a week, but it possessed authenticity, and that was what visitors to the *Isola* wanted. Graziella had been working there for almost a year, making pizzas, preparing salads, waitressing. Lucia was happy for her to bring Rosa with her, and the child would perch on a stool, quietly drawing, or making shapes from dough. Lucia was good to Graziella. She had offered her a job when nobody else would, though she had lost several customers in doing so.

'Good riddance to the narrow-minded hypocrites,' she told Graziella. 'I don't want people like that in my café.'

Nothing intimidated her; when her husband had died, the joke had gone round that her husband, a diminutive man, had been crushed between the buttresses of her thighs during sex. Inevitably, the story had reached her ears, and she had laughed as raucously as everyone else.

Graziella loved her job, and working alongside Lucia. The infatuated men who patronised the café just to get a glimpse of Graziella, more than recompensed for the customers who had left; and they lived in hope that this would be the day she would turn her brilliant smile on them. But though their gaze would follow her with longing, or with lust, they were at all times respectful towards her, even protective, and she never felt threatened. And no, this might not be the life she had mapped out for herself, but when Graziella listened to her daughter's laughter, when she inhaled the sweet scent of her skin, or looked into her eyes, there was nothing more she would wish for.

Nearly all the tables outside were taken, especially the coveted ones abutting the esplanade. Graziella parted the fly curtain and held it for Rosa to go through, ducking as she followed her inside. The interior was cool, thanks to a couple of fans.

Over the wireless, she could hear Lucia coughing. As always it began innocuously enough, then worsened, gathering ferocity. Graziella settled Rosa in her usual chair, near the jukebox, and pushed open the swing doors to the kitchen. Lucia was in the middle of the room, hanging on to her cigarette between her fingers and clutching at her rib cage with her other hand. Rivulets of perspiration trickled down the sides of her face, which had turned a dark purple.

Graziella ran towards her, supporting her as she spluttered and gasped for breath.

'*Madre*, look at you. You need the doctor.'

Unable to speak, Lucia waved an arm to indicate she wanted no doctor.

The coughing spell subsided and she straightened up cautiously. 'You see, I'm fine now,' she said, with a weak smile. Graziella assisted her into a chair. Her weight was immense.

'You're bleeding. There's blood coming from your mouth,' Graziella said.

'It's nothing. I must have bitten my tongue,' Lucia replied.

'You should stop smoking. Everyone says it's bad for you.'

'Don't you believe it. My papa lived till he was ninety-two, and he smoked all his life. They're just scaremongering.'

'Your papa was lucky…' She hesitated. 'I don't want anything to happen to you, Mama Lucia.'

'Eh. It's not going to, *piccolina*.'

'Well anyway, at least let me take over for the rest of the day. You have taught me how to do it all. You should rest.'

Lucia regarded her with fond amusement. 'What a bossy little thing you are… You are the child I never had, Graziella,' she said.

Gripping the sides of the chair, she pushed herself up from it. The fleshy folds around her face trembled from the effort. 'You see? I'm fine,' she said. 'Now, shall we get on?'

Business was steady. The old islanders drank their Grappa and stared at the tourists in their skimpy swimwear. A young man with a poet's eyes wrote in a black notebook, intermittently looking out to sea, before lowering his head once more. A group of three middle-aged women had rigged up their easels and were painting the view. A girl and boy with dilated pupils softly strummed their guitars.

Graziella went back and forth with espressos, *cassata* ice creams, soft drinks, and carafes of wine. She balanced plates of food, three at a time, on her arms: prosciutto and watermelon, pizzas, *mozzarella in carrozza, insalata tricolore;* Rosa was entrusted with bowls of olives and anchovies.

The day wore on, and the student, whom Lucia employed on a part-time basis, took over from Graziella.

She and Rosa walked to the far end of the esplanade, where it was quieter, down the cobbled ramp, and onto the beach. Kicking off their shoes, they ran together along the grainy volcanic sand to the water's edge, and stripped down to the swimsuits they wore beneath their clothes.

The child flung her sturdy body into the sea.

'I won Mama,' she called.

Her mother laughed. 'You always win, *cara*, you are much too quick for me,' she replied, splashing her and laughing.

From afar, somebody watched them romping in the sea. He would have recognised her anywhere, from any distance.

He was too late. What had he expected?

He turned on his heels. He had planned to stay on the island for a fortnight, but there was no point in lingering. Tomorrow he would take the ferry to Palermo. He would not return.

The sun slid down and the sky was infused with shades of red. The heat of the day subsided and, almost drunk from doing nothing all day, the sunburned visitors, wandered back to their accommodation, carrying their newly purchased rubber flip flops.

The bell tolled for Mass.

'Stefano is coming to see us later,' Graziella said to Rosa as they walked back to the *casetta*. 'He has promised to bring us *calamari*.'

'I don't like how it looks. It's slippery and wriggly,' Rosa complained.

Graziella swung their hands together. 'I agree. But it's delicious if it's fried.'

'So it won't look horrible?'

Graziella stopped herself from smiling; her daughter's face was so solemn.

'You won't recognise it, *cara*. And if you don't like it after trying it, then you don't have to eat it.'

They arrived at the *casetta*. Graziella felt for the key in the pocket of her dress. Gone were the days when you would go out, leaving the door to your property unlocked.

'What's that?' Rosa pointed a stubby finger in a vague direction.

'What's what, *cara mia*?' Graziella paused, key in hand.

'There. Hanging from the fig tree.'

She tugged her mother's arm and they went over to it.

'It's a walking stick,' the child exclaimed. 'Whose is it Mama?'

Graziella made no reply. Struck dumb, she unhooked it from the branch, and examined it. Every detail, down to her father's initials, was accurate. There was no question that it had been made by him. It was as though someone had waved a wand and it had been resurrected from the ashes. Was this some kind of a strange trick? As far as she knew, he had only ever made two sticks with a *lupo* head. One had belonged to him. The other...

When I'm a grown up I'll come back, Roberto had vowed. And she recalled his shy, chaste kiss on the lips, and the taste of aniseed balls on his breath.

What did this mean? Had he kept his word and returned? Was he here, on *Isola delle Pecore*? But bearing in mind he had so abruptly ended their correspondence, and in the intervening years she had heard nothing, why, then, would he return? And if he had returned, why leave the stick for her to discover, rather than give it to her in person? Was this a coded message for her? He had always liked tricks. There was another possibility: that her father's Lupo stick had not been burned after all. Nina had been bluffing to torment her. The grey mound of ash in the incinerator may have just been garden waste, and what she had believed to be the remains of a wolf's ear, was merely a piece of projecting wood. But if that were so, where had the stick been for the last seven years? Who had been its custodian? It was utterly bewildering.

'Mama?' Rosa prompted on a questioning note. 'Yes *cara*,' she said absently.

'Did your papa make the stick?'

'Yes he did.'

'How did it get to our *casetta* by itself?'

'I don't know.'

'Maybe it flew.'

Graziella smiled now: 'That's a possibility.'

'So it must be a magic stick, mustn't it?'

'*Si*, my little Rosa. It must be magic. It really is the only explanation.'

CHAPTER 27

NOW

ROSA

H er voice fades. I click off the recorder.

'You hung the Lupo stick next to your papa's fishing rod. I remember taking it down to make a wish on it. And I acted out stories with it. When I started school I told my friends I had a magic stick that could fly. They were so envious. And they wanted to see it fly, but I told them it only flew after midnight. Oh God, it's all coming back to me Mama. How funny. What an eccentric child I must have been.'

'You were adorable,' she says. 'Such an earnest little girl. All great big eyes and smiles. You wanted everybody to love you. And when you swam in the sea, with your head under the water, your legs worked back and forth like a little frog... so sweet...so very sweet...All a very long time ago...go...'

I watch as her features cloud over. She digs her fingers into her skull as though distressed. I realise that her brain is undergoing one of her sudden transformations.

'He's coming after me.'

'Who is, Mama?'

She makes no reply.

'Mama, nobody is coming after you, I promise.'

But she takes no notice of me. It is as though I do not exist, and she stands up, tugging at her pullover, her eyes wide, and goes to the window. Pushing the curtains further back, she peers up, then down, the quiet road.

I play along with it: 'Would you like me to go and look for you?'

'No. He's dangerous. He might hurt you.'

'Did he hurt *you?* Mama,' I ask, seeking a clue as to what this could be about. She ignores me. '*Bastardo!*' she says spitting the word. And, leaning right out of the window, she shouts it: '*Bastardo! Bastardo!*'

I pull her away before she falls out, and she topples back against the sofa. I grab her arm to steady her, but she shakes off my hand.

'You hurt me,' she shouts at me, rubbing her elbow. 'What did you do that for?'

'I was trying to prevent you from falling out of the window.'

'But I've told you - I have to be vigilant. He's after me. He's probably hiding. He's very cunning.'

Who is this "he"? Is it a fictional figure, or it somebody from her past? Could she be referring to her uncle, the mayor?

Best to divert her.

'Mama, I'm rather cold, would you mind if I close the window?'

The ploy doesn't work. 'You do not seem to understand,' she insists.' 'I need it open in order to keep a proper lookout. He could be anywhere. I might get a knife from the kitchen.'

'You stay there.' I pat her shoulder. 'I'll get it. I'll have a good snoop around'

'Be careful,' she cautions.

'I'll take Tosca and Lupo with me. They'll frighten off any intruder.'

'He may be in the mule shelter,' she calls, as I leave the room.

I walk round the back of the house with the dogs, biting back tears. Another couple of months have elapsed. In the seven and a half months since my stepfather died my mother has become alarmingly worse. The blips are frequent now. The book is progressing ever more slowly, and I fear it may never come to fruition. And Mama fights me along the way, unaware that she is being irrational. We have devised a rota of sorts: I go there three or four times a week, a carer comes in for a few hours when I'm not there, and Gino usually sees her on a Sunday. In between, Liz picks her up whenever she wants to go to the sanctuary. I bring food for her to heat up in the microwave. So far, the arrangements seem to be working smoothly. And I am fortunate in so many ways, I do realise, and I should not complain, but I seem to spend my life stuck in Oxfordshire traffic and I feel tired the whole time, and I have just taken on a new commission: ghost writing a celebrity's story, and God knows how I will fit it in. And next month it will be Christmas...

It is starting to rain. I call the dogs and return to Mama.

'Hello *cara*,' she says in a chirpy tone. 'Liz rang while you were outside. She wants my opinion on a fox that has just been brought into the sanctuary. Would you be able to give me a lift?'

'Of course.'

'At least you will have the afternoon to yourself now,' she says.

'But I don't think like that, Mama,' I protest.

'Little Rosa, anyone would think like that,' she says.

In the car I ask her: 'Mama, earlier, when we were doing your story, you mentioned that I had been baptised. If you didn't take me, then who did?'

'My friend Raffaella,' she says.

'The nun? I remember her.'

'It should have been me. I regretted it almost immediately. I should have put aside my own distaste for religion for something so important. I failed you.'

'That's silly, of course you didn't. I was a few months old and wouldn't have known what was happening. I promise I don't hold it against you!' I tease her.

She doesn't smile. 'You had no idea what was happening to you. It should have been me, your Mama, supporting your tiny body. You needed *me*. I have never forgiven myself.'

'This is crazy. You were a child yourself, for heaven's sake.'

'Childhood had long left me behind, *cara*.'

'Oh Mama.'

Neither of us speaks for a couple of minutes. I turn off the B road, into a small, rural lane, towards the sanctuary.

'So what happened to Raffaella? Do you know if she survived the …'

'Yes, she certainly did,' Mama cuts me short. 'We remained in contact by letter for many years after I came to England. Then - well, you know how it is - you lose touch. But just a couple of months ago, I heard from her. She wrote to inform me that she had terminal cancer. She had something she wished to tell me.'

'What was that?'

'One day I will tell you *cara*. But not now. There is a time for everything.'

With that enigmatic utterance scorching my ears, we arrive at the sanctuary.

CHAPTER 28

NOW

GRAZIELLA

He rang me yesterday. His voice was pleasant: rounded, calming, each word considered. And although I had been prepared, nevertheless, I felt myself trembling.

He explained he was staying for a week, with a colleague in Reading. I told him that I would meet him at the station there. It seemed the simplest idea, and I didn't know where else to suggest.

Liz drove me to Oxford station and more or less put me on the train. She did not pry.

'If you have any problems, ring me, and I shall fetch you,' she said.

So now I am on the crowded train, with my head whirring in time to its motion. It's freezing outside, and my whole body seems to have gone into spasm. I hate the cold. I can feel my agitation growing. And why is everybody staring at me? Do they think I am mad? I reach for my bag, to find the mirror in there and check my appearance... but it isn't there. *Madre, Madre*, I have lost my bag.

People are looking uncomfortable. Did I yell it out loud?

Too bad. They are incidental. All that matters is my bag. Disregarding the other passengers, I clamber down, onto the floor to search there. Eventually, a kind voice cuts through my panic.

'What are you searching for, dear?' the woman asks.

Normally I detest it when a stranger addresses me as "dear", but now I welcome it. I tell her that I have lost my bag.

'But you're wearing it, dear,' she says. 'It's across your shoulder.'

If I could cry, I would do so now. And I confide in this kind person about my illness, something I could never have imagined doing.

The realisation of my own deterioration is a shattering thing.

She remains with me for the rest of the journey. Then waits in the cold with me, outside the station, until a man approaches, and asks if my name is Graziella.

We shake hands formally. He has his father's stature, but the gentlest smile, and his brow knits in concentration when you speak to him.

We find a café near the station and, after ordering food and drinks, talk about our respective lives.

'You first,' he says.

'No, you,' I tell him.

We both have much to say. At one point his eyes water with emotion, and I grip his hand.

All those wasted years.

I am not sure when, or if, I shall see him again, but we shall remain in touch, that is certain.

He kisses me goodbye on both cheeks.

'May God be with you,' he says.

I call Liz to fetch me. I would not be capable of taking the train.

CHAPTER 29

THEN
MOTHER LOVE

I t was early on a Sunday morning, and the island was still lost to dreams. A fine mist obscured the March air, which, in another hour or so, the sun would pierce.

Graziella and Rosa entered the forest, scrambling over gnarled roots and branches. After recent rainstorms the undergrowth was moist beneath their feet, and dew dripped from berries.

Each had a hessian sack tied round their waist - a small one for Rosa. Graziella carried her father's shotgun, and a basket containing a picnic of cheese, *bruschetta*, which she had baked at five that morning, fruit, and a bottle of *limonata*. Apart from themselves, not a soul was about, but the forest hills were full of secret sounds and rustlings of life: scurrying of small feet, the drilling of invisible antlers from rutting stags... And, just as her own father had taught her to identify the various sounds of the forest without fearing them, so Graziella explained them to her daughter. She would learn for herself, one day, it's the humans you need to worry about.

They walked until they came to a particular spot, where wild pear, hawthorn and manna ash grew in abundance. This was where her father had brought her when she had accompanied him on his stick-foraging expeditions. Even now, she could recall the sensation of his enormous, rough hand encasing hers; the hoarse timbre of his voice, played in her ears.

Her daughter skipped beside her. It was, she thought, as if time had dissolved and she was watching an image of herself.

She laid the shotgun and picnic basket on the ground, and opened the neck of her sack.

'I'm going to find mushrooms to put in my sack,' Rosa announced.

'*Va bene*, but you must not wander off where I cannot see you, *cara*,' her mother instructed her.

'Can you see me here, Mama?' the child called, dancing forward then halting.

'Yes, *cara*.'

Rosa ran over to the dark line of pines. 'And here?'

'Yes, but no further,' Graziella called.

'I can see lots of mushrooms. I'm going to pick them.'

'Good, but you must not eat any without showing me first, because they may be poisonous.'

Graziella stooped to gather broken branches, tossing them into the sack as she went, and pausing from time to time to check on her daughter. She had filled her sack with all she would be able to carry, and was about to call to Rosa, when noises attracted her attention: heavy shuffling among the fallen leaves, together with a grunting. She recognised them instantly and, reaching for the gun, darted behind a bush.

Into view, about fifteen metres from where she hid, lumbered a boar; a sow, she quickly realised. The creature's teats swung as she snuffled for nuts with her long snout. In tow were three piglets, and they were all making for the line of pines, where Rosa was kneeling to pick mushrooms. Preoccupied, neither she nor the sow was aware yet of the other.

Graziella felt the slow pumping of her heart. With her breath suspended, she crept forward, tucking herself into the bushes. The sow stopped snuffling and raised her head. Her sight was poor and she was unable to discern a human figure more than eight metres away, but her acute hearing and sense of smell compensated for this lack. Her keen nostrils picked out the child's alien scent, and she emitted a loud *gu-gu-gu* sound of suspicion, and sniffed the air.

Rosa sprang to her feet.

From a distance apart of eight metres or so, they confronted each other. Things happened quickly then; though for Graziella it was as though she were watching the events unfold in slow motion.

Normally a shy creature, the sow was fiercely protective of her young. She pawed the ground.

Graziella could see the terror in her daughter's expression, and gestured to her to stay still. She snapped closed the gun's barrel. Briefly, the animal was diverted and peered about her. Seeing nothing, she returned to the imminent threat.

Graziella took aim; however, Rosa was almost in her line of vision. She might kill her own daughter. She raised the gun higher. It shook in her hands and, as she aligned her eyes to the barrel, she wavered. But the boar charged, and there wasn't a second to think, and she pulled the trigger and fired.

For a moment all was quiet. Graziella dared not look. Then her daughter was running towards her sobbing, sobbing in her arms as Graziella comforted her.

'It's alright cara, it's alright. Mama's here.'

The sow lay on the ground, its glassy eyes still open. It had been a good, clean shot. She doubted the creature would have known a thing. Nevertheless, the sight of it keeled over on its side saddened her. She felt an affinity with it: the sow had only been intent on protecting her young.

They found the piglets bunched together, immobile, instinctively relying on their camouflage to keep them safe. Graziella gauged them to be four or five weeks old.

'*Cara*,' she whispered to Rosa, 'please run and fetch my sack. Tip out the wood. And be quick.'

Her heart rate still hadn't settled. It made her weak to think what might have happened. And meanwhile there were the three small orphans whose fate was dependent on her. They looked petrified, frozen in the same position, as she guarded them, with her arms akimbo, to prevent their escape. She could see Rosa chasing back with the sack, slowing into a walk, as she drew near. Such a sensible child, she thought.

Her lips shaped a "Thank you". Then, gesturing to her to hold open the sack, Graziella lifted up two piglets - squealing now - by the scruffs of their necks and lowered them into it. She knotted it, leaving a gap for air. The third piglet showed no inclination to move, and gently, she slipped it into Rosa's sack, on a bed of mushrooms.

CHAPTER 30

NOW

ROSA

'And we trudged home, with our unusual spoils,' Mama recollects. 'Of course I did not have a clue what I was going to do with them, but I read in the book my teacher gave me, that they thrived on a diet of acorns, beech nuts, roots and worms... I loved that book.' Her features are soft.

'We gave them names,' I remind her. 'You let me help you make a lair for them in the mule shelter, from twigs and leaves and grass. It was such fun. Then Stefano made a proper pen for them, with a mud area for them to bathe in. They loved that.'

'Poor Stefano,' murmurs Mama. 'He was your papa's best friend.'

'No, *your* papa, Mama.'

'My papa is dead.'

Today isn't one of her good days. She is not on good form and seems distracted. I think it may have something to do with yesterday: I couldn't get hold of her on the phone, and rang the sanctuary. She wasn't there. Liz said she had gone to meet a friend in Reading; but, later, when I did speak to her, and asked which friend she had met, she told me to mind my own business. A moment later, she thought better of it and gave me the name of a woman who died years ago.

'Anyway, to revert to the boar babies,' I say, hoping to set her back on track. 'They followed you everywhere. You became their surrogate mother.'

'Yes, I did,' she says. 'Until Funghi's hormones kicked in and he kept trying to escape. *Madre*, he became a thug.' She gave her tinkling laugh. 'He drove his sisters mad. There was nothing for it but to reintroduce him into the wild.'

'I remember we walked him on a lead to the forest, to get him used to it. And when, finally, you let him loose, he followed us back.'

'He was my favourite of the three,' Mama reflects. 'He was the most affectionate of them. He kept turning up at the door, but I had to be hard-hearted, and that upset me dreadfully. Gradually he appeared less and less, and though I was sad, I also felt glad. I could see he was in good health. And then it was the rutting season, and I never saw him after that. I hope he was not shot by hunters.'

'That was the start of your collection of animals,' I comment.

'Yes, I suppose it was. And look where the journey has taken me. So you mustn't be unhappy.'

'Mama, you would tell me if there was anything on your mind, wouldn't you?' I ask her.

'Naturally I would, my little Rosa,' she replies.

And makes her eyes round, in that way she does, when she is fibbing.

CHAPTER 31
THEN
MAMA LUCIA

Graziella walked with her daughter to school. It was her first day there. Graziella deliberately got there early. They walked along a narrow corridor and stopped outside a classroom.

'Is this where I will be having my lessons?' Rosa asked.

'No *cara*. This is for the older children. It was my classroom for two years.'

'When I am older, will it be mine?'

'Yes.'

'Why are we waiting here?'

'Because I want to speak to the lady who used to be my teacher about something.'

The door was ajar, and she could see the room was empty. There were just rows of ink-splodged desks, waiting as though in anticipation. The blackboard had only partially been wiped; some of the writing on it was still legible from where she stood. The last lesson of the day had been algebra. Tempted, she went into the room. Rosa followed.

'What are you doing Mama?'

'I just want to see if I can solve this.'

She had nearly worked it out, when the teacher entered.

'Graziella?'

She swung round. 'I'm sorry. I couldn't resist it,' she said.

The teacher glanced up at the board. 'Well you haven't lost your touch,' she observed, with the hint of a smile. She bent down to Rosa's level: 'And look at you. How grownup you've become Rosa.'

'Mama says you will teach me when I'm older,' Rosa said.

'And I look forward to that,' the teacher said, with reciprocal gravity.

She turned back to Graziella, her eyes quizzical. She had aged in appearance, and her face had lost its roundness. Graziella had heard that she had been widowed several months earlier.

'Have you time to talk?' she asked. 'I promise I shan't keep you long.'

'Five or ten minutes then,' the teacher agreed. 'Would that be alright?'

'Yes, *grazie*, that's fine.'

They sat down, Rosa on her mother's lap. It gave Graziella confidence to feel the warmth of her body through her skirt.

'I'm so sorry about your husband,' she began.

'Thank you, that's kind of you, Graziella.'

'And I wanted to tell you that you were right all those years ago.'

The teacher looked perplexed. 'What was I right about?'

'My aunt. She made me give up school. I was heartbroken... I became the maid to the family.'

'Oh Graziella... Oh my dear Graziella, what can I say? I had no idea. You were so convincing. Why didn't you tell me the truth?'

'I thought I would be thrown out of the house. I didn't know what to do, where I would go. Anyhow, it doesn't matter now.'

'But it *does*. I'm so very sorry.' She shook her head. 'I should have realised.'

'You couldn't possibly have guessed how evil they were... How evil *he* was,' she added, fixing the teacher with a penetrating gaze.

She watched as the teacher's complexion slowly deepened in colour. Her hand fluttered to her mouth, in comprehension. She had no need to speak.

Graziella gave a tiny nod of affirmation, then hugged her daughter to her. 'Rosa is my reward, aren't you *cara*?'

'What does "reward" mean, Mama?'

'It's like a prize. You are my prize, *cara*.'

'I shall make it up to you Graziella,' the teacher said, as they parted.

Walking to Mama Lucia's, she felt a lightness of being within her that almost hurt. Her life was falling into place, she thought. She was twenty-one, she loved and was loved by her child, and nothing could be more beautiful than that. She had a home and a collection of strange animals. She had a job, and a mother figure in Mama Lucia. She had her freedom and, importantly, she had a clear conscience.

What more could she wish for?

The day was warm, but humid and overcast; the upper peaks of *La Montagna della Madonna were* submerged in cloud. The café was in shadow, and none of the lights were switched on. Even more unusual was the fact that Lucia herself was nowhere to be seen. A feeling of foreboding wound round her.

'Mama Lucia!' she called.

There was no response. She tried again. 'Mama Lucia!'

Then, from overhead, she heard an almost imperceptible groan, and she tore up the narrow stairs, two at a time.

She had never been up here before; there were two bedrooms, and the doors to both were closed.

'Mama Lucia!' she called a third time, unable to keep the tremor from her voice.

A tiny crackling cough in response came from behind the door on the left, and she turned the doorknob.

Lucia was sprawled on her back, half across the bed and half on the wood floor. Vomit and blood surrounded her, and the room stank. It was all Graziella could do not to retch.

'*Madre*, what's happened to you?' she cried. 'No, don't try to answer. I'm going to fetch the doctor. *Madre... * Oh *Madre.*'

She ran there as fast as she could, barging past anyone in her way, nipping between cars, mules and scooters, praying under her breath all the while, to any deity who just might exist. It was worth a try.

'Dottore Rugolo!' she shouted outside his house that was also his surgery. She lifted the knocker and hammered on the door with it, then noticed the bell, and pressed that too. She heard purposeful feet, and the doctor himself flung open the door, his displeasure apparent.

'What the ...' he began.

There was no time for niceties: 'It's Mama Lucia. I think she's ... *Per favore*, you must come,' she pleaded, breathless from running.

'One minute,' he said, no longer looking angry, and disappeared indoors. She heard him talking in a hurried tone to someone, explaining an emergency had arisen; then he reappeared, holding his doctor's bag and a car key. His car was just outside.

'Hop in,' he said.

She sat in the front with him, and clung on to her seat as he sped round bends, through the newly erected traffic lights, which had just turned red, and skidded to a halt in the alley opposite the café.

He struggled through the fly curtain, his wispy hair becoming caught, and she disentangled him.

'Grazie. Stupid thing,' he muttered. 'Where is she?'

'Upstairs, in her room. She's been sick and ...'

'Stay down here please.'

He was overweight, and he wheezed as he climbed the stairs.

She couldn't sit down - she was too agitated. The café was empty, except for the resident parrot. It was only just gone nine, and also this was a quiet time of year. Graziella did not know what to do with herself. She went into the kitchen and filled the coffee machine. Switched on the radio. Wondered how Rosa was doing, and pictured her at a desk, among a row of other children.

He came downstairs, wearing a sombre expression.

'As you probably realised, she is dying,' he said.

Mutely, she nodded.

'I could feel a tumour the size of a grapefruit on her lungs. The cancer will have spread to her other organs.'

'I nagged her to stop smoking,' she burst out.

He smiled ruefully: 'That, Graziella, is more easily spoken than put into practice,' he said. And she realised he was referring to himself. 'Anyway,' he added. 'For her it would have been far too late. She has only a matter of hours left. I've given her morphine, but I'm afraid there is nothing else that can be done. She is virtually unconscious now.'

'Can I sit with her?'

'Of course.'

'And can I clean her face?'

'As long as you are gentle.'

'I shall be.'

'You are a kind girl. Life has not been easy for you. I see the *Contessa* from time to time and she speaks highly of you. I apologise if earlier I was rather brusque. I shall return in four hours.'

'I have to fetch my daughter from school by three. Today is her first day.'

He appraised her as though about to make a remark then changed his mind. 'Is there a telephone here?'

She shook her head. 'We use the kiosk near the *piazza*.'

He wrote his phone number on a piece of paper torn from his prescription pad, and gave it to her.

'Call me if you need me. Reverse the charges. I shall inform my secretary so that she will accept the call. And I shall not be late,' he said.

Graziella hung the "CLOSED" sign on the door, then fed the parrot. She was wary of him. He was attached by a length of chain to his perch, and liked nothing better than to lunge at you with his strong beak when you least expected it.

She went upstairs. Lucia lay fully on the bed now. How the doctor had managed to move her, she could not imagine. Her face had taken on a greenish colour, and she appeared to be asleep; a faint rattle accompanied her laboured breathing. She resembled a giant sea creature, Graziella thought. Her eyes travelled round the long, narrow room. It was simply furnished: a couple of landscape prints, a pottery urn, a mahogany jewellery box, the usual wooden cross, and three framed photographs. Her eyes lit on the middle one, and astonished, she picked it up. It was of herself, with Rosa in her arms. She dimly recalled Mama Lucia taking it with her Polaroid camera. Rosa had been a few weeks old. It was winter - not that you would have known it; it was so warm people were sunbathing.

She returned the photo to its place of honour, between the shot of Lucia's husband and another of them together. This endorsement of Lucia's affection for her sent a sharp pain through her.

You are the child I never had.

Don't die, she willed the recumbent figure.

The rancid odour that permeated the room was turning her stomach. There was a basin in the room and, beside it, were a sponge and bar of soap; she took these and tenderly bathed Lucia's face and neck, patting her dry with a towel as she went. She sprinkled her arms with talcum powder, dabbed cologne on her forehead, and massaged her feet and hands. Then she sat and waited.

Some time later, a different quiet descended, and Graziella knew that Mama Lucia had gone.

CHAPTER 32

THEN

PADRE ALBERTO

The undertaker had business to attend to in Palermo, and then had to wait for the ferry crossing to *Isola dell Pecore*. For three days Mama Lucia lay on her putrid bed, completely covered by a floral sheet, except for her two big toes, which stuck out. While Rosa was at school, Graziella sat all day in the darkened bedroom, guarding her like a Caryatid. When, finally, she was taken away, it took three men to lift her.

'Who's going to pay for this?' demanded the undertaker, who was sweating from exertion. 'I'm sorry about your loss, but, well, you know how it is.'

'There's money available,' she said.

He looked at her properly for the first time, and she noticed the little spark of interest flair in his pupils.

She kept her expression neutral.

'I should like the coffin to be a simple one, please,' she requested. 'Lucia hated anything fancy.'

'Leave it to me,' he said.

Everyone was talking about Mama Lucia's passing, in a tone of hushed disbelief.

It was, someone remarked, akin to losing a national monument. And the aphorism was taken up and reiterated by everybody who had known her. But whilst Lucia's popularity was not in doubt, and she had indeed had many acquaintances, her close friends were few. For all her joviality, she had been a private person, and although individuals might claim to have been her intimate friend, they wouldn't have found a single significant snippet to relay about her character. She laughed a lot; she was big hearted; she was outspoken; she was generous. But who knew the inner person? Who knew her inner thoughts and secret longings? Only Graziella. But it was the last minutes of Lucia's life that were, for Graziella, the most revelatory; when she had stumbled upon the photograph of herself with Rosa. The only two people in her life who meant anything to her.

The task fell upon her to organise the funeral. Nobody else offered, and she was both unsurprised, and glad. However, she realised she could do nothing, without speaking to Padre Alberto.

With a heavy sense of inevitability, she walked down the hill and along the mosaic path, which led to the church. It was midmorning on a Thursday, and she gauged that it would be a quiet time for him. She had not been inside the church for five years, and as she pushed open the doors, she could feel the apprehension rising in her.

Looking about her, it seemed to her that no time at all had elapsed since that day she had quarrelled with her teacher and come here, hoping to find solace. The same cloying sense of claustrophobia wrapped round her now, as it had then, causing her airways to become restricted.

Don't let yourself be intimidated, her mother whispered.

She rang the bell. To the side of the confessional box was an-other small door, and she could hear heavy feet clomping along the tiled corridor. In readiness, she arranged her features into a demure expression. The door opened.

When he saw who it was, his lips sucked in, in surprise, and his roving eye seemed to spin.

'*Buongiorno*, Graziella,' he said at length, in his sing-song voice, which always sounded as though he were praying, even when he was not. 'How nice to see you. Have you come to confess?'

She shook her head. 'I am organising Mama Lucia's funeral. I don't know how to go about it.'

He frowned. 'Why are you doing it?'

'She had no living relative. I was closest to her. She became like a mother to me.'

'She was a churchgoer. She regularly confessed.'

'I know. I respect that.'

'Graziella, I would like you to confess.'

'But I no longer believe. It would be hypocritical.'

Unused to being challenged, he studied her as though present-ed with a conundrum.

'It would cleanse you. You need God's forgiveness, for the sake of the child you have brought into the world.'

She could scarcely contain her anger; it bubbled up in her. He was implying she was tainted. Well then, let him learn the truth for once and for all. It would travel no further than the confessional box. Let him be judged himself for his judgement of her.

'Very well then, but can we talk about the funeral arrange-ments first, then I shall confess.'

'If that is how you would prefer to do it.'

'Yes.'

She followed him into his office, a small, dark room that smelt of mould. He was a meticulous man and every item in the room had a particular place.

'The first thing to establish is the date and time,' he told her. And he opened his desk diary and flicked through it, licking his finger before turning each fresh page.

She sat down on the spare chair, without being invited.

He snapped shut the diary. 'I would suggest a fortnight today. Two o'clock. How does that sound?'

'*Bene*...I shall do food for the wake. And my friend, Raffaella Falcone, will do a reading.'

He looked surprised at the mention of the nun's name. 'She is a friend of yours?'

'My best friend.'

He said nothing, but something about his manner seemed to change.

'You will need to put a notice in the *Gazzetta*. You should do that soon.'

'But what do I write?'

He smiled at her then. A kind smile. 'Something short - no more than a few words, but from the heart. Would you like me to help you?'

She shook her head. 'Thank you, but I should like to write it myself - if you are not offended.'

'Not in the least. But remember to give details of the funeral, and the wake. Have you done anything about the coffin?'

'Yes. It's something simple. Mama Lucia doesn't - didn't like fuss.'

He looked approving. 'That's true.'

'I don't know what to do about music for the end of the funeral. She liked Mario Lanza.'

'I will see what I can do. I am an admirer of him myself. I daresay I could borrow a gramophone,' the Padre said. He pressed his fingers to his recalcitrant eye and squinted at her with the other. 'And now it is time for confession, Graziella.'

She slid into the booth and knelt on the dusty cushion. On the other side of the mesh grill she heard him settling himself.

'Forgive me Padre, for I have sinned,' she intoned, in a flat voice. None the less, she crossed herself from past habit. The church was steeped in silence. The only sound was the priest's catarrhal sniffing, and she stifled a nervous giggle.

'What is it that you wish to confess?' he asked, and she detected a salacious note in his muffled whisper, which terminated on an elongated hiss. No doubt he was expecting her to repent for her lack of attendance at Mass; well, he would be disappointed, she thought. Searching her mind for a minor misdemeanour, she recalled an incident which had taken place in the town a few days ago.

'I have been disrespectful to another,' she said.

'In what way?' he queried.

'I told the postmistress that her face was as ugly as a lump of her own shit,' Graziella replied. In the long pause which followed, the urge to laugh again built up in her, until she could no longer repress it. It burst from her in uncontrolled gales, and tears ran down her cheeks.

'That was a vile thing to say,' Padre Alberto rebuked her, when her laughter had stopped. 'You have offended not only the individual concerned, with your vulgarity and loose tongue, but Our Lord himself. You will atone for your sin, so that he may forgive you. That you dared laugh in His presence is sinful itself. Do you repent for your behaviour?'

'No.'

She heard his gasp.

'Why will you not repent?'

'Because she and others have gossiped and spread vicious lies about me. They are the ones who should be doing penance.'

'People are affronted by your lack of morals.' The priest's voice had shot up several decibels. 'You have demonstrated no remorse for bearing a child out of wedlock.'

Very well, she thought. Now let him learn the truth.

'And did the man who raped me at knifepoint, who took my virginity and stole my life, that man who was my *zia's* husband, mayor at the time - did he demonstrate remorse?' she challenged. Trembling with fury, she rose from the stool. 'And where was God when my parents died' - she was shouting now - 'where was He when I was maltreated by the family who should have been looking after me? Where was He when a boy I knew was killed?'

She pushed her way out of the booth, as Padre Alberto emerged from behind the grill. He looked more than a little perturbed, and his sparse hair stood on end, as though he had been ruffling it.

'Graziella - my child ...' he began.

She fixed her gaze on his good eye: 'I am nobody's child, Padre,' she said quietly. 'We have discussed all that I came to discuss. I shall see you at the funeral. Thank you for your advice.'

She made for the inner door, and he seemed to recover himself, and pushed it wide.

'I am deeply sorrowed by your disclosure,' he said, and his heavy tone endorsed the truth of his statement.

She gave a sharp little nod.

'May the lord have mercy on you, and forgive those who have done you ill. Go in peace, Graziella,' he said.

Graziella deafened her ears to his words.

CHAPTER 33

THEN
A SURPRISE

The closed sign remained pinned above the door of Mama Lucia's, and she had written a separate one in English and German, to avoid any confusion; but though the bar might be closed for business, she went there each day, as she had done for the past two years. She dusted surfaces, cleaned out cupboards, sluiced the floor, polished the brass rail, bleached cloths, washed crockery, disinfected the toilet and basin, hung fresh flypaper strips from the ceiling and, with a feather duster, swept the dead flies from the light fittings. A couple of days before the funeral, she began cooking for the wake. From the kitchen emanated aromas of baking that were so mouth-watering, passers-by stopped to savour them. She made *cassata* sponge cakes that oozed rum and candied fruit; lemon and thyme cake; *cannoli*, filled with ricotta and dark chocolate; spiced almond *biscotti*, which warmed the tip of the tongue; miniature pizzas, and her sausages.

She stored the food in the capacious fridge; she had no idea how many would turn up at the funeral, and only stopped baking when it was full. Baking served as a balm for her bereavement and, pottering about Lucia's kitchen, Graziella imagined her looking down on her. She knew Lucia would approve.

Late in the afternoon the day before the funeral, Graziella was drawing water from the well when Rosa announced: 'Mama, there's a man walking along the path to the *casetta*.'

Graziella looked up. A slightly built figure was approaching, and she could see that he was smiling a little nervously. Only when he stood right in front of her did she realise it was her cousin. It was six years since she had seen him, and he now sported a thick, club-cut beard, which radically altered his appearance.

'Giorgio!' she exclaimed. She put down the bucket she had been holding and threw her arms round him. 'I couldn't think who it was. You look so different.'

Awkwardly, he kissed her on both cheeks. 'W-well, you - you look no different, Graziella. Except m-m-maybe m-more beautiful,' he complimented her.

'I can't believe that,' she said.

'It's true.'

He bent down to Rosa, who had been staring at him. 'And you must be Rosa.'

'How do you know my name?' she asked.

'Ah, now that would b-be t-telling,' he replied.

'Giorgio is my cousin,' Graziella told her.

'Are you my cousin too?' Rosa addressed him.

'Yes, b-but I am your m-mama's first cousin, and your s-second cousin,' he said. 'At least, I think that's correct.'

'Why do you talk in that funny way?'

Graziella put her fingers to her forehead. 'Rosa, that's rude. You should apologise to Giorgio.'

He gestured dismissively. 'It's f-fine. It happens all the t-time... I have what is called a stammer. I was born with it,' he told Rosa.

'It's funny,' she said again.

'I know… *Cristo!* Am I going m-mad, or are those wild b-boar over there?' He pointed to the pen.

'Yes. Their names are Lola and Lina, and they are my pets. They had a brother called Funghi, but Mama had to take him back to the forest as he was being naughty.' Graziella could tell he was trying not to laugh. His beard suited him, she thought. It made him look distinguished, older than his years, and she guessed that, as a newly qualified young lawyer, he had wanted to cultivate that image.

They went indoors. Giorgio wandered around curiously. He looked out of place in the humble surroundings, dressed so formally, and carrying an attaché case.

'That s-stick - isn't that like the one I thought my father b-burned?' he asked in surprise, jerking his head to where it hung.

'Yes,' she replied; and told him the circumstances in which it had been found. 'Actually, I wondered if you might have had something to do with it. I thought maybe you had rescued it somehow, then put it somewhere and forgotten about it.'

Just for a second he was tempted to fib. 'No,' he said. 'I wish I could say that I did. But I didn't.'

'Then there is only one possible answer to the mystery,' she said softly, in a musing tone, and her heart gave a tiny leap.

'It's a magic stick,' Rosa chimed in. 'It flies.'

'W-well that's… interesting,' Giorgio said, solemn faced.

Graziella lit the oil lamps.

'I don't know how you manage without electricity, Graziella,' he remarked.

'It isn't a problem. I'm used to it… Giorgio - please will you sit down. You're making me on edge.'

'Oh, *p-perdono.*' He sat where her father used to sit.

'Would you like a lemon tea?'

'I don't want to put you to trouble.'

'Don't be silly.'

He watched her put the kettle on the stove and prepare the tea. Her high ponytail swung as she moved about the kitchen. His feelings for her were unaltered. Here he was, still falling to bits in her company, just as he had done when he was a boy. And his great love for her made his sense of guilt all the worse. He ached with its burden.

The afternoon, more than six years ago, came back to him.

He had wanted to say goodbye to Graziella before leaving the island and going away to college, and had reached the path to the *casetta*, when he had heard faint cries. He had run towards the sounds, which were coming from the mule shelter, then stopped. The cries had ceased, but a voice he knew all too well was shouting and cursing. Giorgio did not dare enter. Instead, he peered through a gap in the slatted wood. Appalled, frozen to the spot like a mesmerised rabbit, he witnessed everything. Only when it was over, did his limbs respond, and then his cowardly legs carried him back down the hillside at lightning speed.

Hardly a day went by when his mind didn't flit back to that afternoon and the part he played in shaping his cousin's life. Sometimes, in his mind he saw himself rescuing her; barging into the shelter, like a hero from a novel, stabbing his father with the knife he would have wrested from him. In reality, he could not be certain he wouldn't react in the same manner again. And he would forever despise himself for it.

She poured the tea into china cups. They were part of a set, which had belonged to her grandmother, and most of the pieces had chipped over the years. Rosa played quietly while they talked.

'It is so wonderful to see you, Giorgio. But why have you left it so long?' Graziella reproved him.

'You know h-how it was at home,' he answered. 'I just wanted to g-get away and never come back.'

'But you didn't come and say goodbye, before you went off to university.'

His fair skin flushed. 'I'm s-sorry... I intended to but...' He shrugged. Her gentle reproach increased his discomfort. His own deception gnawed at him.

'It's alright, I know goodbyes are hard,' she said, wanting to console him. She remembered how sensitive he had been as a boy.

'Actually I'm here f-for the f-funeral of Lucia P-Penta,' he told her. 'She was a client at the firm where I work, in Cefalù.'

'I didn't know that... Are you staying with your parents?'

'You *are* joking. No, I'm s-staying with the p-parents of my f-friend Paulo - you remember him? You d-disliked him. You s-said he was vain.'

'I was probably a bit harsh on him,' she said. 'Looking back on it, he was just immature.'

'He s-still is. But he is a loyal f-friend to me.'

'That's what counts.'

'Yes... Graziella, the main reason I am visiting *Isola delle Pecore* is to actually see you.'

'Me? But why now?'

'You can't guess?'

She shook her head.

Giorgio picked up his attaché case from beside him on the floor. It was fat with its contents and, intrigued, she waited while he proceeded to shuffle through papers and documents.

'Oh, there it is, right at the bottom,' he muttered to himself. And she smiled, recalling how disorganised and untidy he had been as a boy.

He drew out a thick document that was bound with dark green ribbon, and got to his feet.

'Graziella Lupo,' he said, with a small grin, 'it is my p-pleasure to inform you that you are n-now the owner of the café-bar, known as " Mama Lucia's". Congratulations.'

She reeled back in her chair. 'What are you talking about, Giorgio?'

He sat down again. 'Lucia l-left it to you in her w-will. She also left you a substantial s-sum of money. Here - read it for yourself.' He passed her the document.

She undid the knot but, then, overwhelmed, was incapable of reading it in detail; she could only pick out the odd word or phrase: *The last will and testament... Being of sound mind... Wish to leave my business, property and contents...*

Her own name was on the document, repeated several times; and at the foot of each page was Mama Lucia's signature, along with that of Dottore Rugolo, as witness. Carefully she retied the knot, and made to hand it back to him.

'No, that is your copy', he said. 'As is this,' he added, passing her another official document, which he had just fished from his case.

'What is it?'

'The p-property d-deeds.... You should entrust b-both to the safety of the b-b-bank,' he advised her.

'*Madre*,' she whispered hoarsely. '*Madre*.'

Giorgio grasped her hand. That he had been the messenger of good tidings was a kind of reparation for the dreadful wrong he had done her.

CHAPTER 34

NOW

ROSA

'Nearly three hundred and fifty people attended the funeral. The numbers were astonishing,' Mama recalls.

'I can dimly remember it, I think,' I tell her. 'I remember hordes of people, all in black, and feeling frightened.'

'That must have been it. I had to take you with me. There was nobody I could have left you with - the only person I trusted was the schoolteacher, and she was going to the funeral. But the numbers of attendees shouldn't have surprised me. Lucia had been a towering personality in the community for so many years, and I don't just mean in size. Folk travelled from the north of the island and from the hills to pay their respects. They crammed into rusty cars, or came by mule and cart, or braved the bus, whose driver was rarely sober. The babies whom Lucia had delivered over the years, who were now adults with *their* children - they came. And several people from neighbouring islands made the crossing by private boat, or took the ferry ahead of time. Locals turned up on foot, or motorbike, or cycled. The alleys were jammed with every kind of vehicle. You and I sat quietly, on the pew, holding each other's hand. It was such a comfort to have my little Rosa with me. And whilst we waited I listened to all these people boasting about their close friendship with Lucia; but I knew otherwise. And when I overheard them expressing their surprise at the coffin's simplicity, and the single red carnation - well that only proved to me how little they had known her. Then, Raffaella arrived - I scarcely recognised her in her wimple; it looked so rigid and cruel - and we spoke together. She understood how stressful the day was for me, and remained with us for a bit, before joining her colleagues. Minutes after that, Giorgio arrived, with his friend Paulo, then Stefano came, and we all sat together.'

'Your memory for the past is fantastic, Mama.'

She pulls a wry face. 'In between blips,' she comments. And sighs heavily.

I notice her hands are trembling on her lap, causing the small table in front of her to vibrate. A sure sign she is becoming tired. And she is starting to loll in her chair. I make to turn off the machine, but she prevents me, with a gesture.

'After the service, the mourners came back to the café for the wake. I had laid out the food for people to help themselves, and they tucked into the food like famished vipers.'

'Vipers?'

She throws out an impatient arm: 'You know - those horrible birds which eat dead creatures.'

I hide my smile. 'Oh, *vultures.*'

'Yes, that's what I said. And I don't know who they all thought made the food - perhaps they thought the nuns from the convent prepared it - but Padre Alberto made no reference to my efforts. It didn't matter. The important thing was that Mama Lucia was given a good send off. She was escorted out to Mario Lanza. I saw my aunt among the throng, and Giorgio barely acknowledged her, except for a cursory nod. To my relief, her *bastardo* husband was not there... *Bastardo!*'

And my mother spits. I have never seen her behave like it.

'Why were you frightened of him Mama?' I ask, after a pause.

'Frightened of whom?'

'Your *zia's* husband.'

'My *zia* is dead. She choked on a fish bone. Anyway, shouldn't we be going?'

'Going? Where are we going?'

'To the party.'

The switch in her is always seamless; it catches me by surprise when it occurs. One moment you are having a normal conversation, the next you are plunged into a kind of Alice in Wonderland world. For the moment I have lost her. But it has been a long session.

'We've got time for a coffee first,' I tell her.

The dogs follow me into the kitchen, hopeful of food. I fill the kettle and switch it on. I notice the small pile of Christmas cards on the worktop, and glance through them: "*May this be a better year for you…*" "*Wishing you good health for the coming year,*" and so forth. Three of the five cards featured fluffed-out robins. One, unopened, card is addressed to my stepfather as well as Mama, and I open it: "*We haven't seen you both for such a long time. This year we must get together. Have a great festive season.*"

Irritated, I scrunch it up and consign it to the bin. Why do distant acquaintances whom you haven't met in years, have a tendency blithely to assume life has remained static in the interim?

A card, half out of its envelope, catches my eye. The envelope bears an Italian postmark, and the card itself depicts a Madonna by Botticelli. I take it from its envelope. The message, penned in a shaky hand, is in Italian:

"*To my dearest friend.*

I wonder how you are? I have been thinking a great deal about our childhood recently, which naturally, always leads me to tender recollections of you. How long ago it seems, since we were children together, yet it is nothing in reality, is it? I remember how you would jump to my defence when I was picked on in class by the other pupils. You were so strong and courageous, dear Graziella. You never gave up. And of course God bestowed great beauty on you, which we both know was not always to your advantage.

As I said, I think of you often, but particularly now, at this time of year, and I am so delighted that your recent meeting was a success. That has made me very happy.

My health has deteriorated considerably since last we wrote, and I do not think I have long left to me, Graziella. God is calling me, and I welcome what He has in store.

I wish you peace and fulfilment, my dearest friend.

Raffaella."

Normally, a letter like this would move me to tears, however, all I can think of is that strange reference to a meeting.

"I am delighted that your recent meeting was a success".

The sentence spins round my head, tantalising. What does it mean? But it is pointless asking Mama about it. She wouldn't give me a straight answer and, in addition, she would be angry that I had read her private correspondence, and would accuse me of prying. But this much I do know: it is clearly linked to that ambiguous remark she made a few weeks ago.

A few other cards are dotted around the kitchen. They are her only concession to Christmas. She refuses to have a tree, or to let me put up any decorations for her.

'I'm not going to do anything this year,' she told me a few days ago. 'Anyway, it's a Pagan farce. I just want to be on my own and read a book.'

But reading is increasingly difficult for her nowadays. She resisted the idea of talking books and gave a dramatic shudder when I suggested it.

'They smack of loneliness and inadequacy.' she said.

'I know it isn't the same,' I agreed, 'but it's better than nothing. It's a compromise.'

My mother doesn't believe in compromise.

'It's worse than nothing.'

'Oh really, you are so stubborn,' I told her.

'So are you.'

Et cetera.

But after a lot of persuasion, she has consented to join us for lunch on Christmas day.

The electric kettle comes to the boil. I pour coffee into two mugs, search for some biscuits which are not stale, and carry everything into her living room, on a tray.

She is not there. Probably she is in the loo. 'Mama,' I call.

No reply. I call out again. Still there is no answer. I can feel my alarm circling round my bloodstream. I poke my head into each room. Then I become conscious of a draught filtering through the house from somewhere, and notice the front door is slightly open. She must have slipped out while I was in the kitchen. I peer down the lane, as far as I can, looking left and right, desperate to see her familiar figure but, apart for a girl pushing a pram, a big man walking a tiny dog, and an elderly woman cycling painfully up the steep rise of the hill, the lane is empty. I rush out, and ask each of them if they have seen a small woman in her late sixties, wearing black slacks and a red polo neck jumper. They have not. I accost a pair of runners, who look irritated, because it means them pulling down their headphones. I ask them the same question, and receive the same reply.

'Please,' I say piteously, 'she has Alzheimer's. She may be using an unusual walking stick. Will you keep an eye open? The house is number eleven.'

I motion in its direction. They mellow then, and assure me they will.

I tell myself that in the short time she has been gone, she could not have ventured far. But God knows what her mental state was when she walked out. Who knows to where her brain might have transported her? The wailing of ambulance sirens in the distance does nothing to appease me, and my writer's imagination conjures all nature of grizzly possibilities before me.

I return indoors to fetch my car keys, intending to drive around in the hope of spotting her, but just as I am about to leave, the doorbell rings. I can hear two sets of footsteps, and my immediate thought is that it is the police bearing bad news. I go to the door with a sense of dread.

On the wide step, stand my mother and a friendly-faced woman I don't know. She introduces herself as a new neighbour, and I hustle them both indoors into the warm. Mama doesn't resist as I assist her into a chair.

'I was practising the violin,' the woman explains, 'when I heard somebody knocking. Anyway, I went to see who it was, and this stranger walked in. I could see she was confused. But it's probably best that you hear it from your mother.'

Mama's expression manages to combine shame and dignity. Her hair has partially come loose from its jumbo clip, and has slithered down her back. She is shivering, despite my stepfather's thick jumper that she's wearing. It is far too big for her, and the sleeves overlap her thin wrists. I can tell that she is shocked by her experience.

'I apologise for the trouble I've caused,' she says in a subdued tone.

'You haven't troubled me, and it has been a pleasure meeting you. I enjoyed having an audience.' The kind neighbour assures her, and with a cheery little hand wave, she leaves us.

'I was going crazy, thank God you're safe,' I tell Mama, stroking her fingers.

'I'm sorry,' she says stiffly.

201

'It's fine. You're safe, and that's all that matters.'

The story unfolds: from what I can gather, Mama had wandered down the lane possibly with the intention of going to the mythical party she had spoken about - but then had been diverted by the strains of a violin emanating from a house. She followed them and upon entering the house, it seems that she sat down, apparently believing herself to be at a concert.

'Well, aren't you going to play?' Mama had demanded, after a minute.

So the neighbour had resumed her playing. It was not long, however, before Mama came to her senses, and found herself in a strange house, being entertained by a virtuoso violinist.

'You have to see the funny side, Mama.'

It was a stupid, insensitive, remark to make.

'No Rosa, I do not,' she says. 'And now, if you don't mind, I should like to go to bed. I don't feel too good.'

She looks ashen. Remiss, I help her from the chair. Leaning on her stick, without another word to me, she walks unsteadily through the house to her room.

After five or ten minutes, I go in to see her. She is already in bed, a dog either side of her. She is lying on her tummy, her face buried in the pillow. Only her tangled hair is visible to me. I touch the top of her head.

'Mama?'

She doesn't respond, but a muffled sound comes from the pillow. Then, slowly, she rotates her body and sits up. Her beautiful face is ravaged. My Mama, who has not cried in fifty years, is weeping. Sobbing brokenheartedly, as though she will never be able to stop.

All I can do is hold her; hold her tight, and weep with her.

Oh Mama. Oh Mama... It's alright. I love you. It's alright.

CHAPTER 35

THEN
THE NEW OWNER

It was several weeks before the café reopened under its new ownership. Having stayed on the island for as short a period as possible, Giorgio had returned to Cefalù, with the promise to Graziella he would visit again soon. They both knew it was unlikely. Meanwhile, she was kept busy. There was much to think about and do. There were meetings with the bank manager - a kindly, avuncular man - to attend; accounts to be transferred or set up; documents to go through and sign. In the evenings, when Rosa was asleep, she waded through various ledgers. Lucia had colour-coded them, and her handwriting, in blue ink, was big and round, making it easy to read the columns of figures and records; nonetheless, it was time consuming, and rather like learning a new language.

On a practical level, the café itself was in need of some attention.

The stinking toilet, that was little more than a hole in the floor, over which you had to straddle your feet, and the men invariably missed their aim, was replaced by a modern system. It was a necessary extravagance, which she decided on with reluctance. She also thought it important to have a telephone installed. For one thing, it would make ordering from suppliers simpler; the other reason was safety. Were there to be any kind of mishap or accident in the café, she would be able just to pick up the phone and dial the appropriate number. There were minor repairs needed to some of the furniture, which Stefano said he would do, for the price of a beer. He had then pointed out that the blank white wall to the left side of the building was rather uninspiring.

'What do you suggest?' She asked, as they both stared at it together.

'A mural,' he said. 'Leave it to me. I will surprise you. And if you dislike it I shall paint it over in white again for you.'

'You are good to me, Stefano.'

'Somebody has to be, Graziella.'

He worked on a small area at a time, covering the rest of it with tarpaulin to protect it. Once he caught her in the act of lifting a corner that was flapping in the breeze, in order to sneak a preview.

'*Cativa!*' he admonished, startling her. He adjusted the tarpaulin and found a heavy rock to hold it down.

'You are mean, I only wanted a peep,' she grumbled.

He laughed. 'It would spoil the surprise. You must just be patient. Graziella.' He wagged the stump of his left index finger. A fish had bitten off a chunk of it several years earlier.

Nowadays he was looking more and more like an artist, with his loose clothing and navy berretta, and he deliberately cultivated the image. In fact, increasingly, he was finding himself in demand. Recently the pop star had commissioned him to paint an erotic mural for his bedroom, of Neptune ravishing a maiden.

'What a horrible man he sounds,' she had commented, in a disapproving tone. 'You shouldn't have agreed to do it.'

He stood firm. 'The money was too good to quibble, Graziella. And besides, it could lead to more business. I'd be a fool to turn it down.'

'Well, just don't talk to me about it,' she said.

He grinned. 'You sound like a wife Graziella.'

He had reddened then, as had she, and neither knew what to say.

Almost a month after the funeral, Stefano unveiled the mural. With a theatrical flourish, he hauled off the tarpaulin. Graziella gave a squeal of laughter, and the inquisitive bystanders clapped, as they were confronted by a life-sized Marilyn Monroe sucking on a long strand of spaghetti.

Today was her first day as the new owner, and as she unlocked the door to her new premises, Graziella felt much as she had done the day after the big storm, when she had gone to the *casetta*, and it dawned on her that it belonged to her. Now, she experienced the same sense of unreality; as though she were partaking in a masquerade. Any moment now, Mama Lucia would bustle in and greet her in a halo of cigarette smoke, then her arms, like red hams, would engulf her in an embrace.

She took down the old sign from above the café door, and hung up the new one. OPEN FOR BUSINESS, UNDER NEW OWNERSHIP, it now read.

She had just deposited Rosa with the teacher, who was glad to be of help, but now Graziella was wishing that she'd kept her back from school for company. Despite coming in each day to check on the place, somehow today felt completely different. The full magnitude of what she had taken on hit her. She felt daunted; mentally ill-equipped to cope with the responsibilities and challenges she knew lay ahead. Yet again, her life was about to be upturned.

It was early. The streaked October sky threatened rain, and held no warmth, but, without thinking, she hooked a pole to the awning and lowered it down, as Lucia used to do each morning. The room, already bathed in gloom, became gloomier still, so she pushed up the awning again and turned the lights on, to make it more cheerful. The tables and chairs sprung out at her, and for a few seconds she had the illusion they were occupied. She walked through to the kitchen almost stealthily, and pushed open the swing doors. Everything in here was as she herself had left it, after her cooking spree for the funeral, and some of her tension dissipated. She turned on the radio to her favourite station; it was playing *She Loves Me*, by the Beatles, which further cheered her.

'*Yeah, yeah, yeah,*' she joined in.

She liked George best. She thought that he looked sensitive. The music made her feel less lonely. Next she ground coffee beans and filled the coffee machine. Soon the piquant smell of it brewing wafted round the room: warm and homely. Feeling brighter now, she set about preparing for the day, as if Lucia had been there.

Then she waited for the customers.

By midday not a single person had come in. Two or three late tourists, drawn by the Marilyn Monroe mural, poked their heads round, but seeing the café was empty, beat a swift retreat. With each passing minute her despondency grew and, too, her bitterness: that people should still hold a grudge against her.

By two o'clock, when only a lanky mongrel, with a scar down the side of its face had wandered in, there seemed little point in remaining open. It would only dishearten her further. The cool weather and sporadic drizzle did not help, she told herself. And trade always slackened during the autumn months; Lucia had used to comment on it. Perhaps this evening would fare better. Now, anyway, it was nearly time to fetch her daughter from school.

She threw some scraps of pizza and sausage to the mongrel who was still hanging about, but he looked at her with sad yellow eyes and seemed disinclined to eat them, though, clearly, he was hungry. She retrieved the scraps and offered them to him with her fingers. He sidled up closer to her, stretched out his thin neck towards her, then stopped, and looked at her again - as though, she thought, he feared he would get into trouble and be beaten.

'*Dai,*' she encouraged him. '*Dai.*'

Gingerly, he took a morsel from between her fingers, and another… and another, glancing at her every time to confirm he was not going to be punished. When he had eaten his fill, and drunk almost a bowlful of water, he lay down with a human-like sigh of contentment - as though he understood that he had found a new owner - and slept. She fed a few anchovies to the tame gull, which pottered around about with a damaged wing and, leaving the dog sound asleep inside, locked up, she went to fetch her daughter from school.

The evening, too, was hardly less of a disappointment. Stefano, ever loyal, rolled in, along with a couple of his fishermen friends, but apart from them, there was nobody.

The problem was the rival café-bar, Stefano told her - eyeing the dog warily as he spoke. With the closure of Mama Lucia's for a month, the customers had been obliged to seek pastures new. The waitress there was not as beautiful, or as classy as Graziella - that would be impossible, he said - but she was comely enough, and definitely more available, as far as the men were concerned.

'So am I expected to simper and flirt, and to prostitute myself?' she attacked him.

'*Calma, piccolina.* You know I don't mean that. No, leave this to me. It is just a matter of time. But I assure you, soon Mama Lucia's will again reign supreme.'

'I'm sorry,' she said, chastened. 'It's just…' She gave one of her shrugs.

He smiled, showing a broken tooth, following a fight with a shopkeeper who had tried to diddle him. He was a handsome man, and it gave him a slightly raffish appearance.

'It's time to give you and Rosa a lift back to the *casetta*,' he said.

'And Elvis.' she said.

'Elvis?'

She pointed to the dog, whose name she had only that second decided upon.

He looked at it with revulsion 'You're joking.'

Her expression told him she was not.

The child was asleep on Lucia's bed. He carried her downstairs, still half asleep, and outside to the beaten up four-wheel drive truck he had recently bought and laid her on a cushion at the back. Elvis clambered in next to her, watching over her like a guardian. Graziella sat in the front, beside Stefano. He smelt of Grappa, sweat and cigarettes. It reminded her of her father, and made her feel safe. She laid her head against him as he drove, and, not speaking, he stroked her hair with his right hand.

Early the next morning, before taking Rosa to school, Graziella plaited her daughter's hair - long and black, like her own - then went about her usual tasks. She filled the butt with water from the well, beat the rugs, hung the washing on the line, picked a few vegetables, and fed the chickens, the dog, and the two boars. There was no need to feed the cat; he thrived on his own limitless supply of rodents, and grew fatter by the day. She had just returned indoors, when a hand caressed her cheek. The sweet scent of her mother's perfume - like camellias - permeated the kitchen. It had been many months, maybe as long as a year, since she had felt her mother's presence, and this morning she thought she could discern the cloudy outline of a figure in the dark, far corner of the room.

'Mama!'

Hello Graziella, carina.

'I've been waiting for you every day, but you didn't come Mama,' Graziella said. 'I've missed you. I thought I must have angered you.'

No, far from it, cara. I'm proud of you.

'Then why?'

You've become a wise young woman. You don't need me so much now. You have your little Rosa.

'I shall always need you.'

Her mother made no comment. In a gentle tone she said: *Take the Lupo stick with you to the bar for the next few days, to bring you luck, cara,* she said.

'I'm afraid that if I take it with me, something might happen to it. It could get lost or broken, or even stolen. I could take the two-tailed lizard with me instead. That has brought me luck before.'

Do as I say, cara. You won't lose it.

'Are you with Papa, Mama? Why does he never come to me?'

'What is it like wherever you are, Mama? Are you with Papa?'

Remain true to yourself cara, I shall always love you.

There was a small sound, like the rubbing together of crepe paper, or saplings shimmering in a breeze, and her mother was gone. For a moment the perfume of camellias became overpowering, then dispersed into the air.

Graziella understood that it was the last time she would hear from her mother.

Rosa came into the kitchen, followed by the dog.

'I heard you talking to somebody, Mama, but there's nobody here. Was it your Mama?' she asked.

'Yes *cara.* How did you know?'

'Because in my prayers I asked her to come to you. I told her you were sad.'

Graziella swooped her up into her arms to hug her.

'My precious little Rosa. How can I be sad, when I have you?'

They descended the steps to the *piazza.* The market traders were setting up their stalls, and early risers were wandering round, to inspect the produce, even though some of the items were still in their boxes, surrounded by newspaper. Graziella was crossing the *piazza* with Rosa, when whom should she run into, but the *Contessa.* She was casually dressed in masculine-cut slacks and a jumper that would certainly have been cashmere. On her head she wore a man's frayed and dented Panama hat. Despite her being well respected, rumours about her abounded: that she was a man in disguise; or that she had been born male and had undergone surgery to change gender. Others speculated that she was lesbian and her late husband had been homosexual, and that their marriage had been one of convenience.

None of this surmising made an impression on Graziella; she liked and admired the straight-talking *Contessa*, who had only been kind to her.

'Why how very nice to see you, my dear,' the *Contessa* addressed her now, taking Graziella's hand. 'And Rosa too.'

'We're on our way to my school,' Rosa volunteered.

'Are you now? Well aren't you grown up? And who is this poor, battle-worn creature?' She stooped to inspect the dog. Graziella had looped a length of blue cord around its sinewy neck. The fabric was soft and would not chafe the dog's flesh.

'He just turned up at the café,' she explained. 'I couldn't bear to leave him.'

'Mama has called him Elvis,' Rosa said. 'He's my new pet.'

'And does Elvis sing?' the *Contessa* asked her, serious-faced.

The child giggled: 'Dogs can't sing.'

'Oh of course. Silly me.' She winked at Graziella. 'I have been in Rome for a month and returned only yesterday,' she told her. 'My gardener informs me that you are now the owner of Mama Lucia's. Is that true?'

'*Si, Contessa.*'

'Then I am very pleased for you. It is no more than you deserve.'

'It would help if I had some customers,' she blurted out.

'Has it been quiet then?' the *Contessa* inquired.

'Quiet!' Graziella gave a dry little laugh. 'Yesterday was the first day of reopening, and not a soul came. My only customers during the day were the dog, and the seagull with the damaged wing. It would have been deserted in the evening too, had it not been for Stefano, who brought along two of his friends. People don't like me. They think… It doesn't matter what they think. Things are as they are.'

'It is a great shame.' The *Contessa*'s eyebrows knitted together in thought. And she re-lit her cheroot, which had gone out.

'Stefano says it will get better, and to leave it to him. But I really don't see what he can do.'

'Well, perhaps you will be pleasantly surprised. Stefano is a good man, an honest man. I hear he has painted a rather spectacular mural for the café?'

'Yes, he's very talented.'

'I look forward to seeing it… I am busy today, with appointments… But tomorrow…' She scrutinized Graziella closely. 'Have a little faith, my dear.'

'It's kind of you to concern yourself, *Contessa*.'

'Not at all, not at all.'

The *Contessa* gave her usual, sharp nod, rotated on her feet and, leaning on her stick, limped off towards the fish stall, manned by a friend of Stefano's.

The day was warmer than the previous one. Perhaps the sun would encourage the customers to come, she thought, with a new surge of optimism, as she prepared the food. Her mood lightened with the return of the three old men, who ordered their usual Grappa, and set up their game, as if there had been no interlude. Nobody else arrived, but it was a start at least, wasn't it? Her Lupo stick had already brought her luck. And the evening, too, was an improvement on the night before. Stefano came with half a dozen friends this time, and the men drank too much, but were not once disrespectful towards her, and Mama Lucia's rang again with the sound of their laughter.

The next day the *Contessa* came to the café, with her mastiff dog. It was ancient by then, and had cataracts in both eyes and patchy fur that looked as though it had been attacked by moths.

The weather had turned cool again but, undeterred, the *Contessa* wore a lynx jacket and sat outside, drinking bourbon whiskey and smoking her cheroot. Her yellow Lamborghini was parked just outside the café for all to see; and the busybodies were agog with disbelief at the sight of her sitting quietly reading. She was still there an hour later, at lunchtime, and Graziella brought her a plate of *antipasti*, comprising pastrami, slivers of watermelon, *melanzane* parcels stuffed with anchovies, and cubes of sausage. She decorated the plate with basil leaves.

'But this is delicious, my dear,' the *Contessa* praised her, when she had sampled each delicacy in turn. 'Especially the sausages.'

'I make them myself. They were my mother's recipe.'

'You are an exceptional girl, Graziella. I have no doubt you will go far.' Stiffly, she got up from the table and drew out an alligator wallet. 'What do I owe you?'

'Nothing, you have been so kind.'

'Nonsense, that is not the way to conduct business. I insist.'

'But … '

The *Contessa* held up her hand: 'This is an argument you will not win, my dear,' she said, with mock severity.

She came every day for a week, with her dog, and sat in the same place, and it was not long before the old customers returned and newcomers trickled in too: if the café-bar was fit for the *Contessa*, then it was fit for the likes of them.

Then Stefano came in one day with the pop star, whose mural he had just finished, and, after that, customers flocked in.

Unable to manage on her own, Graziella paid a visit to Carlotta one morning, before the café opened. With luck, her dreadful husband would have already left for the warehouse, where he worked as a packer. Carlotta was bound to be at home, albeit asleep. She was now doing night shifts at the new pasta processing factory, which formed part of a small, newly built industrial estate, on the way to the lentil fields.

She lived in a rundown terrace in a rundown alley; the paint hung off the walls in shreds, and the door was rusted and fly-spattered. A home where love was absent, Graziella thought, and a shard of rust dropped to the ground as she knocked. Nobody came to the door, and she knocked again, more forcefully. This time she was heard, and the door was opened, slowly, but only a crack.

'Oh, it's you, Graziella.' Her voice sounded thin and weary. She opened the door wide for Graziella to enter, and a lose piece of plaster fell off.

She went in. 'Ah no - what's he done to you this time?' she exclaimed, staring at the raw, bald patches where chunks of hair were missing. Carlotta shook her head and pulled her stained dressing gown closer round her. 'I can't tell you.'

'You can.'

Carlotta assessed her, through bloodshot eyes. 'It wasn't him.'

'What do you mean?'

'It wasn't my husband.'

'But then, who did this to you? Why would someone …?'

'Because men can, and do. You know that, Graziella.'

'You were raped?'

'Yes… no - not exactly.'

'*Yes- no – not exactly* … What are you talking about?'

'You swear you won't tell anyone?'

'I swear.'

'Well, you know I've told people that I was working nights at the new factory. Well, it isn't true. In fact I didn't get the job. They chose someone else who better understood that kind of work. My husband was livid with me… We badly needed the money. So then… So then he had the idea of … No – I am too ashamed to tell you.'

'But you don't need to be ashamed. And I think I can guess anyway.'

'Can you?'

'Has he made you go with other men for money?'

Tears filled Carlotta's eyes. 'It has been so humiliating... The things they have made me do. And their stinking pricks in me... But last night the man wanted me to do something unspeakable, and I couldn't let it happen. I fought him off. I bit him where it hurts, and then I ran all the way home. Only then did I realise that my head was painful, and that he had pulled out lots of my hair. My husband was in a drunken sleep when I got back, and I slept on this chair ... ' She gesticulated towards it. 'But I dread him finding out.'

She was sobbing hard now, and Graziella drew her close to her and held her.

'Oh you poor, poor woman.'

After a moment Carlotta pulled away. She took several hic-coughing breaths, in an effort to stop weeping.

'When I first knew him he seemed such a kind man. It was what I liked best about him. He was not handsome, not tall, but he seemed so nice. You know - quiet, considerate. He told me I was pretty and made me think I was. Nobody had told me I was pretty before... But he changed soon after we were married; the abuse, the belittling of me. I thought it must be my fault. I couldn't believe a person could change like that.'

'He didn't change. He would just have been on his best behaviour,' Graziella said, with a knowing roll of the eyes. 'He was just an inadequate little man who set out to ensnare a vulnerable woman as his wife.'

'I dare say you are right,' Carlotta agreed slowly. 'It does make sense. All I know is that I simply cannot go on like it. I mean, it was bad enough before... but this. Well, honestly, I would be better off dead. I am sure Christ would understand and forgive me.' And she crossed herself.

'You mustn't say that.'

'Why not? It's true.'

'Well, there are your children. Think of them left at home.'

'The older girl is married - to a chef. They live in Toscana, and I hardly ever see them. There is only my fourteen year old. My Angelina.'

A smile touched her lips, as she uttered her child's name.

'You see?' Graziella said. 'For her sake. At least.'

It seemed strange, she thought, talking to the other woman like this: it was not as if they were friends, and she was young enough to be Carlotta's daughter. Yet here she was, advising her. She had been going to offer Carlotta work, but now a further idea came to her, which could suit both of them.

'I think I might have a solution,' she said.

'Oh, Graziella, I remember how, even as a child, you were full of solutions, which came to nothing.'

'But this really is a good idea.'

A flicker of interest lit her tired face. 'I'm all ears. What is it?'

'Leave that shit of a husband, come and work for me - that's why I wanted to see you. I can no longer do it all on my own. It is too much for one person, you and Angelina can live above Mama Lucia's. There are two rooms, but you and she could share if you didn't mind, so that I could rent out the other. And meanwhile, Rosa could use it when I am busy in the café. I wouldn't charge you, and of course I would pay you for your work. It won't be a lot, but ...'

'You would do that for us?' Carlotta was incredulous. Her mouth was opening and closing like a fish.

Graziella nodded, smiling.

Then Carlotta's expression changed: 'It's no good. He will come after us,' she stated, in a flat tone.

Graziella thought for a moment: 'Not if I get Stefano to speak to him and warn him off. He is very big and strong, with ready fists. He and his friends haven't a good word to say about your husband. They would willingly pulverise him if he so much as threatened you.'

Now, Carlotta's features relaxed. 'Well. If you are sure…'

'I'm sure.'

'In that case,' she said, finally smiling, 'could we move in today?'

CHAPTER 36

NOW

GRAZIELLA

My nights are busy with dreams. They merge with those of my girlhood, which besieged me after Gino was killed. I dream of people who have died, whom I once knew. Of friends gone or going. Sometimes all I can see is their backs as they turn away from me, and I plead with them to show their faces. They taunt me, like jesters. I dream of my parents under water, dripping with green slime and algae, like sea creatures, and I am calling them, beseeching them, like Eurydice, to turn round and look at me, but they don't, and swim past me as though I don't exist. I dream my daughter is a child again. She is calling to me, but I cannot find her, and she continues to cry out for me, like a lamb separated from a ewe. It is torture listening to her suffering. My heart is tight with agony.

I dream Gino, my son, has beheaded Gino, my lover. I dream of animals I have rescued over the years, and of a priest wearing a dog collar; and my husband's beautiful hands. I dream of a thousand different things, with a common theme of loss. But, occasionally, I dream of beautiful, tender sex. Sometimes it is with a stranger, whose features are a composite of men I have known; other times it is with my husband, or it might be Gino, or Stefano. And in these erotic dreams I experience the moment of penetration, and a fullness inside my vagina. And when I wake I am damp with desire.

What is real? What is not?

It is becoming harder for me to distinguish. Hallucinations are symptoms of my disease, I have been told. The brain gremlins like to play tricks. Lately they have, according to an MRI scan, invaded new territory. I wonder how long I have, before I cease to be me.

CHAPTER 37

NOW

ROSA

'Was Stefano in love with you, Mama?'

She glares at me. 'What has that to do with anything?'

'I just ...'

Her fierce expression melts, and her head tilts in that endearing little habit of hers. 'I believe so,' she admits.

She sounds almost bashful, which sets me wondering: Could he have been my father?

'And as far as you were concerned ... did you love him?'

'It is easy to be confused between love and friendship, when you are young and have been deprived of affection for as long as I was,' she replies, choosing her words with care. 'I think that he represented a father figure for me.'

At that time she would have been not quite twenty-three and gloriously beautiful, and I doubt he'd have wanted to be regarded as such. But it would be wrong of me to press her further. One thing is certain: Stefano was not my father. She would admit it, were it the case. After all, there would be nothing shameful in it.

'I can remember when Carlotta and Angelina moved into Mama Lucia's,' I tell her. 'It was winter, wasn't it?'

'Was it?' She looks vague. 'Yes, maybe it was. Yes, I think you're right.'

I can still picture Angelina: a tall, slender, sallow-faced girl, her hair in a fashionably short, straight fringe. I recall being fascinated by the soft covering of black down on her arms, wanting to stroke it. She looked after me in the evenings, when Mama and Carlotta were working, and she read to me, and was endlessly patient with my many questions. I remember thinking how grown up she was, and that I wanted to be like her, and have a fringe and furry arms. I asked her if she would be my sister, and she explained to me the reasons she could not be my real sister, however, we could be blood sisters. So she pricked my finger, then her own - I remember forcing myself not to cry - and then we each made a pledge to the other, and mingled our blood. Summer came round again; I recall it as a happy time. The tourists doubled in numbers, and the bar was packed to capacity day and night. Mama had to hire extra help. It was a memorable summer; I recall being surrounded by strong women, and relishing the sense of security it gave me; and the atmosphere of unity and love, and spontaneous female voices. It was a period of calm. Meanwhile, our menagerie grew, with a variety of animals at any given time. An injured stoat, orphaned wild cats, fox cubs caught in snares, a porcupine with a broken toe, not to mention the rats and birds and bats - all came and went accordingly, as Mama would patch them up as best she could then release them. And when any creature died, however lowly, it would be honoured with a proper burial. I remember the two-tiered box in the kitchen, filled with neatly rolled bandages, jars of herbal concoctions, cotton wool, bits of wood, which could serve as splints, tiny pipettes, and feeding droppers... it was like a puncture repair kit for every eventuality.

That summer we had mains water connected to the *casetta*, and electricity installed, and I remember the excitement of running the taps for the first time, and switching the lights on off, on off. Also I think I can remember a certain wistfulness in my mother's expression. As though she had lost something.

I turn to her now. She is staring at the curtain in alarm, her body shrinking into the high-backed chair.

'What is it Mama?'

She points a quivering finger: 'Who is that by the curtain.'

'There's nobody there,' I assure her; and going up to it, I shake it to prove it to her.

Her expression is fearful: 'He's hunched down. He's a greenish colour. Why can't you see him? Are you being deliberately perverse?'

'No, honestly I'm not, Mama. You have to trust me - there's nobody there. I'm just trying to reassure you.'

'Well you're not. Why won't you believe me? In fact, I think you're in on the conspiracy. Actually, I don't think you're my daughter at all. She is prettier than you. You're pretending to be her. My little Rosa... You've killed my poor little Rosa. You have buried her alive beneath the rubble.'

'Mama, really it's me. Look at me.'

Anguished she screws her face up and tugs distractedly. 'I don't know you, I don't know you,' she moans, rocking in grief. Then she lets out a scream so shrill, the neighbours must be able to hear her: 'Imposter, witch, murderer!'

She shoots to her feet, nimble as a girl suddenly, and sets about attacking me, scratching and biting and punching.

'Mama, no!'

I can't fend her off me, without hurting her, and have to shield myself from her wild blows as best I can. I can already feel my eye swelling.

Eventually, I manage to push her off me, and I escape into the garden. With luck, she will calm down on her own. This is the worst episode yet, by far.

The salt of my tears stings my eye. I sit down on the steel chair by the pear tree, which my stepfather bought as a sapling for Mama's sixtieth. It is a mature tree now, yielding fruit in the summer.

'Rosa?'

Mama has come to seek me out.

'I wondered where you got to, *cara*. I think I fell asleep...'

I get up.

She gives a shocked little cry, and her hand goes to her mouth.

'*Madre!* Whatever have you done to yourself?'

I think fast: 'I was playing with the dogs. They jumped up.'

'You silly girl,' she lovingly chides me. 'You really should be careful, you know what they are like outside.'

She takes me by the hand, back indoors. In the bathroom she makes me sit down, and bathes my eye with eyewash, crooning as she does so: 'Silly girl, silly girl.'

I make lunch for us both. We eat on our laps in front of the television and watch a DVD: *Il Gattopardo*. Thoughtful as ever, Jack gave it to her at Christmas. He had recalled that it had been her favourite novel.

To begin with she is captivated, as the rugged Sicilian scenery is spread out before us on the television screen. She eats messily, dropping bits of fish on the floor, mistaking her knife for her fork, then discarding the fork altogether and just using the knife. She chases the food around the plate to no avail, huffing in her frustration. How can I simply sit here, watching her struggle? I bend down and pretend I am picking up the fork from the floor.

'Look - your fork had dropped. No wonder you had a problem,' I say, passing it to her; and I take the knife from her and re-present it in the correct order.

'Thank you *cara*.'

'A pleasure.'

For the next five or ten minutes we watch the television without speaking. She is immersed in the film, and I have the impression she believes that the events are actually happening. I carry the trays into the kitchen. She has eaten well, I note; nothing left on her plate; and she has drunk her glass of water. My eye is throbbing. Heaven knows how I will drive home. I wash up and return to the living room. For a moment I don't see her. Then I notice her, hiding under the table.

'What are you doing there, Mama,' I ask, in as normal a voice as I can muster.

'Quick, come and join me, *cara*,' she says urgently. 'You'll be safe here. Oh do hurry, will you?'

Without quizzing her, I squeeze under the dining table with her.

'And the dogs. What shall we do about them? They must come too.'

'They will be fine, Mama. They run a lot faster than we can,' I tell her, hoping for a clue soon as to what is going on in her brain. We must look comical, squatting here under the table.

'I'll look after you my little Rosa. I won't let you come to any harm… Oh your poor eye. What have you done to it?'

'The dogs Mama… You remember?'

'The dogs did that?'

'They were playing, getting over excited.'

'You should be more careful, *cara*.'

'Yes I know… Mama, shall we take a stroll round the garden? See if the crocuses are out?'

'Why not?'

I back out from under the table, and help her do the same. She stands in the middle of the room, wearing a nonplussed expression.

'Rosa,' she says, 'What on earth were we doing under the table?'

I can't answer that, so I just shrug.

Her eyebrows raise, and she tuts, and gives a resigned sigh.
'And your eye?'

'The dogs, Mama, I told you.'

She looks at me long and hard, with a skewed smile.

'Yes, *cara*. So you say.'

CHAPTER 38

THEN
STEFANO

The sun slid low behind the hazy *Montagna della Madonna*, red as a cockerel's comb, and at the precise moment the bell tolled for Mass, some of the searing heat left the day, as though a tap had been turned off. The tourists waded out of the sea, dried themselves off; then, with towels slung over their burnt shoulders, idled back to wherever they were staying, to smarten up for the evening. Only a group of local youths remained, to finish off their game of water polo, leaping for the ball, careless of the beauty of their bronzed bodies. Then they, too, departed, at a run, because they were already late for Mass. One by one, the businesses and shops were locked for the night; shutters were bolted. Only old Umberto, who must have been in his eighties, remained open. He made and sold leather belts, bags and wallets; though he was old, his hand was as steady as a surgeon's. It had been Graziella's idea that he pitch his cartful of wares to the side of Mama Lucia's. It would be mutually beneficial; and, as well, the tourists liked to pat and fuss over Umberto's stripy grey donkey, so it became quite an attraction.

The lights round the harbour came on, and Mama Lucia's was illuminated with lanterns. The jukebox blasted out with a hybrid mix of music. Tourists and locals mingled, and young men hauled any available woman onto the tiny dance area, where they proceeded to demonstrate their nonexistent dancing skills, gyrating their hips, and singing along in English, without comprehending the words, and generally showing off.

For goodness sake... I got the hippy hippy shake,
Yeah, I got the shake... I got the hippy hippy shake.
Ooh, I can't sit still... With the hippy hippy shake,
Yeah I get my thrill now... With the hippy hippy shake...

All the tables, outside and inside too, were taken. The student, and even Rosa, assisted Graziella in the kitchen, while Carlotta and Angelina hurried back and forth with drinks and plates of food.

'Now that you're shot of your husband you can shack up with me, Carlotta,' Vincenzo, one of the bus drivers, remarked, studying her generous backside as she set down a plate of calamari before him.

'I wouldn't shack up with you if you were the last man on the planet, Vincenzo,' Carlotta replied, in a severe tone. 'And I think you are forgetting something.'

'What's that, my little viper?'

'That you're already married. To my best friend. God knows how she puts up with you.'

'Ah, so I am. How could it have slipped my mind? Such an excellent woman.' He burped loudly. 'Nonetheless, you do have a delectable arse, Carlotta,' he said, ducking as she took a swipe at him.

'*Porca miseria.* Men!' she grumbled to Graziella, who had witnessed the interchange. 'What is it with men?'

Graziella chuckled. 'Think of them as inferior creatures,' she said, tossing some scraps on the floor for the dog.

'They respect you. They aren't like it with you.'

'I've learned not to honour them with a response,' she said.

She undid her apron. Beneath it she wore a chiffon dress in shades of green. Her hair was in a single long plait down her back. Carlotta watched her apply red lipstick in the small mirror hanging lopsidedly from a nail in the wall, wiping away condensation with her hand. She wore no other makeup. What must it be like to be so exquisite, Carlotta wondered? She likened herself to a beige sparrow, whereas Graziella would be a bird of paradise.

'You look lovely,' she said.

Graziella brandished a hand in dismissal. 'All I know is that I am hot and harassed,' she said.

Graziella escaped from the sweltering kitchen with relief. As she wove between customers, they kept stopping her, hoping to engage her in conversation. Now that she was successful, they wanted to know her. People who had shunned her, particularly women, now fawned over her. Did they really think she couldn't see through them? They were as false as an old grandmother's teeth. And how Lucia Penta would have laughed, in that cynical, irreverent way of hers, at the turnaround of events. On second thoughts, she would probably have been unsurprised. She would have taken it for granted that Graziella would make a success of the business, or she would not have left it to her. And understanding human nature with all its weaknesses, she would have foreseen the outcome.

Buona sera… Ciao… Come va?'… She would respond graciously to each of the sycophantic greetings, lightly touching an arm or hand; her smile not wavering.

She made her way to Stefano's table.

'Cin-cin!' 'Salute!' 'Felice!'

It was his birthday, and the celebrations were underway. He was cagey about his age, but Graziella knew he had been a year or two younger than her father, making him forty-six or seven.

Everyone looked up as she approached.

'Here comes the divine hostess herself,' slurred the pop star, whose latest girlfriend, a statuesque platinum blonde, was balanced on his lap.

Graziella smiled stiffly. He had invited himself this evening, and she could hardly have refused. He was absurd, she thought, with his ponytail and gold bangles, prancing about, pretending to be a young man. She didn't care how famous he was; she liked him no better than when she had first met him. Stefano was sitting at the head of the table, beaming happily; smart in a crisply ironed light blue shirt, his hair - showing a few silver streaks - neatly combed back. She slid into the empty chair next to him.

'*Come sei bella,*' he complimented her, half rising, and kissing her on either cheek.

'*Grazie*' she murmured, self-conscious with all eyes on her.

'You can do much better than that,' jeered the singer, slopping red wine down his pristine white shirt. 'Give the girl a proper snog.'

Graziella could feel her face burning; however, before she could give him a piece of her mind, Stefano intercepted.

'I don't think that would be appropriate,' he said.

And she noticed that even he was blushing, and sensed his annoyance, despite his benign smile.

'A shame.' The singer shrugged. 'Hey we could do with more wine on the table...'

The moment of tension passed. Carlotta and Angelina brought out plates of food, and everyone tucked in and praised Graziella's cooking. She counted eleven people at the table, twelve including herself. Except for the pop star and his girlfriend, all were longstanding friends of Stefano. Two of the men were fishermen, like himself; the other two - brothers - owned the ironmongery. To begin with, they were awed by the presence of the celebrity in their midst, barely speaking or lifting their eyes, but as Stefano plied them with alcohol, filling and refilling glasses, the men lost their inhibitions and fired questions at him, whilst the wives flirted outrageously with him, sticking out their breasts, giggling, and competing for his attention.

The friendship between the singer and Stefano was not as incongruous as it might have seemed: he was the son of a Neapolitan fisherman, and when interviewed, spoke with affection for his humble roots. Graziella gave him credit for that, but his crassness and attitude to women incensed her; however, for Stefano's sake she tolerated him. The singer had put new commissions his way, and the money was not to be scoffed at, particularly during winter's lean months. Fame had come to Mama Lucia's also, when the paparazzi had snapped shots of the singer at the café, with his hand cupping a girl's breast. In the background you could clearly see Stefano's Marilyn Monroe mural, which thrilled him. He talked of little else for days: *his* mural in a national newspaper. She refrained from pointing out that the focus of most readers would be on the girl's breasts rather than a mural. He was so childlike in his excitement, so easily impressed. Why deflate him?

The night wore on. The pop star fell asleep at the table; his head slumped over his plate. The girlfriend looked as though she was trying not to cry. She was gnawing her lip and rubbing her eyes. Her mascara had smudged in panda-rings. Graziella realised she was younger than she had first thought - eighteen at the most - and felt sorry for her.

'Are you alright? *Cosa c'è?*' she asked, pressing the girl's shoulder.

She nodded and managed a wan smile. Clearly, she was not alright.

Conversation had dried up, and everyone looked bleary. The music had stopped, and the other tables were empty now, and Carlotta had cleared them. The student had long gone home, and the leather-seller, who had done brisk business, had left with the donkey hours ago.

'The party is over, my friends,' Stefano announced, clapping his hands.

The singer woke with a start. His hair was dishevelled, his eyes red.

'Eh? Eh? What's happening?' he stuttered.

Graziella went upstairs, to check on Rosa. She was in a deep sleep, breathing heavily, her small white teeth slightly parted.

'It seems a shame to wake her,' Graziella said to Carlotta, who was in the kitchen, drying the last of the glasses.

'Why not leave her with us for the night?' she suggested. 'Angelina would like it.'

'So would Rosa.'

'Then that's decided.'

'You look exhausted,' Graziella commented.

'I'll be glad to get to bed,' Carlotta admitted. 'Though Stefano will have to kick out our celebrity.'

'*Madre*, the state of him,' Graziella said. 'What do women see in him?'

'They say that the girlfriend is a prostitute from the slums of Palermo,' Carlotta remarked.

'There, but for God's grace, go you or I,' Graziella stated, with a shake of the head.

'No, not you, Graziella. You are too resourceful. But me... If you hadn't helped me out I don't know what I'd have done,' Carlotta said.

'It was nothing.'

'It was everything.'

For a few seconds neither spoke, each locked in reflection. Carlotta buffed up the final glass with a cloth and put it away. Not looking at Graziella, she said: 'Stefano is a good man, you know.'

'What are you implying, Carlotta?'

'I'm not implying anything,' she said. 'But if I had a kind, handsome man like Stefano, who was crazy about me, then I ...'

'He isn't crazy about me. We are friends, that's all. He was my Papa's best friend. He's known me since I was born.'

'You must be walking around with your eyes shut, Graziella,' Carlotta scoffed.

⥲⥵

The guests had all departed. The last to leave had been the pop star and his girlfriend. He had vomited over the tablecloth, then, aided by her, had stumbled into his Porsche, and they'd roared off. Graziella had seen them go. The girl had looked terrified. She had pleaded with him that he was in no fit state to drive.

Stefano was waiting for her outside, smoking a cigarette and staring at the sea, sleek and glistening in the reflections from the lights. Except for its lapping, and the whirring cicadas, the air was empty of sound. The tethered boats sat, still and silent.

Stefano stubbed out the cigarette. 'I will never grow bored of this,' he said, not turning. 'If I were to die today, I would die as a contented man.'

She realised that, though he had drunk his fair share, he was as sober as she was. She had never seen him so thoughtful, and she liked this Stefano. She took his arm. They walked, with the dog, along the beach. 'I have been thinking,' she began, - and broke off. 'No, you'll tease me.'

'I won't.'

'You promise?'

His teeth glistened, white in the darkness. '*Giuro.*'

'OK then... I've have been thinking of opening a hotel. A very a small one, I mean. More, an *albergo.*'

As she spoke, she realised how outlandish the idea would seem to him, and her defences were up in anticipation.

He gave a low whistle and, predictably, he laughed. 'You don't do things by half, do you, Graziella?'

She wrenched her arm from under his. 'You promised you wouldn't do that.' she said. 'Now I wish I hadn't told you.'

He made himself look serious. 'I'm sorry, *piccolina*. It just came as a surprise. You've not mentioned it before, and it all seems rather sudden, not to say ambitious. I mean a *hotel*!' He gave another whistle, irritating her further.

'An *albergo*,' she corrected him, emphatically. 'I shouldn't have called it a hotel before. Anyway, what's wrong with being ambitious? It's a good thing to be.'

'Yes, yes, of course it is,' he agreed, keen to redeem himself. 'Ambition is an excellent thing.'

'And the idea *was* sudden,' she continued, less defensive now. 'It came to me a few nights ago. I was lying in bed, thinking how rapidly tourism was expanding, yet that, apart from the big hotel, which not everyone wants to stay at - and the self-catering apartments - again, which not everyone wants, there is very little choice of accommodation. So, I thought, why not do something myself?'

'Why not?' echoed Stefano. He understood her well enough to know she was simply seeking affirmation.

'It would be aimed at the upper end of the market,' she expanded. 'And there wouldn't be more than eight or nine bedrooms. It would be a special place. The rooms would be decorated with shells...I can visualise it, Stefano... And I *know* the catering business, don't forget. I know I could make it work.'

He realised she was in earnest. 'I'm sure you would make it work,' he said.

'But?'

'You have a good life now, Graziella. Why complicate it? Why do you *want* to have an *albergo*? I am no businessman, but even I know it would be a big undertaking.'

'That's what appeals to me,' she insisted. 'I like the challenge of a project.'

He gave a regretful sigh. 'You are too clever for me, Graziella. You will leave me behind. Come on, let's get you home.'

They walked back along the beach, and he drove her to the *casetta* in the truck. It smelt of fish. He accompanied her to the door.

'I've got something I want you to have as a birthday gift,' she told him, as he was about to go. 'But you must choose it yourself.'

He laughed. 'That sounds very mysterious.'

He followed her into the *casetta*; switched on all the lights. She still could not get used to having electricity in the *casetta*, and sometimes she forgot, and would light the oil lamp, before remembering.

'You'll have to come up to my room,' she said.

He looked taken aback, and she laughed.

'It isn't want you might be thinking.'

'That's a pity,' she thought he muttered beneath his breath, as he clambered up the loft ladder behind her.

'And make sure you duck. There's a low beam,' she cautioned - too late.

He swore as he biffed his head.

She rubbed the sore spot. 'Aw, poor you,' she said.

It felt odd for Stefano to be here, in her room, with all her personal bits and pieces dotted about. She became self-conscious, and could see he was equally uneasy.

'This used to be my parents' room,' she told him.

'I often think of them,' he said. 'Particularly your papa of course. We shared many good times.'

She smiled and walked over to the wardrobe.

'What are you doing?' he asked, as she dragged out the hessian bag. And he went to help her.

'I can manage,' she insisted. She laid the bag on the floor. 'You can open it now,' she said, hugging herself in anticipation of his reaction.

He knelt to do so.

'*Porca miseria*,' he exclaimed softly as the sticks rolled out. He sat back on his haunches, his head going from side to side in his disbelief. 'When did you find these?'

'Just before Rosa was born. They were only in the wardrobe, but I didn't find them sooner as the room is so dark; the bag was right at the back, hidden by Papa's overalls, and his shoes.'

'*Porca miseria*,' Stefano said again.

'I want you to take whichever stick you want.'

'But I couldn't. They're yours.'

'You have been so good to me…I know Papa would wish it. I wish it.'

'Ah, Graziella,' he sighed, watery-eyed.

She loved his sentimentality. And it seemed fitting, now, that he should in this room, and it made her feel close to her father.

'Go on, choose one,' she urged.

He sat on the floor, and examined each in turn. She tried to guess which he would choose.

He looked up. 'Could I take the owl? I'm not sure why, but I've always liked owls. There's something other-worldly about them.'

'I knew that's what you would choose.'

'You know me too well, Graziella.'

He got to his feet awkwardly: a big, rugged man, in the confined space of the room. They each took a step nearer the other. 'It's gone two in the morning,' he said.

'I know,' she said, holding his gaze.

'I should go. Do you want me to go?'

She swallowed hard. 'No,' she said, barely above a whisper.

'You must know what I feel about you, Graziella.'

'I think so.'

'But I don't want to take advantage of you. I don't want you to regret anything. You've had quite a lot to drink and perhaps that is …'

'I wouldn't regret it … I *won't* regret it… I want to know want it is like to make love with somebody who cares about me.'

'Ah Graziella… *piccolina mia…* You are still so young, and I am middle-aged. Maybe it is wrong.'

'It isn't wrong. Please kiss me, Stefano. And then make love to me.'

She could feel the swelling through his trousers, as he held her close, and his fisherman's hands encircled her face as though it were a frail flower. His kiss was hesitant at first, almost chaste. An image darted into her head, of a young English boy. She recalled that innocent kiss, the taste of aniseed.

Then she felt the tip of Stefano's tongue prising apart her lips. She shut her eyes, and tried to respond to the snaking little stabs. The sensations were not unpleasant, once she became used to them.

This is Stefano, she reminded herself. *This is dear Stefano.*

'May I undress you?' he asked.

'Yes.'

He did so, clumsily, and fumbled with her brassiere.

'Sorry… Sorry,' he apologised.

She helped him in the end, and took off her own knickers.

'*Dio,* you are so lovely,' he said.

But she felt self-conscious under his scrutiny and lay down quickly on the bed.

He undressed with his back to her, scattering his clothes on the floor, then joined her on the bed. She tried not to stare at his nakedness, but could hardly avoid it.

'I shall not let you get pregnant,' he assured her.

He stroked her and caressed her. He could not have been more tender, and she heard herself making whimpering sounds, but they were for his benefit. When he entered her, he took care not to hurt her, and she liked the feeling of him in her, but was unmoved. That ultimate experience a woman could know eluded her. She was aware throughout that this was Stefano, her friend; her *father's* friend; and on the one hand this brought her all the closer to him, on the other it was as though she were committing incest.

Afterwards, he became emotional again, and she stroked the perspiration from his forehead. He fell asleep with his face squashed against hers, but although she was uncomfortable, didn't want to disturb him by moving. She lay there like it, her eyes open, and thoughts racing, until he rolled away from her in his sleep.

She slept deeply then.

At the crack of dawn he slid out of bed and hurriedly threw on his clothes. She was not aware of him gazing at her, before kissing her goodbye. Then, forgetting to pick up the owl walking stick on his way out, Stefano set off for the harbour in his rattling old truck.

He sang, as he sorted out the nets.

'You're annoyingly cheerful at this ungodly hour in the morning,' observed his friend Nico, who had been at the party, and was now about to depart in his boat. 'I'd have thought you'd be feeling like shit.'

'I didn't drink that much. And I've every reason to be happy,' said Stefano.

'You mean that you and the glorious Signorina Lupo finally got it together?'

'I'm not saying anything,' Stefano replied.

He remembered the boat needed topping up with oil, then he pushed it down the ramp, clambered into it and started up the motor.

Soon he was out to sea. The early mist dissolved, to be replaced by blinding daylight. He was tired, from lack of sleep, but his heart and brain were so full with happiness that it hurt him.

It was not long before a fine catch of bream was netted, and he stood and leant over the side of the boat, intending to draw in the net. But the ground slid from beneath him, and he slipped. In his tiredness he had forgotten to put the cap back on the oil can and the oil had spilled out.

He tottered forward, causing the boat to rock, and lost his balance. He tried to save himself, but fell over the side and became entangled in his own net.

CHAPTER 39

NOW

ROSA

'He had become my dearest friend,' Mama says, ruminative-ly. 'And, yes, there was that one night, but…'

'Would you prefer I didn't include it in the book, Mama?' I ask her, concealing my surprise that she had volunteered the information of her own will.

'No. You may put it in if you wish. I did nothing I was ashamed of. I'd known Stefano all my life. He made me feel safe. He was a link with my father. And it was the first time a man had shown me affection.'

'But Mama, surely Gino showed you love?'

'Gino is my son.'

'Yes, I know. But before him there was also Gino your boyfriend who, you said, was my father.'

'He was killed by a snake… Really, why must you always inter-rupt, Rosa? You know it makes me lose the thread.'

'Sorry.'

'What was I saying?'

'You were talking about when Stefano died; about how you felt.'

'Oh yes. So, as you may imagine, I was devastated. I felt a profound sense of loss. I couldn't believe he had gone. There was something so permanent about him. I recall a strange remark he made, after the party guests had all left. He was staring at the sea, unusually pensive, and told me that if he were to die the next day, he would die happy. I have often wondered if he had a premonition, just as my papa did.

It was the postmistress, Maria Alberta, who informed me of the tragedy. She came to find me in the café. She and I were on civil terms by then, after years of mutual loathing. I suppose in her eyes I had acquired a degree of respectability with the passage of time. Also, I had started attending church again. I thought I should do, for your sake. It was the right thing to do, don't you think?'

'Yes it was. But Mama, we were talking about how Maria Alberta broke the news to you about Stefano.'

'Yes, Rosa, I know we were. Don't rush me...remember she came running into Mama Lucia's like a frantic hen, to find me. I was making polenta, I recall. *I've heard some dreadful news,* she shouted at me, as though I was deaf. *It's Stefano, the fisherman. He's dead.*'

I can remember feeling the blood running out of me. And she proceeded to tell me what had happened.

Are you sure? Are you absolutely certain there's no mistake?' I asked her. But she looked at me with pity, and explained there could be no doubt. 'It was his dolphin tattoo. Lorenzo Torre, the *carabiniere* had himself identified the corpse, and had pieced together what had occurred.'

'Apparently, he looked like a giant octopus, caught up in the net,' Mama says, on a lengthy sigh.

'You didn't go to the funeral, did you?' I ask her.

'No. It was in Palermo, where Stefano's mother lived, having remarried after her first husband's death. I was glad. I don't think I could have borne it. It gave me an excuse not to go.'

'I can remember how sad you were. And I was worried, as you had stopped smiling. I told you I'd look after you.'

'My loyal little Rosa... But yes, it was a difficult time. He had become a fixture in my life. I took for granted that I would see him most days. And if I had a problem, he was the first person I would consult. Mama Lucia's wasn't the same without Stefano. And every time I passed the Marilyn Monroe mural, I thought of him. He had been such a big part of it. And my papa and he had used to meet there every evening, and I don't know who was the worse influence on the other.'

She smiles softly, and a whimsical expression smoothes the few faint lines on her forehead. For a moment she looks like a young woman, and I wish I could capture her like it, in a photograph, right now.

'I went to visit Raffaella at the convent,' Mama says. 'I think I hoped she might be able to make sense of what had happened. A pretty, young novice went to find her for me, and I remember thinking that she was about to throw away her life on a myth. Then Raffaella entered the room, wearing her wimple and, as usual, that upset me. I couldn't get used to her like it, and longed to wrench the thing off her. And when she embraced me, I could feel its unforgiving structure against my cheek as we embraced.

She had already heard about poor Stefano, and did her best to console me. I even told her about my night with him, as I was bursting to confide my confused feelings, and we had always been open with each other. But then she brought God into the conversation, and I became angry. I told her that anyone who believed in God was utterly deluded; it was all an elaborate hoax, and not possible.' Mama smiles. 'I can still recall Raffaella's reply, in that curious, childish lisp that she had.

"If that is the case, dearest Graziella," she said to me, "then half the world is suffering from delusion. And do you really think THAT possible?"

I felt ashamed and apologised - I always seemed to be apologising to her. Nonetheless, it didn't alter my opinions, as you know....'

Mama pauses to take a sip of water from the glass beside her, then continues.

'A couple of months passed. I'd been concerned trade would suffer with Stefano gone, but by then Mama Lucia's was well established and inspired a loyal following. It had acquired something of an arty reputation. And, although I say it myself, the food was good. The *Contessa* had become a regular customer, and now usually came with her lady friend - and also a puppy mastiff, to replace the old one, who had died. The pop star flaunted a new girlfriend, even younger, and a lot feistier than the predecessors. He attached himself to Stefano's friends, and they would play cards and backgammon for money, and as the evening went into night and he knocked back Grappa till he could hardly stand, the fishermen grew rich. He was always the last to leave the bar.

And when the hectic frenzy of the summer season died down, and tourism slackened, there was still business to be had. A different type of holidaymaker was attracted to the *Isola* between the months of September through to June: retired people who preferred a quiet atmosphere; keen walkers; naturalists, who wanted to visit the nature reserve; photographers and artists and honeymooners.

And life, without Stefano in it, continued. I realised that my sadness had passed. But whilst I was able to think of him without pain, I recall feeling a sense of guilt.'

'But why?'

'Because I knew I could never have loved Stefano in the right way. If he had lived, I would have broken his heart - and I would have hated myself for doing so.'

'Are you saying it was fortuitous that he died?'

'Possibly. Callous though it might seem, I think that is what I'm trying to say, *cara*. But it was a long time ago. And it is only with the hindsight of shifting years that I dare to say it. It shouldn't detract from the grief I felt at the loss of a very dear friend. But if he hadn't died, the situation would have become complicated. I could never have loved him in the way he would have wanted; and though I'd have tried my best, it would not have worked. He knew it and I knew it. I would have broken his heart. And hated myself for that.

So you see, he might have died prematurely, but, to quote himself: he died a happy man.'

She falls silent, and slumps back in the chair. The session, possibly the frankest and most truthful, must have taken a hell of a lot out of her, and how normal and lucid she sounded throughout her account. When she is like this nobody would believe there was anything wrong with her.

CHAPTER 40

THEN
THE FALCON

It was the first day of October, but today felt more like the height of summer. The dry, dusty heat stuck in your lungs, making you want to cough; tiny, spiteful insects alighted on bare flesh, and infiltrated clothing. The Lambretta crawled up the coast road, emitting a protesting whine, throwing up dust and pebbles in its wake. The dog loped beside them. At least the recently completed wall had made the road safer, Graziella thought, changing down into the lowest gear.

'*Madre*, I feel like getting out and pushing the thing,' she remarked. She glanced round at Rosa, riding pillion behind her.

'Wouldn't it be too heavy?' Rosa asked, clasping her arms more tightly round her mother's waist. She was still nervous, riding on the scooter.

Graziella laughed. 'It was a figure of speech, *cara*.'

The road twisted and climbed up the mountain's flank. They passed the disused penitentiary, which had been built for prisoners of war; then the old monastery. The road doubled back on itself, and she slowed even further. It would not do for history to repeat itself.

The road flattened out for a bit, widening as it did so, and she heard the roar of a powerful motorbike approaching, she called Elvis closer to heel. The pop star flashed by, on his Ducati, giving a friendly toot.

'*Idiota*,' she muttered.

The lighthouse loomed above them, in phallic pride, weather-beaten from years of exposure to the elements; a few metres on, was a gravel and sand lay-by, and she turned into here and cut the engine.

'This is where the path is *cara*.'

She dismounted from the scooter and lifted Rosa down. The dog was panting hard, and she poured water into a bowl for him. He drank noisily, splashing water onto the ground. It dried instantly. Graziella hoisted her rucksack onto her back. '*Avanti*,' she said, swinging Rosa's hand.

They joined this coastal path, following the ridge, which was broad enough for both of them. The dog trotted, nose to the ground, stopping at intervals to sniff new scents. It was a good twenty-minute walk, amidst Mediterranean brush and prickly pear, to where they wanted to picnic, and their feet became hot and slippery within their heavy boots, but the rough ground and tree roots necessitated wearing them; also, they gave some protection against snakes.

The outing today was Rosa's treat: Graziella had promised they could have a picnic before the new school term started again, after the long summer's break. At last they came to the ruins of a Bourbon fortress. It sat like a camel's hump on the crest of a hill. They sank down onto the tussock ground and loosened the laces of their boots. Graziella unstrapped the rucksacks. It was years since she had been to this spot. Her parents used to bring *her* here as a treat. She would go with them on their round sometimes, and sit on the floor of the cart, knees pointing upwards, against the soft pillow of freshly killed dead chickens. The cart stank. Graziella was still able to conjure up the sickly smell. But, then, she had not minded. On their way back, when the cart was empty, or nearly so, they would stop off in the lay-by, where Graziella had left the scooter; her father would unhitch the mule and, with him leading it, they would set off for the ruins. If they were lucky, they might get a glimpse of the falcons which frequented the area. Sometimes their sharp eyes would pick out potential prey far below, and you would watch them plunge down in a stoop that took your breath away.

'Is this where your mama and papa died?' Rosa asked.

'No *cara*. According to Maria Alberta, the postmistress, who witnessed the accident, it happened higher up the mountainside, past where the big villas are. They travelled up and down the coast road every day, with the mule and cart.'

'Were you very, very sad when they died?'

'Yes, *cara*. Very, very.'

'You won't die, will you? I don't want you ever to die.'

'As you know, we all die, my little Rosa. But I plan to live a long, long time.'

'Maybe one day there will be a special medicine which makes people you love live forever.'

'What about people you don't love?'

Rosa shook her head firmly. 'No, just people you love.'

Graziella laughed. 'Oh *cara*, if only,' she said. Then, because the child looked despondent, she added: 'Still, you never know, do you? Anyway, why don't we admire the view? Then we can have our picnic.'

From up here, the scene below took on an unreal quality. It seemed that they were looking at a photograph, or a painting. The sea was improbably flat and static, and its turquoise was surely exaggerated. The curve of the bay, which formed an amphitheatre round the harbour, was too precise. The miniaturised fishing boats and private yachts seemed unnaturally still; the brightly coloured shop awnings, and the cottages stacked one on top of the other, belonged to dolls houses. They could hear the cries of market traders, happy squeals of children, and barking of dogs - muffled by distances; and made out tiny figures, who seemed to have been caught mid-action, so that it appeared as if they were not moving. The ferry, just chugging away from the port, gave several, throaty blasts of the funnel, and they could see the passengers waving nostalgic goodbyes from the deck-railings.

'Do you like it, *cara?*' Graziella asked.

'I think it's my favourite place ever,' Rosa answered. 'I'm not sad anymore.'

'Well that's good.'

She unpacked the picnic. The food was in various containers, and she laid them out on the grass: oily tomatoes and *pimentos*; creamy pungent cheese made of ewe's milk; ciabatta studded with black olives and garlic; spicy, thinly sliced salami; and for a sweet taste to finish, fat, succulent figs.

'A feast fit for a Roman emperor,' Graziella commented.

'Our teacher told us the ancient Romans lived on *Isola delle Pecore*, once upon a time. And they made lots of pots and things,' Rosa said.

'That's right, *cara*. But before them, people who came from a place called Carthage lived here. Next came the Romans, and after them, the Saracens and the Bourbons. And each civilisation in turn built homes and temples, and forts to keep enemies out. And there were lots of wars as they all wanted to possess not just *Isola delle Pecore*, but all the neighbouring isles as well.'

Rosa dipped a chunk of bread in oil. 'Are those what the ruins are?'

'Yes, *cara.*'

'I don't like wars.'

'I agree. They are horrible... But this happened thousands of years ago.'

'Thousands of years is a very long time.' Rosa screwed up her face, grappling with the enormity of the figure. 'Thousands of years is lots and lots of hundreds.'

'That's right.'

'But why did they have to fight? Why couldn't they just live all together and be happy?'

For that, Graziella had no answer.

They lingered there until late afternoon, when the extreme heat dissipated, and a breeze cooled the air still further. Then they packed up the remains of their picnic, took a last look at the view, and wended their way back to the lighthouse. They had encountered nobody the entire day - only a hare, and a friendly thrush, which had shared their food. Walking back with her daughter and dog either side of her, Graziella experienced a sense of wholeness within her. She needed no man in her life in order to feel complete. Men simply complicated things. How would today have been improved by the presence of a man? Even dear Stefano would have just got in the way.

Narrowing her eyes against the whiteness of the sky, she looked upward. A falcon circled in a wide ark, so high that it was a mere speck. It was female, she decided. It had no need of a male partner to survive. It could provide for itself. She would be a falcon if she were a bird.

CHAPTER 41

THEN

DESIRABLE PROPERTY FOR SALE

On the way home they had to pass her aunt and uncle's house. The ex-mayor and Annunciata were standing in the middle of the street, supervising a man on a stepladder, as he fixed a board to the railings. They were arguing about its positioning, but the wording was obscured from her line of vision by the man's body. Graziella's heartbeat escalated. The cobbled street was too narrow for her to overtake with the Lambretta. A confrontation was inevitable.

She braked, then tooted. The man jumped down from the ladder, enabling her to read the board.

FOR SALE, it said. The mayor's house - *ex-mayor*'s house - was for sale! It must mean rumours of his bankruptcy were true. She had heard that his almond crop had failed, and that he owed money left, right and centre.

In her astonishment she stalled the scooter; simultaneously, her aunt and uncle looked round and saw her.

His face became puce, and he strode up to the Lambretta, and leant over it.

'I should have got rid of you,' he snarled in her ear.

'You don't scare me,' she fired back; though she was trembling.

He raised an arm, as though to strike her, and the dog growled.

'Mama?' queried Rosa in a tremulous voice from behind.

His arm lowered to his side. He hadn't noticed the child.

Annunciata pulled him back by his sleeve. 'Let her go, Guido,' she said tiredly. 'Don't waste your energy on the trollop.'

Graziella zigzagged past them, on the scooter, but not before she had made a mental note of the property agent's details.

'Was that lady your *zia*?' asked Rosa, who had recognised her from a previous encounter.

'Yes *cara*.'

'And is the man her husband?'

'Yes.'

'I don't like him. He's horrible. He made me frightened. And Elvis didn't like him. He growled. Do you like him, Mama?'

'No *cara*. As you say, he is horrible.'

'I think he looks like a pig,' Rosa said, and giggled.

They did not go directly home. Instead, Graziella made a detour. She parked the Lambretta in the alley, a few metres from the *agenzia immobiliare*.

'Why have we come here?' Rosa asked.

'I have some business to do *cara*,' Graziella replied. 'Will you wait here, and look after Elvis?'

She nodded, and took him by the collar. 'This is near Stefano's house,' she remarked.

'Yes, *cara*, that's right.'

Rosa sensed her mother's sorrow. 'Maybe he is catching fish in heaven now.'

Graziella hugged her 'Ah, little Rosa, you do say the loveliest things.'

The alley no longer stank. The slaughterhouse had finally been knocked down and a new drainage system installed. Another slaughterhouse, away from the town, replaced the old one, and now the air was fragrant with the scent of the sweet peas, which entwined round walls and arches and trailed from baskets. The area was becoming sought after, particularly with artists. Who would ever have imagined it, Graziella thought?

The *agenzia immobiliare* was almost opposite the *Gazzetta* offices. After all this time, she still could not think of Gino without pain. Yet she had hardly known him, and she could not remember the colour of his eyes. She was almost the same age now that he had been. It was an extraordinary thought.

Gino...Stefano... Both gone.

There was a large, coloured photograph of her uncle's house in the estate agency's window, but no price was visible. Graziella took her sunglasses from her pocket and put them on. Then she pushed open the glossy yellow door and went in.

The estate agent shuffled up from behind a large desk, and she had the impression he had been asleep. He was middle-aged and, to her relief, she had never seen him before. It simplified matters.

'Can I help you, Signorina,' he enquired, blinking at her through thick-rimmed spectacles.

'My boss would like details of a property which has only just come on the market,' she replied. 'He wishes to know the asking price, and requests a brochure, please. There's a picture of it in the window. It's the house with the carriage lamps,' she explained.

'I know the one... Please... take a seat.' The agent gestured to the leather sofa, then walked over to a tall cabinet, and from it, hauled out a box containing brochures. 'Here it is, at the top. A very desirable property,' he observed.

'If you wouldn't mind jotting down the price for my boss,' she reminded him.

'Ah, yes, of course.' He wrote it on the back of the brochure, then handed it to her. She could tell he was wondering what she looked like behind the big sunglasses.

'*Grazie*,' she said, when he handed it to her.

'*Prego*…were there any other properties your boss would like to see?' he asked.

She stood up. 'Not for the moment. But thank you.'

'Might I ask the name of your boss, for our records,' the agent queried.

'I'm afraid I'm not at liberty to disclose it,' Graziella answered. Then, in an impish mood, knowing he would repeat it to her aunt and uncle, she said, in a confiding tone: 'But I can tell you that he is *very* famous.'

CHAPTER 42
THEN
DECISIONS

She spent the evening doing sums, and working on a business plan, and the following afternoon, having made a prior appointment, she went to see the bank manager.

He was a small, bald, rotund man, who always reminded her of a bouncing football. Over the last couple of years he had been supportive of her ventures, and had offered her sound advice. When, in the early days of inheriting Mama Lucia's, she had gone to him for advice, however busy he might be, he would make time for her. A mutual respect had grown between them. Despite her youthfulness, despite her being a woman, he had, from the start, taken her seriously, and had never been patronising or condescending toward her. She trusted him, and nowadays, they were on first-name terms. But, as yet, she had not discussed her plans for an *albergo* with him: since Stefano's death, she had lost her appetite for the project, but the sale of her aunt and uncle's house was an opportunity which could not be missed.

The ultimate revenge.

First, though, she would have to convince the bank manager of the viability. He cupped her hand in both of his in greeting, and showed her into the office, letting her go first, and closing the door behind them. He motioned for her to take a seat.

'*Allora*, Graziella, what can I do for you?' he asked, squashing his roundness into a chair.

She had rehearsed her opening gambit.

'A while ago I had an idea, and I have thought about it a great deal. It is to do with tourism,' she commenced.

Gratified, she couldn't fail to notice how, at the mention of the magic word, he leant forward keenly.

'Go on,' he said.

Nervously, she flicked her hair to one side. 'Well, you know how fast tourism has been growing, yet have you thought what little choice of accommodation there is?'

He reflected for a minute. 'Well there's obviously the hotel.'

'Yes, but it's expensive and impersonal. People come to *Isola dell Pecore* for its special atmosphere.'

'I must admit, I wouldn't want to stay there,' he said. 'But there are the apartments.'

'Yes, and they are fine. But a lot of people don't want to be bothered with catering for themselves. They prefer to be spoiled on holiday. Where are those tourists supposed to go? Currently their only option is to board in the small spare room of someone's home, with photos of the family next to the bed, and a crucifix on the wall.'

He smiled at that: 'What would your suggestion be then?' he asked. 'What is this idea of yours?'

'I want to have an *albergo*,' she said.

'Do you now?' came his noncommittal response; though she suspected he had guessed.

Graziella unzipped the document bag she had brought with her, and took out a folder. She passed it to him.

'It's my business plan,' she explained, when he looked quizzi-cal. 'I'm certain this could work. Mama Lucia's has never been busier - you've seen for yourself what it's like, and it brings in good money and could easily support another business,' she elaborated, speaking more and more quickly. 'I would rent out the *casetta*, to holidaymakers, so that brings in even more revenue...and I'm not boasting, but this is a business which I now know inside out and am good at, and understand. I've done all the costings, and have enough money for a deposit... and ...'

'Graziella... Graziella, slow down. I don't doubt the truth of anything you are saying. It is certainly an interesting and enterpris-ing proposal, for which I commend you. I look forward to studying the plan in depth. However, you are not expecting me to do so now, this minute, are you?'

Her silence said otherwise.

'You know it doesn't work like that,' he said, his voice kindly. 'In order that I give your plan the attention which it warrants, I must take time to read through it thoroughly, and examine the figures for myself. There are many factors to consider, and for your sake, as well as the bank's, we need to weigh up the risks at stake. It would be irresponsible of me not to do so. Ultimately, you wouldn't thank me for it. I would hate you to end up losing all your money and amassing hefty debts. I would feel culpable. You would have to sell the café, if that happened, and I cannot believe you would want that, would you?'

Crestfallen, she shook her head.

'Is there a reason for your urgency, Graziella?'

'I'm worried that someone will put in an offer for the property that I want to buy,' she told him.

'And what is this property?'

She handed him the brochure.

His smile grew larger. He knew of the family rift. He himself had no liking for the Carluccios. 'I see,' he said, pinching his chin, then releasing it. 'Yes, now I do see the urgency.'

She saw the mischief in his eyes. 'There would be a nice symmetry to it,' she murmured, smiling also.

'That's as maybe,' he said, a little severely now, 'but it is no reason whatsoever, to be reckless. This cannot be decided in the heat of the moment, on some whim. It is a decision which could affect your whole life, and you must be pragmatic.'

And she thought she heard her mother's voice.

Head, not heart, cara.

'I will be objective,' he assured her. 'But this is not merely all about figures. The viability of this proposal is also dependent on prediction of the future. Now, of course, few of us are blessed with that capacity ... ' he smiled faintly, 'but, we *can* make a realistic assessment and arrive at a conclusion, whereby, whilst we cannot eliminate risk, we can at least minimise it. You are an intelligent young lady, Graziella, and a good businesswoman. But you must see that this is not a game. Please give me time. I will see you in three days, and give you my decision. If it is of any comfort, I am certain nobody else will buy the Carluccio property before then.'

Everything he had said was logical, and she realised that. A decision of such importance could hardly be made after a cursory glance at a bit of paperwork; nonetheless, her disappointment was immense, and she saw the house slipping away from within her reach.

The bank manager showed her to the door. It was impossible for him to ignore her dismay. He patted her arm to encourage her.

'The advice I give you, Graziella, is no less than the advice I would give my own children,' he said, in a sympathetic tone.

That night, she had a dream, about a young man with laughing eyes, and a soft, golden beard. His voice was soft too; and as mellow as the deep chime of a long case clock. As he walked towards her she noticed he had a pronounced limp, lurching, as though one leg was longer than the other.

You came back, she said.

I told you I would.

But you didn't write.

But I did.

He spoke in Italian, as though it was his native language.

Your Italian is perfect. I can't correct you anymore.

I learned it for you, he said.

And though he was lame, he could perform triple somersaults, run and jump more than two metres high, and run like an athlete. They ran together on the harbour beach; except it was not sand; it was rubble, which hurt the soles of her bare feet and bit into them.

Would you like me to carry you? he asked.

You can't because of your leg, she replied.

I can do anything when I'm with you, Graziella.

He lifted her high, and bore her along, as though she were a princess reclining in a silk-padded sedan. Then the scene changed. They were outside a tall brick house and he led her indoors.

The shelves were crammed with wall-to-wall books, a stuffed owl glared down at them.

Where are we? she asked.

At my house.

It seemed entirely natural that they were naked, and he lay her down on the bed. His tapered fingers explored the topography of her body as though he were blind. His voice came and went in her ear, and she threw her head back on the pillow, in pleasure.

Please don't die; please don't die.

I won't. I'm immortal.

Gino said that.

Who is Gino?

Someone I knew.

Well I shan't die. Not when I have everything to live for. You're my childhood soulmate.

When he was deep in her, she thought she would go insane with the sensations, and felt herself to be on the edge of something extraordinary.

She awoke then, craving.

She touched herself; her nipples, then - tentatively - between her legs. And in her own bed, in the non-judgemental tar-blackness of the night, she turned onto her side and completed what had been incomplete.

She lay for a while, thinking: for their mutual birthday, in three months, she would send Roberto a card. There would be nothing lost - except useless pride, and what did that matter? He was bound to be living at a different address by now, anyway, so he would be unlikely to receive it. He may even be married. But she could at least try. She fell back into a sound, dreamless sleep, clutching her yellow, knitted rabbit to her, that her mother had made.

CHAPTER 43

THEN
A FAIR AGREEMENT

On the afternoon of her second meeting with the bank manager, Graziella left Mama Lucia's with considerable apprehension, but also a feeling of resignation. Although she had the Lupo stick with her for luck, she had already convinced herself that his answer would be negative. And at the end of the day, was it important? she thought, approaching the steps to the bank. She and Rosa were happy as they were. And her aunt and uncle had got their comeuppance. Maybe it would even prove to be for the best.

He greeted her cordially, giving nothing away, and ushered her into the office. As before, he invited her to go first.

He pressed the points of his fingers together, in a steeple.

'Graziella, as you know, I admire what you have achieved,' he started by saying, once they were settled.

And she thought: 'Here comes the "but".'

'I have been through your business plan with the utmost care, and have done my own calculations. There is no escaping the fact there would be a risk attached - you must be aware of that Graziella.'

'Yes,' she agreed, in a despondent tone, wishing now that he would just give his answer, so that she could leave, and forget about the whole thing.

'However, there is definitely a good opportunity here, as you yourself have realised, and potentially this could be a successful and lucrative business... so long,' he cautioned 'as you didn't try to be too ambitious too soon,' he warned her, observing the mercurial changes in her expression.

'I wouldn't.'

'I therefore propose a compromise to begin with. That is, that for the first year you operate on a small scale, without the expense of the extension. There are six bedrooms, you say?'

'Yes.'

'That is ample for you to get your teeth into, to begin with. As it is, there will be substantial refurbishing costs.'

'I allowed for them in my plan.'

'I know, and I am very impressed by your efficiency, which is why I should like to review the situation after the first year of trading... So how does that sound to you, Graziella?'

She put her knuckles to her face. It was going to happen. It was really going to happen. She sat back in the chair, and her smile turned to laughter.

'It sounds very fair,' she said.

⚒

Conveniently, the notary's office was a few doors down from the bank. She'd had dealings in the past with him concerning the café, and knew she could count on his discretion. The door was wide open, and the fan whirred, though today was considerably cooler. He was grossly overweight and perspired profusely and she always dreaded his sweaty handshake.

He looked up as she entered and heaved his whale-like body up from his chaotic desk.

'*Buongiorno, Signorina,*' he said, waddling towards her, hand outstretched; and she braced herself as it came into contact with her own, and had to resist wiping hers on her skirt.

'*Come sta?*' he enquired.

'*Bene, grazie...* Am I disturbing you?' She glanced about the room, at the untidy mass of paperwork that surrounded him.

He had sad eyes, like a hound. 'Not at all. It's always a pleasure. Please take a seat.'

She did, brushing off cigarette ash.

'I'll come straight to the point.' She said, leaning forward in her enthusiasm. 'There is a property I wish to buy. I have just come from the bank and the finances are in place. I'd like to instruct you to act on my behalf.'

'Thank you. I would be delighted.'

'Good... There is one thing, though. The vendor must, under no circumstances, learn that I would be the purchaser. Would it be possible to keep my identity from him?'

He thought a moment. 'Do you have a friend, someone you trust, who ...'

'There is nobody,' she stopped him short. 'Nobody I would wish to involve in my affairs.'

He contemplated her, kneading his lower lip with his finger. 'If that is the case, then I would be able to sign the contract in my own name. That is not uncommon. There would then be a private contract between yourself and myself, in which we would sign an agreement, whereby I become the purchaser, and once completion had taken place I would sign the property over to you, in your name. How does that sound to you? Would you be happy to do that?'

'Yes.'

'I want you to fully comprehend the implications. It puts us both in a vulnerable position; you more than me. If I were unscrupulous I could run off with your money.'

'But you are not, you wouldn't.'

'No, Signorina,' he agreed, smiling.

Even his smile was mournful, she thought; and imagined a lonely existence. He often came into the café, and he was always on his own.

'To start with, I would want to offer considerably less than the asking price.'

'Yes, that is quite usual.'

'And maybe you could emphasise that I am in a strong position to proceed quickly... and also that the property is in need of decorating.'

'Naturally... And I shall need you to give me details of the property and the selling agent.'

'I have it here.'

'You are very organised,' he complimented her admiringly, as she felt in her document-bag. 'Especially for someone so young, if you don't mind my saying, Signorina.'

Graziella shrugged. 'I have had to be. Here is the brochure,' she said, giving it to him.

'*Grazie*' he murmured.

He looked at the cover picture. Frowning, he scratched his head. Dandruff flew out. 'It can't be,' he said to himself, and opened the brochure. He swore then, in delight.

'What a joke!' He exclaimed. 'What a comeuppance! I detested the man. Everyone does. Well, no wonder you are being secretive. What a joke,' he repeated.

'Perhaps, in the conversation with the vendor, you could slip into it - without actually lying - that the purchaser is somebody famous?' Graziella suggested.

His laughter sounded like a rattlesnake.

'I like that very much, Signorina. You can rely on me… Might I ask what you intend to do with the house?'

'I want to make it into an *albergo*,' she told him.

'Excellent. There is a need for a good *albergo*,' he commented. 'Now, I need your signature, to say that you have instructed me to act on your behalf, then let's put in an offer, to the agent, and see where it takes us, shall we?'

CHAPTER 44

NOW

ROSA

Today, Mama almost set fire to the house.

I had not long arrived, and had gone directly to her room. We chatted while she did her hair and put on makeup, then I noticed a strange, sulphuric odour, emanating from the kitchen.

'What's that smell?' I asked.

She sniffed the air. 'I can't smell anything. Maybe it's outside. They've been doing repairs to the lane.'

But she was recovering from a heavy cold, and her nose was still congested.

'It's definitely indoors,' I said. And went to investigate.

A barrage of smoke almost drove me back from the kitchen: thick, choking clouds of it. Sparks danced like red demons across the floor, igniting into small flames, which I stamped on. Coughing, I pushed through the fog. She had left a saucepan of milk boiling on a gas ring; a tea towel on the hob had caught alight. Charred fragments of it floated in the air, settling on surfaces. I didn't know what to do - then remembered the plastic washing up basin in the sink; I filled this with water and flung it over the worktop and floor. Immediately new sparks flared up, accompanied by an angry hissing, and it seemed that I had only made things worse. Frantic, I refilled the basin - time and time again, until the floor was submerged under inches of grey water, which no sparks or flames could survive. Then I became conscious of a different smell. And before another disaster could occur, I switched off the gas ring.

I was leaning against the wall, surveying the wreckage when Mama appeared in the doorway.

'*Madre*, what happened?' she said, holding up her hands in horror.

When I told her, she pulled a face, and punched her fist into her palm. Then she went into the garden, though it was raining. I followed her.

'Leave me *cara*, if you don't mind,' she said.

And I did as she requested, and set about clearing up the mess.

CHAPTER 45

THEN
EXIT THE CARLUCCIOS

"*Ciao Roberto,*
I hope for you happy birthday, and is very good occasion," Graziella wrote ten days before their mutual birthday, with the aid of the dictionary and phrase book next to her. "*I think many time for when we are child, and we laugh much. I am wish for you the good health.*
Felicitations, Graziella"

It had taken her a long time to draft the message, as she sought the appropriate word and its spelling. If her dream were accurate, then he would have a fine time teasing her about her English, as she used to tease him. But that would be to presume he would receive the card and, if he did, that he would reply. Both seemed unlikely.

The card had a view of the *Isola* on it; and she enclosed a photograph of herself - she had debated over this, particularly as he might be married - but then she thought that it was too bad.

She was about to seal the envelope, when she thought for a second, then added a postscript:

"*I have not husband, but I have beautiful child, name Rosa.*"

It was important to her that he understood the status quo. If the truth deterred him, then so be it.

She sealed the envelope, kissing it for luck, and posted the card in the letterbox.

⟞⟝⟞⟝⟞

Completion of the sale took place a few days into the new year. The Carluccios would be no more. They were leaving the *Isola*. And good riddance most people said.

Nobody seemed to know where they were going. The florist thought they were heading for Cefalù where Giorgio, their son, was raking it in, as a lawyer. According to Annunciata herself, they were no longer estranged and he had agreed to help.

Unlikely, disagreed the hairdresser. More probable they were going to Catania, where the daughter had been living, since the demise of her extremely old, extremely rich, husband. She and her father were very close.

However, the postmistress, had it on good authority that they were moving into a small apartment in the wrong part of Palermo, which the former mayor had used as a love nest. And Maria Alberta's sources were usually the most reliable.

The village was buzzing with talk as to the identity of the famous person who had bought the property. Another pop singer? Maybe a film star?

Villagers stood about, watching four burly men carry out crate, after crate, after crate from the house, then loading them onto two lorries. The former mayor was shouting at everybody in turn, his wife, the removal men, the inquisitive bystanders.

'Get out of my way, get out of my way, have you come to gloat?' He bellowed at them all.

Nobody took the slightest notice of him, and the crowd grew bigger and noisier, and called out obscenities in return.

266

Graziella experienced a twinge of pity for her aunt, half hidden in the shadows. She looked old; haggard from disillusion. But this was the woman who had made her life misery. When had her aunt ever demonstrated pity towards *her*? Graziella hardened her heart: her aunt was merely getting what she deserved.

The ferry was in and had been offloaded. Their job done, the removal men drove the two lorries, with the Carluccios' worldly possessions, to the harbour, up the ferry's ramp, and down into the bowels of the boat.

Annunciata emerged hesitantly from the shadows. All that remained now, was for the exiting owner to hand over the keys to the notary. Annunciata took them from her pocket and passed them to her husband - who elbowed her out of the way, with a glare. The notary waddled over and took the bunch of keys from him, with a polite, '*Grazie.*'

A grunt came in response.

The onlookers had grown bored; disappointed that they weren't any closer to learning the identity of the mystery purchaser. Then, just as they were deciding it was time to go back to work; just as the Carluccios were about to set off, on foot, for the ferry, Graziella walked up to the house.

'What is *she* doing here?' the former mayor demanded.

The notary passed the sets of keys to Graziella.

She jangled them back and forth.

'Welcome to my *albergo*,' she announced.

And, as pre-arranged with the journalist from the *Gazzetta*, his camera was at the ready, and he was able to home in on the aghast expressions on the faces of the previous owners.

CHAPTER 46

NOW

ROSA

'I've had a bit of an accident,' Mama said on the phone, sounding barely audible.

I was less than calm. 'What kind of accident?'

'I was hurrying to the phone... I fell.'

I had been dreading this. 'Ah no. Are you still on the floor?'

'Yes. I think my ankle is broken.'

As a vet, she would know. I could hear her wincing in pain, down the phone line, and her long releases of breath, in an attempt to alleviate it.

'I'm coming over now,' I told her. 'Give me ten minutes.'

'I rang 999. The ambulance should be here soon.'

'Please get the paramedics to wait, if they arrive first, then I can follow in my car,' I said.

When there was no reply, I was worried: 'Are you there Mama?'

'Yes, *cara* ... *Cara*, I'm so sorry to be such a nuisance.'

And her apology was a blade driving through me.

'Don't apologise. Don't you *dare* apologise, Mama. Just... just don't you *dare*. You are NOT a nuisance.'

A fortnight has passed since then. I remind myself - and her - how comparatively lucky she was; it could have been her hip; she might have had to be encased in plaster to the thigh, instead of just below the knee.

She tells me to shut up.

'If you don't have anything intelligent to talk about, then don't speak at all,' she says.

Against her wishes, I organised a live-in carer for her.

The first woman lasted a day and a half. Within seconds she had forgotten Mama's name and kept calling her Gretel. Her own name was Daisy, and she was extremely overweight.

'How are we getting on, Gretel, dearie? Do we need the lav yet?' she asked, while I was there.

I saw Mama's eyes narrow. I waited.

'When I was a student at veterinary college, I had to treat a cow suffering from bloat after gorging on spring grass,' Mama said, in that very precise English of hers. 'Its name was Daisy. It became known as Daisy the Fat Cow. You have prompted me to remember her,' she said, her eyebrows arched with innuendo.

The poor woman's complexion had gone a deep, magenta shade. I thought she might cry. When we were on our own, I rebuked Mama, she denied all knowledge of having made the remark. But then, moments later, she muttered: 'Anyhow, she does look like a cow. She should go on a diet.'

I rang the care agency: 'There seems to be a personality clash between my mother and Daisy,' I said.

Daisy packed her bags with obvious relief. The following day her replacement arrived. Mama bristled in readiness.

But how could anyone fail to love appropriately named Truthful? As far as I'm concerned, she could stay forever. Tall, with skin like dark silk, apple cheeks, and a lilting voice, she is a PhD psychology student, taking a year out to fund her studies. What could be better? I feel as though I can breathe.

Mama took to her immediately. We have even done a bit more on the book. However, her heart isn't in it, and it's difficult to keep her on track. It's a whole year since we started on the project, and I did not think then, when I mooted the idea to her, that it would take anything like this length of time. Nor did I know how all-consuming it would become to me, but that is what has happened. When I am working on it, I find myself living Mama's experiences. So immersed do I become, that it is as if I have stepped into her skin. It's as though we are interchangeable. As though I *am* her; it is the most peculiar sensation.

I have learned a lot about Mama on our journey, enabling me better to understand her. And, too, I have learned a lot about myself. Most of all, it has helped me to understand our relationship.

Transcribing her story has truly been an act of love and, as it draws towards its conclusion, I realise how I shall miss it.

But that single, enormous, question remains unanswered: who is, or was, my father?

The day is overcast, but dry. For a change of scene, I take Mama out in the wheelchair, with both dogs keeping pace alongside.

'I'm a bit tired now, *cara*' she says after a while. 'I should like to go home, if you don't mind.'

So we turn back. Her head lolls.

My poor Mama is much reduced nowadays, and sometimes a pleading look will enter her eye. I hate that look and fear it. I would rather not know what it signifies. Frequently, words seep away from her, and sentences die. She no longer attempts to resurrect them: it is too frustrating for her, too much effort. The curtailed sentence dangles like an irritating loose thread. Her resignation is a new thing. It is far worse than her resentment.

But intermittently there will be a reminder, a spark of her old self, and it can last for many minutes, before it extinguishes.

Just as we turn into the driveway, the sun comes out from behind clouds. Mama lifts her face up to it.

She smiles softly.

'I knew him straight away,' she says, in a dreamy tone.

'Who, Mama? Who are we talking about?'

'Papa, of course,' she says, in a normal voice. 'Your Papa. Only ever him.'

CHAPTER 47

THEN
THE ENGLISHMAN

Work on the house had not begun immediately. It had been delayed by the planning authorities. Consent had been required for change of usage, and this had necessitated the approval of two separate bodies. Graziella had been warned that they were a pedantic bunch, but hadn't been prepared for the extent. They nitpicked over every detail. She suspected it was because she was a woman. They were all elderly men, and it was obvious they disapproved of her.

Finally, in early April, the decorators were able to start. It would take approximately six weeks, the contractor had told her. He had been a good friend of Stefano; he had quoted her a fair price for cash, and she knew she could trust him to carry out her instructions and oversee the job.

She was glad, now, of the delay, and used the time productively. She ordered furniture, lighting, and bathroom equipment for the *albergo* from a cut-price store in Palermo, whose catalogue she had seen; bought metres of white muslin and calico, and made beautiful curtains which the light shone through; and her mother's old sewing machine once more whirred until late into the night.

Her daily routine was unchanged. She got up every morning at five - earlier, if she was sausage making or baking. The next hour would be taken up with the animals, the chickens, and attending to the vegetables. Then she would wake Rosa; they would have their breakfast together, and Graziella would take her to school - either on foot or on the Lambretta, depending on the time.

Today was no different, yet - and she could not have explained it - she felt it to be so.

She chatted for a few minutes to her old school teacher, then she walked along the esplanade, and crossed the road to Mama Lucia's. The aroma of espresso coffee welcomed her. Angelina was outside, wiping the tabletops. She looked up.

'*Ciao*, Graziella… Mama is in the kitchen,' she said.

Graziella walked through the café. Carlotta was rolling out pizzas.

'*Buongiorno* Graziella… Coffee?'

'*Per favore.*'

They sat down together.

'I feel that something is going to happen today,' Graziella said.

'Good or bad?'

'Good, I think. Yes, good. I can't explain it.'

Business was steady through the day, which was the most one could hope for at this time of year. The pop star, dressed from top to toe in white as usual, swaggered in, with a man he introduced as his agent. They were both smoking enormous cigars. The agent looked Graziella up and down, as though assessing the worth of a car.

'You could be a movie star,' he told her. And he took a card from his pocket and gave it to her. 'Call me,' he said.

She handed it back to him.

'Thank you, but I don't want to be a movie star.'

He looked astounded: 'Every girl wants to be a movie star. It's every girl's dream,' he protested.

'Not this one,' she said lightly.

The *Contessa* and her friend sat where they always did, under the shade of the awning and watched the antics of the young mastiff and Elvis, as they played. A group of men pored over charts and spreadsheets in a corner of the bar, before turning to the serious matter of eating. A couple of fishermen had a heated argument over whose patch of sea belonged to whom, and they almost came to blows; and a few tourists wandered in, fresh off the ferry.

Graziella prepared *antipasti*, and platters of seafood served with a lime dip; she poured carafes of wine, and chatted with customers, smiling all the while; and that same inexplicable feeling that something was going to happen, persisted.

By siesta time, the café had all but emptied. The jukebox played to itself. It was early, too soon to fetch Rosa, and she took off her shoes, changed into shorts, and walked down the esplanade's ramp, onto the almost deserted beach. The dog rolled in the sand, chased into the sea, then tore back to her, before making a circuit of the beach, and returning to her. She laughed aloud at his antics; and tried to imagine what it must feel like to be him; to feel the sand between the pads of his paws, and to want to run for the sheer joy of it. Inadvertently, she sighed, as her thoughts took her down a reflective path. Her one-time dream of university, and studying to be a vet, seemed a world away.

She glanced round - had felt someone behind her, as though she was being followed. But there was nobody.

She had brought a bag with her - for shells. She was collecting them to decorate the *albergo*. And now her thoughts were diverted to the night of Stefano's birthday, when she had told him of her idea. He had left her bed, happy; not an inkling of fate's plan for him. Or did he? she wondered, recalling that remark of his, which had turned out to be so prescient.

She had half filled the bag with shells of all sizes when, from behind her, a voice said, 'Boo!'

She wheeled round.

He stood there grinning. Time peeled back.

'Would you like an aniseed ball?' he asked, in perfect Italian, before she had a chance to speak. 'They're hard to find nowadays.' He held out a small bag.

She took one, but did not put it in her mouth. As she stared at him, her smile grew. His voice was mellifluous, as in her dream, but he was clean-shaven, and recognisable as the boy she had known. His hair was still gold. His eyes still laughed. The restrictive calliper had gone, and in its place he wore an orthopaedic boot, which allowed more movement, but still looked uncomfortable. He carried a plain stick. These details all registered on her within the space of a second or two.

'It's really you,' she stated, laughing.

'Indeed it is,' he said. 'Aren't you going to have your aniseed ball?'

'Later,' she said, and stuffed it in her pocket.

'Perhaps you would prefer these?'

He had bought her lilies - she hadn't noticed them on the ground behind him. It was only the second time in her life she had been given flowers.

'Thank you, they are so beautiful.'

She was still recovering from the shock of seeing him. She longed to throw her arms around him, as she would have done when they were children. However they were no longer children.

'Am I allowed to give you a hug?' he asked, and she laughed, remembering his English manners.

'Of course.'

His arms wrapped round her, warm and secure. It felt completely natural, and her heart turned.

They sat together on the beach. 'What is the dog's name,' he asked.

'Elvis,' she replied.

'A!' He had a bark of a laugh. 'You like Elvis?'

'Yes.'

'And this Elvis has clearly had a bad time,' he remarked.

'He was a stray. He was in a dreadful state, so I took him in,' she said. 'I have lots of animals.'

'You always liked animals. You wanted to be a vet.'

'I did want to… But life got in the way.'

'It's not too late.'

'Yes it is'

He leant on an elbow to appraise her: 'There is much to catch up on, Graziella. I dreamed of you,' he said, in a rush. 'It was a few months ago, before I got your card. It was the weirdest dream. I was carrying you on a kind of sedan.'

She sat bolt upright, '*Madre* - but I don't believe it,' she exclaimed. 'I had the same dream, at around the same time.'

They stared, heat flushed through her body.

'Why did you stop writing to me,' she asked him.

He frowned. 'But I didn't - at least not for long. I stopped writing for a month or two, as I was going through a difficult patch, but then I resumed. I apologised, and explained everything to you. I must have written a dozen letters too, before giving up. I assumed I had offended you.'

'But I never got those letters, I only received the earlier ones,' she said. 'So then I stopped writing.'

'What a confusing muddle,' he said.

'It would have been my *zia's* doing,' Graziella said slowly. 'She must have intercepted the letters and destroyed them.'

'Your *zia*? But why? What has she got to do with it?'

'Like you say, there is much to discuss. And you? What are you doing now?'

'I'm a hospital doctor. I want to specialise in paediatrics.'

'*Un dottore!* I shall have to curtsey before you,' she said.

He reddened. 'I'm still pretty junior,' he confessed.

And she recollected how self-effacing he had always been.

'I often wondered about you - whether you would become a doctor. And you have. You are very clever.'

'Thank you, Graziella. I appreciate that.'

His seriousness was belied by the glint in his eyes. He lay back and turned his face to the sun. 'It's good to feel the warmth. It's been so cold in England.'

'Have you only arrived today?'

'Yes... I'm staying in an apartment. It seems fine, but I hardly noticed it. I just dumped my luggage, then went in search of you.'

'Aw, you must be tired after the journey,' she observed.

She lay down in the sand beside him.

'I was just impatient to see you,' he said. 'I felt like a teenage boy again... But I shouldn't be telling you that, should I? I wouldn't score any points for tactics.'

'The teenage boy has become a beautiful man,' she said softly, stroking the blond hairs on his wrist. 'Who cares about tactics? We are both adults.'

And she thought that her mother whispered in her ear: *Go with your heart, cara.*

'You were always forthright, Graziella,' Roberto recalled. 'You never suffered fools. That fierce look would come into your eyes. You didn't care what people thought of you.'

'You remember all that about me?'

'And more. I remember everything,' he said, and sat up again, in order to look at her properly.

'I went to the *casetta* first, but nobody was there,' he told her. 'Just the oddest collection of animals. Then I saw the postmistress, and asked where I might find you. She directed me to Mama Lucia's café...'

And now, thought Graziella, *it will be all round the town that I have an English visitor.*

But she found that she did not mind.

'And I was on my way there, when I saw you,' Roberto said. 'So you work at the café, then?'

'Actually, I own it,' she said, unable to hide her pride.

'Good God, Graziella,' he swore in English, 'how did ...'

She cut him short: 'I shall explain later,' she said, getting to her feet. 'As you say, we have years to catch up on, but now I have to fetch my daughter from school.'

'Oh yes, of course,' he said in a deferential tone.

He stood up also. She recognised in his expression that particular look he wore when he wanted something but didn't like to ask, and it filled her with a rush of tenderness.

'Do you want to come with me?'

'Will she mind?'

'No, but she will ask you a thousand questions.'

He gave another of his barks of laughter; then he took hold of both her hands and regarded her in an assessing manner, and she felt her eyes merge into his, and her throat locked.

'And if she asks who I am ...' he spoke with slow deliberation '... what would you *like* me to tell her?'

His meaning was clear. She licked her lips; had the strangest sense of being back in her dream. Perhaps he would fade out and disappear.

But the pressure of his smooth-skinned hands around hers reassured her; and the perfume from the lilies was real enough.

'I would *like* you to tell her,' she replied, with the same emphasis on the word, 'that we were childhood sweethearts, and that you never stopped thinking of me.' She watched his expression carefully; the pleasure in it. She continued: 'But it's too soon for her to digest that. I think you should simply tell her that we were child-hood friends.'

'That's good enough for me,' he said.

As they walked to the school, heads turned.

'Is it because of my limp?' Roberto asked her.

'No, of course not, how can you think that? It's because people aren't used to seeing me with a strange man. You have no idea what this place is like.'

'But you're happy here aren't you?'

She shrugged. 'It's home.'

'And your parents... How are they?' he enquired, as they approached the school building.

She stopped walking for a moment. It seemed incredible that he didn't know. But naturally he would not. How would he?

'Graziella, what is it? What's happened?'

'There was an accident,' she told him. 'They were both killed. I'll have to explain later.'

He looked shocked: 'But that is awful. How long ... '

At that moment a bell rang. The children poured from the building, into the alley, laughing and chattering like excited star-lings. Through the iron gate, Graziella spotted Rosa waving to her.

'I'll have to explain later,' she said hurriedly. 'I promise we will have time later, just the two of us.'

Roberto hung back at a discrete distance, as Rosa hugged her mother's legs.

'My story was read out in class. It got a star,' she gabbled, disre-garding the man a few metres away.

'*Brava, cara.* I told you it was good, didn't I?' Graziella praised her.

She beckoned to Roberto, and Rosa realised the golden-haired man was with her mother. He had eyes that laughed, she thought, as he came forward to meet her.

'*Cara*, this is Roberto. He is a doctor from England, and his surname is the same as ours,' Graziella introduced him.

'Is it also Lupo?' Rosa asked, addressing him.

'Yes, except it is in English,' he said.

'How do you say Lupo in English?'

'Wolf,' he replied. And he snarled, and pretended to bare his teeth, making her laugh.

'Are you a friend of Mama's?'

'Yes. A good friend, from a long time ago.' He glanced at Graziella as he spoke.

'Mama had another good friend, called Stefano, but he died.'

'That is sad. I'm very sorry,' Roberto said, judiciously. And he glanced again at Graziella - who made a helpless gesture.

'What was your story about, Rosa?' he asked, to divert her.

'An ant... He had been trodden on so he takes his revenge.'

'And how did he do that?'

'He finds this magic Lupo stick hanging from a tree, so he makes a wish with it, and turns himself into a big mosquito, and he stings everybody who has ever stung him.'

Roberto burst into laughter. 'But that is a quite splendid story. No wonder you got a star for it. Really, you must be a writer when you grow up, Rosa,' he said.

Graziella watched them together; she could well imagine he would make a fine doctor, with his gentle humour, natural empathy, and that deep, soothing voice, which she could not get used to.

She knew she would never forget this moment, when, outside her daughter's school, she had fallen irrevocably in love with the English boy from her childhood.

He turned back to her. Abruptly, he stopped laughing. There was no mistaking the expression on her face.

They stared at one another.

Smiled, stared… smiled, stared.

Unaware of what had just occurred, Rosa said: 'We have a magic Lupo stick at home. We found it hanging from the fig tree, where Mama says her papa used to sit.'

'How extraordinary,' Roberto commented solemnly. 'That is indeed extraordinary.'

⛧

'You look radiant, and I know why,' Carlotta greeted her.

Graziella laid down the flowers, and the bag of shells, on the worktop. She gave an exasperated little laugh.

'*Madre*, surely it can't already have circulated? That must be a record by anyone's standards.'

'And surely,' Carlotta responded, 'you should know better than to be surprised, Graziella.'

'Apparently so.'

'Was he the English boy from the family who camped near your *casetta*?'

'Yes, that is him. How did you know?'

'Maria Alberta described him. She said he was blond and had a limp.'

'*Porca miseria!*' Graziella shook her head. 'Does the woman really have nothing better to do?'

'Probably not. Gossip is her life's blood, and she would die without it. But she is on your side nowadays, Graziella.'

'Maybe. Anyway...' She combed her fingers through her hair. 'I have a favour to ask. I was wondering if ....' She stopped again.

Carlotta made it easier for her: 'Would you like Rosa to stay with us tonight?'

Grateful, she nodded. 'We have years to make up for. So much talking to do.'

'And so much of something else,' said Carlotta.

Graziella threw her one of her looks.

⛧

Many people remembered the English family from twelve years previously, and in particular, the golden-haired boy with the funny leg, who had almost died when a *vipera* had sunk its fangs into him. The father had charged through the sleeping town with the boy in his arms, yelling for the doctor. And that evening, several of those, including Dottore Rugolo, had gathered at Mama Lucia's, curious to see him. They slapped him on the back as though he were a returning prodigal son, complimenting him that he had become a fine looking fellow, and praising his Italian.

They brought with them their individual recollections: the school teacher remembered how all the girls in the class had wanted to sit next to him, but Graziella had insisted that, as his friend, it was her right.

Maria Alberta, fanning herself to keep her menopausal flushes at bay, remembered airmail letters bandying back and forth between the two children.

Raffaella had baked a cinnamon cake for the occasion, and recalled Roberto offering to carry Graziella's school books for her.

'She refused,' the wimple-clad nun added; but that was not the point.

He looked utterly taken aback by the attention, Graziella thought, sorry for him, but amused.

'Have you forgotten what Italians are like?' she whispered to him - at which he smiled.

Dottore Rugolo asked what he did as a job.

'Actually, I'm a doctor,' he replied, rubbing the side of his head, in that self-conscious little manner that she recalled well.

'In London?' the *dottore* enquired.

'Not any more. I was a student there, at Guy's Hospital, but when I qualified I moved to Oxford. I prefer living there. It's a lovely city.'

Rugolo nodded. 'So I have heard. The university is famous, of course. You are in general practice?'

'Actually, I am doing paediatrics,' Roberto replied.

'*Eccellente!*' the old doctor approved.

'There's some way to go yet,' Roberto said, not wishing to exaggerate his status.

'Well, I am sure that with hard work, you will succeed. And without wishing to be personal, who better than yourself could understand what it is like for a child to spend long periods in hospital? It cannot have been easy for you,' Rugolo observed.

'I would be lying if I said it was,' he admitted. 'But the staff were amazing. They made life as bearable for me as they could. Without a doubt my choice of career was influenced by my own experiences. I wanted to put something back into society. I want to help children such as myself. Though, thank God, they will not be suffering from polio.'

'Thank God,' echoed Dottore Rugolo.

Graziella went into the kitchen.

'Your face,' Carlotta said, as they chopped vegetables into a great pile. 'I've never seen you look like this.'

'Like what?' she asked.

'So happy.' Carlotta said.

'I'm nearly always happy.'

'Don't be difficult, Graziella. You know what I mean. And I am going to risk you getting cross, and say something else.'

'What is that?'

'If you and Stefano had got together, it would have been a mistake. I realise that now. You need somebody who is your intellectual equal. Someone like Roberto.'

Graziella felt a stab of disloyalty toward Stefano.

'*Comunque...* My life is my business,' she said.

Carlotta shrugged. The pair had become close over the years, and were forever bantering. 'Oh, by the way' she said, 'that wretched seagull stole the last of the pastrami. I swear I shall wring its neck one day.'

'Don't you dare. The customers love him.'

'You shouldn't encourage him to come inside.'

At that moment there was a scraping sound at the window: the gull was pecking at the pane to be let in.

Laughing, Graziella carried out a platter of seafood.

Roberto was standing in the centre of the room, expertly shuffling a pack of cards a customer had let him borrow.

'I want you all to watch what I am doing very carefully, so you can satisfy yourselves I am not cheating,' he addressed the circle of people. 'You are happy that I borrowed the cards from a total stranger to me, therefore they cannot be marked?'

They all concurred.

'Very well,' he said, assuming an air of solemnity, to heighten the atmosphere. 'Shortly I am intending to demonstrate my telepathic skills to you. But before I go any further, I need a volunteer to assist me...'

He cast about the room. His gaze lit on Graziella.

'Ah, no, Roberto,' she protested.

'Ah, si.'

Taking her hand, he positioned her.

'You need to be a bit more central,' he said, gently pushing her. 'A bit to the right... Stop... And forward a little ... And a tiny bit more. That's perfect!'

By now, they were all laughing. He had their full attention, and they watched as he made a fan of the cards, holding it up for everyone to see.

'Next, I am going to ask my very lovely assistant to choose any card.'

His gaze held hers. The gold flecks in his eyes danced.

He continued: 'Under no circumstances must I see the card of your choice - this is all about telepathy, remember, so Graziella, I would like you to blindfold me... Oh, I forgot ... I'm not wearing a tie. Does anybody have one I could use as a blindfold?'

This provoked more laughter.

Dottore Rugolo stepped forward, undoing his tie.

'Thank you,' Roberto said. 'In fact, Dottore, I should like you to remain here, as witness. Graziella, please tie the blindfold round my eyes now, and Dottore, please verify that it is in place, and would be impossible for me to see through it.

They did as requested. The room was steeped in quiet.

'Please take a card, Graziella,' Roberto instructed, extending his arm.

She took one, showed it to Dottore Rugolo and passed it back to Roberto.

He then replaced it in the pack, which he proceeded to shuffle, before removing the blindfold.

Please let it work, Graziella prayed.

His forehead furrowed as he riffled through the pack, muttering to himself. Then his face cleared. He drew out a Jack of Clubs.

'I believe this was the card you picked, Graziella?' He passed it to her.

Speechless, she showed it to Dottore Rugolo.

'Now, that is very clever,' he said, shaking his head in bafflement. 'How in heaven did you do that?'

'Telepathy, like I told you,' he answered - grinning as they all clapped.

※+※

It was comparatively early. The sky was the colour of a ripe peach. Hand in hand, they walked to the *casetta*. They had attempted to slip away from the café with as little fuss as possible but, inevitably, nudges and lewd comments accompanied their early departure.

'Speaking of magic,' Graziella said to Roberto, 'I know it is your Lupo stick I currently have in my possession.'

'I don't know what you are talking about Graziella,' he told her.

'I am being serious Roberto,' she said. 'I don't understand why you went off without seeing me. What was the point of just leaving a stick for me?'

He held her face between his hands. 'I did see you,' he said. 'Almost as soon as I got off the ferry, I saw you and Rosa. You were larking about in the sea. You looked so happy... It was stupid, I realise now, but I assumed ...'

'You assumed I was married?'

'Exactly so. Then I had the idea of leaving the stick somewhere you would find it. At least then, I reasoned, you would realise I had kept my word about returning to the *Isola* as an adult. You remember my pledge?'

'Of course. And at the time, adulthood seemed a lifetime away,' she recollected, in a tone of tender reminiscence.

'The ferry to Palermo was still in,' Roberto said, 'and I managed to get onto it just as it was about to sail.'

'Lost chances,' she murmured.

'Yes, but I'm here now.'

'Yes.'

The last of the light slid from the sky.

'Listen,' Roberto said.

And as she spoke, the cicadas struck up with their orchestra.

Back at the *casetta*, they all but fell into each other's arms. His mouth tasted not of aniseed balls, but peppermint; the scent of his skin reminded her of bamboo wood. She wanted to retain the sweetness of his mouth, the sensation of his tongue exploring hers, and wanted, cat-like, to nibble the soft fullness of his lower lip.

I love you, love you, love you, each of them said.

She helped him up the ladder to her room.

He undressed her as though she were made of porcelain, and when he gazed at her, it did not feel strange or intrusive. She wanted him to find her beautiful.

286

When she undressed him, he was embarrassed by his withered and scarred leg, and apologised for it.

'Don't be so ridiculous. That is absolutely *ridiculous*,' she chastised him.

He smiled at her ferocity.

As in her dream, his fingers and tongue explored the topography of her body as though he were blind and, instinctively, she reciprocated.

'You are so beautiful.'

'You are too... No, don't roll your eyes. You are...You *are*.'

His upper body was strong, and he lifted her gently onto the bed.

As he penetrated her she cried out in pleasure. His soft voice was hypnotic in her ear: *Is that nice, darling? And that? And this...*

She arched her back and drew him deeper into her, and it was as it had been in her dream. He held her tightly as she came, and called her "his darling" again, in English. Afterwards, spent, they lay in a damp tangle together, and she wanted to cry with happiness.

'My Roberto,' she crooned, as he stroked the angles of her cheeks, and she nuzzled her face into his neck.

'The building where you live - is it tall and narrow, and made of red brick?' She asked him. 'And you have lots of books everywhere?'

'Yes. You've described my flat in Oxford. But how did you know? How on earth could you possibly have known?'

'I saw it in my dream.'

'That's remarkable.'

'And in my dream you also spoke perfect Italian. Where did you learn it?'

'I became best friends with an Italian medical student, and he taught me. I told him the reason was to impress a beautiful girl. Being a romantic, he appreciated that.'

Graziella laughed lightly.

'Tell me about your parents,' Roberto said. 'How did they die? And what happened to you then?'

'You could be here forever.'

'I can think of worse fates.'

'The accident happened on the coast road…' she began.

She missed out nothing. When she told him about the rape, tears came into his eyes, and he covered his face in shock. She told him about Gino, and finding herself pregnant, and inheriting the café-bar from Mama Lucia. She explained about Stefano - bringing him up to the present, and the purchase of the mayor's house.

'Remarkable,' he would interject from time to time - a favourite word of his, she had noticed. Twice, he swore in English, smacking his hand down on the bed.

'What you have been through,' he stated, gripping her hand, massaging the knuckles.

'That act that was done to me… Rosa must never learn of it.'

'Of course not. Never, never.'

'She has to believe she was born of love.'

'Absolutely.'

'When you left that day with your parents I couldn't see you off, I was too upset,' Graziella said, her voice sleepy. 'For weeks after you'd gone I didn't know what to do with myself. I felt completely aimless. And I thought about you often. Through everything that happened, over the years, I never forgot you.'

'It was the same for me,' he said.

'I was horrible to my parents for several months. I used to think I was at least partly to blame for what happened.'

'What did happen?'

'My beautiful, sweet mother killed herself. I was at a friend's, and my father had just returned from a cricket match. I found him cutting her down. He was bellowing like a crazed bear.'

'*Povero* Roberto. How dreadful.'

'It was pretty tough going,' he admitted, typically understated. 'It was why I didn't write for a while.'

'And your father?'

'He threw himself into his painting and drank himself into a stupor on a daily basis. He died nearly a year ago. Unsurprisingly, his liver packed up.'

'How much has happened to both of us,' she reflected.

'And now - where do we go from here?' he asked her.

'What do you mean?' All at once she felt worried.

'Well, I can only stay for another eight days, then I have to return to the UK.'

She said nothing.

'You and Rosa could come with me,' he ventured.

'But we can't. How can we? Rosa has school… I have a business to run.'

He pulled her close to him again, and curled his toes round hers; kissed her eyes. 'We will work something out, Graziella, *mia cara,*' he soothed her. 'But for the next eight days, let's try to make the most of our time together,' he said.

The ferry had unloaded its cargo. The usual din of livestock and humans competed with the dissonant metallic banging from trucks as they were driven over the ramp, and the whining of winches. The black-clad widows whom one could never have imagined being young, wept at the return of their middle-aged sons. Bewildered tourists, blinking in the brightness, sweating in the blanket of heat, stood about, uncertain where to go next, and clung onto their suitcases for dear life. Within half an hour most of the people had dispersed, and the bleating, braying, mooing, clucking animals had been carted off. There followed a few minutes of comparative calm, before the intake of passengers gathered for the outward journey.

This time round, Graziella was at the port to see Roberto leave. This time, though she hated the prospect of him going, at least she knew he would be returning. A date had been fixed for two months hence. It saddened her, however, that he would be missing the party for the *albergo's* opening.

'I wish you could be there, but I appreciate your work commitments make it impossible,' she said in a thoughtful tone. 'So I was thinking... maybe I should postpone it. For the sake of a couple of weeks it seems silly not to.'

'No way,' he protested forcefully. 'That would be just throwing away business. I would feel terrible if you did that. Promise me you won't.'

'Call me "darling" in English, and I shall consider it,' she said.

The gold flecks in his eyes danced. 'With pleasure... Darling. My darling. My beautiful darling.'

'*Va bene* I shall not postpone it then.'

'I shall be there with you in spirit,' he told her. 'I shall picture you bustling back and forth, being the perfect hostess.'

'It's not fair - you can picture me in context, but I can't you.'

'Well I spend most of my time at the hospital, on the ward. Just picture me with a stethoscope round my neck.'

'I've never been in a hospital.'

'You're lucky,' he said, with feeling. And touched the wooden handle of his stick. People were already starting to board the ferry, in order to get the best seats. A few feet away, the captain, his confidence boosted by the gold-braided cap which concealed his bald patch, tore himself away from the woman who had been flirting with him, and made for the bridge. When not in uniform he was known to be a shy man. He came into the café sometimes for a pizza or light snack, and if Graziella was serving him, he was incapable of looking her in the eye.

'You look worried. A penny for your thoughts,' Roberto said in English. He had taught her the aphorism.

'*No, non c'è niente,*' she replied in Italian.

'Graziella, I know you. There is absolutely never "nothing" going on in your brain. What's wrong?'

'I *am* worried…. How can this work - us, I mean - if we are in two different countries?'

'It *will* work out. Trust me. I have been thinking about it. When we next see each other we will talk about it.'

'And I'm scared I won't see you again; that something bad will happen.'

'But it won't, I promise. And I shall write. And phone.'

And now stewards were ushering the last of the passengers aboard the boat.

'My beautiful darling,' Roberto said in her ear, as they clutched onto each other; and she felt his voice vibrating against her throat.

Then, refusing the help of a well-intentioned steward, he hoisted his rucksack over his shoulders, turned to gaze at Graziella one more time, and limped across the metal brow, onto the boat. He was the last passenger to board and, standing on the busy jetty, she lost sight of him. The brow was lifted clear, the ramp drawn up, and the doors closed. With a couple of friendly honks, the ferry lumbered slowly out of the harbour. The gap between sea and land widened and the boat gathered pace. Onlookers and passengers alike were waving, and her eyes scanned the homogenous mass of diminishing figures for a glimpse of him, and she wished she were a giantess.

Then she saw him, his multi-coloured T-shirt. It was as though a magnetic compass had been guiding her. He was waving his red and white spotted handkerchief at her.

Frantically, she waved back. Her heart was full.

CHAPTER 48

HELL

Something was wrong. The animals were behaving oddly. At just gone four in the morning, she had been woken by Caspar yowling. It was an unearthly sound, such as a cat might make if it were being skinned alive, and it sent a cold sensation down the length of her spine. She had not seen him since. There was little point in trying to return to sleep; she would have got up shortly anyhow. Today was the opening for the *albergo*, and there was much to prepare in readiness for the evening's party.

Her first job of the day, and the one she enjoyed least, was to clean out and feed Mama Lucia's parrot. She had removed it from the café after it had jabbed its beak into Carlotta's bottom, and drawn blood. Carlotta had threatened to leave.

'That greedy seagull is bad enough, but I'll not put up with having my flesh ripped by a parrot,' Carlotta told her.

Graziella knew it was no idle threat this time.

The parrot sat at the far end of its perch, as if he had been carved of stone. Only his panic-stricken eyes moved, darting this way and that. Iridescent green feathers floated round the room, and she realised he had been plucking out his plumage. Tentatively, she stretched out her arm. He made no attempt to lunge at her.

'What is it? Are you ill?' She said, pulling out the tray in order to empty it.

The bird sidled up to her then, and she braced herself. But instead of attacking her, he lowered his head, to have it scratched, as though in need of comfort.

Outside, the skinny finger of a new moon lingered, but despite the early hour, the mid-June sky already yielded a weak light, enabling her to see without a torch. Usually, when Elvis was first let out in the morning, he would tear round the yard a couple of times, but this morning he stuck close to Graziella's side, as though afraid, his tail between his legs, and whimpering intermittently. In their pen, the two boars were pacing restlessly back and forth emitting shrill cries of alarm. In its cage, the squirrel with the broken leg made a repetitive clacking sound. Only the chickens, when Graziella released them from their hutches, were unaffected, crowding round her, clamouring for their grain.

The obvious stress of the animals disturbed Graziella. She had a deep respect - learned from her father - for the finely tuned instincts of animals. They understood the rhythms of nature, and their highly developed sense of hearing and smell meant they could detect danger when humans could not.

And now, as the sky lightened, and the slumbering village began to rouse, Graziella went about her normal tasks with a feeling of unease that could not be banished.

She pulled up a few vegetables, set them aside and went to wake up her daughter.

'I was having a bad dream,' Rosa said, sitting up in confusion and rubbing sleep from her eyes.

Graziella knelt at the foot of the bed. 'What was it about, *cara?*' she asked.

Rosa wrinkled her forehead. The dream was fast ebbing from her. 'Well I can't remember much of it, but I couldn't find you. I was searching for you everywhere but there were hundreds of people, all just walking about, and you'd disappeared.' Her eyes filled.

'Well I'm here *cara*,' she said. 'You can pinch me if you like.'

But the ominous feeling in her was compounded.

They were earlier than usual, and dawdled on the way to the school. Rosa picked the pink flowers which grew in clumps in the wild area. She had with her the "magic stick" as she referred to it still. It was the last day of term, and the children were permitted to bring favourite objects to school.

'Hold the stick in its middle, so it doesn't drag on the ground and trip you up,' Graziella advised; and she recalled saying something similar to Roberto, when they were children. 'You won't let the boys run around with it, will you *cara*? I wouldn't want it to be damaged.'

'I shan't let them touch it,' she assured her mother. 'Anyway, they already know I can make it change into a serpent, which could bite them with its poisonous fangs.'

They had almost reached the school, when Rosa asked: 'Mama, what is Hell?'

'What made you ask that?' Graziella said, stalling.

'The other day some children were being naughty, and our class teacher told them that if they didn't behave, the devil would come for them and carry them off to Hell.'

'Well, that is nonsense,' Graziella said, in a firm tone. 'She had no right to scare you all.'

'But what is it? Where is it?'

'Hell is a horrible pit made of great flames that are stoked by the devil. But it only exists in storybooks. It is a made-up place. I promise there is no such place as Hell, and no such thing as the devil.'

'But my teacher says that in the bible...'

'Who do you believe and trust more, *cara*, your class teacher or your mama?'

'My mama - you - of course.'

They were at the school gates now. 'Take care of the magic stick,' Graziella reminded Rosa.

'It will take care of me,' Rosa replied lightly. Then, tossing a kiss to her mother, joined her friends.

Graziella watched her run indoors, where she was obscured by the shadows. She experienced a momentary, wistful twinge: her child was fast growing up.

From the school she went directly to Mama Lucia's. The *Isola* was in the midst of a heatwave, and the day was already sweltering, if rather overcast. The dog's behaviour continued to perturb her. Normally, when the weather was this extreme, he would seek the cool of indoors, where the fans would be going full blast, and he would lie beside it, clearly enjoying the sensation of it rippling his fur. But today he could not be enticed inside. Instead, he remained outside, looking dejected; his panting sounded like a pair of bellows.

'Poor Elvis is looking very sorry for himself this morning,' remarked Carlotta, who, though she pretended otherwise, had grown attached to the dog.

'I know. All the animals have been behaving strangely. To be honest it has been making me jumpy,' Graziella said.

'It's just the heatwave. It's getting to everyone. Well, it's certainly getting to me. There's bound to be a storm, and the animals can sense it.'

'Yes, I'm sure you're right,' Graziella concurred, and made an effort to pull herself together.

A couple of hours passed, as they settled companionably to the food preparations for both the café and *albergo*. Graziella rolled out pasta on the marble slab. The marble was pleasingly cool against her hands. The butcher arrived with their delivery, in a stinking mood because his mule had had the temerity to drop dead in the heat.

'The only compensation is that at least he'll make a good few salamis,' he said, throwing down a roughly wrapped side of pork onto the table, and only narrowly missing the rolled-out pasta.

Tourists wandered in; and the regulars. The three shrivelled old men drank Grappa and played dominoes beneath the cypress tree. Angelina scurried to and fro with ice creams, *antipasti* and cold drinks, and made sheep's eyes at a bespectacled German boy who, at first seemed bemused by this interest in him, then surreptitiously began to steal glances at her in return. The sea was dotted with swimmers, and the umbrella boy went up and down the length and breadth of the beach, offering shade to the wilting sunbathers, at an inflated price. Save for the record-breaking heat, all was as usual.

Maria Alberta delivered a telegram for Graziella.

'It's from England,' she announced, with a meaningful little smile.

Graziella waited for her to go, before tearing it open.

"Good luck for the party. I shall be thinking of you. See you in a fortnight my darling. All love, R. xxxx"

Smiling, she put it in the pocket of her dress.

'I'm off to the *albergo* now. I shall see you in a couple of hours,' she told Carlotta, who waved from the direction of the fridge.

'And do you want to come with me?' she addressed the dog, who had not moved from his position.

He understood the words "come with" and got up lethargically. Carlotta was right, she thought. The strange behaviour of the animals was down to nothing more than the heat. A heavy rainstorm was what was needed.

Elvis only followed her as far as the esplanade, and then stopped.

'*Cosa c'è?*' she said, stooping to stroke him.

He gave a feeble wag of his thin tail, and gazed at her with his yellow eyes, as though trying to convey information to her, then he ambled off to the beach. He seemed purposeful; to know what he was doing; and she watched him walk to the end of the sand where it was quiet. He flopped down by the rim of the sea, and appeared to be content there. He was a wise dog, she thought. Most probably, he had chosen that spot so he could cool off in the water when he wanted, untroubled by people. He was used to being independent; he would find his way home when some of the heat had left the day.

It was little more than a five-minute walk to the *albergo*, but the two baskets of food she was carrying were heavy, and she wished now that she had taken the Lambretta this morning. A bead of perspiration travelled down her arm, as she trudged up the winding slope leading to the *albergo*. She went up the three wide steps, with the pair of carriage lamps either side of them, and unlocked the yellow-painted front door. The dark, overcrowded, former mayor's house had been transformed into a welcoming place full of light and translucence. A faint whiff of paint clung to the pale walls. Lilies in tall glass vases were reflected in a shell-decorated mirror, where the mayor's portrait had frowned down, and beneath it, Annunciata's bucolic figurines had lent purpose to her life.

Walking through from the hall into the living room, she thought how guests would appreciate the aura of calm it exuded.

It was at this very moment, the room trembled underfoot.

There was no time to react; no time to escape outside. A second later, the entire room shook with the wrath of Thor behind it. Everything was toppling - china, glass, furniture, pictures, bronzes she had found in a junk shop in Palermo, utensils... tinkling, clattering, thudding and crashing around her ears. She made a grab for the curved mahogany banister, but just then the ferocity of the quake intensified; the banister snapped in two, as though it had been kindling wood, whereby, she lost her balance, fell against a side table, before being thrown against the door, and finally was flung onto the upturned sofa. Instinctively she rolled herself into a ball.

Bits of plaster floated down from overhead, and as the ceiling collapsed, huge chunks of plaster, splintered wood and nails rained down on top of her. She felt a searing pain rip through her, and she knew she had broken several ribs; the dust was choking her lungs, but she was unable to cough, because of the agony. From outside, some distance away, she heard the church bells ringing in a frenzied burst - before they fell quiet; and she realised the belfry must have collapsed. Then came an immense, wrenching sound, and as the earth opened up, like a greedy, cavernous mouth, the house listed to one side. She knew she would die if she stayed there, and screamed out her daughter's name.

With buckled metal joists, cables and masonry collapsing round her, she burrowed her way, mole-like through the house, disregarding her pain. The ground had stopped shaking. It had seemed to her that the quake had endured for hours. In reality it lasted two minutes at most, but in that flicker of time it had created a hell, indeed.

She was met with an unrecognisable, flattened and rubble-strewn landscape of death and despair; of the ruins of homes and ruined lives. It echoed with weeping and wailing and groaning. And silence.

Wherever she turned, there was devastation. Distraught figures ran hither and thither, through dense clouds of dust, calling out names, pushing each other out of the way; slipping in pools of blood, trampling over prone bodies, trampling *on* them. Others stumbled about without direction, like drunken zombies. The dying and the dead sprawled amidst the debris, to be further trampled upon by the terrified dogs, cats, goats, pigs, sheep and chickens, that ran amok. The sky was dark with birds that had taken flight.

Caught up in the midst of this purgatory, Graziella thrust forward nipping in and out, between people, ducking, jostling, in her urgency, gasping with her pain all the while; a single purpose in her head: to reach her child.

The street was awash with victims, and their images flashed into her consciousness and would forever be imprinted upon her brain. The mangled corpse of Maria Alberta; the butcher's partially severed head; the florist's staring gaze; the twisted body of the sweet young student she had employed, Tonino, Gino's brother, swinging ghoulishly from a buckled, steel girder, the pulverised features of the pop star peeping from beneath his crushed Porsche, a baby's tiny, amputated leg, the upturned bus with the scattered remains of its driver and passengers.

Da-dum. Da-dum. Da-dum went her heart.

And now she was standing deep in rubble by the twisted gates of what had been the entrance to the school, and was confronted with the heartbreaking scene of dozens of dead and injured and shocked children, their small faces streaked with tears and grey dust and blood. Several were so far gone that had help been at hand, it would have made no difference. The sound of their crying was pitiful. Mothers milled around, praying and sobbing, and nobody seemed to know what to do; where to go; where to begin.

Where the ground had been wrenched apart, were crater-like chasms, into which much of the three-storey building had slid. An avalanche of windows, doors, glass, furniture, steel, and masonry - layer upon layer, had then filled the void. Nowhere, could Graziella see Rosa. The terrible fear in her grew, made worse by the lamenting of grief-stricken mothers. What must it be like, she thought? How would she bear it?

She spotted her old teacher drifting about in a stupor, nursing her arm as though it hurt.

'Have you seen Rosa?' she demanded, clutching her sleeve, and wincing with the effort of speaking.

'I'm afraid not.' The teacher shook her head mournfully. 'Oh my dear Graziella, this is utterly...' She left the sentence incomplete and raised a hand to her temples. 'But look at you - you're badly injured.'

Graziella ignored her: 'I have to find her... I have to find her,' she muttered.

Through her pain, on her knees, she began to dig. Driven by the adrenalin which coursed through her, she feverishly tore at plaster and wood with her bare hands and fingernails, and threw aside stones and rocks, in the hope of finding a gap in the rubble. Her hands were bleeding, she could hardly see through her swollen eye, and her ribs felt as though she had been sawn in two, but she did not stop for a moment. Then someone had acquired a spade, and passed it to her, and she dug with new zeal.

Others joined in, taking turns to use the spade; and as new small victims were unearthed, dead, dying, or frightfully injured, fresh bursts of wailing would break out. Graziella tried to shut her ears to their anguish. It was too harrowing to listen to.

It could be her next.

She dug deeper, harder. 'You should stop for a while. You're exhausted. And look at your poor hands,' the schoolteacher said.

'I can't. I mustn't,' Graziella told her.

How could she relinquish digging, even for a second, while her daughter lay buried beneath layers of rubble, terrified, possibly injured... dead? And, in that awful eventuality, she would not want to live.

She had no concept of time. Time was irrelevant, as she continued to hack at brick and stone, throwing aside bricks and to reveal another layer.

And now, all the children were accounted for, except her child, and, gradually, people began to drift away, God knows to where. A fisherman then reported that the *Municipio* had escaped lightly, and much of it was intact; it was to be used as a temporary hospital. With this news, others shuffled off.

The teacher came up to her: 'Graziella,' she said, watching her, 'I'm so very sorry but I have to go.'

She explained a mother had asked her to look after two of her children, while she took care of their dying sibling.

'But of course you have to go. I understand that,' Graziella told her, leaning on the spade for a moment.

'I am concerned for you.'

'I just want to find Rosa,' Graziella said.

Only a few stragglers remained on the school site now. She bent her head and resumed digging. Exhaustion overcame her, every part of her body was hurting; she could barely see through her swollen eye; and her ribs felt as though they were on fire, her hands and knees were scraped raw. But, as her hope faded, her physical pain was nothing in comparison to her mental pain.

'*Rosa!*' She tried to scream. '*Rosa!*'

But the pain was too great and no sound came out.

She kept shovelling.

And then she noticed something protruding from the rubble, her heart raced, and she peered more closely. There was no doubt. What she had noticed were the two pointed ears of the Lupo stick.

'*Rosa!*' She called again, renewed hope making her voice strong.

And from the rubble, in response, Rosa's muffled voice: '*Mama!*'

Joy swept through her. Her Rosa, her precious Rosa, was alive.

'Just hang on *cara*' she called, laughing and weeping. 'Mama will get you out, I promise.'

Her pain had vanished. She recommenced digging with renewed vigour, tossing clods of earth and chunks of rubble onto the heap, as though they weighed nothing; calling intermittently to Rosa to reassure her. In return she would be reassured by the response. And each exposed layer brought her closer to her daughter. Then she was through, and Rosa was crawling through the gap which Graziella had made. She had with her the Lupo stick, and, except for minor cuts, she was miraculously unscathed. The blood on her was from the sow to whom she owed her life. Its body had cushioned her from the avalanche of debris.

'Mama!'

Sobbing, she threw herself into her mother's arms.

'It's alright, *cara*, mama's here with you now. You're safe. You're safe.' Slowly, sombrely, they headed for home.

CHAPTER 49

NOW
ROSA

I remember it in a stream of selected images and sounds, edited, perhaps, with the passage of time, and not always in the correct sequence. The shaking ground; everything falling and crashing; the screams of my friends. I remember the colossal groaning, rending - of the earth being riven apart; the gigantic creaking of swaying buildings, then the ear-splitting explosion of noise as buildings collapsed. I remember the horror of being incarcerated, the black blindness of it; as I clasped the Lupo stick to me for comfort, and prayed to God to rescue me from what was surely Hell. And I remember the dead pig's snout against my cheek, and its pungent, sickly smell of shit. And being unable to breathe, because of the dust, and it felt as though I was drowning in rubble.

I remember hour upon unending hour, the absolute terror; crying for Mama.

Then, at long last I heard her voice from my tiny space, so distant.

'*Cara! Cara!*'

And I called back, no longer afraid, because I knew that she would make everything alright. She always did.

'It's alright, *cara*, Mama's here with you now. You're safe. You're safe.'

I remember the slow, difficult walk towards the *casetta*; the devastation; tilting houses, collapsed awnings, and broken glass; and bodies and body parts, strewn everywhere, the blood soaked up by the dust.

I remember the smashed and torn market stands in the *piazza*. And hundreds of watermelons rolling about, causing you to slip, and their fresh, sweet scent as they were crushed underfoot.

I remember the mashed features of Padre Alberto beneath the toppled belfry, and his wandering eye dangling.

And I remember Mama's battered face and body, and poor, scraped hands.

Dodging rocks and ruts and huge crevices, we arrived back at what had been our home.

CHAPTER 50

THEN
AFTERMATH

Part of the *casetta* was leaning to the left, and there was a gaping hole in the kitchen wall. The roof of Graziella's hayloft bedroom had caved in, but Rosa's room, that had been Graziella's before her, had weathered the worst. The sturdy old barn, where the chickens had been housed and which Beppe had converted into a room, was hardly touched.

It could have been worse, she told herself, as they silently surveyed the wreckage. And they were alive. It was all that mattered.

From several metres behind them, they heard a small whimper, and turned simultaneously.

'It's Elvis,' Rosa cried. 'Elvis is alright.'

The dog's tail was wagging, in pleasure at seeing them, but he could not be persuaded to come any nearer the building, and they went over to him. He appeared to be unhurt, and jumped up, licking their faces. But when they again coaxed him to move, he still refused to leave his spot on open ground. His behaviour made her wary. They walked round the rear of the *casetta*, to check on the two boars. The pen had been demolished, and Lola had vanished.

With luck, she could have survived, but if she had fled into the forest, it was likely she would have been killed by uprooted trees falling. Her sibling, Lina, was in a frightful state: when the pen was still standing, she must have tried to jump out, but had then become entangled with chicken wire and twisted corrugated metal. Her stomach had been ripped open, exposing coils of intestine. She lay on her side, half conscious.

'Don't look,' Graziella ordered Rosa, and disappeared into the *casetta*. She returned after some while, with her father's shotgun. Carefully, she took aim. Rosa turned her back and jammed her fingers in her ears.

'She's at peace now, *cara*,' Graziella consoled her, as she sobbed anew, when it was over.

'You won't eat her, will you? You're not to eat her,' Rosa demanded.

'But of course I would never do that. How could you even think it?'

'People eat boar. They hunt them.'

'But I don't. And Lina was our pet. She was our friend. And, well, you don't eat your friends, do you? We will bury her later, *cara*.'

She told Rosa to wait with the dog, and went into the kitchen. The parrot was hanging upside down from its perch, its broken neck impossibly stretched, its eyes bulging. She felt almost as sad about the spiteful bird, as she was for the boar. She had grown fond of it. You had to respect it - it made concessions to nobody. But mainly her sadness was because the parrot had belonged to Mama Lucia. She had loved it. And the affection must have been reciprocated, as it never lunged at her.

Graziella searched for the first aid box, crunching on broken glass and pottery, lumps of stone, splintered bits of chairs and wattle from the ceiling. In the midst of it all, lay the squirrel, dead in its cage. The lopsided floor unnerved her. It made her feel slightly drunk; an impression not helped when, peering through the glass-less window, she found herself looking down into a deep, dark crevice.

Eventually, she discovered the metal box under a large piece of wattle, and grabbed it. She had no desire to linger: there was no time to lose; no time for sentiment. She trusted the dog's instincts.

She carried out the heavy box to the treeless area where Rosa sat waiting, one arm round the dog, her other hand gripping the Lupo stick. As she approached, she could see the anxiety in the expressions of both of them.

'You were ages,' Rosa said, her lip quivering.

'Aw, *cara*, I'm sorry. I couldn't find it. But I am here now.' Graziella consoled her.

Her daughter held the bandage in place for her, as she wound it tightly around her ribs. Its support provided a modicum of relief. Next, she bathed her eye with witch hazel and made a patch for it with lint and tape.

'We'll be alright here. Trust Elvis,' she said.

Worn out, her adrenalin spent, she lay down on the rough ground and closed her eyes. Her daughter curled up next to her, and they slept. The dog remained sitting upright as a lamp post, on guard, his nose twitching.

Dusk was descending when the ground started to shudder again. It woke them from their sleep, and they clung together. For maybe another ten or fifteen seconds, during which a crashing from within the *casetta* could be heard, the shaking intensified, and the fury of the aftershock escalated and reached its peak.

Then, in a curtailed goodbye, it was over.

Painfully, Graziella pushed herself up from the ground. She held out her hand to Rosa.

'That's it,' she told her. 'There won't be another.'

'How do you know?' Rosa asked.

She gestured to Elvis. The dog was ambling back towards the *casetta* as though nothing had happened.

The crashing sound Graziella had heard was the remainder of her bedroom ceiling toppling. She stood in the kitchen, knee-deep in debris, staring upwards with a weary sense of defeat. Above her now was just the yellowish sky. All that remained of the converted hayloft, which for the first seven years of her life she had shared with her parents, was a few dangling wires.

How could such damage as this ever be repaired?

She thought of Roberto: at that moment she needed him more than she had ever needed anyone. She longed to feel his arms around her, longed to hear his voice; her longing formed a restrictive band around her ribs, adding to her pain. But, whilst she was contemplating the wreckage of her home, he would be completing his hospital rounds for the evening. Perhaps he was thinking of her too. In his mind's eye, she would be at the party for the opening of the *albergo*, acting as the gracious hostess, unaware of the catastrophe which had taken place.

She slept with Rosa, in her narrow bed, that night. The dog settled himself at the foot of it. Then, at some stage during the night, loud purring close to her ear announced the return of Caspar; and not long afterwards, she was vaguely aware of the activity of helicopters overhead.

The misery was ghastly to see; grey-faced villagers and tourists drifting and stumbling about, as though in a dream. Now, nearly twenty-four hours later, instead of screams, an unnatural quiet prevailed. It was interspersed by soft moaning and murmuring. New victims were still being recovered, and the dead - God knows how many hundreds of them - had been piled up, in what was left of the *piazza*, and covered with sheets of tarpaulin that the flies had no difficulty infiltrating.

All lines of communication were down, as was the electricity. People were hot, and hungry, thirsty, and frightened. In the *Municipio,* a disorderly queue had formed. The makeshift hospital was spilling over with the wounded; Dottore Rugolo was fighting for his own life, and his three colleagues were finding it impossible to keep pace with the never-ending stream of patients. Matters were aggravated by the inadequate equipment and facilities.

The mayor and his wife were out and about early. Her arm was in a sling, and his leg was bandaged. They carried clipboards, and were liaising with the two *carabinieri,* keeping a tally of each person, counting the living; counting the dead. Locals and tourists alike were questioned, in order to glean information about individuals who were believed to be missing.

The neighbouring islands had been spared the effects of the quake. All that had been experienced was a series of small tremors. Word spread of the calamity which had hit *Isola delle Pecore,* and offers of assistance poured in. Over a megaphone, in a voice that was hoarse through lack of sleep, the mayor announced that food, bottled water, medical supplies, and industrial equipment to clear the streets of rubble, were already on their way by helicopter.

There was no avoiding the grim sights, and as they walked towards Mama Lucia's - slowly because of Graziella's injuries - she could feel Rosa's hand tightly bunched in her own. Sometimes, as when they passed a mutilated donkey that had been crushed beneath a tangle of motor scooters, she closed her eyes shut and hung on blindly to her mother. And now they reached the café-bar. An enormous great fissure had opened up, and the entire building tilted. The fissure had also caused the cypress tree, beneath

which the three old men had played dominoes, to become uprooted. There was a body trapped under it, covered by sacks. But the
shoes peeped out, and Graziella recognised them instantly: they
belonged to Carlotta.

'Dear God,' she exclaimed softly. And in a reflex reaction, she
crossed herself, something she had not done for years.

'Who is it Mama?' Rosa asked. Then she, too, recognised the
pink shoes, and began to cry.

Graziella's concern now was for Angelina, and she called out
her name. No reply came, but looking across to the esplanade,
Graziella saw her talking with Donatella, who appeared to be com-
forting her.

They crossed over the road. From here was a good view of
Stefano's mural of Marilyn Monroe; albeit she was now tilting
perilously.

Then Donatella and Angelina glanced up as they approached.
The girl's eyes were swollen and red from crying.

'Oh Angelina, I am so very sorry,' Graziella said, hugging her.
'What will you do? How can we be of help? You can come back with
us to the *casetta*. It has been badly damaged, but we would manage.
And you and Rosa get on well… We would be like a family.'

'Thank you Graziella,' Angelina said, 'but there will be no
need. It has already been decided.' Then Donatella cut in, curtly,
before Angelina had another chance to speak. 'She has said she
wishes to go to her sister's.'

'Is that what you really what?' Graziella asked her.

Angelina nodded, her head bent low.

Donatella continued: 'The convent has suffered very little damage. Angelina can stay there until she has spoken to her sister, once
communications have been restored.'

'Thank you, anyway, Graziella,' the girl said, looking up then.
'You have been very kind. I shall miss you and Rosa.'

'We shall miss you,' Graziella told her.

There was nothing else to say.

They left for home. They had a big clear-up project ahead of them, on which to get started.

CHAPTER 51

THEN
THE RETURN

It was mid-morning the following day. In the distance, they heard the ferry arrive, giving its usual three blasts of the funnel. The heat today was less intense than it had been; there was even a feathery breeze. On a day like this, benign, peaceful, it seemed hard to believe that, only forty-eight hours ago, a tragedy on an immense scale could have taken place.

On her knees, Graziella was clearing the vegetable area, using some of the rubble to fill in fissures. Little by little the tops of vegetables became visible: *melanzane, zucchini, pimentos*... And, encouraged by this small success, she vowed that, however long it took, she would restore the *casetta*. The *albergo* would have to wait, as would the café.

'Mama, there's someone coming up the track,' called Rosa, looking up from filling the water butt from the well. 'I think it's ... '

Graziella had seen him already. Her natural impulse was to run towards him, to fly into his arms, but her injuries precluded it. During the couple of days which had elapsed, her pain had worsened rather than improved, and now, instead, she walked sedately to meet him, her body stiff and bowed.

He looked like a student, encumbered as he was, with a bulging rucksack over his shoulders, from which jutted a rolled-up tent and ground sheet. Its weight would have been substantial, she thought, and it must have been especially awkward for him, because of his bad leg. In addition, he carried a doctor's Gladstone bag, which he lay on the ground, in order to embrace her.

'Oh God, look at the state of you, my darling,' he said, enfolding her to him with supreme tenderness.

'I'm alright,' she told him, loving his concern; loving him. And she pressed the side of her cheek to his; felt the roughness of stubble, like pumice stone, against her skin. Tears stood out in his eyes, and she blotted them with her sleeve.

'I have been going crazy with worry,' Roberto told her. 'Not knowing whether you were dead... or alive... hearing conflicting reports on the news. There was no way of finding out what was going on. It made me furious to feel so powerless. Luckily, the consultant who is my boss was sympathetic, and said I could take some leave, and I managed to get on a flight to Palermo. I stayed there last night.'

'If you knew how I longed for you,' Graziella said. 'And Rosa was lost for many hours, under rubble, and I hurt a lot, but I dug her out - kept digging and digging and digging - then I noticed the ears of the Lupo stick... I shall explain later... But anyway, we are very fortunate compared to some. There are people with the most terrible injuries, and hundreds dead. More than three hundred as an approximate estimate so far, across the whole island, but it is likely to be more than that... So you see how lucky we are... And the chickens survived and are still laying. And even the well still works.'

He smiled at the stream of words. But her stoicism came as no surprise to him.

'When I came off the ferry, I could not believe the devastation,' he said. 'It may be a cliché, but my heart really was thudding all the way here. I was terrified - well, it simply doesn't bear thinking about.'

From the yard, Rosa observed them picking their way up the hill, circumventing wide troughs where the earth had split open. The rucksack rested on his back like a camel's hump. And it was the same beige colour. Things would get better now that he had arrived. Mama would no longer have to do so much. He would not let her. And, in time, the *casetta* would be mended, and they would all live in it together...

However, at the forefront of Rosa's mind was the real, awful dread that it would happen again. Why not? It had happened three centuries ago. Maybe next time it would not wait so long. She likened it to a crouching beast: it was merely resting, recovering its strength; lying in wait, ready for the next onslaught. Who knew when that would be? The *Isola* had ceased to be her friend. She no longer trusted it.

Roberto undid the straps from round the tent and ground sheet, and allowed them to drop. With a groan of relief, he shed the rucksack.

'I don't know how you were able to lug that great thing about and maintain your balance,' Graziella remarked, as he rotated his shoulders a few times.

'Years of camping,' he said. 'You could say I'm something of a veteran when it comes to camping.'

They watched him unpack. Apart from clothes (not many of those), there were tins of food, an opener, matches, a torch, a rolled up bag containing tools, and another with plastic cutlery, paper cups, cleaning materials, washing powder... and several bars of Cadbury's Dairy Milk Chocolate.

'You have thought of everything,' Graziella marvelled.

He made a rueful sound between his tongue and teeth: 'Not everything.'

He held out a chocolate-covered hand. 'It was intended as a treat for both of you but it's melted of course - as anyone remotely intelligent would expect it to.'

Graziella laughed. He looked so mournful; she recalled that expression of old.

'We could spoon it,' she suggested, laughing again - at how his expression brightened.

Later, he inspected her injuries. They used Rosa's room, while she played outside. It was interesting Graziella thought, lying on the bed, stripped to her knickers, how Roberto's persona had altered the minute he'd assumed his doctor's mantel. All trace of the uncertain boy had disappeared; he became the consummate, assured professional.

His fingers travelled over her bruised, sore body, with a light, confident touch. Under any other circumstances she would have found it erotic. Now, her pain was too extreme.

'Another time,' he said, softly, when she told him this. 'We have our whole lives ahead of us.'

Our whole lives ahead of us. It resonated in her head, weighty with significance.

He wound a firmer bandage around her broken ribs, applied ointment to her eye and re-dressed it, and bathed her hands in an antiseptic saline solution.

'And now, my darling Graziella, you are going to leave everything to me, and you are going to sleep for the rest of the day and all night.'

'But ...'

'If you argue, I'll have to lock you in,' he said.

He kissed her and closed the door.

In truth, it was a relief to acquiesce. She felt her body gradually relaxing; the tension of the last few days evaporating. Sounds swam in her head: the ferry pulling out of the harbour; more helicopters; Roberto in the yard, whistling an unfamiliar tune as he shovelled rubble; Rosa's high voice, talking to the dog; the rustling of the fig tree, still clinging to its roots; the clamouring gulls, announcing a big catch. And, what had become of the gull with the damaged wing she had used to feed? And this led her to think of Carlotta - lying in a mortuary by now. Poor Carlotta. It had been a difficult life.

She slept for nearly fourteen hours, not stirring when Rosa slipped into bed beside her. When, finally, Graziella woke, sleep-hungover, it took a moment for her mind to clear, and to realise that she was in her daughter's room, and not her own. Then she noticed it - the yellow knitted rabbit propped up at the end of the bed. Roberto must have discovered it among the rubble.

CHAPTER 52

THEN
THE DECISION

As her strength grew, and her pain lessened, he felt it his duty to offer his help to the medical team.

'I came for you,' Roberto told Graziella. 'But, as a doctor, how could I just look on and not offer my services? I would feel dreadful.'

'Of course you must,' she agreed. 'I'm proud of you.'

For nearly a fortnight, he went every day to the *Municipio*, assisting with operations, tending to children with frightful injuries.

He would return to the *casetta* in the evening, waxen with tiredness and emotion.

'The children are so brave,' he said, on this particular evening, as they sat together on the ground sheet, by his tent, watching the sun sink behind the mountain. For a moment, the distant sea turned red.

'It's really humbling; a lesson to us all,' Roberto went on. 'And some of the kids are beyond treatment, and all one can do is dose them with morphine.'

'It could have been Rosa,' Graziella said. Not a day went by, without that awful thought grabbing her by the chest.

'But it wasn't, thank heaven.'

He rubbed the side of his jaw as he always did when nervous.

She preempted him: 'You have to go back to Oxford, don't you?'

He smiled crookedly. 'I must leave on Saturday.' He paused. 'I want you and Rosa to come with me... I love you... Marry me? ... Graziella, don't look at me like that. I can't tell what you're thinking'

She herself did not know what she was thinking. Her mind was in turmoil. He had taken her hand, but now she withdrew hers. The marriage proposal squatted between them, ignored.

'I thought ... I hoped ... ' She floundered. 'Can't you stay here? You could be a doctor here... couldn't you? You don't have to be a paediatrician...' As she spoke, she was aware she was being unrealistic.

He knew that she realised it. Carefully, he said: 'Graziella, it's my whole career at stake. I have spent years studying, working for this.'

'And this is *my* whole life - here, on the *Isola*,' she countered. 'Or doesn't that matter?'

'Of course it does. That's unfair.'

'It's you who is being unfair - trying to take me away from everything' she levelled at him.

And the real issue struck him then: apart from occasional visits to the other islands, she had never left *Isola delle Pecore*. Graziella was afraid.

Gently, he tried to reason with her: 'Darling, what is left for you here now? Virtually the entire island will have to be rebuilt. The *casetta* will have to be rebuilt, and the *albergo*, and Mama Lucia's. It could take years. And there will be no tourists,' he pointed out.

He made a small, placatory gesture but her face remained stony, and he floundered on. 'Oxford is a wonderful city. And the flat is in a quiet road - though one day I would like to move to one of the nearby rural villages. I prefer to be in the country rather than a city. You'd like that better also, I think. And you could train to be a vet, and... '

'Stop it,' she cried. 'Stop telling me what to do, Roberto. I don't need you. Rosa and I manage fine on our own. We don't need anyone interfering.'

She stood up.

'Where are you going?' he asked.

She didn't answer. A rod lay across her throat. She ached with disappointment. He had expected too much of her, she thought, walking to the convent. Then, more leniently: they had expected too much from each other.

She pulled the wrought iron bell ring, and heard it resonate within. Except for the damaged archway, and Mary's head missing from the statue, there was no obvious evidence to indicate a major earthquake had recently decimated most of the island. God's reward? She wondered, with a sense of irony.

Nobody came to the door, and she thought perhaps the nuns were all at prayer, at gone eight in the evening. She had no idea of the hours they kept. Certainly, the official time for visitors was long past. And now her annoyance was directed at the convent, for its strict regulations, and at Raffaella, for becoming a nun in the first place.

She yanked the bell pull again. Twice. After a minute or so, she could hear footsteps along the corridor, then the swishing of a nun's habit, followed by the rattling of keys being turned. Luck was on her side: the nun who opened the door to her was Raffaella.

'Graziella!' She exclaimed. 'What are you doing here? Do you know what the time is?'

'Yes, but I had to see you.'

'Let's go into the office, then.'

The small room was dark. The electricity had been restored to the village just that day, but the convent had never indulged in such frivolities as electricity, and she lit three candles. Shadows played on the whitewashed walls.

'Look at you. You're breathless. You can hardly walk,' Raffaella commented.

'I'm much better now... It's nothing. Hundreds are dead - poor Carlotta amongst them. At least Angelina could stay with her sister. But, *Madre*, what a catastrophe. And people have lost limbs. *Children* have done.'

'You know the *Contessa* is dead,' Raffaella said.

'*Ah no.... Ah no...*' Graziella slammed her fist down on the small table beside her. 'I am very sad about that. Don't tell me you still believe in God after this?'

'Graziella, you did not come here, at this hour, to discuss God.'

'No. You are right. Of course not.'

She told her about the quarrel with Roberto.

'He asked you to marry him?' Raffaella queried.

'Yes... Yes he did,' she said slowly. Only now, did it fully register.

'And you said what?'

'I said...'

I don't need you. Rosa and I manage fine on our own. We don't need anyone interfering.

'Well, we *can* manage, and we *don't* need him.' She stuck out her chin.

'We all need somebody. I have God. Why must you always fight, Graziella? For an intelligent woman, you can be very foolish indeed.'

She walked back to the *casetta* in a pensive mood.

At first, she could not see him, and panic rose in her. Then she heard him. He was in Rosa's room. He was telling her a story.

'And the kindly giant was so happy because at last he had a friend,' Roberto finished.

They looked so sweet, she thought.

Turning, he saw her. He smiled uncertainly.

She smiled also. Took a step towards him.

'Could I bring Elvis and Caspar to England?'

'They would have to go into quarantine, but, yes, you could.'

His smile grew; as did hers.

'And I could train to be a vet.'

'Definitely.'

'*Va bene,*' she said, glad for once to concede defeat.

CHAPTER 53

NOW

GRAZIELLA

'So that is it, Mama. The end of the book.'
My daughter switches off her little machine after this, our final session.

I am inordinately weary.

'But not the end of the story.'

'What do you mean by that, Mama?'

I close my eyes. Let her believe I am asleep.

Tomorrow she and her husband - I've forgotten his name, are going to Wales for a few days, for their anniversary. Or is it Scotland? No matter. It will do her good; she works so hard. And she worries about me. But, while the cat is away, the mice, they do play …

What *is* her husband called? It's something short… A, B, C, D … Jack, that's it. I like him. Most importantly, he loves my beautiful little Rosa.

I had love.

I miss my Roberto. I miss the Me that I was. Now I am this purposeless, incontinent, nappy-wearing, rambling, surplus piece of baggage. I can only live in the past. And what a past it was. I should like to reclaim it. Though not all of it.

And is there a God after all? The other day Roberto appeared before me, just as my mama used to, and he told me that there was a God. And I did not imagine it. I was not hallucinating; though any doctor would say I was.

'Mama?'

I raise my head.

'Let's walk round the garden. The physiotherapist said you must exercise,' Rosa says.

'There's no point.'

'Of course there is.'

To please her, I allow her to help me from the chair. I reach for the Lupo stick.

'No Graziella, you need the frame,' says dear Truthful, who has just come in the room. I take it from her. The softness of her smile is beautiful.

Sedately, we tour the garden: Rosa, Truthful, the two dogs and myself.

My hand wobbles. My legs have turned into mashed potato.

'You are doing so well,' Truthful lies.

The morning progresses.

'Liz is picking you up soon, to take you to the sanctuary, Mama,' Rosa says, putting on her jacket to go.

'How kind,' I comment. I'm not sure I actually spoke it aloud, so repeat it. And again... Kind. Nice. Kind. Nice ... I like the feel of the words on my tongue.

Rosa's expressive face looks distressed; I hold my arms out to her, and she crouches to the level of my chair.

'Don't be sad, *cara*. I don't want you to be sad.'

I circle her beautiful, tragic eyes with my fingertip. My finger is as bent as a shepherd's crook.

'You will be alright, Mama? It's only four days.'

'Of course. Truthful will look after me. And Gino is coming.'

'I'll phone, Mama.'

'You are a wonderful daughter, *cara*.'

'And you are a wonderful mother.'

She stands up again. The car keys jangle in her hand. I cannot bear to watch her go. Must not cry. Affect a cheerful smile. Waving now from the window: *Goodbye cara … Goodbye…*

CHAPTER 54

NOW

ROSA

Upon our return, Gino opens the door to us. He looks tired, and his smile of greeting seems forced. There is no sign of either Mama, or of Truthful. Tosca lies in her corner and does not get up. She doesn't react when Lupo bounds over to her. Something is wrong. I sense it immediately.

'Where is Mama?'

He regards me steadily, with solemn, tired eyes. 'I'll tell you in a minute,' he says. And whispers something to Jack, who nods, and goes into the garden.

My skin has become icy.

Something very bad has happened.

'Will you please tell me what the hell is going on, Gino?'

'First you must sit down,' he orders me.

I do so; feel myself trembling. He sits beside me, and, taking a folded letter from his pocket, passes it to me. He puts his arm round me. Mama's writing leaps out at me.

I start to read.

"My darling little Rosa,

When you read this, I shall not be here. I am writing this from my lovely bedroom in Switzerland.

Please do not be angry, cara.

I had to take control of my own life again, and that included dying. I also knew you loved me too much to permit me that luxury. Nor must you be angry with Gino. You know what I am like and I pushed him and pushed him until his resolve was broken down..."

My vision is opaque with tears. Her writing is full of crossings-out, spelling errors, and blobs made by a ballpoint pen, that make it the harder to read. One letter slants to the right, its neighbour to the left; some of the writing topples down at such an angle that ends of words are missing. There are also several lines of rubbish, where she must have had a blip. The letter must have taken her ages to compose and to write.

" There is something I must tell you: you have a twin brother" - And here I give a small cry of disbelief, and Gino's arm tightens around me -

"He is a priest in Palermo, whom I myself only knew about comparatively recently, when I received a letter from my old friend Raffaella. The nuns took him at birth. I believed him to have been stillborn. I do not blame them. At the time, Raffaella believed she was doing the right thing.

Your twin's name is Ricardo, and he is keen to meet you. I have given Gino his contact details. I have also given him the correspondence between myself and Ricardo, as well as a photograph. I have already met him. He came to England and we met at Reading. Ricardo is a lovely man: kind, intellectual, non-dogmatic. I am proud he is my son..."

I recall the day now. I was unable to get hold of Mama, and I rang Liz at the sanctuary. All I was able to glean was that she had gone to Reading to see a friend. Later, when I probed her as to whom she had seen in Reading that day, she had become defensive, then, she told me, mysteriously, that one day it would all become clear.

And now I realise who my father was. Twins run in families. Nina and Giorgio were twins. The mayor, not Gino, the journalist, was my father. Looking back on it, I think I had long guessed it, but had not wanted to confront the likelihood. It comes as no great, explosive shock, therefore. He is an irrelevance to me. He planted an accidental seed that is all. Roberto, whom I soon called Papa, was my father by right. Any anger and sorrow that I feel is not for myself, but for my brave mama and what she endured.

And in her next paragraph it is apparent that she knew I would work out the truth, for she wrote:

"Out of bad came good, my little Rosa. You have filled my life with joy. Love is everything. Roberto loved you and he was your father as much as he was your brother Gino's father.

Cara, will you look after Tosca for me? She will be happy to live with her son. As you know, Liz will keep the sanctuary going. I should like my ashes to be scattered there please, by the fox's pen. And please take care of the Lupo stick. Hang it somewhere you will see it, for luck. Now, my beautiful little Rosa, what is there left to say?

I hope that soon you will meet your brother in Palermo. Afterwards, perhaps you may be inclined to take the ferry for Isola delle Pecore. If you do, then please remember me to her.

Don't be sad, cara. You have much to look forward to. And, just as my own mama used to watch over me, I shall be watching over you. I love you always.

Your Mama xxxx."

With shaking fingers, I replace the letter in its envelope and lay it on the table. I can't see for tears.

Gino presses something soft to my buried face. Its shape is instantly recognisable to me.

I open my eyes.

As I clutch the yellow knitted rabbit against my heart, an extraordinary, iridescent light infuses the room. I find myself rooted to the chair, unable to move. It's as if a magnet is holding me down.

'I am here, cara,' Mama says.
And her voice beside me is clear and youthful.
'Always here.'

THE END

Printed in Great Britain
by Amazon